SEARCHING
for SARAH

LYNN ERICKSON

JOVE BOOKS, NEW YORK

SEARCHING FOR SARAH

A Jove Book / published by arrangement with
the author

PRINTING HISTORY
Jove edition / December 1999

The Penguin Putnam Inc. World Wide Web site address is
http://www.penguinputnam.com

ISBN: 0-515-12699-3

A JOVE BOOK®
Jove Books are published by The Berkley Publishing Group,
a division of Penguin Putnam Inc.,
375 Hudson Street, New York, New York 10014.
JOVE and the "J" design
are trademarks belonging to Penguin Putnam Inc.

PRINTED IN THE UNITED STATES OF AMERICA

10 9 8 7 6 5 4 3 2 1

PROLOGUE

"Would you like something to drink?" The senator nodded toward the wet bar.

"Sure, maybe a glass of wine." Sarah Jamison was thrilled that he'd singled her out. She was a little high on excitement, on the man's charisma. He was a breath of fresh air, a brash newcomer who'd burst onto the political scene and snatched the presidential nomination out from under the noses of the stodgy old Establishment zombies.

He moved to the bar, his broad, tuxedo-clad back to her, and took a bottle of wine out of the small refrigerator. "White okay?"

"Yes, fine." She stood at the center of the pastel Aubusson carpet and looked around. "Your suite is beautiful."

"The Brown Palace does a nice job. Very restful. Here you go."

He was a man of medium height but powerfully built, with a head of curly brown hair. It was said, she remembered, that no bald man since Eisenhower had won the presidency. And he had a magnetic smile.

She took the glass and sipped.

"Let's sit over here," Scott said, gesturing to the Victorian sofa. "Tell me about yourself."

"Me? Goodness, I'd rather hear about your campaign. I'd like to know what I can do to help. Anything. Man the phones, send out mail. Run errands."

"Of course, you're on the volunteer list. I don't know exactly what they've got planned for you, but we can use all the help we can get." He leaned forward, his own drink resting on his knees. "But I didn't ask you up here to talk about politics or the campaign. I get so much of that." He frowned. "Such as the rubber-chicken dinner tonight. My God, do you know how many of those I've been to?"

"I can imagine."

"I need to relax. This campaign, hell, *any* campaign, is pure torture." He rotated his head between his shoulders as if to release tension.

"Senator Taylor," she began.

"Scott."

"Scott." She tasted the name. "Okay, *Scott.* I wanted you to know I feel very fortunate to be associated with your campaign. I've never been a political person, but . . ."

He waved a dismissive hand. "Do you know why my wife isn't here? Why I'm staying here instead of driving home just a few miles away?"

His wife. "No, I really . . ."

"Because she can't stand this crap, the smiling, the ass-kissing, the deal-making."

Sarah lowered her gaze to her lap.

"My wife aspires to be First Lady, though. Oh, yes, Heather wants to live in the White House. That's our bargain."

She took another sip of her wine. Warning signals began to go off in her brain. She'd thought he wanted to talk about a particular job for her here in the Denver campaign headquarters.

"We don't really live together," he said. "Ah, hell, why am I telling you this? You could go blab it all over and I'd lose the election."

"You can trust me."

"I think I can. You know, sometimes I have to let my guard down. Talk to somebody."

"Sure I know. And believe me, Scott, I know about keeping family secrets."

He looked at her, his blue eyes shrewd, sizing her up. He took a long swallow of his drink and then started to say something.

The phone rang shrilly.

"Damn," he muttered. "Excuse me."

"Taylor here," she heard him say, then he listened. She sat there, trying to think of an excuse to leave—a date? A friend she had to meet? An early day tomorrow at the campaign headquarters? She pulled her silvery sweater down over the short dark skirt she wore, then tugged at the skirt so that it covered her knees.

"*Now?*" Scott was saying on the phone in an annoyed voice. "Look, I'm bushed. I was just going to bed." Then, "Okay, okay. But make it quick."

He hung up and turned to her. "Listen, I'm really sorry, but there are a couple of important men I have to see. It'll be quick, only a few minutes."

"Oh, I'll go on back to my hotel, Scott. I'm really tired anyway, and I'm sure . . ."

"No, no, absolutely not. And, hell, if they see you leaving it could very well hit the headlines tomorrow. Just go into the bedroom, wait till they leave. Then we can talk about how you can help the campaign, all right?"

"Well . . ."

"Go on. Just in there. Two minutes."

There was a discreet knock on the door. He turned

away from her, and there was nothing she could do but grab her coat and purse and wineglass and retreat into the darkened bedroom, leaving the door ajar.

God, what a ridiculous situation, she thought, skulking in Senator Taylor's bedroom. *Hiding.* She stood against the wall behind the door, afraid to sit on the bed or go to the bathroom, because Scott's visitors would hear her, and, despite the fact that there was nothing going on, her discovery really could damage his reputation.

Sarah wondered if what he'd said about his wife was true, or if he'd been pulling the old "misunderstood husband" routine on her. When she'd met him at a political rally a few weeks ago, and he'd invited her to work with the campaign team, she hadn't known he was so hot to trot. It was obvious now that he used the power of his charm, which was considerable, to get young women into his bedroom. What an idiot she was! At her age.

She heard men's voices in the other room. Scott and someone else. Curious, she peeked through the crack on the hinged side of the door. She could just make out Scott's shoulder in the black tuxedo jacket and beyond him another man, hatchet-faced, gray-haired. *Familiar,* crossed her mind. A familiar face. She'd seen it— where?—in the newspaper, magazines? On television. Yes, on some news program where gray-haired pundits droned on and on.

The man was talking. Quietly. She could only hear a murmur. Scott didn't ask his visitors to sit down. Two minutes, he'd said. She waited, impatient, wanting to change her position, afraid they'd hear her. The heels she wore pinched her toes.

The men shifted in the vertical slot, Scott's shoulder disappeared, and another man's back crossed her sight line. A slim back, tweed coat, thinning brown hair, then he was gone, and the hatchet-faced man reappeared. He looked angry, his brows drawn together, his cheeks singularly bloodless. "Listen, you moron," she heard him say, "you can't do that. Inside the Beltway there are rules."

"Rules," Scott echoed with scorn. "If I'm elected I make the rules. I'll have the mandate. Don't you come in here and threaten me."

Who was that man? Some high-up government official, although she couldn't place him exactly. Yes, she remembered him on that TV program, pontificating about something or other. Then, finally, she put a name to the face, and she was impressed. The man, the big shot, had certainly come a long way to make this late-night visit.

"You like your nice cushy job?" Scott was saying in a hard voice. "You want to keep it? If I get elected, I may let you keep it, but I'll make sure your funding gets cut back so far you'll have to get a night job. You spooks have screwed up too many times, and the American taxpayers are sick of it. Vietnam, Laos, Panama, Iraq, Bosnia, Russia, for God's sake. It's got to end."

"I was afraid of this," the government man said, his voice under tight control. His companion said nothing, not a word.

Sarah was acutely uncomfortable. She shouldn't be hearing this. She didn't want to know this. Scott's two minutes were up.

"You *should* be afraid," Scott said. "Now get the hell out of here."

Sarah saw vertical strips of the men's bodies shift position, black tuxedo, gray suit, tweed jacket. They were leaving. Relief washed over her. Thank God *that* was over. Maybe she really didn't want to be involved in politics; maybe it was even uglier than what she'd left behind.

"See you in Washington," she heard Scott say as they neared the door. Taunting.

Bodies moved, the strips sliding across her line of sight. A vertical kaleidoscope.

"Oh, I doubt that," the government official said, and

then only the tweed jacket filled the crack, and she heard *pop, pop,* and every nerve in her body jumped, froze.

What? her mind screamed. *What?*

Something hit the floor with a thud, something heavy, a . . . body? Low voices. Whose? *Whose?* Footsteps, quiet, purposeful, approaching the bedroom. Sarah's mouth went dry, her entire body turned liquid, boneless. She slid down the wall, slowly, until she could go no farther.

Crouched there, she could see the fan of light from the living room widen as someone entered the bedroom. The light slid over the ornate, marble-topped dresser and mirror, the lace coverlet on the bed, a brass lamp that winked at her from a night table. Her heart was pounding so hard the man was sure to hear it.

"No one here," she heard him say.

"Okay, I just wanted to make certain he didn't have some bimbo hidden away in there. You know his reputation."

She shut her eyes tightly, tried to shrink into herself. She was clutching her purse strap so fiercely her hand was numb. The wine had spilled onto her lap, and she could smell its vinegary scent. Could *they* smell it?

She sensed the man backing out of the bedroom; perhaps she heard the faint scuff of his feet. She didn't move, didn't breathe, willed herself invisible, like a child with closed eyes thinking no one could see her.

She heard noises from the living room then, drawers opened, cushions flung about, the tinkle of a Tiffany lamp falling. What? Looking for something? Then two voices spoke softly, two pairs of footsteps receded, the door to the suite opened and closed with a well-oiled snick.

Sarah remained huddled behind the door, paralyzed, her mind, her emotions, her life on hold. The lighted clock face on the night table clicked the minutes off as she crouched there; she could see it if she turned her head. If she turned the other way she could see, through the crack in the door, a man's outstretched hand on the rug, its fingers curled under loosely, relaxed. She only looked that way once.

Time jerked by spasmodically. An hour, two hours. Sarah knew that she'd have to move sometime. Eventually. She'd have to force herself to stand up, revive her body, think again, feel again. Leave this place. Fear consumed her, though, its flame burning all reason, all free will out of her.

She couldn't move. If she moved . . . They might be waiting for her out there. She heard the two shots inside her head over and over, the distinctive thud—a dead weight—hitting the floor. Oh God oh God oh God.

The clock read two-forty-three when she gathered the will to move, pressing herself up, her back against the wall. The wineglass hit the carpet with a dull plunk; she cringed. She stood, braced against the wall, shaking, her pulse beating in her ears, her coat and purse held clawlike in her hands. Reason sparked once in her brain. She leaned over and picked up the wineglass, stuck it in her purse.

She took a step, then another. Silently opened the bedroom door and slipped out. She edged into the living room, tried to keep her eyes averted as she stepped past the body lying on the floor, facedown, the arm outflung, the broad back encased in elegant black. The dark pool congealing under his head. She gasped and stepped faster, leaving it behind, him behind. The angry voices, the shots, the dark stain.

She moved like a ghost, like a wraith, to the door, opened it, closed it behind her. The corridor was quiet and dim, the famous wrought-iron railing of the Brown Palace on one side of her, and beyond it, the massive open atrium.

She took a deep breath and tried to stand tall, tried to appear normal. She walked, she strode to the broad marble staircase, then she clattered down three flights and through the elegant, empty lobby, bursting out into the cold air of the October night.

Then Sarah Jamison ran for her life.

ONE

Jake Savelle sat, legs splayed, in his favorite chair, the only valuable thing salvaged from his divorce, and stared out the window overlooking downtown Denver.

He was alone in his two-room dump and he let his body slump, let his face fall into the vacant lines of depression. Out in public he faked it, defending himself against pity, but at home it was too damn hard.

His mind took the familiar path, ruts worn deep in it after eighteen months, and with the perfect vision of hindsight, he pinpointed the exact moment he'd begun his fall from grace: the night someone had pumped two bullets into Scott Taylor's brain.

He rubbed the scratchy five o'clock shadow he was too apathetic to shave and turned his head. Outside it was a brilliantly clear March day, the sun poised to drop below the snow-covered Rockies to the west of Denver. At least he had the view. Okay, so it was only a wedge of splendor between two apartment buildings, but it was *his* wedge.

Peaches' chewed-up tennis ball rested against a chair

leg on the rust-colored shag carpet, and Jake picked it up, idly bounced it on a kneecap while he stared at the sun glinting off the peaks of the Continental Divide. Vail was right there, just beyond that tallest peak. He wondered what the skiing was like in the Back Bowls. Most likely great. Bottomless, untouched powdery snow that would part before his skis and billow up behind in the champagne-dry air. He and Shayne used to love the Bowls. They used to throw all their ski gear into their spanking new Range Rover—their big golden retriever, Peaches, jumping in on top of it—and take off for their Vail condo every weekend they could steal from their busy law practice.

Used to. Now the condo was sold, the profits split. Shayne had the Denver house, the Range Rover, and Peaches, because Jake wasn't allowed to keep pets in his apartment. He sneaked her in on weekends, though, when the landlord wasn't around. You might think the place was in ultra-chic lower downtown next to Coors Field, for chrissakes. A pricey "LoDo" loft.

He threw the tennis ball across the cluttered room and avoided looking at the stacks of legal briefs that awaited his attention on the coffee table.

His former energy and passion for the law had evaporated. Sure, he appreciated the paralegal work a few old lawyer friends threw his way, but that was only marking time. It paid the bills. Frankly, he didn't know which was worse, being treated like a charity case or the humiliation he still suffered from his disbarment.

Jake must have dozed then, because the next thing he knew he jerked to consciousness. The light in the room was dim and golden, and someone was knocking at his door. He unfolded himself stiffly, stood and ran a hand through his hair. *Napping.* With the table piled high with unfinished briefs, he was goddamn napping. Sleeping too much—a sure sign of depression.

The instant Jake pulled open the door and saw David

Carmichael he was filled with dread. "Shit," he said.

But the cop only gave a tired laugh. "No, no, Nina's okay." And he strode in past Jake and headed to the fridge, where he pulled out a can of beer and popped it open.

Jake leaned a shoulder against the door and eyed his friend, trying to gauge the man's body language, much the way he once would have assessed a prospective juror. Like Jake, David was a tall man, six-foot-one, though he was twenty pounds lighter than Jake, who somehow managed to keep his muscle tone, forcing himself out the door every morning to take a jog around the Capital Hill neighborhood. And, like Jake, David was still an attractive man approaching his forties, though Jake had almost all his hair, and Rogaine was miserably failing David.

Nina's cancer was taking its toll on her husband.

It was in David's carriage, in the sag of his thin shoulders, in the rhythm of his stride. Being forced to face his wife's mortality was a damn heavy weight.

Jake followed his lead and took a beer out of the fridge. "So," he said, "the surgery went all right?"

"Yes and no. I mean, they haven't found any new cancer, but she had a bad reaction to the anesthesia, and she's still in the ICU."

David had tossed aside a couple of ratty pillows and settled on the couch, taking a long draw on his beer. Jake sat down in the rickety wooden chair across from him. "But she *will* be okay? I mean . . ."

"Yeah, yeah, her doctor said she'd be fine in a few days."

"And the cancer?"

"For now she's in the clear."

"For now?" Jake scowled. "And just what does that mean?"

"Damned if I know."

"Jesus, David, you're a homicide detective. Don't you know how to ask the right questions?"

David's lip curled again in that weary smile. "Maybe I don't ask 'cause I don't really want to know."

"Mm," Jake said. "You want me to pick Sean and Nicky up from hockey practice and get them some dinner?"

"Hell, Jake, you don't have to do that."

"I'd like to do it."

"No, really."

"It's for Nina, okay?"

"Well . . ."

"What time do they get done?"

"Seven, seven-fifteen."

"We'll grab a pizza or something, and I can bring them by to see their mother if you want."

David thought a moment then shook his head. "Better not. She may still be in the ICU and she looks, well, not so great. You know?"

"Sure," Jake said. He knew.

He looked at David, took a sip of his own beer. David Carmichael was a real buddy, a brother, the whole male bonding thing. Their friendship had begun during the Taylor murder investigation, when David had been one of the detectives assigned to the case and Jake, as chief deputy district attorney, had been working it, too.

Most of the homicide cops had regarded Jake with a jaundiced eye, because they all knew Taylor had been his brother-in-law. And there were more than a few in the city government who'd thought he should recuse himself from the case for just that reason.

Both David and Jake suspected Taylor had been assassinated because he was a threat to the Washington power structure. But Denver's top brass, from the DA to the mayor, had serious doubts about that theory. They had been hoping to sweep the affair under the rug—bad for tourism, bad for Denver's image, and too hot to handle.

It was true that the evidence pointed to a burglary gone sour. The only hint that it had not been an impulse shooting was a small wad of steel wool found on the carpet, which could be used as a silencer. Despite Jake's best efforts, the steel wool had been explained away: a sloppy maintenance man. Another thing had always bothered Jake—the two 9mm slugs in Scott's head. Pretty fancy hardware for a burglar.

When the case had been shelved a year ago, five months after Scott's murder, due to lack of evidence or leads, Jake had persuaded David to help him pursue the assassination theory on the sly. And David had come through, in spite of his sick wife, his heavy caseload, and against police captain Barry Disoto's direct orders.

Now *that* was a friend.

David was draining off his beer and coming to his feet. "I better get on back to the hospital," he said, and he arced a perfect dunk shot into the overflowing trash can across the room. "You ought to clean this place up, pal." He nodded toward the coffee table and the cubbyhole kitchen.

"Um, well, the maid skipped me this week." Jake walked him to the door. "Kiss Nina for me, and don't worry about the boys. I'll watch TV till you get in. And they'll do their homework."

David let out a breath. "Thanks, Jake, and I mean that. You've been a real help since, you know, since the cancer thing."

Jake shrugged. "I'm just after your wife, buddy."

"Uh-huh," David said wearily and he closed the door behind him.

It was good to have something to do. Picking the boys up at the hockey rink, feeding them, and getting stuck playing computer games kept him from thinking too much, from wallowing in his depression. He'd always wanted kids. Though he'd never confess it—at least not to another man—he'd married at thirty for two reasons: one, because he was inept at the singles game anyway and he'd fallen in love with a lovely woman who was a damn good lawyer to boot, and two, because he wanted kids. Boys would fit the bill—boys to go to Bronco games with—but girls were fine, too. Hell, he liked women. Maybe he didn't exactly understand them, but once he'd given up trying, women were okay.

Then, a few months before his brother-in-law's murder, Shayne had announced she did not want to have children.

It had been a blow to Jake—but Shayne was adamant. That must have been the beginning of the end of their marriage, he figured. Maybe it really hadn't been his disbarment at all.

He turned in at midnight and thought about his lost life and ruined marriage and couldn't quite make sense of it. He wasn't stupid. Overzealous, maybe, but not stupid. Yet he hadn't seen the setup coming.

David had warned him. "You better cool it with the Taylor murder thing, pal. Word is that you're pissing off the wrong people," he had told him dozens of times.

Jake hadn't listened. Murder, *assassination*, was wrong, and the thought of a cold-blooded killer walking around scot-free had made him crazy with rage.

Lying in the dark now, his hands behind his head, he felt sick. He should have seen the setup coming. But somehow he hadn't. All he knew was that one day he'd been the honest Denver crusader, and the next day a female juror on one of his cases claimed he'd had sex with her during the trial. The administrative board for the Colorado Bar Association was not constrained by the rules of evidence, and Jake had been immediately and conveniently disbarred.

He rolled over, punched his pillow, and tried to stop thinking. It was no good. His thoughts kept crawling out of the black corners of his mind. How could he have been so damn wrong about everything—his marriage, the Taylor murder investigation, his whole life? It frightened him that he'd screwed up so badly. He felt that if he'd been that far off in his judgment, everything he was, everything he aspired to be, must have been wrong. He no longer knew who he was or where he was headed. He had lost his passion and his direction—a direction that had obviously been wrong. It almost seemed as if his life, his very essence, had seeped right out of him. He was like the man in that old sci-fi movie, the man that was shrinking into nothingness.

And that frightened the hell out of him.

A ringing telephone in the middle of the night meant only one thing to Jake: disaster. It had been one of those god-awful calls that had informed him last year that he'd been disbarred—like the well-meaning associate of his couldn't have waited till morning? Now, as he sat up and oriented himself, his heart thumping against his ribs, he could only think it was one of three people: Shayne calling him to say Peaches had gotten loose and hit by a car. . . . Or it could be his sister Heather. . . . But Jake was sure it had to be David with terrible news about Nina.

He picked up the phone and steeled himself. The digital clock glowed 1:06 A.M.

It was not David. Or Shayne or Heather. Instead, an unfamiliar male voice asked if this was Jake Savelle.

He thought a minute, clearing his head. "Yes," he finally said. "And who is—?"

He was cut off. "There was a woman," the voice said, "in the hotel room at the Brown Palace."

"Listen," Jake began, "who is this?"

"She was a witness. A witness to Senator Scott Taylor's murder," the voice cut in again and then abruptly the line went dead.

Jake took the phone from his ear and stared dumbly at it. Someone in the hotel room? *Scott's* room? A woman. "A witness," he breathed. "There was a goddamned witness?"

He finally hung up the phone, and he could feel a tightening in his chest, both a swelling of fury and a terrible elation. A *witness?* Was it possible?

It was hard to think, hard to even fit his mind around the news. He flung himself out of bed and paced in the darkness—a witness, a witness, a woman. But . . . ?

It *was* possible. *My God,* Jake thought, Scott Taylor—his sister's husband—had been the first candidate in three decades who'd promised a new order, who'd sworn to clean up the Washington morass: campaign finance reform, the works. And Jake, along with millions of others, had been swayed by Scott's passionate belief that politics could make things better. The far-reaching possibilities of a Taylor presidency had given so many renewed hope. He himself had been forced to admit he was having grandiose thoughts about visits to the White House, maybe even getting a posting there. Everything had been damn near perfect.

Except for one little problem: Scott was a womanizer, a dyed-in-the-wool sexual addict.

Jake sank down onto the side of the bed. If the anonymous caller had said anything else about Scott's murder, Jake would have taken it with a grain of salt. But a woman. Oh, yes, it fit.

Suddenly he looked up; he could feel the excitement running through him like electricity. It had been so long, so goddamn long since he'd felt anything.

A witness.

He stood up in the blackness of his tiny bedroom and felt heat emanating from every cell in his body. He was a man on fire.

David Carmichael shook his head in disbelief. ''Jake, pal, you get a call in the middle of the night from some jerk who doesn't even ID himself, and this asshole tells you there was someone in the hotel room and you fall for it, hook, line, and sinker. Jesus, think about what you're saying.''

Jake glanced at the hospital bed where Nina was sleeping then turned back to David. "I have thought about it," he whispered harshly. "I was goddamn up all night doing nothing *but* thinking about it. It fits. You know Scott's reputation. Hell, everyone knew. Even my sister knew."

"Heather . . . ?"

"Damn right. She stuck with him because she believed in him and, if you really want to know, Heather was motivated by the very real prospect of becoming First Lady. She didn't delude herself, though. No one who knew Scott did. There's a good possibility that there was a woman with him."

"So where was this broad when Taylor got shot?"

"How the hell would I know? Hiding, I guess."

"And no one saw her? The murderer just missed her?" David blew out a disgusted breath. "Come on, Jake. Get real."

"Maybe there was a woman," came Nina's weak voice, and both men turned and stared at her pale form, which barely raised the sterile sheets.

She licked dry, cracked lips and tried to push herself up against the pillows. Jake was by her side in a flash, helping her up and then pouring a glass of water from a lavender plastic container. "Here, drink this," he said, and he couldn't help noticing that her bony fingers shook. "I'm sorry, I thought we were whispering," he offered.

"Oh, sure, it was more like two male dogs growling over there."

David took her free hand, held it, and looked shamefaced. "How are you feeling?" Jake asked.

"Like I was ridden hard and put away wet," Nina said, and she gave them both a little smile.

God, Jake loved this woman. When his life had come unraveled she'd been there for him, making sure he'd eaten, including him in all the family stuff. Even with her illness, even though he knew how tough it was for her, she'd been his friend.

He stared down at her and smiled. "I'll go now," he said, "let you two talk. I'm sure—"

"Oh, no, you don't," Nina said. "Not until you and David come to some sort of a decision about this witness."

David shook his head. "Babes, please, you don't understand. You know how many people make anonymous calls to the cops every day? Ninety-nine percent of them are either kooks or somebody out to screw somebody else. Jake's caller is probably some ex-con trying to mess with his head." He stroked Nina's arm. "And another thing, Captain Disoto would go ballistic if I went to him with an unsubstantiated story about a witness. He honest-to-God believes Taylor stumbled in on a burglar—bad timing."

Nina closed her eyes for a long moment, and even Jake knew she was about to chew David out. He felt like a total ass. He had no business buttonholing David in Nina's hospital room and dumping on him in front of her. Especially Nina, who believed almost as fervently as Jake that Taylor had been assassinated for his political beliefs.

Jake met David's gaze and tried to convey an apology. Then Nina opened her eyes. "Help him, David."

"Babes," David began, but it was no good, and by the time Jake made his escape from Denver General, he felt like a number-one heel for dragging Nina into this mess.

By the middle of the week, he wasn't feeling much better. Despite that pile of work awaiting him—despite a few concerned calls from lawyer friends awaiting those briefs—Jake had spent the better part of three days in the public library going over newspaper and magazine accounts of the last three months of Scott's life, looking for any hint of a liaison. Both Jake and David figured that if a woman existed, then there had to be some clue as to who she was: a mention of an aide, a photo of the candidate with a pretty young thing close by, adoration in her eyes. Something. Anything.

When he wasn't in the library, his eyeballs falling out of their sockets from scanning microfiche, he was on the phone to former campaign workers, but it was always the same story: "Gosh, Mr. Savelle, I really can't help you." And the one person who would most likely know if Scott had been with a woman that night—other than his wife, Heather, of course—was Scott's former private secretary, Anne Schaffer, and she'd hung up on Jake the instant he'd posed his first question. *Bitch,* Jake had thought, but then he'd revised his opinion: *Loyal bitch* was more like it.

There was another problem with Jake's renewed investigation: his sister. He had almost forgotten what finding a witness, a *woman,* in Scott's hotel room would do to Heather. God only knew, she'd been through enough when Scott was alive. And now, if such a person existed, the old wounds would be reopened. Was it fair to Heather? Wouldn't it be better all the way around if he let it go?

But he couldn't. He could no more ignore this new information than he could stop the blood from pumping through his veins. He tried hard not to think about Heather at all, but still he did, and when she phoned him on Thursday night and asked him to a dinner party at the Cherry Hills Country Club that coming weekend, Jake begged off. "I, ah, promised Shayne I'd keep Peaches this weekend, and I can't leave her alone in the apartment. You know."

"For Lord's sake," Heather said, "if you don't want to socialize, just say so. I only thought getting out a little would do you some good."

"I do get out," he said defensively.

"Of course you do," she shot back. Then her voice softened. "Oh, Jake, really, I'm only trying to help."

"I'm okay. Honestly."

"You're sure?"

"Scout's honor."

But after he hung up he felt a stab of guilt. Shouldn't

he at least have told her about the possibility of a witness? Talked over the implications?

On Saturday Shayne really did leave Peaches with him. She stopped by at noon, and he met her out front on Lawrence Street, girding himself for the inevitable confrontation, straightening his shoulders and putting his old insouciant smile on his face. Pity from his ex-wife would destroy him.

Peaches leaped out and jumped up on him the minute he opened the car door.

"New car?" he asked Shayne, eyeing the leather interior, trying to keep the edge from his voice.

"Well," Shayne said, her eyes hidden behind big round tortoiseshell sunglasses, "the old Range Rover had almost forty thousand miles on it." Then she did that thing with her streaked blond hair—that thing that had always made his stomach coil with longing—she reached up and twisted it into a quick knot at the back of her neck. Magic.

He looked away. "Wow, forty thousand miles. Wonder you didn't have a breakdown."

"Oh, Jake, come off it," she said. "I'm doing all right and I'm certainly not ashamed of it. I can't help it if you screwed up your life." Then she rested her head on the steering wheel. "Sorry. That was uncalled for. I only hope that you, well, learned something from it." She straightened. "Jake, you're still a good-looking man. You're smart and you were a damn good lawyer. If you'd . . ."

"Go on," he said tightly.

"You know, get over it, get on with things. I mean, look at how you're living. I don't want to sound like a snob, but really, *look* at this place."

Jake pivoted, scanned the old brick building, then shrugged.

"Okay," she said, "whatever. If you don't want advice I won't offer it."

He said nothing.

"I have to go. I'll pick Peaches up tomorrow around five, if that's okay."

"Sure." Again he shrugged. And then he couldn't help himself. He glanced at the skis in the roof rack—two pairs—and said, "Got a date in the mountains?"

She hesitated. "Yes," she finally said, "I do."

Wisely, he let it go.

Still, when she'd driven away, he couldn't stop the thought of Shayne with another man from sitting like a stone in his gut. And he wondered what it might have been like if he hadn't pursued the Taylor murder investigation—if he hadn't gotten himself disbarred. Would Shayne have stayed with him?

He looked down at Peaches, who was sitting docilely by his feet now, her big, brown golden-retriever eyes beseeching him, her feathery tail dusting the sidewalk.

"Okay, girl," he said, "so I'm a sap at heart." Then he grinned. "And I suppose *you* want to go for a run."

She sprang to her feet and barked.

"Figured," Jake said.

Wearing a knit ski cap over his dark hair, which badly needed a decent trim, a turtleneck and blue sweatshirt, and his navy blue sweatpants, Jake put Peaches on her leash and headed along Lawrence, straight through downtown Denver toward the Auraria campus.

He started out sluggishly despite the cold March afternoon. His mind was not on the run; he was thinking about Shayne and their marriage and how it had gone wrong.

He knew he was beating himself up. A few days ago, when he'd gotten the anonymous call, he had felt the old familiar fire in his blood, and he'd dared to believe he was over his depression. But now his odds of finding that witness—if there was one in the first place—were diminishing. The depression was creeping back. And seeing Shayne again . . . He could have done without that. It wasn't that he still loved her. The love had died. But, damn, it hurt somehow to realize she was going on so easily with a new life while his had flickered out like a spent match.

He crossed Speer Boulevard with the light, and jogged toward the entrance to the campus, trying to clear his head. What he *needed* to do was keep his hopes up, concentrate on the search. Was there some angle he'd overlooked? Something David hadn't considered? Was there someone else close to Scott that he should call?

Call, Jake was thinking, Peaches loping along by his side, he must have phoned a hundred people this past week, and a lot of the calls had been long distance. He could hardly wait to see his phone bill.

"Long goddamn distance," Jake panted and he stopped short, leaned over with his hands on his knees, and tried to catch his breath.

If the anonymous caller had been local there was no hope of tracing him. But if the call had been long distance, then maybe, just *maybe,* one of the phone companies had a record, and David had the authority to access those records.

Jake straightened, still panting, his breath a white plume suspended in the cold air. Peaches looked askance at him, and Jake had no idea he was grinning.

He'd made the run down to the Auraria campus in thirty minutes. It took him less than twenty to get home and dial David's number.

TWO

David Carmichael looked up from his desk, saw Capt. Barry Disoto approaching, and mumbled under his breath, "Ah, shit."

"What?" the woman on the other end of the phone said.

"Sorry." David shifted the receiver to his left ear. "Can I phone you right back, Nancy?"

"Oh, sure," she said, "I'm at your beck and call, detective."

He hung up just as his captain sat on a corner of his desk. "So, David, am I interrupting?"

"No, sir," David said. Actually, he'd damn near been caught checking out those long distance phone records for Jake with his contact at US West. If Disoto knew . . .

"I want to hear all about how your wife is doing," the captain was saying. "Did she get the flowers okay?"

"Yes, and she wanted me to thank you."

Barry Disoto waved a dismissive hand. "And her exploratory surgery? No complications?"

"No, sir, well, a slight reaction to the anesthesia, but she's home now and doing just fine."

"Glad to hear it. I don't know much about bone marrow transplants . . . Now, that is what she had last year?"

"Yes, that's right, sir."

"And this was follow-up surgery?"

David nodded.

"You know," Disoto said, "if there's any problem with the department's insurance . . . I know how tough these companies can be on experimental procedures."

David nodded again. Tough wasn't the word. Brutal was more like it. And there wasn't a damn thing Disoto or anyone else could do about it.

Disoto stood and casually scrutinized David's desk. "Any progress on that north Denver double murder?"

"Not much, sir. I've got my informants asking around."

"Drug-related, most likely."

"That's our thought."

"Well, keep on it, detective."

"You bet, sir."

David liked Barry Disoto. All the guys in Homicide did. Movies and detective novels tended to portray police captains as fat, loud, stressed-out bullies. Disoto couldn't have been more different. He was tall and trim, distinguished in appearance, with an air of quiet competence. He always went to bat for his subordinates with the police commissioner or mayor or even Internal Affairs no matter the circumstances. A good man. And it bothered David to go behind his back.

Nevertheless, as soon as Disoto disappeared into his office, David called Nancy at US West again. He didn't have time for this, and the whole thing was better off left alone, but Jake Savelle could be a real pitbull when it came to his lofty standards of right and wrong and justice, and he wasn't going to let this go until David checked it out.

A witness in the hotel room, he thought, mentally scoffing, *no damn way.*

"It's me, Nancy," he said when his contact at the phone company came on the line. "Got anything on that call to Savelle's number?" *A witness,* he was still thinking, *right.*

But Nancy surprised him. "I do have a record of a call from Princeton, New Jersey, to Jake Savelle's number on the night of the twelfth, three-oh-six A.M. Eastern Standard Time."

"Really?" David said.

"Really, detective. Have I ever lied to you?"

"Ah, no," he said, then, "Can you pin the number down for me?"

"It's from a pay phone on the Princeton campus. If you need an exact location, I could go into the competition's records, but if I get caught . . ."

"No, that's all right, Nancy. If I need it that bad I'll call you back. I must admit, I am surprised. Princeton, huh?"

"Princeton, New Jersey."

He hung up and sat back in his chair. What the hell was going on here?

"Princeton?" Jake said, and then he promptly burned the side of his hand on the baking sheet he was removing from Nina's oven. "Damn."

"Run it under cold water." Nina shook her head.

"What do you think it means?" Jake asked David, who was filling the cooler for the trip to the Colorado Springs ice hockey play-offs.

"Run it under cold water, Jake," Nina repeated.

"I don't know what it means," David replied. "Like I said before, odds are it was some nutcase who's screwing with your head. You were pretty infamous for a while there, pal."

Jake grunted, staring at the raised red welt on his hand

as the cold water eased the pain. "Maybe. But Scott had just returned from campaigning up and down the East Coast before that rally in Denver. And, if my memory serves me correctly, he went on that trip alone. Heather was down with the flu or something, and she stayed in Denver."

"So?" David said.

"I don't know. Maybe Scott met someone in the East. Maybe he invited her here to Denver for a liaison."

"So?"

"Maybe she was from Princeton and was married and the call I got was from a pissed-off husband." Jake turned to Nina. "Sorry, that was crude, but it's a scenario that could fit."

David closed up the cooler and frowned. "What it is, pal, is science fiction. Now let's get all this stuff into the van and hit the road."

Sean's team won. It was a close game, two-two until the last forty seconds. And there was only one fight between hockey dads out in front of the Olympic Center, which Jake and David broke up, David muttering, "Assholes," the whole way across the parking lot to the van.

Nina held up wonderfully, although Jake worried about her. She was so thin, and she was obviously weak from the recent surgery. He would have put his arm around her in the van when she swayed a little, but he knew she was too proud to allow it. He envied David his family, a wonderful, loving wife, two big strapping boys. Jake caught himself. Hell, he was damn near broke, living in a two-room dump, no prospects for the future. A family? Fat chance.

He'd tried all evening to keep from thinking about the call from Princeton. This was not the time or the place—it was Sean's big night—and God only knew David was sick of hearing about it. Still, by midnight, when Jake arrived back at his apartment, it was stuck as firmly in his head as a tune he couldn't stop humming. Was there a connection between Taylor's East Coast campaign trip and the anonymous caller? And how did the hypothetical woman fit in?

Jake stripped down to his boxer shorts and T-shirt and lay in bed thinking, probing his memory as he would a sore tooth: Had he ever sent someone from Princeton to jail?

Dozens of cases and trials pressed on his brain, running together. Hadn't there been a hit-and-run driver—five, six years ago—a repeat DUI case, that Jake had prosecuted? The man had been sentenced to fifteen years hard time. And hadn't that man been from somewhere in eastern Pennsylvania? A place called Media? Was it close to Princeton? Had the man followed Jake in the press, learned of his disbarment, and could that man be out of prison by now, paroled, and seeking revenge?

But even to Jake's suspicious mind the scenario was too farfetched to consider.

The following day he caught up on some of the paralegal work and made three deliveries to three separate law firms. By four he was back at the library scanning microfiche. It was a boring, tedious job, frustrating, and the only thing keeping him going was the notion that if he actually found this mystery witness—and if the truth could be wrung out of her—then perhaps he might be reinstated to the Colorado bar. A lot of ifs.

He sat back in the library chair, legs stretched out, hands behind his head, thinking. Photographs. The newspapers and magazines contained mostly shots of Scott on the typical campaign trail, waving to crowds, kissing babies. Where would he find candid photos? Mob scenes? *Women*.

He almost hit his head with his palm. Tabloids. They'd loved Scott Taylor. My God, he'd been wasting his time with the straight news.

An hour into his new search he spotted his first possibility in the background of a tabloid photo taken in Philadelphia two weeks before Scott's murder.

A woman. Standing off to the side. Staring at Scott. There was something about her. . . . Still, the photo was too grainy to tell him much. He printed it out and kept on with his search. An hour later there she was again, at a rally in a Philadelphia suburb called Rosemont, standing behind Scott, smiling at the back of his head. Pretty lady. Dark-haired, pale skin from what he could tell. Young. Well, under thirty-five. To Jake that was young.

He made a copy of that photo, too, and then left the library and drove straight to an all-night Kinko's near the University of Denver where he had a couple of blowups made of both photos. It was the same woman, all right. The question remained, was this *the* woman.

At nine-thirty he phoned David and told him about the photos.

"Hell, Jake," David said, "so some bimbo was in a couple photos with Taylor. You've got nothing."

"Two photos from Philadelphia," Jake reminded him, "and New Jersey and Princeton are right across the river. It's a little too coincidental for me."

"Coincidental, pal, is the operative word. And even if there is some connection to this Princeton telephone call and some woman who allegedly witnessed the murder, how are you going to find her? It's crazy, Jake, the whole thing is right off the wall."

"There has to be a way. Maybe the photographer—"

"*Right.*"

"Okay, but someone has to know who she is. If Scott was having an affair, one of his campaign people would have known. Anne Schaffer, his private secretary, she'd know."

"Yeah. And didn't you tell me she hung up on you already?"

"This is different."

"Is it?"

"If you were to talk to—"

"Because I'm a cop you think she'll pour out her heart? Gimme a break. What she'd probably do is call my captain and complain I was harassing her." Jake could hear David's sigh over the line. "Ah, hell, let me sleep on it, okay?"

"Okay," Jake said, "and thanks. I know you could get your ass chewed over this."

"Bitten right off is more like it," David said, and he hung up.

It was Jake who contacted Anne Schaffer again, because David got tied up on a new homicide case, high profile, involving the shooting of a uniformed patrol officer. The whole department was called in on it, and Jake figured it would take days to investigate the crime scene.

Schaffer lived in Parker, Colorado, a booming suburb south of Denver. The phone was in Jake's hand when he abruptly changed his mind, deciding to drive to Parker and talk to the woman in person.

He dressed for the occasion, wearing a navy blue suit, white shirt and tie. It had been a long time, and as he fumbled with the knot on his tie, he felt rotten. Damn it, he should still be at the DA's office. It rankled him that his peers had so quickly accepted the juror's story that Jake had had sex with her during a trial. Her word against his. And they'd believed her despite a lie detector test he'd insisted on taking, one that had come out in his favor. Okay, so the DA had checked her bank accounts here in Denver for signs of a payoff. But that's as far as the so-called investigation had gone. Jake knew someone had conspired to get him disbarred: "Get rid of Savelle, he's rocking the wrong boat on this one."

Hell, Jake thought as he slipped on his overcoat, everyone with half a brain knew Taylor had been assassinated for his radical platform—assassinated because the polls showed him to be the clear leader in the presidential campaign. But no one in politics gave a damn about the truth, not when it came to power and position and money.

Even Shayne, his own wife, had begged him to reconsider. "Jake, you're a fool, an obsessive fool. You don't get it. No one wants to know the truth. Drop it. Please."

Well, he hadn't dropped it. And she'd been right.

Jake drove a used British racing green BMW he'd picked up cheap after the divorce settlement. The car was okay in the summer, but it was squirrelly on the icy roads of winter.

Today was no exception, especially after the storm. And Anne Schaffer lived on a shaded hillside, a steep incline past snow-covered horse pastures. He didn't even try to negotiate her driveway, but walked instead, his wingtips getting soaked. He hardly noticed. He felt he was close to a breakthrough in a case that had defeated him eighteen long months ago. It was worth any inconvenience. If, of course, Ms. Schaffer would talk to him this time.

She was as cold as the icicles hanging from her eaves when she opened the door and saw him on her front stoop.

"Oh, God," she sighed, disgusted.

But Jake was persistent. If nothing else, ex–chief deputy DA Jake Savelle was persistent.

"You and I both know that Scott was murdered—*assassinated*—because he posed a threat to the Establishment. It's very hard for me to believe you can sit back and live with this knowledge knowing the murderer is walking around free. I don't know about you, Anne," he said, still on her stoop, "but at least I sleep at night and can look at myself in the mirror."

Anne Schaffer eyed him coolly. "I loved Scott Taylor," she said. "He was practically a son to me. How dare you suggest I'm involved in some sort of a cover-up?"

"Let's be honest. You were aware of every woman he

ever looked at. I know how much you cared for him. I also know you're still protecting him.''

She was stubbornly silent.

"But it's wrong,'' Jake went on, pressing home his point. "*Murder* is wrong, Anne. Even not wanting to open old wounds cannot justify your reticence to speak up.''

"What about Heather? She's your sister, Mr. Savelle. Have you considered what reopening the case might do to her?''

"Of course I have.''

"This purported witness you spoke of on the phone the other day, you said the caller told you it was a woman. A woman in the hotel room with Scott.''

"I know that.''

Anne Schaffer glanced down at the large manila envelope in Jake's hand. He could see a shiver run through her.

"I have two photos,'' he said.

Slowly she nodded.

"Would you look at them?''

"Would you go away if I told you no?''

"Maybe,'' he said. "But I'll find out who she is eventually.''

The woman was quiet for a long time, and then she stepped aside and allowed him entrance. Jake contained his relief, but the fire in his gut was sparking to life.

He never sat and Anne never invited him to. She stood in the middle of the living room and opened the envelope, pulled out the photos, glanced at them, then put them back in the envelope and carefully handed it to Jake.

He was ready to burst. She knew who the woman was.

"Anne?'' he said gently, in his best witness-stand coaxing voice. "Tell me who she is.''

"Her name is Sarah, Sarah Jamison.''

The fire inside him leaped into flames.

"She's from Philadelphia. Scott . . . He met her while he was campaigning there."

"Uh-huh," Jake got out.

"I wouldn't know at which function. There were so many." She expelled a long, quavering breath. "I believe she was a campaign volunteer. Now, if you'll leave my house, please. And don't contact me again. I won't talk to you or anyone else."

Jake nodded solemnly. "Thank you," he said. "You did the right thing, Anne."

She didn't say another word, only showed him the door. He walked down the slippery drive, the snow crunching beneath his feet. By the time he was in his car he could no longer contain his excitement.

"Sarah Jamison," he said aloud, switching on the ignition, "Sarah Jamison." A name for the face. The name of the candidate's mistress? He felt a thrill pulsing in his gut. At last a door had opened—perhaps only a crack. But, by God, he could get his foot in.

That afternoon, in his jeans and a ratty Denver University sweatshirt, he sat on his couch and booked a flight to Philadelphia. While he waited on hold, he pulled out the photos and laid them on the coffee table, on top of the unfinished briefs. He studied the face of Sarah Jamison.

She was no more than thirty-five. She appeared slender, though it was hard to tell because in both shots she was wearing a coat. She had longish, curling hair, very dark brown, and incredibly pale skin. He couldn't tell the color of her eyes. Dark, probably, or maybe only shadowed. Her features were delicate. Not exactly beautiful, but intriguing.

Then Jake caught himself. No, he decided, the phone still to his ear, it was her smile that intrigued him. It was somehow elusive, the extraordinarily feminine smile of da Vinci's Mona Lisa, though this woman was hardly a Madonna type.

Scott Taylor's mistress.

If it was true that she'd been witness to his murder, if Sarah Jamison had indeed seen the crime, then why hadn't she come forward? Fear? Fear for her own safety?

He finally got his flight booked and then hung up and sat back against the cushions and mentally ticked off what he'd need to get done before the trip. God only knew how long he'd be away.

Pay rent. Call Shayne and let her know he couldn't baby-sit Peaches next weekend. Of course he'd bring David up to speed. He could ask the lady downstairs to keep his mail for him.

What else?

Pack. Was it warmer in Philadelphia than here? Sure. And humid.

Jake made his mental list with the feeling he was forgetting something. The rest of the afternoon passed with that same notion nagging him. It wasn't until dinnertime that he finally allowed himself to acknowledge it—that one last chore before he got on the plane.

He had to let his sister know what was going on.

And suddenly, realizing he could no longer avoid telling Heather, the wind went right out of his sails.

Heather Taylor looked up from the book she'd finally found time to read, frowned, then glanced at her watch as the doorbell chimed again. Nine o'clock at night. Who in heaven's name would come by at this hour?

When she saw Jake standing on the threshold she was unaccountably relieved. It was only her brothoer. But then she saw his face, his expression, and foreboding furled inside her breast.

"Sorry I didn't call first," he said, his hands jammed into the pockets of his parka. "But I just wanted to stop by and talk for a minute. I hope it's okay?"

"Of course it is, come on in. Can I fix you a drink? Or would you like coffee? I have decaf." She covered her misgivings with chatter.

"Ah, no, nothing. I'm fine."

"Well, then, let's go sit by the fire."

"Sure," he said.

Heather had a beautiful home. It was built of lichen stone, wood, and glass and sat protectively nestled in the trees off a fairway at the exclusive Cherry Hills Country Club. She'd decorated the five thousand square feet of space herself, every inch, her taste so impeccable the house had been featured in *Architectural Digest*. She was terribly proud of her house—one of the few perks she'd procured from her marriage to Scott, who'd come from Denver oil money. She had thought of selling the house after his death—dozens of friends had inquired why she hadn't—but, really, why should she? It wasn't as if she couldn't bear this place without Scott. That didn't bother Heather in the slightest. Her reply to her friends had been simple: "I can't bring myself to part with it." Which was true.

Jake sat in Scott's favorite leather chair near the fireplace in the sweeping living room, and Heather returned to her couch across from him, her book still open on the glass table beside her.

"Well," she said, "I can't remember the last time you dropped by."

"It's been a while."

"Months."

"Mm."

"So why the visit? Not that I mind, of course." She almost mentioned that she had just run into Shayne at a gallery opening in LoDo, but she bit back her words. Jake was still sensitive about Shayne leaving him. And Shayne had not been alone.

Heather shook off her thoughts, smiled, and fixed her attention on her little brother. "Well," she said again.

"I'm going to Philadelphia," he began, and she noticed his gaze slide away.

"Philadelphia?"

He nodded. "It has to do with Scott."

"Scott? But . . . ?"

Jake held up a hand. "Let me tell you what's happened." He took a breath. "It started with a phone call, an anonymous call late the other night." He paused, as if to form his next words with great care. Heather knew that pause. She shifted uneasily in her chair.

"The caller claimed that Scott had not been alone when he was killed."

Heather opened her mouth to say she didn't understand, and then she clamped it shut. *A woman.* Jake was going to tell her Scott had been with a woman.

"He said there was a woman in the room. A witness."

"Frankly," she said, "I don't give a damn. Or is it 'Frankly, *my dear,* I don't—' "

"Heather."

"You mean I'm not amusing?"

"This is deadly serious." Jake leaned forward, elbows on knees, hands clasped. "This woman may have witnessed the whole thing."

"You mean . . . ? Oh. Oh, God. If this, this woman saw the murder, then it's going to come out . . . The press, everyone will know . . . Oh, God, oh no. Scott's dead. What good would it do to drag all this up?"

Then suddenly she knew. It was Jake. All Jake. *That's* what this was about, her brother and his damnable sense of right and wrong. Nothing was gray to him. It never had been.

She looked up sharply. "Just drop it, Jake. This won't get you anywhere. And even if it did, even if this woman saw who killed Scott, it doesn't mean you'll be vindicated."

"This isn't about me."

"Oh no? I suppose you're doing this for *me.*"

"Heather, please."

"Please nothing. You haven't changed one bit since you were a child. You're obsessive. Remember in school when that boy—I don't even recall who it was, but he pulled my ponytail and even though I begged you not to get involved because he was three years older and twice your size, you just had to. He hit you so hard you still have a scar. And do you know what you said?'' She was so furious she was trembling. ''You said you couldn't let a wrong pass like that. It wasn't even *your* hair he pulled. God, Jake, can't you see? I don't miss Scott. I was almost relieved when he was killed. My marriage was torture. Oh, sure, he left me quite comfortable.'' She made a gesture with her hand. ''But Scott was a cheater and a liar, and I paid for all this. Oh, did I pay. And now you want to drag me through the mud?''

Jake remained silent.

''Answer me, goddamn it, why are you doing this?''

''He was murdered. It's that simple. And the murderer is walking around as free as a bird. If we don't have the law, Heather, if we choose to ignore the rules because it suits us, then we've lost our mortal souls. How *can* I ignore this?''

''For me,'' she cried. But it was no good. This was Jake Savelle, crusader. Goddamn him.

He finally stood. He made a move toward her, but she shied from him.

''I'll go now,'' he said quietly. ''Nothing has happened yet. Maybe nothing will. I only thought you should know.''

Heather fought back tears of rage and pain and could only shake her head at him futilely.

''Are you all right?'' he asked.

''No, I'm not.''

''I'm sorry,'' he tried. ''I didn't mean to upset you.''

''The hell you didn't.''

She watched him put on his parka, pull on his gloves, and when he turned to her, his eyes seeking her understanding, she showed him her back and waited for him to leave.

She heard his car start up, heard it pull out of her driveway. Hugging herself, she stood at the window and stared out at the black night. Bitterness seeped through her; Scott, her dead husband, was tormenting her from the grave. Through Jake. Oh, Jake had known about Scott's affairs, but the two of them had always gotten along so well, like brothers. The up-and-coming young senator celebrated for his protean political talents and the incorruptible, fearless young prosecutor.

Birds of a feather, Scott and Jake. Both so careless of other peoples' feelings.

God, how she wanted to phone the one person she could count on. Pick up the receiver and dial his number. But she couldn't; he was at home—oh, yes, at home with his wife.

THREE

Born, bred, and schooled in the West, Jake felt like an intrepid explorer in a new land. Philadelphia was so old, so tradition-bound. He couldn't comprehend the city's age—over three hundred years. The very air felt different.

He took a room on Broad Street, in a rough area not far from Temple University. He would have liked to stay in Society Hill and dine at Bookbinder's, but his financial situation wouldn't allow it.

On his first full day there, he walked to the public library where he knew he'd find the Philadelphia and vicinity phone books. It was warm out, and softly humid, and he was already sweating in his trousers, sweater, and sport coat three blocks into his journey. He would have taken a cab—there were plenty—but he had no idea how long he was going to be in the East or how long his credit card would hold out till he was cut off.

His first shock came when he discovered there were a hundred or more Jamisons in the greater Delaware Valley. He sat back and realized he'd have to phone damn near all of them. The odds of one of the three Sarahs listed being *the* Sarah Jamison were probably not all that good. Not the way *his* luck had been running.

In a stroke of genius, Jake talked the hotel manager into cutting a deal for local phone charges. The manager agreed to a flat rate of ten dollars.

"Better than the Hilton," Jake muttered, then he took the steps to his third-floor room and began the task of dialing every last number on his list.

As he'd suspected, none of the Sarahs were the Sarah he wanted. By the thirty-fifth Jamison on his list he was beginning to despair. What if the woman he sought wasn't even from here or was a student at Temple or Penn or God knew where else? Hell, Scott had liked them young. But Anne Schaffer would surely have told him that much. She'd said Sarah Jamison was "from Philadelphia." She wouldn't have lied. But maybe she'd had the wrong information.

Of course, Jack realized on the fiftieth call, maybe Sarah Jamison or her family was unlisted. In that event, he would have to solicit David's help to get the number. He'd really hate to call and ask, and he hoped it wouldn't come to that.

He struck pay dirt, with a Roger Jamison, on the seventy-eighth call. "My name is Jake Savelle," he began on the line to a woman who'd answered the phone by saying, "Jamison residence." "I'm an acquaintance of Sarah's. We met in Denver during the Scott Taylor campaign. I was wondering if she is home, or if . . ."

"Miss Sarah is away, sir."

Jake's heart began to beat heavily.

"Oh, too bad," he said, "I'm only in town for a short time."

No reply.

"I don't suppose you have a number where I might reach her?"

"No, I don't."

"Gosh. Could you get a message to her, then?"

"That won't be possible."

"This *is* the Sarah Jamison who was with the senator's campaign?"

"Miss Sarah was only with those people"—*those* people, he noted—"for a very short time. As you no doubt know, the senator was killed."

"Yes, yes, of course."

"Now, I'm sorry I can't help, Mr. . . . ?"

"Savelle, Jake Savelle."

"Yes, well, good-bye, Mr. Savelle."

"Good-bye," he said, and he hung up.

The listing had been under Roger Jamison III. Jake circled it and snatched up his jacket and headed straight back to the public library. He tried to temper his excitement, but it was no good. He was so close, so damn close he could practically taste the sweetness of victory.

Two days later, his eyes sore from the strain of searching library, newspaper, and courthouse records, Jake was beginning to put together a picture of Sarah Jamison and her family. He was fortunate that they were a prominent clan, and that the newspapers followed the Philadelphia socialites with some interest.

The Jamisons of Bryn Mawr—a Main Line suburb—were evidently very old Philadelphia. And whereas a lot of old money had disappeared over the generations, it seemed that Roger Jamison was well heeled. At least he owned a large bank that boasted ten area branches. And Sarah's mother, Elisabeth, was a sculptor of some renown. He learned that Sarah was thirty-three years old; he learned where she'd gone to school, that she'd been a horseback rider of some merit, a debutante, and that the whole family was listed in the Social Register, and its roots dated back to an English colonists' ship called *The Welcome* that had sailed to the Colonies in the mid sixteen hundreds. It boggled his Western mind. And he wondered how a girl raised like that, with all that tradition and money and opportunity, could have ended up in Scott Taylor's bedroom.

He ran across two other items that held his interest. Sarah had had an older sister, Constance Conway Jamison, who had died in her teens. The society page obituary said only that the young girl had died at her Bryn Mawr home. Nothing about an accident or extended illness, and surely that information would have been mentioned. Jake had to surmise that there was something not quite right about the girl's death. And, sure enough, later that same day in the library, Jake ran across a piece in a not-so-social paper that stated Constance had taken her own life.

"Damn," Jake whispered to himself. That had to have been rough on the family.

The second item of interest was a graduation announcement for Sarah's only brother, a boy who would be in his early twenties now, Phillip. The kid had graduated from the Haverford School four years ago. Did this Phillip know where his sister was? Perhaps they were close, especially after the loss of Constance. But where was the kid now? College? Home? Traveling the world on a trust fund? Jake made a mental note to find out.

The following afternoon he rented a midsize white car that would serve to get him around.

He was uncertain about how to approach the family, a rare state of affairs for Jake Savelle. But he'd cook up something to tell them. He'd always been good at improvising, a fast thinker on his feet. Well, what trial lawyer wasn't?

The one thing he did feel confident of was that someone—Roger or Elisabeth or Phillip—had to know Sarah Jamison's whereabouts, and he'd damn well stay here in the East until he found her.

The argument began in the dining room. It always began in the dining room, Phillip thought as he looked up from his plate and met his father's eyes.

"Not one more dime," Roger Jamison said. "You'll get your usual monthly check on the first."

Phillip pushed the plate away. The early meal before he returned to college after a two-day visit had been his mother's idea, food equaling love in her mind. He wasn't hungry. He *was* in need of money, having lost over two thousand dollars betting on March Madness basketball with his social club brothers.

"I'd really like to get this course under my belt before graduation," Phillip said, tight-lipped. "It's expensive, I know, but the lecturer is first rate."

Roger also nudged his plate aside and absently signaled for the maid to remove it. He picked up his cocktail and drained it. "What kind of a fool do you take me for? Do you think I don't get copies of your grades?"

"My grades don't have anything to do with this," Phillip shot back.

"His grades weren't that poor," Elisabeth said from the other end of the long dining table that had been her great-great grandmother's. "He did have that dreadful bronchitis at midterms."

Roger glared at her. "It's no goddamn wonder this boy is failing. You believe every word he says." He turned back to Phillip. "The answer's no. No check. You'll wait till the first. I'm sick and tired of you coming home at will and trying to con me. You lost your money betting on college basketball, didn't you." It was not a question.

"You know," Phillip said, his face growing scarlet, "it wouldn't matter what I did, you'd find fault in it."

"You're a liar, boy, you always have been. An ineffectual liar."

Phillip shot up from his seat, almost knocking it over. He stared with undisguised hatred at his father, and his shaking hands were balled into fists at his sides. It wouldn't have mattered what he told the old man to get the money, the answer would have been the same. And there was his mother—her eyes nervously avoiding everyone, an emotional cripple. The old man had bullied her into submission, just like he'd bullied Sarah and Constance. Pushed Constance so hard with his drunken fits and brutal accusations, destroying her self-worth, that she'd killed herself, probably to show him, to have the last word. Phillip had only been a child, but he remembered.

And Roger had tried to do the same to Sarah. Anyone else would have been forced to examine what had gone so horribly wrong in his family after the suicide of a child. But not old Roger the Third. He'd merely turned his drunken venomous words onto Sarah, who, in spite of her gentle disposition, had managed to survive by living her life wholly apart from her family, mentally when she'd been a teenager, and later physically, rarely seeing either her mother or her father. Instead, she searched for herself outside this insanity.

Phillip continued to glare malevolently at his father, and a scene came rushing back to him, a suppressed memory. He was upstairs in bed—he was seven, eight years old?—and something awakened him. An argument. He wasn't sleeping well anyway, hadn't since the night Constance had slit her wrists in their parents' bathroom. The screaming, the wailing, the terror, the police, the ambulance, no one coming to his dark bedroom till hours later . . .

But on this night, a few months after the funeral, it was his father, drunk, confronting Sarah in her bedroom next door that had awakened Phillip. He'd forgotten the incident until now, the vicious words from his father, Sarah's pained voice.

"Where the hell have you been? It's two A.M.!" Roger, staggering drunk, in Sarah's bedroom door.

"I was at Barbara's. I told you. You said I could—"

"Not till this hour I goddamned didn't. You were out whoring with that slut friend of yours."

"Barbara isn't—"

"You're both *sluts*. And I know her parents are in Bermuda, you little . . ."

"They aren't! They were home tonight, we didn't—"

"*Look* at you. A skeleton. I don't know why any boy would even be interested." Slurring badly. "You didn't win that horse show last week because you're so goddamned skinny you couldn't hold your horse . . ."

"I am not," Sarah sobbed. "You called Constance a fat pig; now you think I'm too thin. Nobody can please you. I don't even care!"

Phillip had put his pillow over his head and shook and cried and tried so very hard to block out his sister's pain and his father's cruelty. It hurt so bad. . . .

He refocused on Roger now in the dining room and his face twisted. Constance had escaped the best way she knew how, in the process wounding her parents in a brilliant coup of retaliation, and he admired her endlessly for it. And Sarah . . . Sarah had gone on an odyssey in search of herself. Yet Phillip hadn't yet been able to tear himself from this madness. It was as if the misery of his existence was a shroud he wore, a cloak too comfortable to discard. His weakness terrified him.

"Get out," Roger was saying. "Go back to school and get out of my sight." He ignored Elisabeth's strained voice saying, "Roger, please. Please."

"You know," Phillip said, icy control solidifying in him, "you, *you* killed my sister."

"Phillip! No," Elisabeth choked out.

He went on, relentless. "You destroyed all your children."

"Sarah is not—" Roger began.

"You don't even know the half of it," Phillip pressed on. "And if I'm a liar and a wimp it's *you*, both of you"—he pivoted toward his mother—"who made me what I am. So live with it. Live with your dead child and your lost one and me." He studied their faces and felt a surge of power—*yes,* it was as if he'd shot arrows straight into their breasts.

"Screw you both," he said. "I'm going up to get my stuff and I'm out of here." He made his exit, shoulders squared, a great exit, he thought, and he knew he'd win the day.

Five minutes later Elisabeth tapped meekly on his bedroom door and handed him a check for two thousand dollars. She was teary-eyed and contrite, her hands trembling. She air-kissed his cheek and left.

Roger wasn't as quick to take the bait. It wasn't until Phillip was starting up his Porsche in the courtyard out front that his father came to him, drunker than he'd been at dinner, check in hand. Pitting them against each other was a family tradition. Constance had tried to do it; Sarah knew the game. But no one played it as deftly as Phillip.

He started the engine, refusing to meet his father's eyes. He'd gotten what he wanted—two checks—one from each guilt-ridden parent. The irony was that they'd always confused money with love. They were unable to provide the emotional safety net their offspring so desperately craved. So they wrote checks. This, too, Phillip had learned, was a family tradition.

He roared out of the courtyard and down the long lane to the road. He wasn't sure if he felt elated and triumphant or sick with whirling confusion. He drove too fast along the winding road, taking a single-lane stone bridge at sixty. He was thinking about Sarah—Sarah could explain his feelings to him—and he wondered if she were happy and safe. He knew he could phone her, but she'd made him promise only to call in a dire emergency. Still, he needed to hear her voice.

He was lost in thought, not so sober himself after the long afternoon at home, and he took a dip and an immediate curve in the road so fast that he almost forced an oncoming car off into the dirt, a piece-of-shit white rental, he noticed idly as he sped by, downshifting, hitting the gas again.

He looked in his rearview mirror and said, under his breath, "Asshole," then he disappeared into the dusk, his hard-won checks folded safely in his pocket.

FOUR

Still rattled by the near miss, Jake parked his rental car
at the entrance to the Jamison estate. Were all Pennsylvania drivers that crazy? He sat there for a minute, studying the place. The countryside was green, brilliant, an
unlikely green to a Western eye, even this early in the
spring. Rolling verdant hills bracketed by thick wood-
lands, leafed out in early pastel green. White fences, stone
walls, horses frolicking in the fields in golden evening
light. The Jamison house—the manor—sat behind ivy-
covered stone walls and a small stone house. A guest
house? The scene was out of a period piece, an English
movie; it reeked of money and privilege, and Jake felt
like a brash, raw Westerner: Davy Crockett visits the East.

He took a deep breath and got out of his car. Smoothed
his hair back. Strode up the immaculate stone driveway
as if he knew what he was doing.

What if Sarah herself opened the door? What would he
say? How would he get her to talk to him? But he dis-
missed the notion as unlikely. Why would the woman

he'd spoken to on the phone have lied to him? Nah, Sarah wasn't living at home.

Mrs. Jamison answered the door. A slender, once-pretty lady with dark hair, the bones of her face sharp under her skin. Apparently she had the same pale skin as her daughter.

Jake put on his act. "Mrs. Jamison? Elisabeth Jamison?"

"Yes?"

"Well, it's so nice to meet you. My name is Jake Savelle. I met Sarah in Denver when she was there with the Taylor campaign."

"You know Sarah?" her mother asked in a reedy voice.

"I sure do. I know it's crazy, me just knocking on your door like this, but Sarah knew I was going to move to Philadelphia. And she was so nice, she said to look up her folks. So"—he smiled a genuine, fourteen-carat smile—"here I am."

"Mr. Savelle—" Sarah's mother began.

"Who in hell is it?" came a voice from inside the house.

Elisabeth Jamison turned. "It's a young man, a friend of Sarah's." Then to Jake, "I'm so sorry to keep you on the doorstep like this. Please come in. Roger?"

Threadbare, probably priceless Persian rugs covered a polished wood floor. The furniture was dark, heavy, more formal than Jake was used to, with touches of brass and copper and honey-colored pieces of early American stuff that should have been in a museum. And there were three or four rooms serviced by the elegant entrance hall. A living room, library, dining room, and what appeared to be a formal office, one that would suit an upscale stockbroker's ad.

The ceilings were all low, not vaulted or beamed in this stately home. So very different from the open floor plans and high ceilings popular nowadays. Elegant, yes,

Jake decided, the smile plastered on his lips, but claustrophobic to someone raised in the vast spaces of the mountain states.

A heavyset man with white hair was coming through a set of French doors. He had on a banker's suit, matching vest, in a dark pinstripe. The double-breasted jacket fell open over his belly. Two spots of red stained his cheeks, his bushy white eyebrows met in a frown, and in his hand was a tall glass of what appeared to be bourbon.

"Mr. Jamison, it's so nice to meet you. Sarah spoke of the both of you so often," Jake said glibly.

"She did, did she? Wonder what she said," Roger Jamison growled.

Jake smiled until it hurt.

"Come in and sit down, Mr. Savelle." Elisabeth graciously laid a hand on his arm.

"Jake, call me Jake, please." He followed her narrow back into the living room. Many-paned double doors looked out onto a pool and, beyond that, acres of manicured lawn and flowering shrubs.

"Would you like a drink?" Roger Jamison held up his glass.

"Do you have a soft drink?" Jake asked. "A Coke or something?"

"A Coke?" Sarah's father laughed. "Elisabeth, would you get our guest a Coke?"

Jake realized with a bit of a shock that Roger Jamison was not exactly drunk, but well on the way. Voice too loud, too hearty, face red. The thickened skin, the bloat. Yes, Roger was a drinker.

Elisabeth handed Jake a glass that tinkled with ice cubes. "Thank you so much, ma'am."

He sat down on a pale lemon brocade sofa, across from Roger, feeling suddenly that, like Alice in Wonderland, he'd fallen through the rabbit hole into a world where things were a touch off.

Elisabeth sank gracefully into a chair and leaned forward eagerly. "So you know Sarah?"

"Oh yes, we were great friends."

"Have you seen her recently?" Elisabeth asked. "She's been—"

"Elisabeth."

"Sorry, Roger, it's just that it's been so long, and I . . ."

"I don't think this young man needs to hear about all that," Roger said.

"Oh, sure, I saw Sarah, let me see," Jake pretended to think, "a few months ago. In Denver."

"Oh, thank God," Elisabeth said. "I've been so worried. Was she all right?"

"Fine. Just fine. She's a beautiful girl. You must both be so proud of her," Jake lied smoothly. "But she's busy, you know, real busy. Probably hasn't had a minute to call home."

"What is she doing?" Elisabeth folded her hands tightly in her lap.

"Oh, she's, well, I guess last time I saw her she was, um, running a gift shop. Managing it, you know."

"A gift shop," Roger said sarcastically. "Send her to the best schools, and what does she do?" He raised his glass to salute his folly and drank.

"A gift shop," Elisabeth repeated, "how nice." Her lower lip quivered and her eyes glistened with tears.

"Now, Elisabeth," Roger said.

"Roger, please, can't you see how relieved I am? Stop trying to bully me." A tear followed the fine network of wrinkles under her eye. "Did she look all right, Mr. Savelle? Sometimes she gets too thin."

"She looked fine, Mrs. Jamison."

"Oh dear, I'm silly, aren't I?" Elisabeth pulled a linen hanky from her pocket and dabbed at her eyes.

"Would I be acquainted with your family?" Roger was asking. "French, are they? Savelle."

"I doubt it, sir. My father died a long time ago, and my mother resides in south Florida. Warm weather." Jake smiled charmingly.

"Hm. What brings you to Philadelphia?"

"Well, I got a good offer at a law firm here."

"Which one?"

"Uh, Ralston and, uh, Frank."

"Don't know it. Must be one of those new ones."

Jake smiled and smiled, nodded in agreement. Now that he knew Sarah wasn't here, that her parents obviously had no idea where she was, he felt an urge to escape. This was not a happy house. But he fought the urge; he might pick up some crumbs of knowledge about the mysterious and apparently missing daughter.

"Do you happen to remember the name of the gift shop Sarah manages?" Elisabeth was asking, her head tilted oddly, as if listening to secrets only she heard.

"Actually, I don't. I was never there. I'm sorry."

"Oh."

"Elisabeth, don't badger Mr. Savelle. If Sarah wants to get in touch with us she will."

Neither of them was going to call him Jake, he guessed.

"Yes, I know, I just . . ." Elisabeth subsided and touched the hanky to her eyes.

Roger drained his glass and set it down. "Excuse me, I have some work to do. Nice meeting you, Mr. Savelle." The man stood with some effort, and extended his hand. He swayed a little, and Jake could smell the alcohol on his breath. Conspiracy hung about him like heavy chains. Jake stood quickly and shook Roger's hand. *Work.* Sure, he thought as he sat back down and Roger left the room.

Elisabeth asked him, "What did you and Sarah talk about? She spoke of her family?"

"She certainly did."

"Did she tell you I am an artist?"

"Oh yes."

"She was always proud of my work," Elisabeth mused. "Would you like to see it?"

A lonely woman with a drunk for a husband, one daughter dead, and another who hadn't been home in a long, long time. He felt pity for Sarah's mother, and a bizarre curiosity. "I'd love to. Are you sure you don't mind? Is it too late?"

She waved a thin hand. "Not at all."

She led him into a butler's pantry then through the kitchen, down a corridor that suddenly became unfinished, and into a large room with a central table, a stool, and a welter of spatulas and knives and plaster spatters.

"This is where I work."

"Wonderful," Jake said.

She was a sculptress. Funny nothing of hers had been in the house. Bronzes mostly, horses, a lot of horses, and busts of people. Faces, all around him, bronze, blank faces, burnished, lovingly crafted. A few of marble, some unfinished plaster casts.

"Roger doesn't like them in the house. But I sell some. There's a shop in West Chester that carries my work. Not"—she smiled gently—"that I need the money, but so that I can share them with people."

"They're very beautiful."

"Did Sarah tell you about the series I did of the family? Years ago. When Constance was still alive." Another tear formed in her eye. "Constance died, you know. When she was eighteen. A riding accident. We sold that horse."

A riding accident? Jake remembered the obituary of Constance Jamison. Elisabeth was lying. Yet he could swear she believed her own words. Did she use fantasy to dull the pain as Roger used alcohol?

"I'm so sorry."

"This is Constance." Elisabeth put her veined hand on the head of a young girl, touched it as if it were alive, the way a mother caresses a child's head to assure herself of its safety and well-being. It was painful.

"She was seventeen when I did this one."

It was hard to conjure up the image of a living girl from the bronze—it lacked coloring. A straight nose, curly hair, fine, curving lips, a pretty if unfinished face. A young girl, after all. Yet there was a brooding quality to the bronze of Constance, something in the eyebrows, a tension. What secrets was Elisabeth Jamison keeping?

"It's beautiful," he said.

"She was very lovely. Wild, though. Constance was so wild." She sighed. "And that is Sarah." Again the maternal, achingly intimate caress. "She was only sixteen."

He stepped around so that he could study Sarah's face. Sixteen years old. There was a tranquility in this bronze, quite different from her sister's. Same curly hair, tied back into a cascade of curls frozen in metal. A poignancy in her expression, a tiny smile tilting up the corners of her mouth. The bemused Mona Lisa smile. Not happy, exactly, but hopeful. Or was he imagining things?

He had seen that smile in the grainy tabloid photographs. But surely she was harder now, not the vulnerable teenager anymore. Yes, she certainly must have changed a lot, taking up with the likes of Scott, a married man. How many had there been before him? And how many since? What exactly did Sarah look like in person now? Jaded, blasé, too many miles on a youthful body?

He had a sudden sharp desire to meet her in the flesh, to judge for himself what the years of fast-lane living had done to her.

"She seems very mature for sixteen," Jake said, just to say something.

"Does she? She was dreamy as a child, then she was, well, I guess you could say unsettled. She never discovered her path in life. She was such a free spirit."

Elisabeth spoke as if Sarah was dead. Was she? Could that be possible? But no, it couldn't, or her parents would

have been notified. No, Sarah, it seemed, had gone to
ground. He experienced a burst of satisfaction. She must
have witnessed the murder. It made sense. The whole
damn crazy thing was beginning to make sense.

"And that's Phillip. He was my late-life child. He takes
after his father more than the girls did."

A smiling head with heavier features, an ordinary looking boy.

"Where is Phillip now?" Jake asked out of politeness.

"He's a senior at Princeton. A very good student. They
were all good students, although the girls never applied
themselves . . ."

Jake felt his heart skip a beat, and her voice faded to
a background mumble. *Princeton?* My God. Could the
anonymous caller have been . . . ? But Elisabeth had
stopped talking now, and he had to respond.

"Princeton's a marvelous school," he said. "Phillip is
a lucky young man."

"Oh yes, yes, he is," she said, but her tone was thin
and lacked veracity.

Jake wanted to get out of there with a kind of desperation. He needed to think, to consider. He needed more
than ever to find Sarah. And Phillip, he needed to talk to
him, too. He started conjuring up excuses in his mind,
excuses to leave this echoing, sad house, this poor woman
who lived among bronze heads from the past, a lonely
museum curator.

"My gosh," he said, glancing at his watch. "It's so
late. I really do have to get going. Work tomorrow morning, you know."

"I'm so glad you came by." She turned away from
her display shelves. "And if you see Sarah or, well, if
you hear from her, please tell her we're thinking of her.
All the time. We miss her so."

"I certainly will, but now that I've moved here to the
East, well, I probably won't."

"Of course."

"Thank you again for your hospitality, Mrs. Jamison. And thank Mr. Jamison for me. I enjoyed meeting you." God, he sounded like an idiot.

She was leading him back through the house, a thin, erect figure in a high-collared silk blouse and a straight skirt. Elisabeth Jamison seemed fine, on top of things, until you heard the quaver in her voice or looked into her eyes.

She was opening the front door. "Good-bye, Mr. Savelle. Come back again sometime."

"Thanks, I will. Good-bye." *Idiot,* he berated himself again.

The heavy door closed behind him, and he began to stride down the driveway, gulping in the fresh, humid night air. That house was stifling. He'd never in his life been exposed to such an aura of dark secrets and frenzied pain. Had Scott been aware of this facet of Sarah's life? Had he been playing father to her? Had he taken advantage of her vulnerability?

Or had Sarah done the seducing? Maybe she was a high-class adventuress whose address book was crowded with famous men's names. Or maybe she'd had a more serious relationship with Scott. Love?

An unaccountable irritation filled Jake at the thought. He brushed it aside. What the hell did he care? Scott was dead. Finding the woman was all that mattered.

Phillip Jamison walked downstairs to the pay phone in the front hall of his club at Princeton. No way was anyone going to trace Sarah through his phone records. Hell, he'd seen enough cop movies to know that. It was late, and no one was up, but he was careful anyway, just in case. He'd already figured out what to say if anyone saw him.

He had the forbidden number memorized, although he'd only called her once before in a year and a half. Usually she called him, but that wasn't very often, either.

He couldn't stop himself; he guessed it was the fight

with his parents that had capped it; he felt a desperate need to talk to her, because she *knew,* she understood. He didn't have to analyze or explain. He didn't have to start at the beginning.

He punched in the numbers, figuring it was two hours earlier there. Still, maybe he'd wake her up, but she wouldn't mind. Not Sarah.

His gut hurt. It always did after one of his family's knock-down-drag-out fights. Sure, he got what he wanted, but at what cost? Constance had paid the ultimate price, and sometimes Phillip, in an infantile fantasy, imagined himself dead and his mother and father crying over him, revering his memory.

He'd learned to put up a good front, but sometimes he had to let the pain out, like steam from a pressure cooker, or he'd explode. Sarah would listen, give advice, she'd help. She always had. Sarah, who'd been more of a parent to him than anyone.

The phone rang, once, twice, three times. Did she have an answering machine? Not that he'd leave a message. He couldn't. Four times. He was going to hang up when there was a click in his ear and a sleep-clogged voice saying, "Hello?"

"Sarah, it's me."

"Phillip? What time is it? What's the matter?"

"Nothing. Nothing's the matter. It's not an emergency. Sorry. But I had to talk to you."

"Damn it, Phillip, I thought you understood . . ."

"I'm on a pay phone, don't worry."

"That's not the point. You promised."

"I know, I'm such a mess, though. I went home and we fought. The same old thing. I can't stand them, I really can't. You know what it's like."

"Don't go home," she said flatly.

"I know. I shouldn't. I was out of money. I know that's a shitty excuse, but I thought, I don't know. I always think it'll be different and it never is."

"It will never change. Deal with it. Stay away from them."

He couldn't talk, couldn't answer. He felt it swelling up in his throat, a poisonous goiter. Tears squirted from between his clenched eyelids.

"Phillip? Phillip?"

"I can't. I can't anymore. I want to go away, like you did. Anywhere. Be a ditchdigger or a carpenter or something. I can't take it anymore."

"Phillip, calm down. This will pass. You'll feel better in the morning. You know that. Just hang on and believe it, things will get better."

"What's the end? Tell me, what's the end? Is it like Constance?"

"No."

"I know why she did it. Oh boy, do I know."

"We both know. We're stronger than that."

"You are. Me, I don't know." He wiped at his eyes with a fist, like a little boy.

"You are, believe me."

"Sarah, I miss you."

"I miss you, too. But I'm here. You know that. In time . . ."

"How long?"

"I don't know. When I feel safe."

"Never. You'll never feel safe. I'm quitting school, goddamn it. I can't stay here another second with these dumb, naive *kids*."

"Don't quit. Listen to me. You've only got a couple more months. Don't quit."

"I can't stand it anymore!"

"You can, yes, you can. Only a few days. Take it day by day. You can do it."

"Shit, Sarah." A sob.

"I know."

"I want to leave all this and come out there where you are. I'll work. I can work."

"No."

"I hate them," he hissed.

"I know. Look, next summer . . . If you keep it secret you could visit me here."

There. He'd gotten what he wanted. He usually did. But at what cost? At what cost?

"I'd love to," he said.

"It's a secret."

"I can keep secrets."

"Yeah," she said drily. "I know."

"Sarah, I keep thinking. Why don't you go to the police? Turn yourself in and tell them. Get it over with. Then you can go on with your life."

Silence.

"Sarah?"

"I refuse to discuss it. I'll hang up if you mention it again."

"Sarah, please . . ."

"Not another word."

"You can't run forever. You can't hide forever."

"I told you . . . God, what have you done? What in hell started this? Damn it, Phillip, tell me the truth!"

"What truth?" Gooseflesh rippled on his arms.

"Have you said anything to anybody? *Have you*?"

"No, I wouldn't do that. I promised you. Christ, what do you think I am?" His voice was so smooth, so practiced, so goddamn *truthful* he could hardly believe it.

"For a minute there . . ."

"I'm sorry I scared you. But this call was about me, you know, the usual spoiled brat, poor little rich boy routine." Oh, could he lie. He'd learned to do it with his mother's milk.

"Okay. You better now?" she asked, concerned.

He deserved long, drawn-out torture for doing what he'd done to her. "Yeah, I'll live."

"Not funny, bro."

"Shit, it's just a figure of speech."

"Hang in there. I'll see you this summer. It's beautiful in Colorado in the summer. You'll love it."

"And I won't go home anymore."

"Good idea."

"Bye, Sarah. Thanks."

"Bye, Phillip."

He hung up, swamped with guilt. Torture was too good for him. He knew full well why he'd made that phone call to the lawyer in Denver. The disbarred lawyer. The nut who wouldn't drop the Taylor murder case.

And he recognized, too, why he'd called Sarah. Sure, it was the fight with the mater and pater, but it was more, much more. He'd wanted to feel her out, to see if he could confess what he'd done. Get some kind of absolution for betraying her secret to the one man who would pursue the information like a bloodhound on a scent.

Well, she wasn't ready to forgive him, and he might have put her in danger. He was so goddamn selfish. And he knew why he'd done it, despite all the risks. It was so he could have his sister back.

FIVE

Jake used a false name when he phoned Princeton to locate Phillip Jamison. He'd thought and thought about it and finally decided that if he showed up as Jake Savelle the kid would feel like a cornered rat, get defensive, and refuse to talk. Worse, he might contact Sarah and she'd run, go to ground so deep no one would ever find her.

The one thing Jake did know was that he'd have to be damn careful.

He used the name John Van Sant. He'd known a guy in law school by that name and plucked it out of the air. He only prayed that the Jamison kid hadn't seen pictures of him in the paper, or if he had, it had been so long ago he'd forgotten what disbarred Chief Deputy District Attorney Jake Savelle looked like.

He used the same tired story with Phillip—he'd met Sarah in Denver during the Taylor campaign. Would love to meet her younger brother, whom she'd spoken of so often. The kid wasn't in, probably at class or the library, but Jake left a message for him with his Philadelphia hotel phone number.

It worked. When he got back to the hotel that afternoon Phillip had replied: He'd be glad to meet Mr. Van Sant tomorrow at four o'clock in front of his club. And there were even directions.

Jake went over his story on the drive to Princeton the next day. "John Van Sant," he repeated out loud in the car. "John Van Sant." He wondered whether Phillip suspected who he really was, or if he figured John Van Sant had been sent by the one man on earth who had the most to gain by discovering Sarah's whereabouts. He had to be very cautious, cagey. Even if Phillip had made that call—and Jake was ninety-nine percent sure he had—the kid wasn't going to own up, and perhaps he was regretting that he'd done it in the first place.

Princeton was another revelation to Jake. Huge old trees, venerable buildings. The campus looked as if it had been there forever, grown up out of the ground into its present form. Everything seemed *right,* the way it always had been and always would be. Ivy League. Definitely not Denver University.

Sarah's younger brother looked like Roger must have forty years ago, before the bloat and the sag and the white hair. Pleasant in appearance, dressed in threadbare jeans and a T-shirt, like all the other kids, all the other young, optimistic, rich kids. Brown hair, even features, heavy shoulders.

"Where are you from?" Phillip asked after shaking his hand. "I mean, where did you meet Sarah?"

"I'm from Denver originally. That's where I met her. But I moved to Philadelphia recently."

"Denver."

"Yes, the campaign. The ill-fated campaign. Awful thing." He shook his head sadly.

Phillip led him inside, and Jake was instantly reminded

of every frat house he'd been in. Here, though, they were called clubs. Of course. This *was* Ivy League.

"Have you seen her lately?" Phillip was saying as they sat in the living room.

One thing Jake had learned as a trial lawyer was how to read people, an innate ability to spot the truth. He knew that he couldn't feed the same exact story to Phillip as he'd used on Roger and Elisabeth. The kid knew damn well his sister wasn't managing any gift shop in Denver. Phillip was on a fishing expedition.

"No, not for ages. That's sort of why I'm here. Where'd she disappear to?"

The college kid shrugged. "I don't know. She left Philadelphia over a year ago. No one's heard from her."

Liar. "But she always told me that you two were so close. I can't believe she wouldn't have contacted you." Jake smiled innocently.

"Well, she hasn't." Phillip looked at him hard, a little too intensely for a seemingly casual student. "When did you say you moved here?"

Shit. "Midwinter. It certainly is a change from the West." Another smile. Was he laying it on too thick?

"Did you move to Philly for a job or something?"

Jake nodded. "Better offer. I'm in financial management."

"Uh-huh."

Tactfully, Jake switched subjects. "So, what're you majoring in?"

"English, the usual stuff. My old man wanted me to go into the family bank, but no way."

"I got you."

At that point Jake was sorely tempted to cut the crap and tell Phillip outright that he knew the kid had phoned him and that he had to find Sarah. Phillip had yet to tell a single truth. It was in his voice, in his body language, and Jake would love to skewer him the way he'd skewered lying witnesses in cross-examination. He didn't dare, though. *John Van Sant. John Van Sant. Keep up the act.*

"You want something to drink?" Phillip asked.
"There's a machine down the hall."

"Sure, a Coke would be good. I can't get over how
warm it is here in March. It's snowing back in Denver.
The altitude." He was chattering.

Jake fished out some change from his pocket, and the
Coke cans thumped down the chute. They walked back
to the living room and sat again in the old leather chairs.

"You know, my old man almost had a coronary when
Sarah left to work on Taylor's campaign. He hated that
man. Said he'd ruin the country. A bleeding heart lib-
eral." Phillip shook his head, remembering, and Jake filed
the information away. Just how much had Roger Jamison
disliked the candidate? Hated that his daughter—his only
surviving daughter—was having an affair with Taylor?
Interesting.

Jake fed out a little more line. "It's really too bad
Taylor never had a chance to prove what he could do. He
might have been a great president. We all had very high
hopes."

"Yeah. And look who got elected. Surprise. The boring
old vice president. Politics as usual," Phillip said scorn-
fully.

"Are you into politics?"

"God, no."

"But Sarah was."

"Only because of Taylor. She never had been before."

"I was sure hoping to hook up with her. I called your
folks"—a little white lie—"and they said they didn't
know where she was."

"They don't."

"But I was sure you would. Has she left the country?
Doing Europe or something?"

Another shrug of the broad shoulders. "I really don't
know."

"Damn. I thought maybe she'd be around, you know,

and I'm relatively new in town. It'd be nice to know a native.''

''She'd never come back and live here again. She despised it.''

''New start in the West, huh? Well, Denver's overflowing with people doing that.''

''Listen, Mr. Van Sant''—emphasis on the name—''I've got a class soon. It's been swell talking to you. Sorry I can't help you find my sister.''

''Yes, too bad. Well, Phillip, thanks for your time. I appreciate it.''

''No prob.''

Jake walked back across campus to his rental car, thinking. Phillip knew where Sarah was, but the kid wasn't talking. He was trying to protect his sister. She'd probably sworn him to secrecy.

The question remained: Why in hell had Phillip called Jake and told him there'd been a woman in the hotel room the night of Scott's murder?

It made no logical sense. But Jake had learned people were rarely logical. He reached the car and got in, turned the key in the ignition. There were several reasons Phillip might have made that call. Jake went over them in his mind as he drove through the verdant New Jersey farmland on the way back to the city.

Phillip hated his sister, some kind of sibling rivalry caused by that screwed-up family, and wanted to get back at her. Or an inheritance thing. Phillip wanted to ruin Sarah in their father's eyes, get her disinherited.

It was a possibility. Jake went over Phillip's reactions in his mind, but he couldn't decide how the kid really felt about his big sister. The young man had been very carefully controlled.

Did Phillip want the murder solved? Did he truly want to remedy the injustice of Scott's murder?

Christ, no. He'd never known the man.

Did the kid really not know where Sarah was and hoped Jake would ferret her out?

Unlikely.

Maybe Phillip hadn't made that phone call.

Sure he had. *Remember,* Jake thought, *the call came from Princeton.*

Maybe he'd made the call then gotten scared at what he'd done. So scared he'd deny it till his dying day. Because if his sister found out he'd done it, sicced Jake Savelle on her, she'd never forgive him.

So *why* had he made that call?

Jake drove across the Delaware River and back into Pennsylvania with a frown on his face. He'd hoped to get something out of the Jamison boy, anything, a hint as to her whereabouts. And he was beginning to wonder if he ever would.

Jake learned something over the next few days: He was never going to make a good gumshoe. He really hated the work, the digging, the repertoire of lies he was becoming so adept at telling. He sat one afternoon in the tidy office of the headmistress at the Agnes Irwin Country Day School—Sarah's alma mater—waiting for a Mrs. Barthol, and he asked himself just how long he could keep this up.

"Mr. Savelle?" he heard behind him, and he stood up and greeted the elderly woman and wondered if she'd been headmistress here since the last century. She wore a dull plaid wool skirt, frilly blouse with a knit vest, thick stockings, and heavy-soled shoes. Her two fat Welsh Corgies lay by her chair, obviously used to accompanying her. A Dickensian character. So proper, so WASP, that he was taken aback and stammered out his come-on line.

"It's so, ah, good of you to take the time to see me," he began, and he didn't sit down again until she was seated behind her desk, hooded blue eyes assessing him.

"I'm a friend of Sarah Jamison," he went on, "and I've recently moved to Rosemont. I met Sarah in Denver a year or so ago, and I knew she went to school right here in Rosemont, so I took the chance to stop by and see if you might have a recent address for her.''

''Sarah, yes,'' Mrs. Barthol said, her gaze still pinioning him. ''I remember her well. A fair student, a lovely personality. Sarah made a lot of friends here. I do recall that she fell short of her potential, however.''

''Um,'' Jake said.

''Yes, Sarah, a very warm young woman. And we may have a current address for our newsletter. But I'm afraid we don't give out that information, Mr. Savelle.''

''Of course you don't,'' he said quickly, flashing a congenial smile. ''The trouble is that I lost a piece of luggage on the move here, and my address book was in the bag.''

''Oh, my,'' she said without a bit of sincerity.

''Yes, well, I was hoping you'd make an exception.''

''Have you tried her family?'' the woman said, ignoring his request.

''I'm afraid they don't seem to be in town right now.''

''That's unfortunate.''

''I do realize I'm asking a lot. . . .''

The woman studied him for a moment and then rose. ''I'll compromise, Mr. Savelle,'' she said. ''If we do have a current address for Sarah, I'll have the school secretary drop her a line informing her that you're looking for her and giving her your telephone number. If Sarah wishes to contact you, I'm certain she will.''

''Thank you,'' Jake said.

''Now, if you'll pardon me for a minute, I'll check to see if our files are up-to-date.''

Again, Jake thanked her, and the moment she left her office, followed by her two Corgies, he walked to the wall of bookshelves where dozens of yearbooks were kept, found the year he was looking for, and he swiped it, tucking it into his trousers at the back, realizing his sport coat would barely hide it if anyone was looking. By the time Mrs. Barthol returned to inform him there was no current address on Sarah Jamison, he'd broken into a sweat.

This really sucks, he thought, making a hasty exit, muttering his thanks and disappointment the whole time as the old woman walked him down the corridor, past classrooms and pretty little girls in their crisp school uniforms. When he was finally outside, he drew in a long breath and promised himself that when this was over he'd never tell another lie in his life.

The Lamp, Sarah's yearbook, came in handy, and two days after having *procured* it, Jake had spoken to several of her old classmates who still lived in the area. With each one he collected more names—married names—and his list grew. He wasn't getting any closer to finding Sarah, but he was learning an awful lot about her.

Like any good lawyer, he compiled notes on yellow legal pads, not knowing if he'd need them, but figuring he was better off prepared than not.

On his sixth night in Philadelphia he sat propped against the backboard of his bed, bent over the notes and the open yearbook, Sarah's seventeen-year-old face staring up at him in the lamplight from the bedside table. He chewed on a slice of pizza from a box next to him, and he studied her face.

He had learned a lot about her. The trouble was, he was getting disparate pictures. There was Mrs. Barthol's brief assessment: lovely, warm, though apparently not academically motivated. One of Sarah's former classmates had described her as uncontrollable, getting caught smoking in the girl's bathroom. Another had told Jake she was warm but shy, and yet another had said she was introverted and insecure.

According to the classmate he had just finished speaking to on the phone, she was gracious and ladylike.

Jake had written in his notes descriptions of her as sweet, a loyal friend, a nurturer. There were more words scribbled in his horrible crabbed handwriting, such as lost and withdrawn. No one who'd known her parents thought much of them: very wealthy, very Philadelphia blue blood, very dysfunctional.

The only thing Jake could gather from all this no doubt useless information was that Sarah Jamison was an enigma.

To him the whole thing seemed a bit like the parable of the blind men and the elephant; who you thought Sarah was depended on which part of her you had touched.

He was beginning to form his own image of her. He picked up another piece of cold pizza, took a bite, and looked at her picture again. She was not a classic beauty; her features were softer, and there was that secret smile that continued to intrigue him. Aside from her appearance, he was beginning to see her as warm and intelligent, possessing unique strengths, but a woman who was dancing with her own shadows.

It was a miracle she had survived at all in that family, with its dark pride and ugly secrets. Yet her upbringing explained why she'd been attracted to Scott Taylor in the first place, why his charisma, his strength and self-assurance had drawn her like a moth to a flame.

He was revising his notion of her as a vamp who seduced powerful men, leaning toward the vulnerable, needy version of Sarah. Yes, that suited her better.

He found himself imagining a first meeting with her. He saw her in detail, her face, those now-familiar features. The smooth, pale skin, the curling dark hair. Her clothes were fuzzy in his head, the background fuzzy as well. But her body language, her expressions, they were all there.

"It's good to meet you," he said in his fantasy. "You can't imagine what I've gone through to find you."

The scene split into two from there. One in which she was friendly, polite, responsive, actually grateful that he would protect her so that she could come forward to tell her story. The other was different—she was terrified, furious, hated Jake for finding her. He could hear her voice in his head, tense, scared. "How *dare* you do this to me? How dare you?"

His reply to her eluded him. He never could figure out what he'd say.

He swung his legs off the bed and went to the window, hands in his khaki pockets, staring down at Broad Street. A cop car tore by, lights flashing, siren whelping, and he realized he was beginning to obsess over Sarah Jamison, the same way he'd obsessed over Scott's murder. And then he asked himself if they weren't one and the same— Scott's murder and Sarah's disappearance. If he solved one he solved the other; they were so intertwined as to be inseparable.

He thought long and hard about his deceased brother-in-law, and he couldn't help wondering again if Scott had taken advantage of the woman's vulnerability.

The notion turned his stomach. He would have preferred remembering Scott as a high-spirited womanizer, not a lecher who took advantage of young women.

He phoned David that night and brought his friend up to speed despite having nothing concrete to report.

"You want my advice?" David asked. "Drop it. This latest crusade of yours is only going to destroy more lives. You can't bring your brother-in-law back, Jake. Think about your sister."

Jake ran a hand through his dark hair. "I have. I do every day."

"Then think about yourself. Haven't you lost enough over this case already?"

"You might say that."

"Then for chrissakes let it lie. Get on with your life."

"I'll think about it," Jake said.

"No, pal, you won't."

It was true. He wouldn't drop it. He was incapable of dropping it. And David knew it.

"Ah, shit, Savelle," David said, "keep me informed. You're an asshole, though, you know that?"

"Yeah, I guess I am," Jake had to concur.

Later that night, tossing on the sagging mattress, smelling the pervasive stale human odor of the sheets, Jake tried to figure out why he was staking his life on the pursuit of one woman.

He'd already lost everything in the same kind of compulsive pursuit. He'd been warned then, but he hadn't listened. David had just warned him again, but he was true to form—pursuit at all costs.

If he was wrong this time, too, if Sarah was not the witness, if he never found her, he'd lose all over again. All his renewed faith in himself, his reason for being would siphon off. The thought frightened him. He'd be empty then, a flaccid, useless creature.

His whole damn life hung in the balance, and Sarah Jamison was the fulcrum.

SIX

The Washington heavyweight sat in the comfortable leather chair at the head of the conference table and surveyed his domain. One of his recruits was giving a report on the results of a wiretap, but the heavyweight wasn't really listening; he was presiding. It was his domain and he'd protect his position at the top with all the means at his disposal.

His secretary opened the conference room door a discreet crack and slipped in. She leaned down and whispered in his ear. "Damn," he said under his breath, but the truth was he didn't mind this sort of interruption. It merely served to strengthen his aura of importance.

"Gentlemen, I'm so sorry, but you'll have to excuse me a few minutes. A call. National security. Daryl, please take over. No, no, Ted, go on with the report."

He strode down the sterile corridor to his office and took the call on a secure line. It had nothing to do with national security; actually, it was even more crucial.

"I'm here," he said.

"You sitting down?" came the familiar voice.

"Yes."

"There was somebody in the Brown Palace hotel room that night. A woman."

The man sat back in his chair as if someone had pushed him. He was stunned, his thoughts flitting wildly. *Christ Almighty.*

"No," he said, "it couldn't be. You looked."

"I missed her, I guess."

"How do you know?"

"The intelligence is reliable," was all the voice said.

"Who was she?"

"Name's Sarah Jamison."

"Where is she now?" His brain churning, starting to make sense of the situation, to look for remedies.

"Don't know. But Savelle is on the scent. Obviously she got scared and went to ground."

"Well, that's better than going to the cops." He swiveled in his chair, frowning. "Okay, let's say it's true. She hasn't talked in eighteen months. Maybe she won't."

"Listen, when Savelle gets hold of her, and he's a god-damn pitbull, she'll talk. She'll spill her guts."

"Shit."

"Yeah, we're in it up to our necks."

"There's only one solution. You know what it is."

"I was afraid of that," the voice said drily.

"There's no choice, you know that. Don't crap out on me now. Look, there might be some more money in it for you. I'll work on that angle."

"You do that."

"Find her, this Sarah person. Find her and shut her up. *Before* she talks."

"I've got as much at stake as you do, don't you forget that for a minute. I'll find her and I'll make sure she never says a word."

"Think you can buy her off?"

"No way, not when Savelle locates her. Not a chance."

"Okay, then you take care of it. I'll be waiting to hear from you."

"It might take a while."

"What kind of time frame are we talking here?"

"Weeks, maybe a few months, but I doubt it."

"You need cash for expenses?"

"I'll let you know."

"You find the bitch."

"Don't worry, I've got it covered."

The heavyweight hung up and his frown deepened. How the hell had they missed this woman? Jesus H. Christ, was she some sort of pro?

Jake's stack of notes on Sarah was growing, piling up on the peeling veneer of the dresser and bedside table, piling up so high he couldn't believe he did not yet have a single solid clue as to where the woman was. Well, he had to give her credit: She'd pretty much vanished into thin air.

He'd spoken to over twenty of her former classmates from the Agnes Irwin School and two former college roommates from a two-year stint she'd pulled at the University of Pennsylvania.

The descriptions of Sarah were proliferating. One college dorm roommate had called her brilliant but a lost soul. The other roommate had said Sarah was one of the strongest women she knew, considering her sick family. Everyone Jake had spoken to found her caring and loyal.

A good friend of hers from her riding competition days told him on the phone that Sarah was one of the most graceful, beautiful women she had ever met. "The pity is," the horseback rider said, "she had so much potential, but every time she turned around, her father put her down. The man is a bastard and a lousy drunk."

"Oh," Jake had said.

He was hoping for a break tonight, meeting with a former boyfriend of Sarah's who'd gone to the Wharton School at Penn. The man had agreed to have a beer with

Jake at a downtown bar on Chestnut Street. Maybe Sarah had dropped him a card in the last eighteen months? Something with a postmark? Anything that would give Jake a hint as to her general location would be fine with him, because he was reaching the end of the line. And even if he weren't, he was already way over budget on this wild-goose chase.

The financier Jake met at the popular after-work spot was nearer to Sarah's age than Jake's, though he looked ten years older, with a belly and hair that had receded halfway back to the crown of his head.

When Jake sat down with Mark Klinker, the man was polishing off a Philly cheesesteak sandwich, grease dripping from what was left of the roll. Over the loud din Jake gave him the usual line, that he'd met Sarah in Denver, had recently relocated to the area, and she'd given him a few names to look up. "But, damn, now I've lost her address and phone number."

"Sarah gave you my name?" Klinker looked up in surprise. "Wow, I wouldn't have thought she even remembered me."

Jake sipped on his own beer and smiled. Inside he was sinking. Obviously, Klinker had no idea where she was.

Still, the man was outgoing and liked to talk, and Jake gleaned more for his notes—useless notes, he thought in frustration.

"Sarah was something, all right, a real catch on campus. All the guys were hot for her." Mark Klinker winked. "I don't know why she finally picked me, but we kind of started out as friends. She was just the type men gravitate to. She had this way of making you feel special, you know, needed or whatever?"

"Uh-huh," Jake said, noting the wedding band on Klinker's finger. He supposed Mark had found someone else who made him feel needed.

"But, boy," the man was saying, "she was some kind

of a prude, you know? Well, I'll bet you do know. Sure."
Another wink.

"Mm," Jake said, taking a quick sip of his beer. Were they talking about the same woman, Scott Taylor's mistress? A prude?

"At first," Klinker went on, signaling the barmaid for another beer, "I thought it was maybe me, you know? But then I heard around campus that she wasn't easy. Anyway, it was a long time, months, I think, before we made it."

Jake smiled and nodded.

"Frankly," Klinker said, "I'd have thought Sarah would be married with three kids by now. She liked kids."

"Mm."

Klinker cocked his head. "Has she been married?"

"No, no," Jake said. In truth, he'd never considered that she might have been married.

"Well, she left Penn after a couple years. I think it was a shame, but maybe she needed to get away from her family. She had a sister, an older sister, who'd committed suicide a few years before I met her, and I think the wounds were awfully deep. I always thought Sarah would make it, though, you know? She's a survivor."

Survivor, Jake thought. He'd add that to his notes, although he supposed he already knew it.

"Yeah, I always believed she'd get the hell out of this stuffy area and make something of herself."

"Oh, she's doing fine," Jake said, as if he knew.

Klinker drained his beer, checked his watch, and stood up. Jake, too, stood and tossed several bills onto the tabletop.

"So you haven't heard a word from Sarah in a long time?" he asked casually.

"No, it's been ten years at least. And it's just as well, you know?" Klinker waved the wedding band under Jake's nose. "The little lady wouldn't understand."

"Mm," Jake said, then he thanked the man and they parted.

He strolled down Chestnut Street and into Society Hill and the waterfront area, the damp March evening air enfolding him. Tomorrow, he realized, he was going to have to book a return flight to Denver. After all the lies, all the people he'd spoken to, only one of them, apparently, knew where she was, and young Prince Phillip wasn't talking. Jake's bitter frustration returned, consuming him. He strode straight past Independence Hall and the Liberty Bell housed in the Mall directly across from it and never even looked up from the old, cracked sidewalk.

Jake woke up late and bolted out of bed. Christ, he was going to miss the shuttle train to the airport.

He started jamming things into his suitcase, trying to locate the damn room key, wondering if he could do without checking the hotel bill. He might make it yet if he could just—

The phone rang.

He almost didn't answer it, but some unfathomable hunch made him pick it up.

"Jake Savelle?" A woman's voice.

"Yes, this is Jake."

"Oh, good. My name is Christina Abbott, you left a message on my machine several days ago?"

Jake glanced anxiously at his watch. "Ah, yes, that's right."

"I was out of town. Your message said something about your being a friend of Sarah's?"

"Yes," he said, phone against his shoulder, fumbling with the strap on his suitcase.

"You aren't from Philadelphia?"

"No, ah, I met Sarah in Denver."

"Oh, not Aspen?"

Something in Jake seized up. "No, we met a while ago in Denver, and we lost touch."

"Well, I haven't heard from her in, oh, I guess it's been since Christmas, three months, anyway, so maybe I can't help. . . ."

Jake sat on the side of the bed, his heart beating a strong tattoo against his ribs.

". . . But if you'd like, Mr. Savelle, we could meet for lunch."

"That would be fine."

"And where are you now?"

"Downtown."

"Oh, well, do you have a car?"

"Ah, no."

"Then catch the Paoli Local out to Bryn Mawr, oh, say around eleven-thirty, and walk across the park to the Barnes and Noble, and I'll meet you . . ."

Jake pulled a pen out of the inside pocket of his sport coat and wrote furiously. *Aspen?* She'd said Aspen. Was that where . . . ?

"I'll see you around noon, then," Christina Abbott was saying.

"Noon. Great, see you then. And thanks." Jake got the words out past the lump of pure anticipation in his throat.

He got to Bryn Mawr early on the local Main Line train, and spotted the bookstore immediately. Sarah's old school friend had directed him to a tiny café near the store, and he found that easily, too. She arrived right on time, and he knew her on sight—hell, he'd looked through Sarah's yearbook dozens of times. What he hadn't expected was the instant come-on from the exquisitely turned out Main Line blond beauty, Christina Abbott—*Mrs.* Abbott.

She stuck out a slim hand and took his. "It's Chris. And I hope I can call you Jake?"

"Of course."

"My, if you'd told me how handsome you are, *Jake*, I would have made it an hour earlier."

He didn't know what to say. Jake Savelle, at a loss for words?

They took a table in a corner of the cute French-style café and she smiled. "I'll have a salad, and would you like a glass of wine? A Merlot, perhaps?"

"That would be fine," he said, and he thought: This is going to be an interesting afternoon.

It was interesting, and it was immensely rewarding. Jake learned everything he needed to know and then some. He felt caught somewhere between claustrophobia, wedged in a small corner with the flirtatious woman, and overwhelming elation as Chris prattled on and on about Sarah.

"Sarah is so tough. She always was," Chris told him over soft, yeasty rolls. "Everyone thought that bastard father of hers had destroyed her, but they didn't know Sarah. Well, you know how strong she is."

"Oh, yes," Jake said, spreading butter on the fragrant roll.

Chris was laughing, a tinkling sound. "God, Sarah and Barbara and I used to have these slumber parties, and Sarah's old man used to come in and just yell at us, the worst things. We'd ignore it at the time, but I knew it hurt Sarah. And we all knew what it had done to Constance. Did Sarah ever mention her sister? Oh, my, I hope I haven't . . ."

"I know about Constance." There, he thought, finally a truth.

"Phew. Well, anyway, Sarah was always the strong one. I knew she'd escape somehow. She was such a great friend, I miss her. During my divorce"—Chris bit her lower lip enticingly—"after my *first* marriage, that is, Sarah took me to the mountains, the Poconos, where she'd been working at one of the resorts, and we just kicked back and cried and laughed until I got over it. She really has a big heart. And I'll tell you, although you must already know, men are drawn to her like magnets. God, I used to be so jealous.''

Jake took it all in but, damn, he'd been imagining Sarah as the sexual victim of a powerful father figure—Scott. And now this woman, this very close friend of Sarah's, was telling him that needy men gravitated to her? Not exactly the femme fatale that he'd first conjured up, but a brand-new take on Sarah Jamison. A nurturer of lost souls. Is that what Scott had seen in her? He was tempted to ask Chris if Sarah was in the habit of dating married men, but he tabled the question.

He listened to Chris, but his thoughts were on Sarah. He couldn't help picturing her, trying to match her to her friend's stories. The intoxicating smile, the delicate features, the halo of dark, springing hair. How good a listener she was. How she cared about people.

Jake frowned inside his mind, trying to get a handle on the new Sarah. Not a husband-stealing vamp, not a vulnerable sad sack, but a nurturer.

Something Chris was saying made him pay attention. ''So I naturally assumed you met Sarah in Aspen. But on the phone this morning, didn't you say Denver?''

''Ah, yes. Around the time of the Taylor campaign.''

Chris shook her head. ''That was a pity. I know Sarah was very excited about the man's candidacy. Of course, Sarah thought he was such a gentleman. I wasn't so sure. At any rate, she was thrilled to be asked to work at the Denver campaign headquarters.''

''Yes,'' Jake said.

''And then we lost touch for a while,'' Chris reflected. ''But I finally got the card over the holidays and I was so relieved to hear that she was with Bill Lovitt at his retreat there.''

''Ah, Bill . . . ?''

''Oh, of course you wouldn't know him. Bill used to work for Sarah's father at one of the branch banks, but then he moved to Aspen and opened one of those executive retreats, you know, for stressed-out CEOs and such. Anyway, I'm sure Sarah must be very happy there. And *I'm* happy for her.''

Bill Lovitt. Jake's blood was surging, and he was having a hard time keeping his true emotions from showing. He had her. At last. And so close to Denver he felt stupid for not knowing that in the first place. *Aspen.*

He looked up at Chris, and one last question taunted him. Just what was Sarah's relationship to this Lovitt character?

He didn't ask. He hadn't asked Chris about Sarah's liaison with Scott or with other married men, and he wasn't going to bother about this Lovitt character, either. Hell, Jake thought, turning his full attention back to Chris, smiling, he really didn't give a damn.

Det. David Carmichael drove out to pick Jake up at Denver International Airport at five in the afternoon. It was raining, a gray April Fool's Day drizzle, and the distinctive peaked roof of the main terminal dripped water onto the windshield of his car as he waited in the Arrivals lane. It was probably snowing in the mountains, David thought, the late-season powder hounds were probably going nuts on the ski slopes.

Jake strode out the big doors. He looked like hell, unshaven, circles under his eyes, rumpled. *Jesus.*

''Thanks, David.'' He slid into the passenger seat, tossing his bag in back. ''I couldn't face the bus.''

''No prob. Nina's got dinner.''

''Aw, hell, she didn't have to do that.''

''We're worried about you. Look at you, you're a mess. You probably forgot to eat.''

''I remembered, all right. Mostly I couldn't afford it.''

''So, you get anything new on her?''

''You bet your ass I did.''

David pulled out of the airport onto Pena Boulevard

and shot a sidelong glance at his friend. "Really," he said.

"Yeah, listen, I'll tell you all about it later. I've been trying to get it straight in my mind, so you don't think I'm crazy."

"You found her?"

"Maybe." Jake laid his head back on the seat. "Maybe. Christ, I'm tired."

Nina had dinner ready when they drove up. The boys were starving, shooting baskets in the driveway, in the drizzle, waiting for the men to get back.

"God, Jake, you look awful." Nina kissed his cheek. "Worse than I do."

"Sweetheart, you look great," Jake said. "Beautiful. A sight for sore eyes."

They sat around the kitchen table, kind of squeezed in with the added chair for Jake, but they were used to it; he ate at their house a lot.

Fragrant stew, salad, rolls. Ice cream for dessert.

"God, this is the best food I've eaten in weeks," Jake said.

"The most, too, I'd venture to guess." Nina peered at him. "You're skinny."

Sean and Nicky were punching each other in the biceps, seeing who would yelp in pain first.

"Boys," David said, "come on, lay off. You're at the dinner table. We've got company."

"It's only Uncle Jake. He's not company," Nicky said.

Nina rolled her eyes.

"Hey, listen, that's one of the best compliments I could get," Jake said. "It's good to be home."

The boys went upstairs after dinner to do their homework, Nina went into the kitchen to see to the dishes, and David sat Jake in a chair in the living room.

"Okay, talk," David ordered.

"Where to begin?" Jake shook his head. "I used every trick in the book. You would have been proud of me.

Fake names, improvised stories. Lies. Lots of lies. I spoke to her parents, her brother, school chums, boyfriends.

"She's an enigma, David. I can't put my finger on it, on her. Everyone I spoke to gave me a different opinion."

"Anyone know where she is?"

"Wait, I'll get to that." Jake ran a hand through his hair. "She comes from an old family. They live on the Main Line, that's what they call it. Out in the country around Philadelphia. Rich, horsey people, you know. Her folks"—he let out a low whistle—"wow, weird people. The mother's a mess, the father's a drunk. Her older sister, Sarah's older sister, committed suicide when she was a teenager. Seeing the parents, I can almost understand it."

"Cut to the chase, Jake."

"So, I asked a million questions. Sarah, she's nebulous, you know? I can't figure her out, and I can't deal with someone if I don't know who she is, how she thinks. One person says she's this, the next says she's that."

"Do you need a personality sketch to find her?"

"Well, not so much to find her, but to approach her after I do. I mean, I need to know how she'll react." Jake smiled. "She's pretty. Well, from her pictures. She was a horseback rider, hot stuff, I guess."

"Rich people," David remarked.

"Mm. And her brother. What a piece of work. The kid's a senior at Princeton. Lies like a rug. I know damn well he's in touch with her, but he wouldn't tell me a thing. I'm sure he's the one who made that call. It had to be him. I don't believe in coincidences."

"But why'd he call you then not admit it?"

Jake was slow in answering. "I'm not sure. That family, Jesus, they add a new meaning to the word dysfunctional. I was thinking maybe he wants to get back at her or something, but he's chicken to do it in the open. Hell, I don't know."

"You think her brother knows where she is, then?"

"Yeah, but he wouldn't say a word. I actually got my lead from an old friend of Sarah's. This woman—and, boy, was she a piece of work—got a Christmas card from Sarah just this last December. It was postmarked . . ." He shook his head again, and David waited. Jake always liked to make his points with a dramatic flair. "You won't believe this, but it came from Aspen."

"Aspen, Colorado? *Here?*"

"Uh-huh."

David blew out a breath. "So she didn't run far."

"Nope. She just went over the mountains. This friend of hers told me that an old family employee runs an executive retreat somewhere up there. His name's Bill Lovitt. I figure she's hiding out right there among all the uptight execs. Out there in the pristine wilderness."

"You think she's still there?" David asked. "I mean, she could have moved on."

"Sure she could have. But that's where I start. Me and all the rest of the overworked CEOs."

"You're nuts, Jake, you know that?"

"Yeah, so you've said. It just pisses me off that I spent all that money going back East when she's right here in Colorado."

"This isn't about money, though, is it?"

"Hell, no."

"It's about finding that girl, Sarah Jamison."

"She's not a girl. She's thirty-three years old. She's a woman. A terrified woman." Jake pushed himself out of the chair and started pacing restlessly. "And she's not dumb. She knows what she's doing. What she *did*. It's up to me to convince her to tell the truth. Goddamn it, David, I've got to get her to talk. She's a witness, right? She owes it to me, to society, to Heather, to tell what she saw that night."

"Get off your soapbox, Jake, for chrissakes."

"I can't. Sorry, that's me. I'm going to find her and I'm going to get the truth out of her."

"And who're you going to drag down with you this time, huh?"

"I don't care. You know I'm right about this. We're talking murder here. She witnessed a cold-blooded murder. She owes us."

"You've got to get over that way you have of seeing everything in black and white. The truth is that everything's gray, shades of gray. Why do you think you've got the monopoly on moral righteousness? Like I said, you're a real asshole sometimes."

"I need to do this, David," Jake said with ferocity.

David sighed. It was no use talking to Jake. He never listened. There was no deterring him.

"You think I should drop it?" Jake was asking. "Now, when I'm so close? No way."

"You make it sound easy. It probably won't be so easy. Sometimes, Jake, you're blind, deaf, and dumb."

"I won't give up," Jake said. "Don't bother trying to persuade me."

"Okay, okay, but there's another problem here. Or should I say, another facet of the same problem. Disoto found out that I traced that phone call. He went ballistic. 'The case is shelved,' he kept yelling. 'The fucking case is shelved.' "

"Shit."

"Yeah. So I had to admit what was going on. That you were back East looking for the alleged witness."

"She isn't alleged."

"He's mad, he's on the warpath, and Captain Disoto on the warpath is not a pretty sight."

"He has no power over me," Jake said.

"No, but he does over me."

"So, stay out of it."

"Fat chance. You won't let me."

"Shit, David."

"You already said that." David cut the air with his hand. "Will you sit down? You're driving me nuts."

Jake sat. On the edge of his seat. He was thin, intense, unshaven. "So, what're you going to do?"

"I made a deal. I do any investigating on my own time. I keep Disoto abreast of every development. He decides if there's enough to reopen the case."

"What if I go to the DA? I've still got some friends there. Take some pressure off you."

"Forget it. They'd laugh in your face."

Jake popped up again, pacing, pounding a fist into his hand. "I've got to find her. It's the only way. Then I'm vindicated. You're vindicated."

"Okay, so you find her. You know what you're like? That character, you know, Don Quixote, tilting at god-damn windmills."

"She's not a windmill, she's a real live person."

"Okay, but you're just like him anyway, and I'm the idiot sidekick, Sancho Panza. I should know better."

Jake stopped and stood there. "But you know I'm right, don't you?"

"What I know is that if you keep this up, I'm afraid this time the powers that be won't be satisfied with destroying your career. Whoever it is doesn't want anyone nosing around this case. Whoever it is plays for keeps. They killed once, they'll kill again. Be warned, pal."

"Who is it? Who the hell is it?"

David shrugged.

"When I find Sarah I'll have the answer. She knows who killed Scott."

"Maybe."

"That's why she ran. It's so clear."

"To you."

"Yes, to me." He pounded his fist again. "I know why she ran, I know where she ran to. I just have to see her, get to her, convince her. I can do it, David, I know I can."

"You seem awfully sure of yourself. Hell, she's a total stranger. You haven't a clue how she'll react."

"I know her. I just spent weeks getting to know her. Okay, so maybe we haven't met face-to-face but, damn it, I feel as if I've been living with her."

David snorted derisively. "Christ, Savelle, you're in love with this phantom female of yours."

"The candidate's mistress?" Jake laughed. "You must be crazy."

SEVEN

The April rain that fell on the high plains of Denver turned to snow the minute Jake drove up into the foothills of the Rocky Mountains. By the time he passed the exit to Evergreen, it was coming down hard, hard enough that the snowplows on I-70 couldn't keep pace. The highway after the Eisenhower Tunnel, near eleven thousand feet, was a nightmare and, although the chain law was in effect, he didn't even have snowtires on the old BMW, with its treacherous rear-wheel drive. On the western slope of the Continental Divide, he pulled over and waited for a snowplow then followed the lumbering orange truck with its blinking blue light over Vail Pass, where the road finally descended and the snow let up.

"Thank God," he muttered, his palms slick on the steering wheel. Hell, he and Shayne had made this drive dozens of times every winter, but they'd been in the Range Rover, which was built to take brutal Rocky Mountain winters, not to mention spring and autumn, in the high country.

He drove and thought about Shayne and couldn't help wondering who it was his ex had been skiing with that weekend before he'd left for Philadelphia. Was she serious about someone?

He gassed up in Glenwood Springs, where the roads were melted and wet, then turned onto the highway leading to Aspen.

It had been years since the first time he'd visited the small though celebrated mountain mecca—home to the rich and famous. He'd been in college, and he and his roommates had come for a weekend during the World Cup races in early March. Now, *that* had been a weekend. Up early to ski, then off to watch the downhill races, then more skiing, then, après ski, too much to drink at the eight-thousand-foot altitude, then a nap, then an all-nighter in the best damn bars, discos, and saloons in the world. By Monday he'd felt like checking into a hospital but, hey, he was young then, twenty-one, and able to bounce back.

Not anymore.

The former country road was now a four-lane highway almost all the way to Aspen, and whereas it had been bracketed by ranchland on both sides twenty years ago, it was now lined with bedroom communities and business parks.

Jake took the hint and stopped in Basalt, eighteen miles short of the ski haven, and got a room, almost affordable. He used a new credit card, one that had been conveniently awaiting him in the mail when he'd gotten back. Funny, now that he was living hand-to-mouth, he received more plastic in the mail than when he'd been flush. The banks must have intuition, knowing he'd never be able to pay off the monthly balances.

Jake checked into the motel and then made the drive on up to Aspen on icy roads. In April. He shook his head. Still, the drifts of snow in the open fields were melting, and green grass showed on slopes with southern exposures. It had always amazed him how fiercely the Rockies clung to winter and how grudgingly winter gave way to spring.

The single road that ran the length of the Roaring Fork Valley rose and wound past the road to the Snowmass Ski Area. At a traffic light, he glanced up to where the sun struck the ranks of fourteen-thousand-foot peaks. There was nothing like it, nothing in *this* world.

And apparently, he thought as he drove past the airport outside of Aspen, a lot of folks must have thought the same thing. Very affluent folks. The runway was lined with private jets. Hundreds of them. Everywhere he looked, on every hillside, behind every strategically placed berm, was evidence of the influx of wealth to this inaccessible valley. These were not houses or vacation chalets, these were trophy homes. Every-goddamn-where. When he'd last visited here there had been wealth, sure, but nothing like this.

He cruised down Main Street, which was lined with tall, stately cottonwood trees, their branches snow-laden, and behind them Victorian lodges and homes, all color-fully painted, all in perfect, remodeled condition. The streets were as Jake remembered, quaint, tidy, hinting at bygone days. Still, Aspen had obviously been discovered and gentrified.

And Aspen Mountain. That hadn't changed. It had been said that the mountain resembled a huge white wave cresting over the town, and it still did. The only difference he could see was a new gondola proceeding up the run called Little Nell.

Yeah, he thought as he waited at a light, maybe the town had grown, maybe it had been taken over by the rich and famous, but the ski mountain that had made Aspen a premiere resort would never change. He longed to ski it again, ached to feel the snow beneath his boards. *Maybe. Someday.*

He found a parking spot in downtown—which at least

had kept some of its old silver mining–Victorian charm—
then went about the business of locating Bill Lovitt's retreat.

It wasn't hard to learn exactly where the retreat was.
In the first place he walked into—an espresso coffee-
house—he was provided with all the information he
needed.

He bought a latte and asked the counter girl, "You
wouldn't know where an executive retreat run by a Bill
Lovitt is located?"

She didn't get a chance to reply. The man waiting di-
rectly behind Jake said, "I don't mean to eavesdrop, but
I do the plowing at Bill's place. It's called the Rocky
Mountain Retreat, about fifteen miles or so out of town.
You know where the road to Old Snowmass is?"

By the time Jake walked outside to sit in the warm
April sun on the patio, he knew exactly where the place
was and how to get there. So, he mused, Aspen had re-
tained a little of its small-town flavor—everybody knew
everybody else's business. He guessed that was good. He
sat there and sipped on the steaming latte and put his
mind on the problem at hand—Sarah Jamison.

He *could* drive out to the retreat and try to find her—
if she were still there, of course. He could confront her
right off the bat, in true-to-form Jake Savelle fashion. But
if she spooked and tried to run, then what was he supposed to do? Handcuff her, tie her up, kidnap her?

He contemplated the situation, studying the few ave-
nues of approach open to him. The main thing was not
to alarm her.

It occurred to him that she might not even be using her
real name. And in that case it would be dumb for him to
stride up to the desk and ask for her. If she got wind of
it she'd be gone like a bat out of hell.

The only completely safe route was for him to meet
her without her knowing who he was. That would mean
he'd have to check into the retreat under false pretenses

and scout the territory before charging ahead.

There would be some problems with that approach, though. He'd have to use a credit card, so he couldn't register under a different name. And he needed time. Time to feel her out, gain her confidence. How much time? How long would it take to get close to Sarah Jamison?

Using his real name was a gamble, but he had no choice; he could only hope that no one would remember him from his ordeal in Denver. Especially Sarah. But even if she did, there was no reason for her to believe he was at the retreat to confront her. Hell, he'd pepper the truth with lies: He was a barrister in need of a good rest. He had to make it work. He could do it.

That evening in his Basalt motel Jake put into action Plan A and made a reservation at the Rocky Mountain Retreat under his real name. When a man answered the phone and took the information, Jake was relieved as hell. So far so good. Except for the five-hundred-dollar-a-day charge, of course.

His second call did not go as smoothly. "It's me, Heather," he said to his sister.

"Well, thank you for finally getting in touch," she said coolly.

"Hey, there was nothing concrete, so I didn't want to bug you."

"I've been sitting here on pins and needles, Jake, dreading the whole thing. Where are you, anyway?"

"I'm, ah, in a motel near Aspen."

"What?"

"The witness may be living here. I don't know yet. It's going to take time."

"So there is someone . . . a woman?"

"It looks that way."

"God. I can't face what's going to happen."

There wasn't anything he could say. Heather was right—if the Jamison woman came forward, the story would hit the headlines like an atom bomb. Scott's name, *Heather's* name, would be on every tongue in the nation. And so would Sarah Jamison's.

"Let's take it one step at a time," he finally said. "Nothing is etched in stone here."

"You, Jake," Heather said, "your damn ego is what's etched in stone." She hung up.

It crossed his mind fleetingly that he could drop it. Drop the entire thing before it went any further. The notion flew through his head and then was gone.

The weather cleared entirely by the next morning, and Jake followed the directions to the retreat along a dirt road through a broad, rolling valley, past stands of empty-branched aspen trees shading stubborn snowdrifts, past rambling split-rail fences that enclosed cows and horses in the summer, past pale green spring growth that followed the retreating snow. Capitol Peak loomed over the valley, pure, glistening white in the spring sun.

The country was magnificent, empty except for the buildings of the retreat itself, and even those were crafted of native materials: wood and river rock and pine logs that formed a twenty-foot sloped ceiling in the great room and extended out over a long summer porch that ran the length of the building. Upstairs, behind a balcony formed by the tall ceiling and a narrow landing, were the simple, functional guest rooms where the overworked, stressed executives were housed. No phones, TVs, or fax machines.

After all, he thought derisively as he was led to his room, it had to be very unnerving to lay off fifty thousand workers. It would sure make *him* tense and maybe even give him a bad headache until, of course, he did a stint at a peaceful retreat at five hundred bucks a night.

The dress was casual among the guests and staff: sweaters, jeans, boots, parkas, a few workout suits. The twenty guests were mostly male, but there were two or three women, keeping to themselves, evidently disinterested in anything but R and R.

Everyone, much to his relief, was on a first-name basis. Other than filling out the registration card, which was kept in confidence—he was assured—no one knew or seemed to care who the hell he was.

If there was any difficulty at all, it was in trying to act the overworked CEO type. He suffered no such stress. In truth, he was elated, feeling that he was closing in on his prey, and thrilled at the prospect.

By dinnertime he had yet to spot Sarah. He'd seen cabins on the hillside behind the main lodge, and he assumed that was where the employees lived. Still, he'd spotted very few workers, and certainly not Sarah, who he knew he'd recognize in a flash. Nor had he met Bill Lovitt, the owner and operator of the retreat. It occurred to him that Bill and Sarah might be cozily shacked up in one of those cute cabins on the hillside, and that was why neither one of them was in evidence. He guessed he'd meet Bill at dinner. Would he have the nerve to ask Lovitt if there was a Sarah Jamison working here?

Bill was not there at dinner, and Jake was spared having to ask any awkward questions by overhearing a useful turn in conversation at the table. Studiously he applied himself to the fresh rainbow trout, the medley of steamed vegetables, and the wild rice pilaf, and listened as the man next to him asked another guest, "Now, tomorrow Sarah's taking us snowshoeing, right?"

The man next to Jake nodded. "I think so."

Then someone said something else, but it was lost on Jake. *Sarah. At last.* His heart damn near burst from his chest.

Morning dawned cold and brilliantly clear. Very cold for April, well below freezing. It seemed odd to Jake after his warm interlude back East. But this was the Rockies, the lodge stood at nine thousand feet, and the snow was still thigh-deep under the pines.

He rose and greeted the diamond-sharp day with a

smile and an anticipation so urgent that there was a tremor in his belly.

Breakfast was hearty. Jake told the man sitting next to him that he'd slept better at the lodge than he ever slept at home. It was a bald lie; he'd been awake half the night, too excited to sleep.

"God, isn't it true?" the man replied. "No worries, no tension, no *meetings*."

He finally met Bill Lovitt at breakfast. Lovitt was a short fireplug of a man, balding, with a fierce walrus mustache. Jake couldn't imagine him as a big-shot banker in Philadelphia. Maybe he hadn't fit in, and that's why he'd left for the wilds of Colorado. And then Bill introduced him to Muriel. His wife.

"So nice to meet you, Jake," she said. "I'm sorry we weren't here last night, but Bill had promised to take me to one of the winter concerts in Aspen."

"No problem," Jake said, "your staff took great care of me."

"Oh, good, that's what we want." And then she went into the kitchen, a petite, plump lady with a pretty face and a genuine smile.

Muriel Lovitt. Bill's wife. A happily married couple? A bizarre frisson of relief shook Jake.

After breakfast he got his parka, hat, and gloves and went outside to where Bill was gathering the guests for the snowshoe walk, handing out equipment.

"You can use ski poles if you want," Bill was saying. "Now, make sure you have the snowshoes on tight enough. Push your foot all the way to the front, Wallace, that's it."

"Do you have a pair for me?" Jake asked.

"Sure, we've got plenty," Bill said. "Now, if any of you have just come up from a lower altitude, take it easy. You need a few days to acclimate. Sarah is well aware of the symptoms of altitude sickness, so no one's to panic. And don't forget sunscreen."

"How long is this walk?" Jake asked, trying to appear anxious, as if he didn't run five miles at a stretch whenever the mood struck.

"Three miles, that's all. And no one will push you, don't worry. Everybody goes at his own pace."

Jake took the snowshoes and a pair of long cross-country poles, sat down, and pretended to fiddle with the contraptions. He searched the area, trying not to be obvious, desperate for a glimpse of Sarah. Across from the lodge, beyond the plowed driveway, was a large shed. Was she in there? Or was she still in her cabin?

And, why, if Bill Lovitt was a friend of her father's, had she come here to hide? Jake was sure the Jamisons did not know where their daughter was, so did that mean Lovitt was in on it with Sarah? Or had she lied to the old family friend, too?

Sarah, Sarah, what have you been doing?

He sat there, breathing in the cold clear mountain air that tingled inside his nose, almost unable to contain his impatience. *Sarah, where are you? You're late, goddamn it. Late.*

Four or five people were gathered, strapping on the webbed snowshoes, trying them out. There were two types here, Jake noted: the out-of-shape executives and the lean, mean greyhound types, who probably worked out with as much energy as they exerted to downsize their companies.

He was still fumbling with the straps, watching for Sarah, his body thrumming with expectation. Trying to look cool, a young captain of industry on vacation. Damn it, where was she?

He glanced down at the binding on one of the snowshoes then looked up again, and somehow she'd materialized out of thin air.

That first glimpse of her was like a blow, swift and deadly. His breath caught in his lungs. *At last. At goddamn last.*

The world narrowed down to a single entity; time ground to a halt. She was moving toward him, striding across the white snow quickly, long legs, dark curling hair pulled back haphazardly into a ponytail. Smiling. Sarah Jamison was smiling, a little bit in a hurry.

"Sorry, everyone, I'm late. Sorry, sorry," she said, and her voice rang in his ears like the tolling of a bell.

The color—that's what held him, the dark hair catching the morning light, the white skin, green eyes, red plaid shirt. Except for those overenhanced tabloid photos, he'd never seen her in color before. Green eyes . . .

Suddenly everything around Jake, every tree, every branch, the snow on the ground, the steps on which he sat, the very air possessed a shimmering intensity. There she was. Right in front of him. He could reach out and touch her, speak to her. She was real.

"Hi," she said, turning to him. "You're new, aren't you? I'm Sarah."

As if he didn't know. As if he hadn't studied her pictures over and over, imagined her a thousand times. "Oh, hi, Sarah, I'm Jake," he said, his voice sounding strange to his own ears. Trite, false in the face of this wraith turned into flesh, and he found that he had to force his world back onto its axis.

"Okay, Jake, everybody. Are we all ready?"

She was taller than he'd expected, coltish, with the warm smile that was so familiar yet at the same time curiously altered in her living body.

"We're going out into the horse pasture, okay, Bill?" she said, kneeling to strap on her own snowshoes.

"How long will it take?" a man asked, tall and very big in the belly, his face red before he'd even started to walk.

"That depends on your pace, Owen. No one's to get too out of breath. Any bird experts among you?" She smiled genuinely. "We should see some of the regular winter birds, maybe a few early migrating ones."

She was the same yet entirely, blazingly different. Easy in her body, athletic. She wore jeans and hiking boots, the red plaid shirt, tail out, a fleece vest over it. He watched in mute fascination, and it hit him that she was practically a tomboy, not the seductive mistress of famous men. Not Bill Lovitt's mistress. Yet she'd been with Scott, or had Jake been wrong about everything?

"Okay, everybody ready? Try to get into a rhythm, and it'll be easier. This way, right along that track, see it?" she was saying, and Jake realized that her voice did not sound as he'd thought it would. He'd imagined it as demure and soft, but it wasn't at all. It was husky, filled with a resonance that promised—what? He had no idea; he'd lost every shred of faith in his own judgment.

The sun came up from behind a sharp-edged peak, throwing clear light on the snow. Everyone put on sunglasses and followed Sarah.

"That girl," Jake heard a man say to another, "is what my son would call hot."

"What takes the cake," replied the second man, puffing as he trudged through the snow, "is that she's nice. *Nice.*"

"Think I could recruit her?" the first asked.

"Not a chance."

Jake didn't say much. He put one foot in front of the other, trying to fit his mind around the new reality. He needed to refigure, replace the fantasy with the real. He'd thought he'd known Sarah Jamison.

He had to talk to her, delve into her psyche, get close. How? She had a cheerful, enthusiastic way about her. Camp counselor style. No innuendos, no come-hither glances. Straightforward.

The air warmed, and Jake began to sweat. He took off his parka and tied it around his waist. Others were shedding layers with equal alacrity.

"Water break," Sarah called out.

She had an easy manner. It seemed genuine to him,

friendly; she seemed the kind of person you felt comfortable confiding in. He couldn't fit her into the mold he'd prepared in his mind: witness to a nasty murder, sex object, insecure daughter of a dysfunctional family, sister to a messed-up young man, sister to a girl who'd committed suicide. He kept trying to tie the two frayed ends of the rope together, but they refused to meet.

Maybe her old school chum Christina had been right about Sarah. She was tougher than anyone knew. She didn't need nurturing, not from Scott or anyone else. *She* did all the nurturing. Maybe she *had* escaped her past, her family, and found herself.

When the group started up again, he was glad for the physical exertion. The fresh air cleared his head, and he started to study his quarry. Staying behind her, but not right on her heels, he followed her up a long slope. The rest of the pack fell behind, and he and Sarah stopped on the crest to wait.

"You're in pretty good shape," she acknowledged, wiping sweat off her forehead with her forearm.

"I try. But I think this had more to do with the macho thing, you know, hating to be left in the dust by a lady."

She laughed. Something warm spread in his stomach, and all he could think was that this was what had drawn his brother-in-law to her, the unpretentious, unconscious femininity in the tomboy facade—if it was a facade.

He watched as she leaned over and tugged at a heavy wool sock above her hiking boots, and he fought the image of her in Scott's arms . . . his bed . . . hotel sheets twisted around her . . . hair spread on white pillows. What the hell did he care? He was there to get the truth out of this woman, to see that justice was done.

"The altitude doesn't seem to bother you," she was saying as she straightened.

He shook off his thoughts and came up with a reply. "I'm from Denver, so I don't have to acclimate as much," he explained, "not like the guys from sea level."

"Oh, wow, do I know that feeling," she said.

"Where are you from?" he dared to ask. It was a normal, natural query, wasn't it?

"Back East."

The rest of the group was catching up, so he desisted from singling her out. The others would think he was trying to hit on her.

But he still couldn't help watching her, and he kept finding new things to digest. The fine dark curly hair would not stay put. Wisps kept escaping from the rubber band, springing into a halo of curls around her face. There were a few golden freckles across her nose. Her lips were pink, her cheeks, too, from the sharp air and exercise. She had a long graceful neck and when she threw her head back to laugh, Jake had to swallow hard. Her hands were small and strong-looking, with short nails. When she took her sunglasses off, her eyes crinkled, a deep green flecked with hazel, and her eyebrows curved strongly, very dark.

None of her pictures, nor the bronze head, had prepared him for this, and he thought, okay, all right, she had a unique allure that drew even him. He should have factored that possibility in, but it was no big deal now that he recognized it.

Back at the lodge for lunch, Sarah mixed with the guests, very careful to bestow her attention equally on everyone. Including the women, who didn't seem to resent her in the least.

Jake sat and ate, hardly tasting a thing, unaware of anything but Sarah, watching, assessing, feeling her out as if she were a hostile witness in the box on cross-examination.

And she'd be hostile as hell if she found out why he was there.

"Jake, right?" she said, approaching him after lunch. "I have a hard time with all the names." That sincere, open smile.

"That's me."

"You interested in snowmobiling this afternoon? You can drive it yourself."

"That sounds like fun." A noisy, diesel-spewing machine, but she had asked, and he wasn't going to disappoint her.

Three women joined them and one of the men, the red-faced one from Chicago. Owen.

Actually, Jake had more fun than he liked to admit. He became pretty proficient at driving the thing, only got stuck once. Sarah showed them all how to handle the snowmobiles, and he watched her small, competent hands on the handlebars, on the switches. He tried to imagine those same hands on a horse's reins, guiding, calming, urging. There had been one newspaper photo of her going over a jump flat on the horse's neck, her eyes, her focus beyond the camera, on the next jump, he guessed. And her hands on the reins on either side of the horse's black, shiny neck. He had stared at that picture for a long, long time.

Dinner that night included the Lovitts and Sarah, and it was a lively affair. Lots of talk—Bill Lovitt knew the corporate world and he knew how to converse with these magnates. Muriel was charming, Sarah vivacious, stunning in a bright red turtleneck sweater.

After dinner they moved the tables back, put on music, and the Lovitts tried to teach the guests the Texas two-step. They had a way of putting everyone at ease. Nonthreatening, Jake guessed. And Sarah placed no conditions on anyone except that they have a rousing good time.

The women guests learned quickly; the men had more difficulty. Some just sat and tapped their feet and laughed at their comrades.

To dance with Sarah. My God. He wanted to feel her skin, touch her, breathe in her scent up close. He found himself, to his shame and irritation, annoyed as she switched partners, encouraging, smiling, in the arms of a dozen men. He tried his best and finally caught on to the step—quick quick slow slow—until he could do it for a whole song, dancing with Muriel and Jan from the kitchen, then the female guests. It was amazing to see how the women let down, relaxed, enjoyed, and how the men concentrated, frowning, swearing. Always competitive.

Finally Sarah turned to him. "You got it?" she asked, her face glowing, damp from the activity.

"I think so," he said, abruptly ill-at-ease, palms sweaty. What was he, for chrissakes, a junior high school kid at his first dance?

She moved in his arms like a dream, warm, sinuous, and she smelled of something tart and sweet, like fresh apple cider. Or something citrus-flavored. Sarah Jamison in his arms.

"Quick quick slow slow," she counted out as his damn feet fell behind.

And then, before he could really get into the rhythm of the dance, before he could say anything witty or genuine or pithy, she was gone, Alan from New York holding her in a death grip while she counted out the rhythm for him.

He *was* irritated. He wanted Sarah to himself, needed time with her. He resented every second she spent with the others. *They* weren't here to solve a murder case with Sarah's testimony, for God's sake.

He hung around after the dance lesson was over, itching to get a word with her, but Bill Lovitt came over and asked him about his supposed law firm in Denver, and when Jake looked around a moment later Sarah was gone.

EIGHT

The next day was chock-full—skiing on Aspen Mountain for those inclined, among other activities. The moment Jake heard Sarah would be skiing he was so inclined.

She drove the van into Aspen, a half-hour trip. They all rented equipment at a shop that had an agreement with the Rocky Mountain Retreat. Jake hadn't skied since his disbarment, and he was astonished at the new, wider skis. Doubtful at first, the minute he got off the lift and took a few turns he was sold.

"Great, aren't they?" Sarah said. "I told you."

The group split into three—those who preferred the easier runs, led by Muriel; the intermediates, led by Bill; and the skiers who wanted to try the black diamond trails. Sarah was their leader and Jake, sending up a swift prayer, joined her. Of course.

There were only four of them: Sarah, Jake, one of the ladies, Colleen, from San Francisco, and a small, wiry New Yorker named Douglas. Jake was by far the best downhill skier of the quartet, and Sarah openly admired his technique.

"But I've lived in Colorado most of my life," he explained. "We grow up on skis. I'm not really so great."

"The hell you aren't," Douglas said. Competitive.

They warmed up on the easy runs, then switched to the steeper ones studded with moguls. Jake was enjoying himself, it was nice to be good at something, better than any of the others. It was especially nice to reach the bottom of a run first, rest nonchalantly on his poles, and wait for the others. Wait for Sarah.

She wore a shimmering emerald green parka over black stretch pants, and her legs were long and lean.

"I'd only skied in New England a little and some in the Poconos," she was telling Colleen on the quad chairlift that went to the top.

"Well, you're pretty good," Colleen replied. "Frankly, I think I've hit a permanent plateau. No time to practice."

"I used to be okay," Douglas said. "But I haven't had any time lately. This is great, though. And I can brag to my ex-wife. We were planning a trip here, but she decided she had to find herself instead. Screw her."

"Now, now, Doug." Sarah shook a gloved finger at him. "You know the rules here. No bitterness, no stories from the past."

"Sorry, I stand corrected," Douglas said meekly.

They met the rest of the contingent for lunch at the Sundeck Restaurant. Everyone was red-cheeked and cheerful.

Jake felt that little stab of annoyance, noting how the men all wanted to take a run with Sarah after lunch, asking her which trails were best. And she responded, friendly and concerned, uncritical, utterly undemanding.

On one of the runs after lunch, an easy trail called Silver Bell, Jake hung back and watched her as she traversed the slope in wide turns, graceful, athletic, the long lean muscles of her thighs bunching and contracting with her movements.

Shayne had been a very good skier, he remembered as he stood by the trees at the edge of the slope, extremely competitive, though she was not nearly as athletic as Sarah. Or as even-tempered. Shayne never would have had the patience to deal with this crew. Hell, she'd never had much patience with him. Then he shook off his musings and caught up quickly with the group. He was here to feel out Sarah. This was business.

He took the last gondola ride up with her when everyone else went into the Little Nell bar at the base of Aspen Mountain for an après-ski drink. His legs were tired, but he couldn't pass up this opportunity. They had the six-person gondola car to themselves, seventeen uninterrupted minutes to be alone with her.

"Aren't you tired yet?" she asked.

"Aren't you?"

She smiled. "I'm not admitting it if you aren't."

"Okay, then, I give. Yes, my legs are shot. I haven't skied in two years."

"Mine too. There, are you happy now?"

"Absolutely."

"So, you're from Denver?"

"Uh-huh."

"It must be a nice place to grow up."

"It is. My folks came from the South, but they never regretted moving."

"And you're a lawyer?"

"Yup. The fine old firm of Isaacs, Rose, and Woods." He named a very prestigious one—may as well go for the big lie.

She cocked her head. "I thought . . . Oh, well, it's none of my business."

"What?"

"No, really."

"Don't leave me hanging."

"Well, I thought I overheard Bill or Muriel mention your last name and it rang a bell."

Shit. "That's interesting."

She shrugged. "It happens to me all the time. Something sounds familiar but I can't quite place it. Are you famous, Jake?"

"Hardly."

"What kind of law do you practice?" she asked innocently.

"Oh, I do boring corporate stuff." Christ almighty, he thought, he had to steer her away from this subject.

"I bet it's not so boring."

"Listen," Jake said, "I suppose every single guy who comes to the retreat asks you this, but humor me, okay?"

She looked at him, head still cocked, eyebrows raised questioningly.

"What's a beautiful girl like you doing out there on that isolated place?"

She didn't miss a beat. "I love working there. Come on, you can see how great it is. And"—she smiled—"I get to meet lots of interesting people."

"Well, what I mean is, it's not exactly a career move."

"Not everyone wants a career."

"What did you do before you came here?" But he knew, he knew everything about her, except the most important thing, who she'd seen in that hotel room.

"Oh, a little of this, a little of that. You know, mostly resort work."

"And you prefer this job here?"

"Yes, my God, yes." She thought for a minute. "You know when you're young and you have fantasies about what you want to be when you grow up? Well, this is my fantasy. Only it's come true."

"I'm envious," he said truthfully.

"You don't like practicing law?"

He shrugged. What a liar he was. He'd give an arm to have his career back. A leg, too.

"Maybe you could come for the summer. It's wonderful at the retreat in the summer. We have horses, hiking, fishing, barbecues."

"You like horses?"

"Oh, I love them. Do you ride?"

"Hell, no, I'm allergic to the beasts." *She speaks the truth,* he thought. *She hasn't lied, only evaded questions.*

They skied down, stopping a few times to rest their legs, and met the crew in the bar. Jake was tired, but tired in a good way, physically fatigued, his skin tingling from the wind and the sun. He felt he'd made a few small strides toward approaching her. He'd tried very hard to mold himself into the kind of man he believed would attract her, and he thought she liked him, although she was so damn nice to everyone it was hard to tell.

Back at the retreat he showered and changed then drew aside the curtain in his room and stared at the staff cabins. He frowned. He still didn't have any sense as to what she'd do if he told her who he was and why he was really here. For all her apparent openness, she was ultimately unknowable.

Another healthy dinner, a fine wine to accompany it. No dancing tonight; everyone was too done in. Sarah excused herself after dinner and left for her cabin, and Jake was tempted, so terribly tempted to go for a walk in the chill spring evening, happen upon her cabin—it was the third one past the big blue spruce—and knock on her door.

No, he couldn't. It was too soon. He might ruin everything, the fragile rapport he had with her. Or was the rapport a figment of his imagination?

He finally got it on the third day: All the men at the retreat were a little in love with Sarah. He watched her show Wallace how to wax his cross-country skis; the man was acting like a foolish young boy. And when she measured the Los Angeles studio head for pole length, he put his arm around her and made a joke that caused Sarah to laugh.

Goddamn it, Jake resented all the men who could relax around her, show their admiration, flirt harmlessly. He couldn't. He had to be cautious, inching his way into her graces, deceitful. Lying at every turn.

He thought often of coming clean with her, confessing who he was and what he wanted, but he knew he couldn't. It was too late for that, and there was too much at stake. Ironic, he thought: To uncover the truth he had to live a lie.

Sarah was *his* discovery, he thought as he watched her demonstrate cross-country ski techniques in the field beside the lodge. Not theirs. He was the one who'd pursued her across the country, who'd learned every detail of her life, who'd pried and questioned her family and friends. He was obsessed a little maybe, like Heather had said, and he had to constantly fight the feeling that Sarah was his, that he owned her.

Of course he didn't, and if he gave that impression she'd be furious and frightened. Rightfully so. *Watch your step,* he told himself, staring at the graceful swing of her arms as she skied around the track, hearing her voice call out encouragement to the rank beginners.

She skied over to where Jake was standing, pushed her hair back. Her forehead shone with a film of sweat. "Come on, why don't you try it? Great for the old heart and lungs."

"No, I don't think so," he said, realizing he was sulking. "I'm still tired from yesterday."

"You sure? We're just going out on a flat track today."

"No, really."

"Okay. Maybe tomorrow?"

"Sure, maybe."

Moron. He might have made a few more points with her. He had no time for petty considerations; he was here, squandering his time and money, for one reason—to gain her trust and convince her to come forward as a witness. What the hell had he been thinking?

That night, in his room, he lay on his bed, hands behind his head, staring at the ceiling. Five hundred more dollars. Two thousand chalked up on his new credit card. How long could he keep this up? How long before he'd be forced to approach her? Something had to happen soon, or he'd have to make it happen.

He finally managed to snatch an opportunity the next day. At breakfast he heard Muriel discussing errands with Sarah, things she had to do in Aspen. A list. Wine. Some specialty items to pick up at the Butcher's Block.

"I couldn't help overhearing you," Jake said, approaching the women. "Do you think I could catch a ride? My car is the pits on icy roads, and I've got to pick something up. I promised a friend I'd bring him a souvenir."

"Sure," Sarah said, "no problem. It might take me a while, though. If you don't mind waiting?"

"Not a bit. I'll walk around town, window-shop."

"Okay, half an hour, out front."

"You sure you don't want to go on the snowmobile picnic, Jake?" Muriel asked. "It'll be a lot of fun."

"No, really, I have to get this done. And we'll be back this afternoon, won't we?"

"We better be," Sarah said and she laughed.

It was a warm day for the mountains, fifty degrees, but the sky was overcast, a uniform pewter gray.

Sarah drove the van. Halfway into Aspen, she peered over the steering wheel. "It's going to snow."

"Oh?"

"It always snows when it gets gray and warm like this. The wind'll come up this afternoon, and it'll blow in."

"It's so warm, though. Won't it rain?"

"It might start as rain, but at this altitude it'll turn to snow. You'll see."

"Hey, I believe you."

She shot a glance at him then switched her eyes to the road again. "You could have told me what you wanted to buy, you know," she said. "I could have picked it up for you."

"I needed a break from the health regimen."

"I knew you were fibbing."

He forced a grin. "Lousy liar, huh?"

"Yes."

"Can you handle the truth?" he asked.

"Sure."

"I wanted to spend some time with you."

"Hm. Why?"

"You interest me."

"What, like I'm some kind of laboratory specimen?"

"You know what I mean." He saw her cheeks flush. Was he going too fast?

"You flatter me," she said quietly.

"I like you." *Lies, more lies.*

"God, I don't know what to say. I like you too, Jake. What's it been, three days? I hope you're not imagining something that isn't there."

"I'm not imagining anything," he said meaningfully. "The other guys, they're older, married, most of them. I'm single and I'm not *that* much older than you."

"What does age have to do with it?"

"A little."

She was silent for a time, passing sloping fields, moth-eaten with melted snow. "Were you ever married?" she asked.

"Yes."

"Divorced? Children?"

"Yes to the first, no to the second." He looked at her profile. "And you?"

She stared straight ahead. "I've never been married."

"That's hard to believe."

"Why?"

"Because you're desirable, because you like men and they like you."

"Maybe I'm not really what I appear to be."

"Oh, come on, Sarah, you've got some deep dark secret?"

"No, of course not. I was just warning you. Nobody's what they appear to be."

"You're a closet cynic."

She flashed a bright smile at him. "No, I'm not. I'm just realistic."

His mind whirled—*was* he pushing too hard? Was she trying to tell him something, to hint at her past? Or was this all just innocent conversation?

"Yeah, well, reality can be pretty brutal," he said.

"You sound as if you've had personal experience."

He sighed, laying it on thick. "My divorce, it was only last year. She left me."

"That's too bad." Trite words, but spoken with sincerity.

"She found someone she liked better. Ah, shit, I shouldn't be dumping this on you."

"Consider it part of the retreat's services. Go on, tell me."

"Nothing much to tell. Shayne came home one day and announced she wanted a divorce. And the dog."

"The dog."

"She took our golden retriever."

"You like dogs?"

"I like this dog a lot. I get her for weekends, just like I would a kid." He decided to keep going, constructing his story as he went. "And, you know, the worst thing was Shayne's timing. She picked a bad moment for me. I didn't need that, too. Damn, I don't like thinking about it."

"What happened?"

"I'd just lost a big case. A bad loss. I was representing a group of people who lived near high-tension electrical wires, the kind that march across the countryside. There was a statistically elevated incidence of cancer among them. These were ordinary blue-collar people, no money to fight the big guys. They were dying, suffering, their kids had tumors. I tell you, it was heartbreaking. We took the case pro bono, and I worked on it like a demon. If I'd charged those hours, well, suffice it to say, I worked on it for two years. And we lost. I lost. Those poor slobs didn't get a dime from the utility company. They're still dying out there.''

"God," she said.

"It was a bad time for me."

"You tried, though. You did your best."

"It wasn't good enough."

"You can't always win."

"No, but I should have this time. Okay, so let me lose a couple of corporate cases, they can afford it, but this one, this one mattered."

"At least you care. You're not one of those zombies who's lost his moral center."

"How do you know I'm not?"

"I know. I can tell."

"Psychic Sarah."

"No, just a feeling."

"Feelings can lie," he said tightly.

"Not always. Now who's the cynic?"

"I guess I am. I learned the hard way. If you put yourself out on a limb, somebody's going to come along and saw it off."

"I know the feeling. It's pretty awful, to have your life changed, destroyed by someone else. When it's totally out of your control, and you lose everything." She halted, then said slowly, "But it's always about what you do, the choices you make, isn't it?"

"Yes." His heart beat a little harder. What was she referring to? Witnessing the murder? Her sister's suicide? Her father's psychological brutality? All of the above?

She could be describing him, too, his life taken from him. Were they alike, then? Under the surface, were he and Sarah the same?

She dropped him off at the corner of Mill and Main, across the street from the century-old Hotel Jerome, an Aspen landmark.

"I'll be back at noon, right here," she said. "Is that okay?"

"Sure, don't worry if you're late. Can I take you to lunch?"

"I'll grab some sandwiches at the deli, and we can eat them in the car on the way back."

"Ah-ha, the stressed-out ranch hand."

"No, not really. It's easier, that's all. See you, Jake."

The first thing he did was call David from a pay phone.

"Lucky you got me, pal, I'm running off to a double homicide in LoDo."

"Interesting."

"So, you found her?"

"I did," Jake said with a touch of smugness.

"And?"

"Nothing yet. I'm trying to come off as a good guy. We'll see. I can't afford this place much longer anyway."

"So you're living in the lap of luxury. What's it called again?"

"The Rocky Mountain Retreat. Beautiful spot, isolated, below Capitol Peak."

"More to the point, what do you think of the Jamison woman?"

Jake hesitated. "Hard to say. She's entirely different than I thought. Kind of a cowgirl type. Pretty. Easygoing."

"Do you think she's capable of seeing Taylor murdered then running?"

"I don't know."

"If she's so darn nice and easygoing, how come she didn't run to the cops and tell us what she saw?"

"My best guess? She was scared. Whoever she saw in that room frightened the hell out of her."

"Okay, so do I inform Disoto you've found her?"

"Well, give me a couple more days, then tell him. I'm afraid he'll do something rash, rush in, scare her so bad she'll never talk."

"You're hanging me out to dry here, Jake."

"I know, I know. Give me two days."

When he hung up he considered phoning Heather, but he'd only upset her, so he didn't bother. Then he strolled around Aspen, people-watching, checking out the bars and shops and trendy clubs. The ski season was almost over, most of the snow in town melted, leaving dirty piles in the shaded areas. The mountain that loomed over Aspen was white, though, north-facing, and there was still some good skiing up there. Maybe he'd go once more, ask Sarah if she wanted to ski with him another day.

The town was emptying out, he could tell. The pace was quiet, with few people in the streets. Locals were winding down from dealing with the hectic crowds of the season, and they stopped to chat here and there on the brick-paved malls, over coffee, on street corners. It must be a relief when all the tourists leave, and the locals have their town back.

The buildings were beautifully renovated, from the stately brick Hotel Jerome to the Wheeler Opera House to all the charming Victorians surrounding the downtown area. So different from Vail, which was only thirty years old and had chosen to go with Bavarian-style kitsch.

He walked, poked around in shops, even tried on an atrociously expensive sport coat in a men's shop. He bought a book in Aspen Drug, then he sat on one of the wooden benches in the street mall and thought about how to deal with Sarah.

There was something between them, something ephemeral but real. She liked him, okay, but that could mean so much or so little. How could he make her like him enough to trust him with her secret?

He felt a real reluctance to deceive her, to hurt her—and, he had to face it, he wanted her to think of him as a wealthy, respected lawyer, not the loser he was.

She was so different from the image he'd built up in his mind. Nicer, better, warmer, kinder. He had to keep reminding himself that she'd had an illicit affair with Scott, that she'd witnessed his murder and never gone to the police. A crime in itself. It was impossible to fuse the woman he was getting to know with what she'd done. He didn't want them to mesh; unaccountably, he wanted his lovely, pristine Sarah to be the true one, the only one.

His overriding problem, as he saw it, was in shoving aside his reluctance and deciding when to pounce. When to get inside her defenses and drag the truth from her. Would she hate him then? Oh, yeah.

She picked him up right on time, the back of the van filled with grocery sacks, long baguettes wrapped in butcher paper, cases of wine. On the seat between them was a paper bag filled with sandwiches, bags of chips, cookies, and soda pop.

"I'll have to work off these calories," he said between bites of a turkey club sandwich.

"You don't appear to be exactly pudgy," she said, cutting her eyes at him.

"You want me to drive while you eat?"

"No, I can manage. Sometimes I even eat salads while I'm driving."

"Christ."

"Inborn talent, I guess."

"We should do this more often," he said.

"What?"

"Go out together like this."

"Tomorrow's my day off."

"Is it?"

"Uh-huh." She pulled out around a slow truck and

gunned the van past it. Eating her sandwich at the same time.

"Listen, I don't want to get you in any trouble with the Lovitts. Maybe it's not cool, us being . . . ah, friends like this."

She shot him an amused glance. "Bill and Muriel? They've been pushing men at me ever since I started working for them."

"But you didn't take them up on it?"

"No."

"Now I'm flattered."

She looked straight ahead, but he could see the corner of her mouth curve up. Suddenly, without warning, he wanted to touch her there, feel the smoothness of her skin, run his hand through her hair, down her long neck, along her arm. He realized he was in danger of losing himself in a counterfeit realm of his own making. But, damn, he was human.

He stared at the passing scenery and reminded himself that the woman sitting next to him was only a receptacle for information, that was all, like a safe with a complicated lock. He had to open it—he had to open her.

"Can we get together tomorrow?" he ventured.

"Sure, we can do something."

"I'd like that."

"How long are you staying?"

"Two more days."

"Two days," she repeated. "Well, you are running out of time, aren't you?"

"I sure as hell am."

He continued to stare out the van window, consciously keeping his eyes off her. Guilt settled in his stomach. What he was doing was wrong, unethical, goddamn obsessive. He had the urge to pivot toward Sarah and confess, throw himself on her mercy, like a criminal pleading in front of a judge.

It was too late for that, though; the game was too far along.

He said nothing, and then Sarah's prediction came true—the first big snowflakes spiraled from the leaden sky.

She flipped on the heater. "Brr, just got cold in here," she said.

"Yes, it did," he replied without inflection.

NINE

Sarah had precious little time to herself during the winter season. She almost always spent her free time alone, hiking or skiing in the solitude of the mountains. She asked herself often, on these excursions, if she were avoiding reality. *Trying* to avoid reality. Because no matter how many miles she trekked into the high country, no matter how far she removed herself from civilization, that reality dogged her. She wondered if she would ever truly heal, ever truly put enough time and space between her and that hotel room. Perhaps she was deluding herself. Perhaps she would always live in the shadow of the past.

On this morning off she would have gone cross-country skiing alone. But that was before she'd met Jake Savelle. She wasn't exactly sure why she'd invited him along or packed a picnic lunch. She had simply asked him, impulsively, choosing not to examine her motives.

Jake was stuffing the litter from their lunch into a backpack in front of a cross-country ski hut, and she sat at the picnic table, her head tipped back. The sky was clear sapphire blue, except for a few puffy clouds haloing the highest peaks, as if reluctant to release their hold on the earth. The sun was warm, and snow fell from tree branches, slid off the hut roof, in soft, wet plops. Chickadees whistled their spring mating question.

For a few short hours she had been content. She enjoyed Jake's company. Something about him felt right; it had since the moment they'd met. She put away thoughts of their respective situations: her living in the mountains and Jake two hundred miles away in the city. This was enough for now.

"Should we get going?" he asked.

"Soon."

She stole a glance at him as he kneeled alongside his skis and adjusted a binding. He was a good-looking man, not model-handsome, but he had strong, intense features, with a bony jawline and straight black brows over blue eyes that had a piercing quickness.

There were things about Jake she hadn't yet gotten a handle on. Most of the men who came to the retreat were thoroughly groomed—hundred-dollar razor-cuts, always clean shaven or if they sported a beard or mustache, it was trimmed to the last hair.

Not this guy. He had a great head of dark hair but it needed a good haircut. And he had a perpetual five-o'clock shadow. She couldn't quite imagine him in a courtroom, clean shaven, hair no longer curling behind his ears, suit and tie impeccable. At first she'd thought he was laid-back and casual, but over the last few days she'd seen something different in him. There was an intensity and alertness in those blue eyes, as if she were a hundred-thousand-dollar horse he wanted to bet on. And there was something else that she'd gotten glimpses of, a shadowy disillusionment that he concealed with wry humor and a careful distance. It made him doubly attractive to her, that tinge of something secret and tragic.

Jake was standing now, dusting the wet spring snow

off his knees. He glanced up at the peak that towered above him. "Do those clouds mean it's going to snow again?"

"Maybe," she said, "but I'm so full I can't move yet."

"We could spend the night in the hut."

She shook her head. "No. No sleeping bags." Then she waited for him to come up with the obvious male cliché, that they could keep each other warm.

But he didn't. "You're right," was his reply.

"It's so beautiful here, isn't it?" She sighed.

"Beautiful," he repeated, "yes," but the heavy weight of his gaze was on her.

She led the way back to the retreat. It was all downhill, the tricky part of the trip on cross-country skis. Jake was a beginner at the Nordic style of skiing and struggled, trying to make the unfamiliar equipment turn. He laughed at himself as he fell time after time. Once she had to help pull him out of a tree well.

"I can't get used to the damn heels coming up," he said. "I keep trying my downhill moves, and they don't work."

She braced, tugged on his arm, and he hoisted himself out of the hole. And she thought that perhaps he didn't let go of her hand as soon as he might have.

She had some work to do that afternoon, and they parted at the shed that housed the outdoor equipment.

"That was great," Jake said, "thank you. I'm sure you have better things to do with your free time than lead me around."

But she shook her head and closed the shed door, latching it. "What I like about this life," she said, turning to him, "is that I don't have to live on a schedule. I can do what I want when I please."

"Nobody can do exactly as they please," he said.

"This is close enough for me."

"Lucky girl."

"Don't we all make our own luck?"

"We all make our own mistakes," he said thought-fully.

She tilted her head and studied him. "Now, what is that supposed to mean?"

"Oh, hey, nothing. Sometimes I've been accused of thinking too much."

"You're not supposed to be doing that here, Jake."

He raised a hand. "I know. It's a hard habit to break." He studied her for a moment, then seemed to come to a decision. "Would I be really out of line if I asked you out tonight? A movie or something?"

She hesitated only a fraction of a second, mentally sifting all the possibilities, the consequences. "A movie. Sure, why not?"

"Good," he agreed.

"There is this Swedish film . . ."

"Sounds fine."

"You probably hate foreign films."

"No, no, I like them." He paused. "Dinner?"

"Oh, let's grab some Mexican at the Snowmass Conoco on the way."

"Sounds like a gas station."

"It is, but they serve food inside, the best chicken tacos you've ever had." She grinned. "You game?"

"Goddamn right I'm game. What time?"

"Six-thirty, okay? That'll give us time to eat on the way to town."

"I'm looking forward to it," he said, almost solemnly.

"So am I." And she was. It was foolhardy and she was a little afraid but, damn it, wasn't she allowed a life?

"A date?" Muriel Lovitt put her hands on her hips and surveyed Sarah in the kitchen. "And makeup, too."

Sarah touched her lips. "Is it too much?"

"No, you look wonderful. Happy," Muriel dared to add.

Sarah did not have to say a word, they both knew what

a difficult time she'd had this past year and a half, though neither Bill nor Muriel knew the details. Sarah had told them only that she needed a place to stay, and that her whereabouts had to remain secret.

"Even from your father?" Bill had asked, skeptical.

"Especially from my father," she'd said with no further explanation.

She had asked only for room and board in trade for as much time as they needed her, but both Lovitts had insisted she receive a check, just like the other staff.

Strangely, she had often thought, the retreat felt like her first real home. And the nightmares that had been so frequent when she'd first arrived came less often. Someday, maybe, someday they'd disappear forever.

She looked up from her musings and smiled at Muriel, who was studying her. Who *knew* her. Who also had to have seen the extra attention she was lavishing on the good-looking lawyer from Denver.

Muriel smiled back. "Go on to your movie. Enjoy yourself. You've earned it."

"You're sure you don't need a hand here in the kitchen? I could—"

"Get out of here, Sarah."

Jake was early, she found when she'd zipped up her parka and walked out front to meet him. But, then, she was early, too.

"How do you think the highway is?" he asked.

"Fine, all melted."

"Let's take my car, then."

"You sure? I know the roads."

"Humor me," he said, dangling his car keys from a finger.

They ate gourmet chicken tacos at a bare wooden booth in the convenience store at the gas station. Young couples, grizzled ranchers, local construction workers filled the place.

"I told you the tacos were good," Sarah said.

"This is quite a place. How many stars does Michelin give it?"

"Oh, not too many."

She couldn't quite figure Jake Savelle out. On one hand, all her instincts told her he was a good person, fun, outgoing, genuine, successful. On the other hand, he didn't exactly fit into the mold. He was too young to be at the retreat, and he didn't seem all that stressed out, not the way the other guests were. Oh sure, he'd told her about his divorce and the case he'd lost. Typical problems for the Lovitts' guests. But it was almost as if—she searched her mind—he'd made up that sob story to gain her sympathy. Of course he hadn't, but something didn't quite mesh.

One thing she did know: he was a very intense man, a go-getter, sure of himself. She liked that. What she liked even more was a certain reluctance she had sensed in him. Well disguised, but there. It was as if he were being careful around her. Whereas most men came on to her with brutal directness, as they would a corporate acquisition, Jake seemed to be deliberately holding back. She was endlessly curious as to why he was interested in her and at the same time so cautious. His divorce? Or had another woman just burned him? A whole string of women? She'd love to ask him, but there was a distance to Jake Savelle that she was afraid to probe.

They got back into his car after dinner for the trip to Aspen. A small car, not the typical pretentious four-wheel-drive monsters that navigated the local highway.

He parked a couple of blocks from the Wheeler Opera House, where the art films played, then they walked together, side by side, stopping to glance in shop windows, studying art in the now-closed galleries.

"My mother is an artist," she said, peering in a window at a sculptor's exhibit.

"Oh?" he said, his arm touching her shoulder as they stood together. "Back East?"

She tensed then relaxed. Oh, right, she'd told him she was from the East. "That's right. She's a sculptor."

"Famous? Someone I should know?"

She shook her head and they moved on. "It's more of a hobby, really."

"Huh," he said, and she felt that curious tension in him. He certainly ran hot and cold.

They climbed the long flight of stairs to the ornate Victorian theater and found seats in the center section.

"This is a great place," he noted, looking around.

"Completely redone," she said, "like everything in town."

Their shoulders were practically touching. Would he reach for her hand when the lights dimmed? She wondered, with a childish thrill, what his skin felt like.

One of them had to say something. "God," she ventured, "I hope you don't hate this movie. It got very good reviews at Cannes."

"I like any movie. Well, *almost* any movie."

The lights dimmed and the screen came to life.

The movie began with the hottest sex scene Sarah had ever witnessed. She bit her lip and didn't know whether to laugh or cry as the Swedish actor nibbled and sucked on every available inch of the actress's voluptuous body. Someone behind them whistled. Someone else gave a catcall. In typical, irreverent Aspen fashion.

Jake leaned close, his mouth brushing her hair, and whispered, "You didn't tell me you were into skin flicks."

"Oh, totally," she said lightly, embarrassed.

The sex scene went on and on and on, the actors achieving multiple orgasms before the story had even begun.

"I don't think so," Jake whispered at the male's fourth erection.

It was a dreadful movie. No plot. Just sex, a murder, then more sex, and it had an unhappy ending. People

booed when the lights came on and Sarah shook her head.
"Well, so much for the movie idea."

"I could use a drink." Jake took her elbow and guided
her out. "Is the Red Onion still here?"

"Right up the street."

"Buy you a cocktail?"

"I should buy *you* one."

He helped her into her parka. "No," he said, "the
movie was a good idea. I actually liked it."

She gave him a look. "You're joking."

"No, not in the least," he said, but she saw the tiniest
twitch of his lips.

"Oh, you almost had me. Almost."

"I had you, Sarah."

"No. Really."

"Liar."

Strangely, as they strode side by side along the brick
mall with the pines and aspens glittering with tiny white
lights, she felt as if they'd known each other a long time.
There was one difference, though, one major difference.
You didn't have giddy sensations in the pit of your stomach with someone you had known forever. What she felt
for Jake was new and fresh and terribly exciting. Something was happening between them, she dared to think,
something that came along so rarely you couldn't let it
pass unexplored—there would be too many regrets.

She walked beside him and caught herself and felt her
heart sink. How could she even dream of a relationship
when she couldn't tell him the most important thing about
her? Thank God he was leaving in a few days. She'd
forget him and go on with her life. She had no choice.

They entered the Red Onion and were confronted by
hoards of Friday night revelers and loud music.

"Holy cow," Jake said over the din, "I remember this.
Want to go someplace quieter?"

But she shook her head. "It's fine."

He found them two seats in what the locals called Beer

Gulch, a horseshoe-shaped area with a long, scarred wooden table surrounded by a continuous padded bench.

Sarah held their seats while he fetched them two draft beers then sat down, so squashed together he had to put his arm behind her shoulders on the backrest of the bench.

"We won't stay long," she said. "I'm a cheap drunk. One beer and I'm okay, but two . . ." She shrugged.

"Interesting." He sipped on his beer. "Does that run in your family?"

A sudden cloud descended on her, but she managed to hold it at bay. She wouldn't think about that, her horrible father, the drunken rages, the long childhood nights of fear. She forced a smile. "My family? Heavens, no. They're quite good at drinking."

He was quiet for a moment too long, and his eyes became shuttered, opaque. Then the expression was gone, but his gaze still held a whisper of his thoughts. Or was she imagining it?

"What?" she said.

He took another drink, then leaned forward and set the glass on the low table. "Nothing."

"There was something."

He smiled. "No, really, I was just thinking."

"About?"

Again, he smiled. "Nothing. Nothing to do with you." He moved his hand from her shoulder and gently tucked a loose curl behind her ear. "Really," he said. Then, "Do you know Denver very well?"

"Not at all," she replied, which was true.

"Not a city girl, huh?"

"No. I like the city, shopping, theater, museums, you know. But I'm more the outdoor type."

"Yes, you are."

She turned to face him. "So," she asked forthrightly, "are you involved with anyone?"

He sat a little straighter. "No. Actually yes. There's Peaches."

"Peaches?" My God, she sounded like a stripper or something.

"That's right," he was saying, his head bent to hers. "She weighs about sixty pounds, has a ton of red-gold hair, the most beautiful brown eyes, and she's got a bad habit of jumping on you."

Sarah looked perplexed and then got it and laughed. "A dog. You really are a comedian, aren't you?"

"Most people would disagree."

"Then what are you? *Who* are you? You aren't like the other guests."

"Oh? And how am I different?"

She thought a moment. "I don't know exactly. You just don't seem, well, uptight like the others."

"There are those who would disagree with that, too."

"Your law partners?"

He shook his head, grimacing, as if in irony. "No, not them. Just friends, I guess."

It occurred to her at that moment that this was a man she could confide in. It was true that she knew very little about him, his friends, his likes and dislikes. What had his wife been like? Did he still ache for her? Questions. She had so many questions about him. Yet she felt instinctively she could trust Jake. Other than her brother Phillip, she'd told no one her secret. Hadn't even considered telling. Until now.

Whoa, she suddenly thought. Was she so weak, so lonely, that she wanted to confess to the first guy who came along?

"You're awfully quiet," he said, and she had to force herself back to the noisy bar, to the light mood, to him.

"Just thinking," she said.

"About what?"

"About you, about us. What's going on, Jake?"

He shrugged, his dark blue eyes on her vigorously. "I don't know. What do you think?"

"Something."

"Yeah, something, all right."

She smiled. "Maybe we should just leave it at that. Something's better than nothing, isn't it?"

"Usually it is," he said soberly, but there was a suggestion in the words, in his tone, that kept her sleepless and confused the entire night.

TEN

Time was running out, and Jake spent half the night reviewing his options. He could confess to Sarah in the morning, get it over with. Use all his considerable powers of persuasion to convince her that coming forward was the right thing to do, and that he would, absolutely and unequivocally, guarantee her safety.

The problem, he knew, was that she could tell him to go to hell and be gone in a flash.

He rolled over in the bed and punched the pillow. He realized that course of action was a bit premature. One more day, he told himself, if he could work on gaining her trust for just one more day the odds of garnering her cooperation would be that much better. But, damn, he was impatient, every cell in his body urging him to come out with the whole truth and put the ball in her court. She was a decent person, as far as he could tell. She'd do the right thing.

Or she'd take off so damn fast, run so damn far he'd never find her.

By morning, his nerves were raw, and unfocused irritation seized him. When he spotted Sarah heading toward the van, it took all his control to shake off his mood and stride up to her. *One more day. Twenty-four hours.* He could do it.

"Morning," he said. "More errands in town?" He plastered a smile on his face, a mask so uncomfortable his skin felt as if it were stretched across a drum.

"More errands," she replied, and she returned his smile. Hers was genuine. "I'm the regular gofer around here."

He nodded toward the van. "Mind if I tag along?"

She regarded him mock-soberly. "Are you trying to get out of a healthy activity again?"

"You bet your ass." He widened his stupid smile. "I guess I'm just not cut out for this kind of life. I'll do better tomorrow, I promise."

"I'm not doing anything interesting, really."

"That's okay. At least it's civilization."

He sat next to her in the front seat of the van and cast about for some neutral subject, his mind sluggish from lack of sleep.

They ended up talking about the Swedish movie, and the differences in culture between the States and Europe. She was well read, had solid opinions on a lot of topics.

"So, you must have gone to college back East," he inserted into the conversation when he saw an opening.

"That's quite an assumption."

He shrugged. "Well, I just figured, you know, since you're from there . . ." He knew precisely where she'd gone to college, two years at Penn.

"You happen to be right, but I never finished." She looked straight ahead, evading his gaze.

"Oh, why not?"

"Family stuff. Not very interesting."

"Family stuff is usually the most interesting."

She turned to face him then, for a split second. "Look,

do you mind if we leave my family out of it? They're really boring."

Boring. Right. "Okay, sure."

They rode in silence for the next few miles. It was hardly companionable. He knew he was strung out, and it was showing through the well-worn nice-guy facade; the twenty-four hours that he'd told himself he could handle suddenly seemed like an eternity. This had gone on long enough.

Now. He should confront her now, while they were alone.

He cast her a swift sidelong glance. She was fiddling with a cassette. His mind flashed back to the lunch in the car. No. Bad choice. Not in the damn car. Soon, though. The first opening he saw.

In town, they stopped at a deli for Bill Lovitt's favorite mustard sauce, the dry cleaner's, the shoe repair shop, the liquor store for kirsch for the cook, who planned a cheese fondue that night. And all the time, while he carried on a conversation, he kept thinking: *Now? Should I tell her now? Or wait?*

He gave up temporarily over lunch, realizing he was too damn tired to handle her reaction—whatever the hell *that* was going to be. And Mezzaluna, where they stopped to grab a bite, was sure not the place to confront her anyway.

"Should we get lunch to go?" Sarah asked, standing at the marble bar.

"Not on your life," Jake said, his annoyance showing, "no more eating and driving. Not with me in the car."

"Well, okay." She raised a dark brow at him.

Cool it, he told himself. The last thing he needed was for her to get pissed off at him.

They enjoyed Mezzaluna's pot-stickers while sitting at a big glass window and watching the activity outside— not very many tourists, a few decked-out mountain bikers already on the streets, although the trails they'd normally frequent were still mud and snow. Joggers, mothers with children, construction workers.

"It doesn't look like a resort anymore," Sarah noted. "We're going into off-season."

"Where were all these folks during high season?"

"Lost in the crowd."

"Working their butts off, you mean."

"That too."

He felt a little more human after lunch and sat back in his seat, his eyes resting on her as she gazed out the window, pensive, a fist under her chin. "Penny for your thoughts?" he said.

"Oh. I wasn't really thinking anything. Maybe that it's off-season." She turned and gave him one of those Mona Lisa smiles, and somehow the stark black of her turtleneck sweater made her eyes seem even more green than they were.

"Do you get a vacation?"

"I can if I want. I don't know yet."

"No family visits back East planned?"

"Hardly," she said, leaving it at that.

He could own up right now, he knew, seize the moment. But then the waiter stopped by and the check came and Jake gave up. He stood, reached into his back jean pocket, and tossed a few bills on the table in a blasé gesture.

"Thanks for lunch," she said.

"My pleasure." Then, when they were out on the sidewalk, he turned to her. "Say, do you have to be back at the retreat right away?"

"No, not really."

"I could use a walk." He envisioned a private spot, someplace where he could be alone with her—a captive audience. "How about it?"

She considered his proposal then nodded. "Sure. Why not?"

They drove down Mill Street and parked near the busy

post office. He noted that she put the van keys in her right parka pocket and zipped it up. If she tried to run, he'd keep her from getting at the keys. What he'd do then was a mystery. *Something.* He couldn't let her escape. Not when he was this goddamn close to the truth. Eighteen long months, and he was almost there. They walked across the parking lot toward a path that cut down toward the Roaring Fork River and he felt his inner fires burning. This was it.

RIO GRANDE BIKE TRAIL, a sign read as they entered a deeply wooded area. The grass was green along the edges of the path, and the tall cottonwood trees were covered with barely swelling buds.

Sarah was telling him something about the trail running along the old railroad right-of-way. "The Denver and Rio Grande," she was saying. "This is the route all the silver used to be hauled out on a hundred years ago."

"Interesting." He was taking in all the cyclists and joggers and lady power-walkers, the dogs loping alongside their masters—a lot more people than he'd expected. What if Sarah took advantage of the crowd to get away? Would she go that far?

". . . brothers or sisters?" he heard her asking.

"Huh?"

"Do you have any brothers or sisters?"

"Ah, yes, a sister."

"Does she live in Denver?"

"Yes."

"And your parents?"

"After my father passed away my mother moved to Florida. She's into tennis and bridge."

"That's nice for her."

"Yes."

A dog ran up to Sarah then, wet from an icy plunge in the river, tail going a mile a minute. She stopped and played with him and eventually tossed a stick.

Everyone loved Sarah, Jake thought. Even dogs. He'd

never considered that about her. In spite of everything he'd learned, it hadn't occurred to him that she was a special person, loving, caring, nurturing.

How did that fit in with her being Scott's mistress? He couldn't imagine this woman who played with dogs and cared deeply for everyone around her as an adulteress, sneaking around to a married man's hotel room. What had her relationship been with Scott? *What had it been?*

"So where did you go to school?" she was asking.

He cleared his mind. "I went to DU Law, then I got a job with a good firm, paid back my school loans, and here I am."

"Why did you come to this retreat?"

He thought quickly. "It was one of the senior partner's ideas. He knew what a mess I was over my divorce and losing that utility case. He suggested it. Even thought I could be reimbursed through my medical insurance."

"Is it working?"

He paused for a moment. "No." *Tell her now.*

"That's too bad."

"I'll survive."

"People usually do."

"You say that as if you know what you're talking about."

"Oh, no. I'm just philosophizing. Silly of me."

"No, it's not silly. You're right, of course. But nowadays people want a quick fix. They don't want to suffer while they're going through the survival things. Hell, I'll admit it. I suffered. Still am."

"It gets better, though, doesn't it?"

"Sure, the pain fades, but you never quite forget it."

She was silent, walking beside him, and he was sure he could read her thoughts: *No, I won't ever forget it, and I'm still scared to death by what I saw in that hotel room and I want to stay here and never never think about it again.*

He glanced at her. Exactly when had he started caring

more about Sarah's feelings than the truth he was after? Had it been when they'd skied together and he watched her turn down the mountain, laughing and full of the thrill of the sport? Or when they'd gone on the picnic, and she'd reached down to pull him up and he'd held her hand for a heartbeat too long? Or was it when she'd joked about that dreadful Swedish movie, and he'd first noticed her dimple?

He shook himself mentally. This was all beside the point, as any trained legal counselor should know. The point was to solve a murder, and now was a good moment to do just that.

"Do you spend a lot of time in court?" she was saying.

He stopped short and took her arm, turning her toward him. "Look," he began, "I'm not the man you think I am, Sarah. There's something I have to—"

"You can tell me anything," she said calmly. "I won't judge you."

Jesus. "You don't understand."

The tilted head, the serious green eyes. "You're still married, aren't you?"

"No, damn it." He continued to hold her arm, but the moment had passed, his resolve had been defused. He felt very weary, used up. Letting go of her arm, he started walking again, walking doggedly, and Sarah caught up with him, and for a time they strode together in silence.

At dinner that night he was uncharacteristically quiet, grappling with his dilemma. Even when the other guests tried to draw him out he was barely polite.

He felt like a bulldog who had Sarah's neck in his jaws and he couldn't let go. Once, he'd considered his tenaciousness a fine attribute, one of his strong points. Right now, at this dinner table with Sarah's eyes searching him out, puzzled, he despised that tenacity. It was a sick compulsion.

But like any compulsion, he couldn't shake its power over him. He couldn't leave Sarah alone; his mind was still scheming and twisting, working out ways to corner her.

He finally pretended to eat, he finally pretended to enjoy the other guests, he joked with Bill Lovitt and flirted with Muriel. He finally spoke to Sarah in a quiet, intimate tone; his words were false, but his feelings, his voice were genuine. If he'd met her in any other circumstances, something might have come of their relationship, and he wondered at the irony of it.

"Come outside," Sarah said after dinner, "I want you to see this."

"What?"

"Come on." She pulled him. "It'll just take a minute. No, you don't need your coat. Rough it."

Outside, their breath froze in white puffs.

"Okay," he said, "so?"

"Look." She pointed up.

He raised his eyes. The moon was rising, sliding out from behind the shoulder of a mountain. Huge, brilliant.

"It's almost full," she said. "Just look at it."

But he couldn't. All he could do was stare at her, the way the moonlight cast her face in silver.

He finally made his escape, begging off when she told him they were all going for a moonlight cross-country ski.

"Oh, come on," she urged.

"Can't," he said, his breath hanging in the cold night air.

"Not even for hot cider or mulled wine?"

"Nope. I have some work to do."

"*Jake.*"

"Sorry."

She regarded him for a moment. "I won't tell."

"Thanks."

"But tomorrow we *are* going skiing. You have to promise or I'll rat on you tonight."

"Sure. Skiing."

"Are you all right?"

"Sure. Fine," he said, and he left her standing there staring after him.

Locked in his room, alone, he almost vomited. He paced instead, breathing hard. Then he thought about David. He needed him here. *Now.* He needed his calmness, his expertise. He sure as hell needed his objectivity.

He sat on the side of his bed, head hanging, and pictured Sarah out there skiing in the moonlight with the others. Sharing the mulled wine. Tossing her head, laughing, the men unable to take their eyes from the glow of the moon on her face.

He finally forced himself to pick up a magazine, and he tried to read, to concentrate. It was no good.

The knock on the door sounded like a gunshot.

"Jake?" he heard through the solid wood.

Sarah.

"Are you in bed?"

"Ah, no."

"Can I come in for a moment?"

All his senses told him to get rid of her. Even as he opened the door and saw the glow on her cheeks from the cold night air, he wished he could muster the strength to tell her to get the hell back to her cabin and leave him alone to wrestle his demons.

"Listen," he got out. "I think you ought to—"

"I only wanted to check on you," she interrupted. "All night you've been . . . well, on edge. I just thought . . ."

She was lying. The lie was written all over her face, in her body language, in the way she averted her gaze as she tugged off her gloves and unzipped her parka, shrugging it off.

He stared at her, and it was as if the cold mountain air clung to her like a gossamer gown.

"Say something?" She finally met his gaze.

But still he didn't. He was trying to fit his mind around the fact that Sarah Jamison was offering herself to him.

He could so easily take what she was offering. Here. Now. The two of them, alone. Hold her close, caress her the way a woman wanted to be caressed. And she would open to him, a winter blossom.

He stepped toward her and she didn't move, and then he reached out and laid the back of his hand against her cold cheek. Still she did not move. He tilted her face up then, and she met his eyes with an intensity that matched his, and lust streaked through him like lightning.

Jake kissed her, covered her mouth with his, tasted her, smelled her, and he felt himself becoming heavy and slow, turning to liquid, a warm, viscous honey flowing in his belly.

She opened to him, her mouth, her body moving against his. He felt the sharpness of her hipbones. Her cool hands were on his back, on his neck, his shoulders.

He knew with certainty he could take her right now, make love to her. His bed was only a step away, and he was awash in sensation, so full of her. She was willing, her breath coming fast, gathering his shirt into her fists, twisting. He was aching for her, he—

He couldn't do it.

He pulled back, held her by the shoulders. Her face was stamped with passion, her lips bruised. A small sigh of disappointment came from her throat.

"This is wrong. I can't do this," he muttered.

She cocked her head, regarded him with a puzzled look, not quite hurt. Not quite. "What's wrong?"

"Nothing. It's not you."

"Jake," she said.

"No." He put up a hand as if to ward her off and stepped back. "Go to your cabin, Sarah."

"Jake," she tried again, confusion spreading across her face. "Can I help? I know there's something. . . ."

"You're right. There is."

"Do you want to talk?"

"No. Not now." The moment had finally arrived, the

moment he'd waited all week for, and he couldn't go through with it.

Somehow he got her to leave. Somehow he promised that he'd ski with her in the morning. He even promised he'd discuss his "problem" with her. What a joke.

"Shit," he said out loud. "You stupid son of a bitch." And he didn't know if he was angry at himself for kissing her, or if he was angry because he'd let her go.

ELEVEN

David Carmichael sat at his desk in Homicide, his head in his hands, the phone receiver held between his ear and hunched shoulder. "I had to tell Disoto," he said. "I waited as long as I could, but my ass is on the line here, Jake."

"Okay, okay, I understand. It's all right. Things are coming to a head here, anyway."

"Is she talking yet?"

"No." A pause. "Well, not about that."

"What are you going to do?"

"I'm going to lay it on the line. I've let this go on too long as it is. It's time."

"Got a clue how she'll react?"

"No."

"Damn, Jake, does she have any idea who you are or why you're there?"

"None whatsoever."

"Oh, this is gonna be great. I can see it."

"I know. Don't you think I know? That's why you

have to come up here. Meet her, help me talk her into confessing. She'll feel safe with you."

David let out a string of oaths.

"Look, it's the only way. I've thought it all out. Can you fly up here?"

"Christ, Jake . . ."

"I'm asking a lot, I know."

"You have no idea how much, pal. Look, you did your best, you found the girl, she's not gonna talk. And I don't have any authority to hold her."

"She doesn't know that."

"She'll run, Jake. We both know Taylor was assassinated, and we're way out of our league here. Hell, if I were her, if I witnessed an assassination, *I'd* run, too."

"We can protect her."

"Can we?"

"Of course. But you're going to have to be here when I confront her. I'll need backup. Can you get up here? Fly? You'll be back in Denver within a day."

David expelled a ragged breath. "All right, damn it, I'll try to get there tomorrow. I've got a few loose ends to tie up here first. Court this morning."

"Thanks, and I really mean that."

"Meet me at the airport?"

"Sure. Let me know when."

"Savelle, you are one giant pain in the ass."

"You know it's the right thing to do."

"Do I?"

David hung up and closed his eyes, head still, resting on his hands. Sweet Jesus, that man was a bulldozer, pushed and pushed until you caved in. Relentless.

Sarah Jamison. So, Jake had located her and even befriended her. David found himself feeling sorry for the woman, because Jake was going to bulldoze her the same way Jake had just bulldozed him. And if Jake got her to talk, if she'd really been a witness to the murder, then, by God, the shit was going to hit the fan.

He pulled himself together and stood up, thinking he'd have to make sure Nina felt all right, that the boys would promise to help out while he was gone. He went to his captain's door and knocked. He had to keep Disoto informed. No way was he going to pull this off secretly.

"Come in," came the captain's voice.

David stood in front of Disoto's desk. "Savelle just called me."

"Oh, hell, what now?" Disoto asked. "That maniac."

Jake hung up the pay phone at the Snowmass Conoco and turned to leave. His eyes rested on the booth where he and Sarah had eaten dinner, and he looked away.

She trusted him. Okay, that had been the plan all along. He'd wanted her to confide in him, but the situation had become warped. He hadn't planned on . . . He searched his mind. Hell, he hadn't planned on caring about her. And last night. What a goddamned mess he'd made of that.

He was relieved as hell that David was coming. He could get through today if he knew there'd be an end to it, and tomorrow the two of them would confront her and she'd be forced to come clean. The one thing he regretted, the only thing he regretted, really, was last night.

Jake steeled himself as he drove back to the retreat. Screw it, he thought, this situation with Sarah was no different than hundreds he'd faced in the courtroom. There was always new evidence or a witness who refused to cooperate at the last minute. Glitches. He'd learned to be quick on his feet, to roll with the punches, to react to those glitches effectively. That's what being a trial lawyer was all about.

It was just that this time the glitch was his emotional involvement with a witness. Well, he'd deal with it. He'd go skiing and keep up the act and tomorrow David would be here. Reinforcements.

Twenty-four more hours.

"So, where'd you disappear to?" Sarah asked playfully when he got back to the retreat, as if nothing had happened between them.

"Do you really want to know?"

She tipped her head. "Don't I?"

"Promise you won't tell anyone?"

"My lips are sealed."

"I phoned my office." He could play the game as well as she could. Oh, yeah. "I just had to know how a certain case was going."

"Naughty boy."

"I know."

"We're going to Aspen Highlands today. You still want to come along?"

"You bet," he said, his act now seamless.

Aspen Highlands had some of the steepest out-of-bounds skiing in the state. You had to walk along a knife-edged ridge past Loges Peak to get to the runs down Highlands Bowl, a huge white expanse above timberline that had been known to avalanche in the past, but was now controlled by the ski patrol and presumably safe.

"I've never done Highlands Bowl," Sarah mused as they got off the lift at the very top of the mountain that afternoon.

"I remember when three patrolmen got killed in an avalanche in the Bowl," Jake said. "It hit the Denver papers, TV news, the works."

He realized everyone was looking at him as if he was kidding. "No," he said, "it's true. But that was years ago. It's safe now."

"Safe?" Sarah turned to their companions. "Did you hear that? He says it's safe now."

Douglas smirked. "Anyone who skis those runs is nuts."

"Oh, I don't know," Colleen said. "I bet it'd be a thrill. I wouldn't try it, but if you were good enough . . ."

One of the other women sighed, swinging a ski pole.

"I wish I had the nerve. I buy and sell commodities, deal with millions of dollars every day, but I'm chicken when it comes to steep slopes."

"I'd say that's smart, not chicken," Douglas put in.

"It's only been open about three years, Bill told me. It used to be a closed area," Sarah said.

Jake eyed her. "I'll do it if you will."

"You *are* nuts," Douglas said.

"You're serious?" she asked.

"I am that. You game?"

She studied him a moment. "Okay."

"Okay?"

"You're really going?" Colleen said, aghast.

Sarah grinned. "I said okay. Let's do it."

Well, Jake thought, when she threw down the gauntlet, she sure did it with aplomb.

They didn't talk much, trudging along the sharp-edged ridge at eleven thousand feet, huffing and puffing, and sweating. But Jake couldn't stop looking at her, the long legs, the bright green parka against white snow and blue sky. Her hair tumbled around her headband, and the muscles worked in her calves above her ski boots.

"Wow," she said when they reached the take-off point. "Holy cow."

They stood alone on the ridge, Highlands Peak jutting up ahead of them, the white bowl beneath their feet. The entire Castle Creek Valley lay below, wending its way up to even higher peaks. It was gray-green in the lowlands, the snow mostly gone. Paragliders floated off Aspen Mountain across the valley from them, the canopies like brilliant blooms in the sky.

"Let's go before I get paralytic," Sarah said. "It's *steep.*"

"You go first. I'll be behind you. Take it easy." Jake gave her a reassuring nod.

When he saw that she was skiing the bowl comfortably, he took off after her. Big swoops down the huge expanse on soft spring corn snow. Ecstacy, utter freedom. The swish and glide of his skis, the wind in his face, perfect turns, one after another, until his thighs burned.

Sarah waited at the bottom, grinning, high as a kite, her cheeks glowing pink.

"Oh, my God," she said. "I did it! I really did it!"

"What a rush." He was still winded, exhilarated. They looked at each other, eyes locking, sharing the moment, knowing it would pass too quickly.

"Thanks," she breathed.

"For what?"

"For letting me do that."

"I didn't let you."

"I wouldn't have done it if you hadn't come along. You know that."

"Well, hey, you're welcome."

"I mean it, Jake."

She was killing him with refined and exquisite torture. He had to look away. "We better get down before they call the ski patrol to rescue us," he said.

Strategically, he withdrew to his room when they returned to the lodge. He couldn't face her, and he was afraid he'd give himself away. He only had to last until David arrived tomorrow. The time was ticking away, he told himself. Then he thought: Yeah, like a bomb.

When he finally had the guts to go downstairs, Sarah was telling everyone the story of their great adventure.

"It was incredible," she was saying. "The view from up there was, well, I can't even begin to describe it. Majestic, all those words they use." She laughed then, utterly unself-conscious, charming. "I was scared to death."

She saw him walk into the room then. "There he is, the hero of the day."

Spontaneously, everyone clapped. The mood was happy, excited. Sarah had done that, gotten them all animated. She had that presence, the kind Scott would have noticed. Yeah, Scott would have been straining at the bit to get her in the sack.

Mock-serious, Jake bowed to the guests. He put a big smile on his face. "If Sarah hadn't taken off first, I would never have done it. I would have walked back the way we came," he announced.

The evening was agony. He smiled, acted nonchalant, swallowed the excellent food, but it stuck in his throat. *Only a few more hours,* he reminded himself over and over.

After dinner he had every intention of escaping early, pleading exhaustion, but Sarah approached, touching his arm.

"Are you leaving tomorrow?" she asked. "Muriel told me . . ."

"Yes, I really have to go back."

"Duty calls," she said lightly, but he detected a note of disappointment. "Will you try to come back in the summer? I promise to teach you to ride."

"It's hard to say."

"You're busy, right?"

"I sound like everyone else, don't I?"

"Right now you do." She wasn't smiling. Her green-flecked eyes were serious, meeting his with such blazing honesty his stomach clenched.

"Hey, Denver's not so far away. Come into the big city and visit."

"Sure."

"We'll keep in touch."

"You're a lousy liar, Jake, but I think I said that to you before."

"I'm not lying, Sarah."

"The hell you aren't." A spark of anger, and then she walked away.

She knew, goddamn it, she *knew*. She saw through him as if he were a newly washed pane of glass.

He climbed the stairs to his room as soon as he could.

And then he paced, feeling trapped, claustrophobic. Knowing she was so close, downstairs. Or maybe she'd returned to her cabin. Maybe she was packing, getting the hell out of there. He'd screwed up royally.

He'd been doing so well last night. Until the lie became too much for him. That's when it all started to unravel.

It was a good lie, though, the kind the cops used on suspects and witnesses all the time. David had told him so many stories, the way they tricked perps in the stark interview rooms. *The good lie.*

But Jake wasn't a cop, and he'd never known you could suffer so much from a lie. What he didn't know was that his suffering had only begun.

Sarah sat in her small, cozy cabin, feeling more upset than she'd been in a long time. She'd made a fool of herself, snapping at Jake like that. He was a busy man; she'd known all along he couldn't stay forever. He had a law practice, responsibilities, for God's sake. A life.

Maybe they *would* be able to keep in touch. Denver wasn't so far, as he'd pointed out.

He'd backed off, though. She knew it, felt it. He'd changed since last night, and he couldn't hide it. She played with a dark curl, twirling it absentmindedly around her finger, trying to determine the next step.

If there was one.

Maybe Jake was just gearing up for his return to the real world. She'd seen a lot of the guests do that. Or maybe he simply wasn't interested in more than a casual flirtation to lend spice to his week at the retreat. She could have sworn it was more than that, but she'd been wrong before. Maybe her judgment was compromised by how she felt about him.

There was one other possibility that Sarah had to consider: Jake knew, sensed somehow, that she was living a lie. That every word and mood and gesture were false. Maybe it showed more than she thought.

She drew in a deep breath. He was a smart man, shrewd, used to reading people—that was his job. Stupid of her to try to fool him.

She rose and looked at herself in the mirror. Pale, hair all over the place, spots on her shirt from helping in the kitchen. Scared. Yes, she was frightened. Frightened of what she could lose—was losing—with her sick denial, her attempts to evade the past. *Oh, Daddy, you did a good job. You trained us well. Run from anything worthwhile, anything difficult.*

The window of her room let in the pure silver light of the moon, and she moved to it, holding on to the sill with white-knuckled fingers. It was cold and clear out, black shadows stippling silver snow. There were no lies out there, only life and death. A kind of purity.

Jake didn't trust her, it was obvious. She'd done something . . . Or maybe it was just the way she was, some character flaw that he recognized.

She could let him go. He'd return to Denver and forget her. It was safe that way.

Or she could, for once, try to grasp what she'd been offered. A new start, a relationship, Jake Savelle.

Oh, God. She walked around the room, trailing her fingers over the familiar surfaces: dresser, bed, chair. Her safe haven for so long now. Her womb, her cocoon. Wasn't it about time she left it and faced reality?

She'd tell Jake. She'd confess, tell him the whole story, throw herself on his mercy. He was a lawyer. He could protect her. He'd know what to do, wouldn't he? If he hated her for what she'd done, if he rejected her, well, she'd have to take the risk. She'd live with the results of her decision. It was worth it, Jake was worth it. Maybe even she was worth it.

It was time.

She brushed her hair out, put on a clean sweater, and pulled on boots and her green parka. Before she could talk herself out of it, before the Jamison cowardice could kick in. She left her cabin, closed the door behind her, and took a deep breath of the pine-scented night air. Across the snow, at the end of the path that lay at her feet, rose the bulk of the main lodge; she could see Jake's window, knew which room was his. Had known since the first day. His light was on, a rectangle of brightness up on the second floor. She could go in through the kitchen door—no one would see her—and up the service stairs.

She closed her eyes and swallowed, her heart pounding, her mouth dry. She was so terribly afraid. She'd be putting her life in his hands. She took a step on the moonlit path, then another. This was the right thing to do. For the first time in her life she was making a real decision, a hard decision, not taking the easy way out.

Another step. She straightened her shoulders and made her reluctant feet move. *Come on, you can do it,* she told her feet. *Cowards.*

She couldn't live in fear anymore. Fear owned her, owned her life. She wasn't certain what she would do after this, wasn't certain of anything except Jake. He was her beacon.

She didn't understand him completely—he had hidden corners, too—but didn't every human being have secrets? She'd find out all there was to know, though. She'd lay her cards on the table, and he'd be forced to match her hand.

She crossed the snow, her footfalls crunching, her jaw clenched. *This is the right thing to do.*

In the distance, beyond the lodge, the mountains rose, pale with patches of black pine forest. Coyotes were yipping and warbling out there. She could hear them singing to the full moon. The raccoons were probably out, rifling the garbage. And the foxes, with their small delicate feet and luxuriant bushy tails.

God, she loved this place. It had provided her refuge when she needed it. But now, now perhaps she didn't need it anymore.

She looked up at the brilliant silver disk hanging in the black velvet sky. Just risen, huge, gigantic. She'd heard somewhere that when the moon was low in the sky it appeared much bigger, something about light rays bending in earth's atmosphere. It was called the moon illusion. A lie, she supposed, but not an ugly one like hers.

The moon illusion.

She slowed and lifted her face to it, bathing in its glory.

The blow to her arm came before she registered the report from the rifle. A terrible blow that staggered her and snatched her breath from her lungs.

Shocked, she looked down. Stupidly, uncomprehending, she saw the dark stain spreading on her parka. Her mind understood nothing, but her body knew better. Her knees buckled, and as she fell the moon spun crazily in the black sky.

TWELVE

The high-powered Washington politico took the early-morning call in his bathroom, where he'd been standing at the mirror, shaving, a towel wrapped around his torso. When he heard the voice on the other end of the line, he closed the door on his wife, who was fluffing the pillows on their bed.

"What the fuck are you doing calling me at home?" he whispered harshly, steam enveloping him from the recent shower.

"Savelle found the woman."

The man slumped down onto the toilet seat, his heart falling to his stomach. "He . . . he's actually spoken to her?"

"Yes. But the problem is already taken care of."

It took the Washington man a moment, then he rasped, "You mean she's—"

"You don't need to know the details."

"But you *got* her?"

"I think so."

"You *think* so? Either you did or you—"

"I hit her. With a thirty-thirty at less than a hundred and fifty yards. But it was night—"

"Shit. Then she might still be . . . ?"

"I don't know. I'll find out in an hour or so."

The politico thought hard for a minute. "If she's still . . . viable, then finish the job. We can't let her talk. And you know goddamn good and well I won't take a fall alone. You get my meaning?"

There was silence.

"Keep me informed. But not at this number, use the secure line."

"Right."

The man hung up. Outside the bedroom door he could hear his wife calling to their two kids. "Rise and shine, school bus will be here in thirty minutes."

School bus.

He tried to collect his thoughts, to squelch the panic, but it was impossible. The steam mingled with his sweat and poured off his chin, dripping on the tile. And all he could think was how in hell had they missed her in the hotel room?

It was the major screwup of his career. Of his entire life.

Cop that he was, David began taking notes before he and Jake had even driven out of the Aspen airport.

Jake switched on the wipers as he steered toward Old Snowmass and the Rocky Mountain Retreat. "Christ, look at this snow," he said. "You're lucky the flight made it in."

"I wasn't sure I *was* going to make it," David said.

"I don't know why we have to stop at the retreat first. I need to be at the hospital, David, I need to be there when Sarah wakes up."

"See this snow?" David pointed out the window with the eraser end of his pencil. "If the shooter left tracks, or if there's any brass around, this will sure as hell cover it up. We gotta check. And now.''

Jake stared through the glass and the mesmerizing *swish, swish* of the wipers. David was right, of course, but all he could picture was Sarah, waking in a strange room—in a strange *hospital* room—cops at her door, unfamiliar faces. Muriel Lovitt was there. Okay. And Bill was checking in and out. Still . . . *he* needed to be there, damn it, he needed to talk to her, tell her . . . Tell her what? That this was his fault? That she took a bullet because of him? *God Almighty.*

"All right," David was saying, "what have you told the Aspen cops?"

"It's the county. The sheriff. I told them nothing."

"Nothing?"

"Look, I talked my way into her hospital room; there were cops swarming the halls and I overheard something about a stray bullet from a hunter's rifle. A night poacher. What the hell else would these rural cops think? That someone made a hit on an employee at an executive retreat?" Jake laughed bitterly.

"Hey." David looked up from his notebook. "Don't get angry with me, pal, you're the one who pursued this. I warned you."

Jake clenched his jaw. Oh, yeah, he'd been warned. And warned. And David's predictions had come true. Except for one thing—Sarah Jamison was still alive.

David sighed. "Sorry, didn't mean to snap at you but, hell, Jake, you just never listen when you're on a crusade."

"A crusade," Jake said tightly. "I'm the one who should be lying in that hospital room."

"You weren't the target. Now, let's do some work here before we get to the retreat. And stop worrying about Sarah." David shot him a glance. "She'll be okay. You said so yourself. She's got full protection right where she is. We'll be there soon."

"Uh-huh," Jake said. Full protection? A bunch of small-town cops, who don't know the bullet was intentional?

"She means a lot to you," David said, "I can see that. We'll protect her, Jake, I promise. Okay?"

"Sure. Whatever," Jake ground out.

David was full of questions then, scribbling in that illegible shorthand of his in the ubiquitous cop's notebook. He wrote down what time of night the guests had heard the shot, where Sarah's body was found, the weather conditions. Then he got down to brass tacks. "Okay. Who other than you and me and Disoto could have known her whereabouts?"

"Her brother. He knew."

"Okay. Phillip Jamison." David scribbled. "Who else? A parent?"

"Not her mother." Jake shook his head. "I'm positive there's no way. But her father, Roger, he's hard to read."

"Okay. Roger Jamison. Who else from back East?"

"An old girlfriend. Christina." Jake gave him the details.

"Anyone else?"

"I don't think so. Possibly. But in my gut I think the people I talked to were telling the truth."

"I want a list, anyway."

"The list's in Denver."

David made a notation. "How about your sister? Did you tell Heather?"

"Yes. But . . ." Jake saw him writing down her name. *Jesus.* "Not Heather," he snapped.

"Why not?"

"Because . . ."

"Hey, she basically detested her husband. *You* told me as much. What if Heather was involved from the very beginning?"

It took Jake a moment. "You mean . . . in the Brown Palace? You mean with Scott's murder?"

"It's not that farfetched."

Jake swore. "You can put away that cop's hat you're wearing when it comes to my sister. Hell, she wanted to be First Lady. For chrissakes, she didn't *off* her husband."

"Mm," David said.

"Not Heather," Jake repeated.

David was silent for a moment. "Okay. Sure. If you say so. Now there's you and me. Obviously we both knew where Sarah was hiding out. And I told Disoto, as you know. I also had to let my partner know I was on a job in Aspen. I didn't give him the details, though."

"Disoto," Jake said as they pulled into the long drive leading up to the retreat. "How do we know he didn't tell a dozen people?" Then Jake frowned. "Hell, it was Disoto who was so damn quick to shelve the Taylor murder case in the first place. I always wondered about that. Did some high-up muckety-muck get to him?"

David grimaced and flipped his notepad shut as Jake parked in front of the main log structure. "You're reaching."

"*Somebody* put the word out on her," Jake said fiercely. "A few more inches, and that bullet would have gone into her heart instead of her arm. Somebody marked her for the hit and I'm going to goddamn find out who."

"Okay, okay, take it easy." David opened the car door and stepped out into the snow. "We'll get the bastard. Just calm yourself down, Savelle."

"Easy for you to say," Jake muttered.

By the time they reached the area where the sheriff's boys were standing around scratching their heads, three inches of new snow had fallen on the blood-soaked ground. "Hey, don't you think you should throw some plastic over that?" David said to the group.

One of the cops pivoted. "We *know* whose blood it is. And who are you, anyway?"

Jake was silent as David introduced himself, flashing his ID for them. Then he had to come up with a story as to why a Denver homicide detective was there in the first place.

"Hey," David said, shrugging, "I'm just visiting my pal here, Jake, and I thought maybe I could help out."

"Well, thanks," the cop said, "but we got it covered."

"Mm. What do you think went down?"

The cop eyed him for a minute then seemed to relax. "We believe a night poacher got careless. The edge of the field is littered with deer and elk tracks and someone made a bad mistake."

"Mm," David said again. "You find any casings in the snow?"

"Not yet."

"Footprints?"

"Nope. There are dozens of tracks all over the place. The guests." The cop lifted his blue parka-clad shoulders and dropped them.

"Mind if Mr. Savelle here and I take a look around? He's a friend of the victim's, Miss Jamison."

"Go ahead. You know what to do if you come across any evidence."

"Yeah, yeah," David said, "don't contaminate the crime scene."

When they were out of earshot of the local police, Jake put a hand on David's arm. "Why didn't you tell them the truth?"

"Look, we want Sarah in Denver as soon as she's able to travel. We can't protect her up here, and I'm sure these boys have no experience whatsoever when it comes to witness protection. We have the safe houses, the manpower, the know-how."

It was David's assumption that the shooter used the woods above the field as cover when he'd had Sarah in his crosshairs. "I would have," David said, and so they searched the heavily wooded area above the main lodge. There were hundreds of game tracks, now just dimples in the new snow.

"What a great hunting area," David commented as they trudged through the woods, stepping over deadfall, their feet sinking, city shoes getting soaked.

"Do you think our guy used a scope? Like a night-scope?" Jake asked.

David shook his head. "Don't know. You said there was a full moon. Watch that branch there. He could have done the job without one."

"It would have been hard, though."

"Oh, yeah, and he missed his mark, didn't he?"

They spent a half hour in the woods and got nowhere. The snow was piling up, and Jake was itching to get to the hospital.

"Is this worth it?" he asked, cold, wet, impatient.

"Probably not. Even if I find something, the new snow's gonna make an ID almost impossible. I can't imagine our guy leaving his brass behind, either. Even you wouldn't be that dumb."

They did spot what looked like a trail of human foot-prints leading out of the woods toward the back of the staff cabins, but they could have been made days ago and by just about anyone. The footprints were ruined, anyway, by the wet snow that was still leaking from the gunmetal gray sky.

"Let's get out of here," Jake said, his hands jammed in his parka pockets, his bare head ducked.

"Okay, all right, we'll go visit your little lady."

"She's not my little lady."

By the time Jake pulled onto Castle Creek Road and drove up to Aspen Valley Hospital, half the morning was gone. He was at the height of frustration and anger: *My fault, my fault,* was the mantra pulsing in his brain.

There were still cops in the corridor leading to Sarah's room, talking, sipping coffee, apparently waiting for her to make a statement, see if she had seen or heard anything before she'd been hit.

Outside her room, they ran into Bill Lovitt. "Is she awake?" Jake asked anxiously.

"Not really." Lovitt gave Jake an assessing look. "I want an honest answer. You aren't what you said when you came to the retreat, are you?"

Jake shook his head.

Lovitt seemed to digest that. "All right. Then I have to assume this was no hunting accident."

Again, Jake shook his head.

"God," Bill Lovitt breathed.

Then David stepped up to the plate. "Mr. Lovitt," he said, having introduced himself, "did you by chance tell Sarah's parents where she was? It's all right if you did. We understand that you'd only do so to save them unnecessary worry." David, in his good ol' boy voice. Lovitt's new best friend.

Bill Lovitt looked shamefaced. "I spoke to Roger Jamison last year. I only told him because, well, like you said, I knew he had to be worried."

"It's okay," David said kindly.

Roger Jamison, Jake was thinking. Just how much had he hated his only surviving daughter keeping company with the brash, *married,* upstart politician from Colorado? Enough to pull strings to have Scott Taylor murdered? But this *hit* on Sarah . . . Jamison couldn't have had anything to do with that. Still, maybe his contact, whoever had killed Taylor, had gone out on his own. . . .

Ah, hell, Jake thought as he turned toward the door to her room, none of that mattered at this moment. Sarah was the only thing that counted.

A part of him wanted to be with her the minute she woke up. Another part dreaded it. How in God's name was he going to explain all this to her?

Anger and guilt swirled inside him, and then there she was, lying against the sterile sheets, so small, so fragile, the bandage on her arm, IVs stuck in her.

At his side, David whispered, "Take it easy."

But Jake wasn't listening. His focus was on Sarah, wounded, unconscious from a stream of drugs flowing into her veins.

My goddamn fault.

He tuned out the quiet conversation David and Muriel were having by the window. He was unaware of the snow falling outside the window, darkening the day. He stared down at her, frowning. After a time she made a small sound and twisted her head groggily. He thought she tried to smile, but he'd had surgery himself, a knee in college, and he knew she was still under.

"Want some coffee?" David asked at one point, but Jake shook his head. A singular, unfamiliar pain began to grow in his gut, a hunger. He'd find the man who did this, find him and hurt him as he'd hurt Sarah.

For the first time in his life, Jake knew what it meant to be in a killing mood.

Awareness came to Sarah all at once as if she'd been prodded with a sharp point. She lay without moving for a time, and she knew something horrible had happened. She couldn't quite remember, but she knew it deep inside, with the absolute certainty with which nightmares are believed in the darkest hours.

Instant terror kicked her senses wide open, and she tried to sit up, but the leaden weight of her arm held her back, and then it started coming back to her.

"Sarah's awake," she heard a soft voice say. Muriel. Then she felt a hand on her arm. "Honey?"

"Urhm," she said, her mouth dry.

"You're going to be fine," Muriel said. "You're in the hospital."

She lay there for a time, trying to gather her thoughts. But questions flashed in her brain amidst the roar of fear. *Who? How? Now. Why now?*

She finally opened her eyes and focused on Muriel's face.

"Don't worry about a thing," the woman said. "You're okay. It's just the drugs."

Sarah blinked. "What . . . What happened?"

"Someone shot you. In the arm. It's fine, though."

Shot. She remembered that, the blow, the moon spinning. *Shot.* They'd found her. *He'd* found her. The sudden terror felt like another bullet ripping into her.

"Jake's here, and his friend from Denver, David, who's a policeman."

"Jake," she croaked. She'd been walking across the snow to talk to him, to tell him. . . . The crunch of spring snow beneath her feet, the huge moon lighting the path, the song of the coyotes, the sudden, fierce blow . . .

"You want some water?" Muriel was asking.

"Yes, please. Can I sit up?"

Then Jake was there, leaning over her, his face haggard, his eyes like two chips of blue ice.

"Let me," he said, pushing the button to raise the bed.

She grimaced at the movement.

"Damn," he mumbled under his breath.

"No, it's okay. Go on."

Muriel handed her a plastic glass with a flexible straw. The cold water tasted good. "Who did it?" she asked them. "Did they catch him?"

Muriel answered. "They haven't found him yet. The police are looking all over."

"Oh, God," she whispered.

"You're not to worry. You're perfectly safe now. There are policemen all over the hospital." Muriel smiled at her reassuringly. "They think it was a poacher, a stray shot. An accident."

An accident. She closed her eyes and wished her brain were working better. But she knew it had not been an accident. How had they found her?

She put a hand up to her head and felt tears burn behind her eyelids.

"Are you okay?" came Jake's voice, concerned, ragged.

"Yes, I'm just a little . . . overwhelmed."

He stood beside the bed, looking down at her, his eyes shadowed. After a moment he put his hand over hers, and she was so glad for his presence there. He was a lawyer. He could protect her, couldn't he? She'd been on her way to tell him . . . when had it been?

"How long ago was it?" she asked, trying desperately to orient herself.

"Last night," he said. "It's now"—he glanced at the clock on the wall—"almost eleven in the morning."

She had to tell him. Now. Before anything else happened. She'd been found. My God. How? Her heart clenched in fear. That same awful, numbing fear she'd felt that night in the Brown Palace Hotel.

"Jake?" she said.

"I'm right here. Is there anything I can do?" His gaze met hers, and she recognized, with some small surprise, that he was near the edge, with a kind of whirling madness in his eyes.

She tried to smile. "I'm okay, really. But you're a mess."

"We've been so worried," Muriel put in. "We've been at the hospital all night."

Sarah turned her head away, biting her lip.

"Owen found you," Muriel went on. "We all heard something and he went out to check on it. And Jake drove you to the hospital. He wouldn't wait for the ambulance."

She looked up at him again, trying to decipher his expression. Maybe he did care. Maybe there was something. . . .

"Are you in pain?" he asked. "Should I call the doctor?"

"No. It's okay, just feels heavy."

"You were lucky." He gave her a weary smile. "If it had been a few inches to the right, it would have—" His voice clicked off, and he switched his eyes away.

"Lucky," she breathed.

"She needs to rest," Muriel said. "Sarah, you really do need to rest."

"No." Panic throbbed in her chest, much worse than her arm.

"You folks want to leave and get some sleep?" A strange voice. "I'll stay with Sarah. I wasn't up all night like the rest of you."

"That's David," Muriel explained.

"David?"

A thin man with a lived-in friendly face came into focus. "Detective David Carmichael, Denver Homicide. I'm a friend of Jake's."

"Hi." *Denver Homicide.* She tried to fit him into the picture. Jake's friend. *Homicide.* Why was he here? Had Jake contacted him? But no, no. Everyone thought a poacher had shot her. An accident.

"Hey," David Carmichael was saying, "maybe we all need to clear out of here and let her get some rest."

Sarah saw Jake meet the man's eyes and they exchanged a glance that she couldn't decipher. Then Jake said, "Look, David, you and Muriel go on back to the retreat. I'm going to hang out here. I don't think Sarah should be alone."

"You sure?" David asked.

"I'm sure."

The room suddenly seemed empty, Muriel and the Denver cop gone, the nurses busy elsewhere, and there was only Jake now. And her. She took a deep breath and it rattled in her lungs.

It took all her courage, all her energy, to look up at Jake. "I . . . I need to tell you something," she began. "I was on my way over to tell you last night, when . . . when it happened."

"Oh, God, Sarah." His voice was ragged.

"It's not your fault this happened," she said, "but I have to talk to you. I—"

"Jesus Christ."

"Jake, please, I know it wasn't a poacher. I know why someone shot me. I think I do, and I have to . . ."

He held a hand up to stop her. "Sarah, for God's sake, listen to me. Don't say another word. Just listen." He was unshaven, his shirttails out, his eyes glittering in an odd way.

"It *is* my fault. All of it."

What did he mean his fault? He had been inside, in his room. . . .

He let go of her hand then, and he began pacing. Finally he stopped beside her bed and gave her a flat, sizzling glance that scared her.

"You know who I am? Who I really am?" He loosed the words like vomit. "Well, I know who *you* are. knew . . . hell, I knew weeks ago. Before I ever got up here."

She closed her eyes, felt her arm beginning to throb dully. This was all a dream, a crazy dream. It was the medication. . . .

"I'm the man who was investigating Scott Taylor's murder," he blurted out harshly. "I *was* the chief deputy district attorney for Denver then, and I headed the investigation."

It took her a minute to fit her thoughts around his words. Jake, a DA? The man who had headed the murder investigation?

She stared up at him, her eyes searching his face intently, as if he could take back those words, or she'd wake up any second and . . .

"Yes, Sarah. And I never knew there was a witness until a few weeks ago." He stood over her, the skin of his face pulled so tightly she thought of a skull. "I got this anonymous phone call in the middle of the night. 'There was a woman in the hotel room in the Brown

Palace.' I'll never forget those words. A witness. A woman. You, Sarah."

"Who . . . who told you?" she asked weakly.

"I have an opinion, but no proof."

She squeezed her eyes shut and felt a sob well up in her chest. Who would have betrayed her? *Who?* And then she suddenly knew. It could only have been one person. Phillip. Her own brother. *That* was why he'd phoned her, upset, practically in tears. He'd already talked to Jake. *Of course.*

Phillip. And now Jake. They'd both betrayed her.

She tried frantically to close her mind to this knowledge. Jake was still talking, purging himself, but the only thing she heard was her own inner cry of anguish: *No, no, no more.*

"Listen, damn it," Jake was saying, "I tracked you down. I found out who you were, pretty clever, aren't I? I went to Philadelphia, I talked to your folks, your friends, your boyfriends. I went to see your brother at Princeton. I learned all about you, Sarah, and I knew I had the right woman. The witness."

She put a hand over her eyes. He'd met Roger and Elisabeth, Phillip? He knew them? He knew her whole crazy, sick family? Constance? Did he know about Constance?

"I found out you were at the Lovitts, so I went there. Pretending." He stopped, ran a hand through unkempt dark hair. "Lying. Figuring out how to get you to talk."

"No," she whispered. "No more."

"Yes, Sarah, oh yes. And do you know why I couldn't come right out and subpoena you or have you picked up as a material witness, why I had to lie and sneak around?"

She shook her head, tears spilling out of the corners of her eyes, sliding down across her temples.

"Because I am no longer with the DA's office. I am, in fact, no longer a lawyer. I was disbarred. Lost my license. When everyone wanted to drop the Taylor murder case, I refused and they stopped me; they stopped me, all right.'' He shot her another flat glance. ''Is this making sense, Sarah?''

She mouthed *yes,* unable to talk.

''I knew Scott hadn't been killed by accident. A burglary. Bullshit. I knew it was an assassination, but I couldn't prove it, and someone wanted it covered up very badly.''

He paused then, and she couldn't stand to see the torment in his eyes. *No more no more no more.*

Then, suddenly, he laughed, a harsh, bitter laugh. ''You'll love this one. Scott Taylor was my brother-in-law. Do you get it now? He was family. Okay, he was a philandering asshole, but family nevertheless. I couldn't let it go.''

Jake Savelle. *That* Jake Savelle? No wonder his name had been familiar. The DA who was disbarred for jury tampering. Scott's brother-in-law. It had been in the papers. Yes, yes, she remembered.

''You know now, don't you? You know who I am and why I was at the retreat. You know what I want from you, Sarah. And you know that it was my fault you got shot.'' He leaned over her, his face ravaged, his eyes black holes. ''Someone found out what I was doing. Someone followed me the way I followed you. You know who it is, don't you? Oh, yes, you know, Sarah, *and they want you dead.*''

He spun away, stalking across the room, frenetic. ''So, now you know everything. No more lies. It's over.''

She lay there, spent, silent tears wetting her hair and the pillow. He knew everything, her false life, her awful weakness. He knew she'd been in the hotel room with Scott Taylor. He must think . . .

She felt violated.

''I haven't done this very well, have I? Just dumped it all on you. Not very good timing. I'm sorry, my hand was forced." He pulled a chair over to the side of her bed, its legs screeching across the tile floor, and sat down. "I'm so goddamn tired."

"Am I supposed to feel sorry for you?" she managed to choke out.

"No."

"It was all a lie then."

"Yes. Most of it."

"You were good though, Jake."

"So were you. If I hadn't known . . ."

"Please."

Carefully, he took her hand. She tried to pull away, but it was no good, she didn't have the strength. *Damn him.*

"You can't hide from this now," he said. "Listen to me. Sarah, *listen.* The local cops think it was a poacher, and we're leaving it at that. I have to get you to Denver. You'll never be out of our sight again. You'll be safe. I still know people, I'll get you in to talk to the DA right away. We . . . *they* will put the murderer away. It'll be over. I swear you'll be safe."

"You've got me cornered."

"It's not like that. It's not about me. It's about *you.* You can help us clear this case. You can make justice prevail."

"Justice." She wanted to laugh, felt it bubbling up inside of her, manic laughter.

"Yes, and I won't apologize for that," he said. "The law is all we have. It's what stands between us and anarchy. It matters. It goddamn matters."

She bit her lip and stared at him, this stranger, this man who she'd thought she knew, who . . . who had come to mean . . . too much. Too much.

She took a breath. "What do you really get out of this whole thing, Jake? Come on," she said, "what are you really after? And don't spout that justice stuff. It's more. I know it."

He met her eyes with his, dark blue and deadly serious,

his straight black brows a bar across them. "The whole truth and nothing but the truth?"

"Yes."

"If I can prove there was a plot to assassinate Scott, if I know who did it, then I know who set me up. I can get my license back."

She believed him. Oh, yes. "Of course," she whispered.

"You understand now, why I had to . . . ?"

"Give me a Kleenex, will you?" She took it from him with her good hand and blew her nose. "Boy, you really know how to get a girl when she's down, don't you?"

"I'll never forgive myself for leading someone to you."

"Sure you will."

He shook his head, stroked her cheek with the back of his hand. "I didn't know, Sarah. I didn't know who you were. You weren't like I thought. I do care about you. I'll protect you. I won't let you get hurt."

"It's too late."

"No, it's not. They're going to let you out tomorrow. David or I will be with you every moment. We'll take you to Denver."

"Leave me alone."

"Sarah, I didn't know, I mean that. You and I . . . I didn't mean for that to happen, but it did, and I . . ."

"Shut up, Jake." Her nose was running again, tears spilling from her eyes. She hated him, hated herself. She felt the most unbearable shame. Fear and shame and a sick rage.

Turning away from him, sweeping a hand across her eyes, dashing away the humiliating tears, she whispered, "The truth is very important to you, isn't it?"

He nodded.

"Well, here's one for your books, Jake Savelle. You were someone I could have loved."

Then she found the buzzer, and she pressed it, desperately, over and over.

THIRTEEN

Roger Jamison stood on the stone veranda of his Bryn Mawr house and surveyed the rolling pasture beyond the pool and guest house. It had rained last night, a good, soaking April rain, and the land was lush and emerald green in the afternoon sun.

He was a portly man, the old English squire type, and he put up a desperate front of authority to the world. Inside he was a frightened, cowering, loveless human being, tossed on seas of insecurity and resentment, betrayed by his family, wounded by their emotional desertion but unable to tell them so.

Alcohol was his refuge but, ironically, drink turned him vicious and drove them further away.

He took a long swallow of his bourbon and watched the horses canter across the field. He always liked to see them run. Powerful, uncomplicated beasts. He could stand here forever and watch them, but unfortunately a chore awaited him.

Income tax time was right around the corner, and he'd

stayed home from the office to work on his personal return. *Christ,* he thought, he had a two-hundred-thousand-
a-year chief financial officer at the bank, but he couldn't
utilitize the man's skills—not with his personal return,
too much tweaking to be done with the numbers.

He was thinking about how he could deduct the gardens off the west wing from his taxes, when Elisabeth
found him, the cordless phone in her hand.

"It's for you," she said.

"Well, who is it?"

She shrugged, handed him the phone, and eyed the
glass in his hand before she walked away.

Roger put the phone to his ear while taking another
drink. "Yes?" he said.

"Roger? It's Bill Lovitt here," came a familiar voice,
and Roger frowned.

"Well, Bill, how long has it been?"

"Oh, over a year, I guess."

"Um. And is that daughter of mine still . . . ?"

"Ah, yes she is, Roger. In fact, that's why I'm phoning."

Roger sat on the edge of a lounge and felt a knot form
in his stomach. *Not again,* he thought, he couldn't take
any more bad news about his children. *No.* Never again,
not after Constance. . . .

"There's been some trouble," Bill was saying.

"Trouble." *No. Please, no.*

"Now, Sarah is fine, honestly. It's just that there was
an accident. . . ."

"Jesus H. . . ." The alcohol burned all the way up to
his throat.

"No, no. She really is okay. But she is in the hospital,
and—"

"What kind of an accident?" Roger demanded.
Couldn't the man get to the point? No wonder Lovitt had
left his high-pressure job and run off to Colorado. A goddamn executive retreat . . .

"Sarah was shot, Roger, shot in the arm, but the doctors are absolutely certain she's going to be—"

"Shot? You're telling me my daughter was *shot?* With a gun?"

"Well, yes. The police think it was a poacher . . . you know, deer and elk, but . . ."

"But *what?*"

"Well, you know when Sarah first came here there was that, ah, trouble . . ."

"Hold on, I need a minute here." *Trouble.* He had always suspected Sarah's disappearance had something to do with the Taylor murder out in Denver, but how was *this* connected? What the hell was going on here? "Now, Bill, tell me everything you know."

"Okay, well, I believe it has to do with a man who's staying at the retreat. I think he was connected to that high-profile murder case in Denver and he traced her. You remember the Scott Taylor case?"

"Yes, yes, go on."

"Well, Muriel and I never made the connection until Sarah was . . . injured last night, but we were aware she was with the campaign . . ."

With that whoremonger Taylor, Roger thought, his blood boiling. Hell, he'd done everything in his power to stop the affair. He had called contacts in New York, Washington, Los Angeles, practically begging for intervention because, damn it, he was the last person Sarah was going to listen to. Then Taylor had been killed. He'd all but kicked his heels in the air. He'd never asked, never again contacted the people he'd spoken to—it was enough that Sarah was free from that disaster of a political upstart, that cowtown provincial, who wasn't worth a hair on her head.

"Roger?" came Bill's voice.

"Yes, yes, I'm here. I'm trying to think." Sarah . . . wounded. And Lovitt thought the shooting was connected to a man who'd been working on the Taylor murder case?

"Who is this man who traced my daughter?"

"His name is Savelle, Jake Savelle, and Muriel and I both remember him now from the DA's office in Denver. He got himself disbarred . . ."

Roger was listening with half an ear. Jake Savelle. That son of a bitch had sat right inside this house and lied through his teeth to them.

"Roger? You still there?"

"Look," he said, "you say Sarah is all right?"

"Yes. I'll give you her doctor's name."

"Give me the hospital number. I'll talk to her myself."

"Of course."

Roger walked inside to the library with the cordless phone and drink in hand and jotted down the number. *Damn that Sarah,* he fumed despite his relief. It was always something, with his children.

"All right," he said to Lovitt, "I'll talk to her and find out what's going on here. I wonder if she needs a bodyguard or something."

"Jake . . . Jake Savelle, that is, has a homicide detective from Denver with him. I, ah, believe they plan on taking Sarah back—"

"Taking Sarah?"

"That's correct. I'm afraid she may be mixed up in something much more serious than either of us ever imagined."

Now, there is an understatement, Roger thought. Aloud, he forced himself to say, "Thanks for letting me know, Bill." *My daughter sure as hell wouldn't.*

Then he slumped into a leather chair and hung his head.

Why, why, why? He'd sent his children to the best schools. He'd bought them the best horses, cars, clothes— he'd even shipped them abroad in the summers so they could soak up some culture. He'd bought them skis, sailboats, European racing bikes; paid for nannies, music lessons, art courses. Everything. And what had he gotten for his investment? A weak-willed daughter who had slit her wrists, a wimp for a son, and pigheaded, hard-hearted Sarah.

He drained his drink and went straight for another, dreading having to tell Elisabeth. He poured a double, eschewing his usual splash of water. What had he done to deserve this? His children, his goddamn children, they were going to kill him yet.

It was after eleven that night when Jake returned to the hospital, a pizza box in hand.

David was leaning against the wall outside Sarah's room.

"How is she?" Jake asked, nodding at the door.

David yawned. "Sleeping. Like I should be doing. Is that all you could find, a pizza?"

"Hey, it's late and it's practically off-season here. Everything's shut down. Damn thing cost me twenty bucks as it is. *Aspen.*"

"Yeah, I'll be glad to get back to the real world."

They ate right there, standing in the hospital corridor, the pizza box open on a chair Jake dragged over.

His mouth full, Jake said, "So what's the plan? I think they'll let her go tomorrow."

"I figure the sooner she gives her statement to the DA the better. Then there'll be red tape."

Jake nodded. "Reopen the case, convene the grand jury."

"Will they indict?"

"With an eyewitness? You know what they say: A grand jury will indict a ham sandwich."

"Did she give you any indication who she saw in that room?"

Jake snorted in derision.

"But you asked?"

"Yeah, earlier this evening. I tried."

"Huh," David said, reaching for another slice of pizza. "Pineapple and pepperoni? Not bad."

"So what about Sarah's safety once we get back to the city?"

"I'll get Disoto to arrange for a safe house, might take a day or two, and we'll keep it on a need-to-know basis."

"Like that will really work."

David shrugged. "We do our best."

"Denver," Jake mused aloud. "There has to be a Denver connection."

"How's that?"

"Whoever killed Taylor, whoever shot Sarah has to have eyes and ears in Denver."

"Maybe," David allowed. "Or maybe you were tailed from Philadelphia."

"Possibly, but I always assumed the Taylor murder had a Denver connection."

"Well, we'll find out soon enough."

"It's driving me nuts," Jake admitted. "She's lying right inside that door and she knows. She *knows* who did it. I've waited eighteen months for this. I've lost everything over it, and she knows." He laughed mirthlessly. "And I'm the last person on earth she's going to tell."

David wiped his hands with a cheap napkin, crumpled it, and tossed it in the cardboard box. "Ever occur to you that maybe she *doesn't* know?"

"It occurred to me."

"She may have seen a face, Jake, but that doesn't mean she has a name to put with it."

"Mug shots?"

"If it comes to that."

Jake clenched his jaw.

"Hey," David said, "she probably knows. She ran, didn't she? Whatever she saw, or *who*ever she saw, was enough to make her run like a bat out of hell. She knows, all right."

"Yeah," Jake said, wanting to believe that, needing to.

"Well," David said through another yawn, "it's your turn to man the door, pal. I talked one of the nurses into letting me get some shut-eye down in one-oh-three. Hope you don't mind. I'll spell you in a few hours, okay?''

"That's fine," Jake said. "I doubt I could sleep, anyway."

"Eh, don't be so hard on yourself."

"Hey," Jake said, forcing a Savelle grin, "maybe I like wallowing in self-pity."

He watched David walk tiredly down the hall and then he turned toward Sarah's door. He knew it would be better if he sat in her room—*she'd* feel better with someone there. But it was hard. Going back in that room, seeing her with the IV and bandages, would just about kill him.

He quietly pushed open the door. *Be asleep, Sarah.*

For years, long before her husband's murder, Heather Savelle Taylor had been well aware of the Denver society gossip, that she only stayed with the philandering Scott Taylor because she had set her sights on the White House.

There had been a lot of truth in that. There had also been another reason she'd remained with her womanizing husband: Heather herself had been involved with someone. Not a short-term affair, but a loving relationship that had lasted for twenty years, longer than most marriages, she often thought smugly.

The only trouble was he was married. Not unhappily. He had two teenaged children, whom he adored and would never desert. And a wife he liked, whom he would not divorce because of his Catholic faith.

Few people knew of her long-standing affair. Scott had never noticed, and Heather wouldn't have given a damn if he had. Poetic justice. Her brother Jake had been vaguely aware of it, having known the man since Heather had dated him back in high school. Their mother, who lived in Florida, had suspected, but she'd never said a direct word and was too busy in any case with her senior social life to meddle in the affairs of her offspring.

Heather met with her lover infrequently. She would

have seen him every day, but his hectic, very public position with the Denver police, and his devotion to his family, came first. That was all right. She wouldn't have loved him so dearly or respected him if it had been otherwise. And he was always there when she needed him. Except for that one time so long ago.

Today, she needed him desperately.

They met at their usual rendezvous, the Denver Botanical Gardens. It was their place, where they'd first kissed by the fountain in his senior year at high school. She'd only been sixteen.

She and her high school sweetheart had loved each other deeply, had even planned marriage. But then she'd found out she was pregnant, and her life fell into ruins around her.

She'd gotten an abortion, on her own, because he'd insisted they marry immediately, and she'd known in her heart they were too young; their lives would have been destroyed. When he'd found out his rage had been biblical.

After he had broken up with her over the abortion, she'd gone on to college; she'd met and married Scott. But when Scott had begun what was to become a string of affairs, early in her marriage, she'd turned to her oldest friend, her one true love, for comfort, and he'd welcomed her back into his arms.

Heather arrived at the gardens first, and waited by the splashing fountain, her hands damp on her purse strings. She was wearing jeans and a black sweater and had a scarf tied around her dark hair; her blue eyes were hidden behind big round sunglasses. She never wore jeans otherwise. And her glossy brown hair was one of her distinctive attributes. Dressed this way, her hair covered, she was unrecognizable. As she always was when she met him in public.

He arrived ten minutes late. But he was a busy man. She watched him stride up to her on the tulip-lined path.

He always struck her as distinguished. He was a little over six feet tall, with fine brown hair that was just beginning to thin. He was lean as a greyhound, with a long jaw and a gaunt, strongly hewn face. Not handsome but kind, intelligent, and his eyes were good. When Barry Disoto looked at you, you felt as if you were the only person who existed in his universe.

"Hi," he said, and he took her free hand, squeezing it. "I got your message down at headquarters. Is everything all right?"

Heather shook her head, the moisture in her eyes hidden by the dark glasses. "No, everything is not all right. It's that brother of mine again."

"Jake?"

"Who else?"

They began to walk together along the path, the tulips and daffodils in bloom, the trees heavy with buds.

"Oh, Barry," she said, a catch in her voice, "he's about to dig the whole thing up again, everything."

"Tell me."

"Oh, I'm so sorry to dump this on you again."

"It's all right. Now tell me."

"You remember a few weeks ago, when I told you Jake had discovered there was a witness to Scott's murder?"

"Of course."

"And you said you thought you could control that detective . . . Jake's friend, you know?"

"David. David Carmichael."

"Yes, that's him. Well, it didn't work. I know you tried. But Jake called me from Aspen the other day, and he thought he'd actually located this witness of his, this *woman,* and I haven't heard from Jake since, and . . ." Angrily, she wiped at a tear that slid from beneath her glasses.

Gently, Barry took hold of her arm and stopped her, turning her toward him. "Damn," he breathed, "I was hoping . . . Look, I don't know how to tell you this, but things have gone a lot farther than that.''

"Oh, God.''

He nodded. "Jake found the woman.''

"I knew it.''

"And I'm afraid . . .'' He hesitated, then went on. "I'm afraid she's been shot.''

Her head came up sharply. "Is she . . . ?''

"She's alive. In fact, David is in Aspen with Jake right now, and they're due to bring her in sometime later today.''

"Oh, my God,'' she whispered, "oh, God, Barry. If she . . . if she talks, if the press gets wind of this . . . oh, God, it will be all over the news. Scott, that bastard, with a woman when he was killed. It was hard enough to live with it when he was alive. But this . . . it's as if he's rising up out of his grave to humiliate me one last time. Oh, Barry.''

"Shh,'' he said, and he cradled her head to his chest.

"If only . . . if only whoever shot her . . . Oh, I don't mean that, really, but if she weren't alive . . . to talk . . . Oh, I don't mean that, it's too horrible.''

"Shh,'' he said again, "we don't know yet if she will talk or if she even knows anything. Let's take this one step at a time.''

Suddenly Heather looked up. "Can you . . . can you do anything to stop this, Barry? I don't know what, but you're the boss, the head of Homicide, and it's your jurisdiction. Scott's dead. This won't bring him back. It's not justice. *It's not.*''

"I know, I know.''

"It kills me to ask you, but I have to. You're the only one I can trust. Oh, that bastard Scott, why, why did I marry him? And I keep falling back on you, asking you to do the impossible.''

"That's what love is about,'' he said, and her heart

took wing. Barry would do something to stop this woman. He would. She knew it.

They both drove to Heather's Cherry Hills Country Club home. Separately. It had been a long time since they'd been together, and it never felt right, not because their sexual encounters were anything but perfect, but because Barry always suffered guilt afterward. He loved his wife in a way; Heather accepted that. But she knew in her heart he'd never love anyone as he loved her. If only she hadn't had that abortion. If only she could have seen into the future, known that the abortion was going to leave her barren. She often wondered if Barry had stood by her all these years because of guilt, but then she'd tell herself that it was really love that bonded them.

Her marriage to Scott had been such a farce. A loveless marriage, a childless marriage. Not that he'd ever wanted children. Oh, yes, she thought, it had been a match made in hell.

Barry stood in the master suite and smiled at her. "I like you in jeans, you know that?"

"You're so silly," she said, and she slipped off the sweater and shrugged her jeans down, kicking them aside. She still felt anxious, even afraid, but she was heartened to know that Barry would do everything in his power to protect her. It was enough. It had to be.

"Come here," he said, and she did, in her nakedness, thrilling inside at her boldness, at the way he stood there so stock-still, his eyes moving over her. Then she was in his arms and he bent his head, his lips brushing her breast, and her own head fell back as ripples of pleasure took hold. For a time, Heather was able to forget.

FOURTEEN

The doctor signed off on Sarah that afternoon. Muriel brought her clean clothes to change into, as her old ones were stained with blood, and her parka and shirt had been cut off her in the emergency room.

Her arm hurt now. A dull, deep throbbing. But she'd been refusing pain pills since that morning; she needed her wits about her.

She managed to pull on her jeans, decided to forgo a bra. She got the flannel shirt on with agonizing slowness, the bad arm first. If she forgot, for a second, pain stabbed and made her feel sick. Thank God she was right-handed.

The nurse helped her adjust the sling and drape her jacket over her shoulder.

"There, you're all set," the nurse said. "Now, don't forget the prescription. You may need it."

"I can't . . ." Sarah began.

"At night," the woman suggested. "It's going to hurt for a few days."

It was actually a relief to have such mundane things to

think about. If she let the significant questions creep into her mind, she'd go mad.

Who shot her?

The same man who'd murdered Scott?

She was so afraid. The fear was ugly and familiar and debilitating. She couldn't trust anyone; who knew to what corners of the nation the man's influence reached?

Jake. She supposed she could trust Jake, but only with her physical safety. Her mental stability, her emotional health was not his concern. He didn't give a damn, not anymore, not since the lies were all out in the open. He had her now, and he had no need to treat her with any more care than he would another witness. She couldn't expect anything from Jake Savelle.

The nurse let Jake and David back into her room.

"All set?" David asked.

"I think so."

"The nurse is getting a wheelchair," Jake said.

"I can walk."

"We're driving you back to the retreat," David said. "You can pack a few things. The Lovitts will send the rest when you decide where you'll be. Then we're driving to Denver."

"Well, I guess you boys have it all figured out."

"This is the safest way," David said. "Believe me, Sarah."

She believed him. He had a nice face, tired blue eyes, slightly receding hair. A good face. Yes, she trusted David. But still . . .

They walked on either side of her, down the hospital corridor, past the nurses' station. David had a hand on her good arm. At the front desk, the sheriff was waiting.

"She's been released into your custody, I understand," the sheriff said, glowering, one hand on his holster as if in threat.

"Yes, sir." David's tone was nonconfrontational.

"I'd like to know what in hell's going on," the sheriff said.

"There's nothing going on."

"I'd like your captain's name." The sheriff squared his shoulders. "This whole thing stinks. You know I could hold Miss Jamison as a material witness."

"But why would you want to do that?" David asked in a level voice. "She didn't see anything. She told you that."

They all waited by the front desk, the sheriff posturing, David and Jake acting the innocents, Sarah feeling dizzy and nauseated.

"I mean," David went on, "if you had the poacher in custody, I'm sure Sarah would be happy to come in again."

In the end the sheriff stepped aside. He did not look happy. "Your captain's name?" he repeated to David's back.

"Ah, that would be Captain Barry Disoto, Homicide," David called over his shoulder and they made their escape.

"Christ," David muttered once they were outside. "I hate that brown-nosing crap." He opened the passenger door of Jake's green BMW and helped Sarah down onto the seat. She inadvertently moved her left arm and sucked her breath in.

"You okay?" David asked.

She tried to smile. "I'll be fine. Just ignore my whining."

"You're not whining. I've seen big tough cops shot no worse than you, and they carry on like babies. You're doing great, Sarah."

Jake got in the driver's side, David in back. She went cold at the thought of being closed in a car with Jake all the way to Denver. She moved as far toward the door as she could, then felt David's hand on her shoulder. Reassuring.

Jake drove. She looked out of her window, not seeing a thing, thoughts batting about in her head: Who shot her? Who had followed Jake to her?

The road to the retreat was familiar but strange to her now, as if she'd never lived there, never been one of the staff: nice, outdoorsy Sarah. That life seemed so distant, unreal. She wanted desperately to remember it, to hold it close, to keep it, but it was already slipping away.

A new Sarah was awaiting birth, and she had no idea what this one would be like.

Jake pulled up near her cabin.

"Do you need any help packing?" he asked, his eyes not meeting hers. Carefully focused elsewhere.

"I'll get Muriel to do it."

"Okay. David, you can stay here. I'll go pack my own stuff."

Muriel came running across the snow, Bill behind her.

"Oh, Sarah, this is such a shame, you leaving like this. I can't believe it. Everyone's so upset."

"God, Muriel, play it down. I don't want your business hurt."

"Oh, don't worry about that. Do you have to leave so quickly?"

"Yes, Mrs. Lovitt, I'm afraid she does," David said.

"But why? She's just out of the hospital. Look at her, she's still pale as a ghost."

"I'm okay, Muriel."

"I can't believe this, detective," Bill Lovitt said, "dragging this poor girl off to Denver so soon."

"I'm not a girl," Sarah said softly, laying a hand on Bill's arm, "and I do have to go."

"It's awful," Muriel said, "just awful."

"We'll take good care of her, I promise," David said.

"Why, Sarah?" Muriel asked. "Why are they doing this?"

"Shush, Muriel," Bill said. "I guess Sarah knows what she has to do."

"I'll keep in touch," Sarah said. "As soon as I can, I'll let you know where to ship the rest of my stuff." Her throat grew tight. "Thanks, thanks for everything. I loved being here."

"I'd hug you, but your poor arm . . ." Muriel said.

Muriel helped her empty her drawers into a duffle bag; the bathroom stuff went into another, helter-skelter. David stood at the door, alert. Too alert. Then Jake came back lugging a suitcase, put it in the trunk of his car.

"I can't say I'm very pleased with your staying here," Bill Lovitt said to him, "on false pretenses."

"Send me the bill," Jake replied, his face blank.

"Don't worry, I have your credit card number," Bill said.

Sarah barely heard the exchange, her feelings alternating between anxiety and sadness and anger. She had a headache, an unrelenting ache behind her eyes. From the drugs, she supposed.

Bill put her bags into the trunk of the BMW. Muriel hovered, near tears. David was edgy, his eyes scanning the area. Did he have a gun? He must, she thought. Oh my God, he had a gun.

They got into the car, but this time Sarah insisted on sitting in back. As Jake turned around to head out the driveway, she felt claustrophobic—the headache, Jake in the car, David and his gun. She was leaving the safety of the womb, and she wanted to scream out her pain and fear. But she held it in, the way she'd done her entire childhood when her father went on his tirades, held it in, pressed it down, told herself she could handle it, she could face it, she could bear it. Because she had to.

David turned around in the passenger seat. "You comfortable back there?"

"Sure."

"Let us know if you need to stop or get hungry or anything."

"Okay."

Two hundred miles to Denver. And then what? David had told her she would talk to the DA first. Then they'd reopen the Taylor murder case. Then she'd have to testify before the grand jury. And, later, at a trial, unless there was a pretrial settlement of some sort.

He made it sound so easy: She tells what she saw, the guilty party is arrested, charged, tried, and convicted. But she knew it wasn't that easy. It couldn't be; it never was. It could drag on for a long time, years maybe, and she'd be afraid, worrying about every noise, every shadow. For years.

Where would she go? What would she do? How would she live?

She laid her head back on the seat as Jake drove, every mile, every minute, bringing her closer to the nightmare she'd hidden from for a year and a half. Closing her eyes, she tried to relax, but her brain churned unceasingly. Hatefully.

Was she glad she'd finally been caught? Glad that the running and hiding and pretending were over? Was it a relief?

Not yet, she thought darkly.

"We're going to drive straight to my house," David said, turning again. "I think that'll be the safest place until we arrange something else."

"Your house?"

"I'd rather not leave you at a motel, and Jake's place . . . well, I didn't think . . ."

"You're right," Sarah said quickly.

"Nina won't mind. She'll like the company," David said. "Nina's my wife. And there's Sean and Nicky, my kids."

"Oh, I can't," she protested.

"No arguments."

She shifted her sore arm because her shoulder was getting stiff, and realized she didn't have the energy to argue. His house. Fine. "Then what?" she said.

"I'll arrange a safe house for you. With guards."

"Am I worth all this?"

"Yes." Jake spoke for the first time.

"Will I be prosecuted?" she found the courage to ask.

"Not if you cooperate with the district attorney's office," Jake said.

"And you would know, I suppose."

"Yes, I would know."

What a bastard he was. He'd pretended to care about her, but she'd only been a pawn all along, a pawn in his plan to vindicate himself. She had the information he needed, and he was dying to find out what she knew. She could tell, just looking at the back of his head she could tell. He was bursting with his need to know, consumed with it.

She could give them the name right now. It would be easy, simple; it would take her ten seconds. Get it over with. And they would be shocked, but they'd believe her. Yet something inside her, not entirely rational, perhaps, warned her not to give out the name until she was sitting in the DA's office with a tape recorder, a court stenographer, and guards all around her.

Perhaps it was mere spite, though; perhaps she was being vindictive, a spurned female, but she wouldn't tell Jake Savelle yet. Not on her life.

She studied the back of his head, his shoulders. Dark unruly hair, a red-and-black plaid wool shirt. Had he forgotten about the danger? Did he think he was immune? He certainly didn't seem worried about his own safety or hers, not the way David was. All Jake cared about was delivering her up like a sacrificial lamb.

"We can make a nature stop up here at the Vail exit," David said. "Sarah?"

"I'm okay. I'd just as soon get this drive over with."

She stayed in the car while Jake pumped gas. Dusk had fallen, and it had turned cold, a cold, clear spring evening. David stood guard close by.

Darkness made her paranoia swell like a malignant tumor. She shrank back against the seat of the car as Jake drove up to the summit of Vail Pass. Behind them the sky still reflected a faint tinge of light from the setting sun; ahead it was black. She turned to watch the passing cars. Was that man in the Explorer with the skis on top really a vacationer? Or that station wagon Jake was passing—full of kids, a mother driving . . . was she really an innocent, or were the kids her cover? That pickup truck could hold secrets in its camper top. They could have waited for her, they could be following right now.

And what about her safety in Denver? Until she talked, no one knew who they were dealing with. Could David and his police department protect her? Could they stand up to the pressure that might be brought to bear on them? What if the federal authorities suddenly wanted her? What would she do then?

They descended the long, steep grade into Denver just after seven o'clock. Sarah noticed that Jake needed no directions to David's house, so he must know the Carmichaels quite well. Obviously he and David were not merely acquaintances through work.

"Stay for dinner," she heard David say.

"I don't think so," Jake replied.

"Sure, come on. Nina will want to see you."

"Better not, David."

"Just come in for a minute then, so Nina can say hi and check to make sure you're okay."

Jake made a sound of disgust. Was he embarrassed at all the fuss? But Sarah couldn't muster the energy to really wonder. She was tired, the headache persistent, and her arm throbbed like someone was beating on it. She flexed her fingers, but even that hurt.

"Here we are," David said as Jake pulled into the driveway of a two-story suburban house. "Sarah, I'll get your stuff."

She creaked as she got out of the car, stiff from sitting so long.

"Jake?" David asked, but before he could continue, two teenaged boys appeared from inside and then Nina Carmichael was there.

She was a thin woman with skimpy blond hair, and frail looking, but her smile was genuine when she introduced herself and showed Sarah inside.

The house was pleasant, ordinary, with some good pieces of furniture, a big sectional, upholstered in bold stripes, a few lovely antiques.

"I bet you're starving," Nina said. "Probably didn't eat a thing in the hospital. I didn't."

"You were in the hospital?"

"Didn't David tell you? I had a bone marrow transplant last year. Cancer. Believe me, I'd rather be shot in the arm."

"I'm so sorry to hear that."

Nina waved a hand. "Oh, hey, I'm used to the idea now. You learn to live with things."

David arrived with Sarah's bag.

"Honey, put it in the guest room, will you? Jake, are you staying for dinner?"

Jake stood just inside the front door, looking uncomfortable. "I better get home," he said.

"Oh, come on, Uncle Jake," the boy named Sean said. *Uncle Jake.*

Then everyone chimed in, wanting him to stay, but he begged off and turned to Sarah. "There should be a patrolman here shortly, and you'll be perfectly safe for now. Are you all right with this?"

"I'm fine," she said flatly.

He turned to go then hesitated. "For the record," he said, "you're doing the right thing."

"Small consolation," she said, and she turned her back to him.

Five minutes later, after Jake had driven off and a patrol car appeared on the street, Nina called them all to dinner.

It was a simple meal—spaghetti, salad, garlic bread. Everyone passed plates, reached across one another, talked a mile a minute. Teased each other.

The dinner was illuminating. Sarah thought of her own family meals—her father drinking, her mother near tears, the cold words, the awful tension. She'd thought all families were more or less like hers. But apparently she was wrong.

"Where are you from?" Nina asked. "Or did David tell me?"

"Philadelphia."

"Oh, that's right. You know, my folks still live back East. Boston. I love those old Eastern cities. Denver's a great place, but what they think is old here"—she rolled her eyes—"is 1890."

"I noticed that, too."

"Nicky, stop spattering tomato sauce all over. David, will you please control your son?"

"My son? I thought he was yours."

Nicky looked at Sarah. "They do this kind of stuff all the time." He grinned, displaying braces. "They think it's funny."

"It is funny," Sarah replied.

"It's boring," Sean said.

Nicky was the oldest, the one with braces. Sean took after his mother, slim and blond. Nicky was the sincere one, Sean the mischievous one.

"Why didn't Uncle Jake stay?" Sean asked.

"He was tired," David answered.

"He always eats here when you make spaghetti, Mom."

"Uncle Jake had to go home," Nina said firmly.

"Maybe he had, like, a date," Sean said.

"A date? With a girl? You gotta be kidding," his brother replied, tearing off a hunk of garlic bread and chewing it, laughing with his mouth full. "A date?"

It was so clear to Sarah that the members of this family loved one another. You could see it, hear it, feel it. She watched them, surreptitiously studying each one. There was no tension, no derision, no discomfort, just easy conversation and jokes and ribbing.

"Dad, your forehead's higher again today."

"And your braces are shinier."

"Stop it, you two."

"Mom, did you know Sean wore the same undershirt for two weeks?"

"Did not."

"Did so."

"Did not."

"Make them stop, David. They sound like idiot children."

"They are idiot children."

Sarah ate and answered questions put to her, but mostly she listened.

No wonder Jake was a constant visitor. *Uncle Jake.* He would bask in the affection of the Carmichael family. He was alone, divorced, probably lonely, too.

It occurred to Sarah once again that Jake had visited her family in Bryn Mawr, and he must have seen the Roger and Elisabeth act. He must have noticed the strain between her parents, felt their emotional sickness. It shamed her that Jake knew so much about her family, about her. He must have had a preconceived idea of her. She wondered what it had been. Had she lived up to the Jamison tradition?

Did Jake know that her closest friend on earth, her sister Constance, had committed suicide to escape her family? She hoped not. She couldn't bear his pity.

"You must be so tired," Nina was saying, jerking Sarah back to the present. "Do you have some pain pills? This would be a good time to take one. Then you'll sleep like a log."

"They gave me some, yes."

"I can tell that you don't want to take them but, you know, Sarah, I learned that you heal better if you're not in pain. Honestly. Listen to the voice of experience."

"Well, maybe I will."

David got up and started piling dishes and carrying them to the sink. "Boys, hup to."

"They're taking awfully good care of me. Afraid I'll faint on them or something." Nina put a hand on Sarah's arm. "I'm pretty tough, though. I humor them, you know. My three boys," she said fondly. "Let's get out of their way."

Was she really safe in this house, in a police detective's house? She glanced at the dark windows, wondering if anyone had followed her to Denver, if they knew, if they would locate her despite David's precautions. She wanted to curl up in a corner, in a dark place, but she couldn't.

She had to make conversation with Nina, who, of all people, didn't deserve Sarah dumping her fears on her.

"You have a wonderful family," Sarah said in the living room.

"I do, I know. I'm very lucky."

"I envy you."

"Oh, look at me, though. I'm so skinny and pale. That awful convalescent look. I hate it."

"You look great."

Nina laughed. "You don't have to lie, Sarah. But, my God, you should have seen me without a hair on my head from chemo. I tried wigs, I tried everything. I was a sight to see, let me tell you."

"But you're recovering."

Nina shrugged. "For now. You learn to take one day at a time."

She felt a sudden fierce need for Nina to be healthy, to live. For David and her sons. It was too cruel that this woman . . . But she wouldn't think about that. Instead she smiled and said, "I'm sure you'll recover completely."

"I think so, too," Nina said.

Before Nina showed her the guest room, David took her aside and pointed out the patrol car parked in front of the house.

"He'll be there all night, so don't worry."

"I'll try not to."

"You're upstairs. No one can get to you. No one knows you're here except me and Jake and my captain. The patrolman thinks he's there to watch for burglars. You're safe, okay?"

"Okay." *Safe.*

"Now, go take one of those pills and get some sleep."

Lying in a strange bed in the Carmichaels' guest room that night, Sarah kept seeing Nina's face when she said, "I think so, too." Such faith, such love, such caring. That was what a family was supposed to be. Not like hers, not a cruel drunk of a father, a pathetically unhappy mother, a sister dead at eighteen, a terribly confused brother. And she herself, someone who made bad choices, her judgment skewed. But she shouldn't blame that on her family; she had to take responsibility for her own decisions.

"I think so, too," Nina had said, all the love in the world in the words.

God, how she envied Nina Carmichael.

Despite taking the pain pill, Sarah didn't sleep well. Every noise, every creak of the unfamiliar house awakened her. She had dreams, wisps of emotion and image that she couldn't recall the next morning. She felt empty and unsettled.

When she got downstairs Nina was doing the breakfast dishes.

"David went to work, the kids went to school, and Jake called to ask how you were and to say he's going to the DA's office today to set things up for you," Nina said. "And don't worry, the patrol car's still outside."

"Aren't you afraid that your family could be in danger for harboring me?"

"Honestly? No, I'm not. I trust David. He's very good at his job."

"You're awfully brave."

"Not really. And it's only for a couple of days. David's working on a safe house for you right now."

Sarah put her head in her hand. "I really got myself in a spot, didn't I?"

"David and Jake are getting you out of it, don't worry. Want some coffee? Eggs, toast, cereal?"

"Coffee, please, and maybe a piece of toast. I feel so damn helpless with this arm."

Nina sat across from her at the kitchen table and joined her with her own cup. "Jake said you worked up in the mountains and that you loved it up there. He said you were a pretty darn good skier. You know, I could tell that he felt terrible about taking you away from all that."

Sarah felt her face harden. "Do you know what Jake did? Has he told you that?"

"Not exactly."

"Nina, he pretended to be a guest at the place I worked. He lied to the owners, to me, to everybody. He was slick, I'll say that for him."

"Oh, dear."

"I guess you can tell that I don't like him very much."

"I did . . . sort of notice that, but I didn't want to . . ."

"He lied to me. It was my fault. I was such a sucker, I fell for his line. We all did."

"Jake has a line? I sure would like to hear that."

"Is it true that his wife divorced him when he lost a big case, something about people getting cancer from high-tension wires?"

Nina looked blank. "Well, yes, Shayne divorced him, but we all thought it was because of his disbarment. I never heard him mention a case like that."

"Oh, God, I'm such a dope. I believed him," she said.

And then she had to listen to the sad tale of how Jake had been unjustly disbarred, divorced, and lost everything of value in his life. How depressed he'd been.

She sat listening, nodding occasionally, wishing Nina would drop the subject. She didn't want to hear about Jake's life; she didn't give a damn about him. She was sorely tempted to say that he'd caused his own problems, that he'd made his own bed and could lie in it. But she didn't want to erode Nina's faith in him.

"How is your arm?" Nina finally asked, and Sarah was immensely relieved Nina was off the Jake Savelle bandwagon.

"It hurts," Sarah replied. "Stiff today."

"Well, let's take a look," Nina said.

With some difficulty, Sarah finally got a shower. But as she stood under the blissfully warm spray, an image popped into her mind without a bridging thought: the shower scene from *Psycho*, the naked woman, the hand with the knife, the blood swirling away down the drain.

What if someone could get into the Carmichaels' house? Killed Nina or knocked her out. Came up the stairs, into the bathroom? She felt so defenseless. Her heart began that sick pounding, and she grew nauseous. It couldn't happen. There was a policeman outside. No one was going to get in.

She finished her shower quickly, stepped out onto the rug, turned the lock in the bathroom door, then took in a deep breath. She listened carefully, but couldn't hear anything suspicious. Only the jazz station Nina was listening to filtered faintly through the bathroom door.

She was crazy, totally paranoid.

It took her a long time to dress, refasten the sling, dry her hair. She kept glancing out the window at the front of the house. Instead of comforting her, the patrol car seemed ominous, a reminder of her danger. She could see the policeman inside it, sitting there, reading the paper and drinking coffee, on his radio once. He must be so bored. How could he stay alert?

It was a sunny day, warm and sunny. Sarah knew because she saw people on the street dressed in shirtsleeves. How good it would feel to sit outside in the sun or take a walk. But she was afraid.

It was better when Nina was in the same room. Then she could stave off the feeling of doom for a few minutes at a time, putting on such a good act she almost believed it herself. For a few precious moments here and there.

She took a nap that afternoon despite herself. Wrapped up in a hand-knitted afghan on the couch in the television room, watching talk shows. When she woke up, she didn't know where she was for a second, then it all came back and with it the slow, turgid beat of her heart.

Where was Nina?

"There you are, awake at last," Nina said, peeking in the door. "You were out cold."

Sarah struggled upright. "I guess I must have been tired."

"I used to sleep on that couch all the time when I was sick," Nina said. Then, "By the way, Jake called again to ask how you were. David checked in, too. Everything's going along fine."

She was okay, she told herself, sitting there in the comfortable room. Nothing was going to happen to her. David had it covered. He'd never in a million years put his family in danger, never.

She finally got up, tried futilely to fold the afghan with one hand, and went into the kitchen. The bright, sunny, homey kitchen, where Nina was pulling cookies out of the oven.

"They're always starving. The boys, I mean."

"They must eat a lot at their ages."

"Endlessly," Nina said, rolling her eyes.

"Can I help you do anything?"

Nina eyed her arm. "Probably not."

She didn't want Nina to feel as if she were clinging to her, so she tried to read in the living room. But she couldn't concentrate, so she got up to look out the window. The trees were budding into the lacey pale green of spring, the grass was turning green, too. A little boy rode his tricycle on the sidewalk. Such a peaceful scene. It was ludicrous to imagine she was in danger, that someone could creep up and shoot her on this bright spring day.

She was safe here. Nina was in the kitchen, the boys would be home from school soon, David would be home from work. She peered through the curtains and checked on the patrolman again. God, he was tuned out, his head down. Asleep? She wanted to run out there, bang on the car window, scream at him. But she wouldn't; she was afraid to go out there.

Her eyes searched the block, her nerves jangling. There was a utility truck parked across the street. US WEST, it read. The phone company. In how many movies had she seen this exact setup? It wasn't really a utility truck, it was being used by the man after her, by the hitman. At this very second they were surveying the house, watching, listening, waiting.

And when they finally made their move, when it was dark, the patrolman wouldn't notice them until it was too late. They'd kill him, and force their way into the house . . .

She shrank back from the window, cold with fear, and stood against the wall, crying silently, afraid Nina would hear, rocking back and forth.

Ridiculous, she told herself. She was perfectly safe. This was a cop's house, for God's sake.

She was safe here. Of course she was. She was safe here.

FIFTEEN

Jake was at the top of his game. He sat across from District Attorney Thomas Hurd and attempted to keep the grin off his face. It was hard, though; vindication was tasting so very sweet.

"I have to say, Jake, I'm shocked. I honestly believed a burglar killed Taylor. All the evidence pointed to it. The room being torn apart, Taylor's body position . . ."

"A burglar with a nine-millimeter? A small wad of steel wool found on the carpet? Not to mention Scott Taylor having made enemies of half the politicos in Washington? Come on, Tom."

Hurd glared at him. "Oh, I'll bet this feels real good. Admit it, Jake. Coming in here cold and shoving my face in it."

"That isn't the point."

"Isn't it?"

"Well," Jake allowed himself a measure of smugness, "that's a fortunate side effect."

"Okay, did she say who she saw in that room?"

"You get no information until she makes the formal statement."

Hurd leaned forward, his shrewd black eyes burning into Jake's. He didn't like being put in this position and Jake knew it. "What if this is all bullshit? What if this woman just wants to incriminate a boyfriend who broke up with her?"

Jake shook his head. "She's the real thing. No bullshit."

"Who's representing her?"

"I've taken care of that." He hadn't yet, but he wasn't about to let Hurd know that. He was planning on representing Sarah himself. If she'd let him. A big *if*.

"Anyone I know?" Hurd asked. "Lenny or Howard?"

"Neither of them."

"I like to know who I'm going to deal with, if he's a prick or cooperative."

"Oh, he's a prick all right," Jake said evenly. "Now, there's one more matter. A very important one. She doesn't talk without full immunity."

"Well," Hurd said, "this witness of yours disappeared for eighteen months, Jake. Immunity? I'm not so comfortable with that."

Jake stood and spread his hands deprecatingly. "No immunity, no statement. I guess we're done here, then."

Hurd cleared his throat. "I suppose I could have my secretary type up an agreement."

Jake pivoted. *"Full* immunity, Tom."

"Goddamn, Jake, I haven't even heard this woman's statement yet. I mean, was she involved?"

"Absolutely not."

"But she was there?"

"Yes, hiding. She was, shall we say, a guest of the candidate."

"I see." Hurd rapped a pen on his polished desktop and regarded Jake. "All right," he finally said. "Full immunity from prosecution. However, if there's anything you haven't disclosed to me, *anything*, such as this woman being even remotely involved in this affair, I'll go after her, Jake. And you know I will."

"Yes, Tom," he said, "I'm sure you will."

"Her name?" Hurd asked.

"Jamison," Jake said, "Sarah Jamison."

It took a half hour for Hurd's secretary to prepare the document. Hurd signed it and asked Jake to have Sarah sign it and bring it with her when she came in. Then they set a date: tomorrow morning at ten o'clock.

When Jake was leaving, Hurd said, "Is the killer going to be hard to get at? Is this someone who's buffered, well-protected?"

Jake did not know. All he really knew was that Sarah had been frightened enough by who she'd seen to run for her life. "Sure, you can get him," he replied. "Hell, Tom, who could stand up to you?"

He left the city building on West Colfax and dodged the traffic across to Fifteenth Street, where his car was parked. He used to have a parking space behind the Civic Center, paid for by the county. Even as he shelled out seven bucks for parking he was smiling—nothing was going to ruin his high. Jake Savelle's fire was burning bright.

He stopped at his place on Lawrence and changed clothes, putting on jeans and a sweater. Then he stood looking at the Writ of Immunity Hurd had signed. All he needed now was Sarah's signature. She'd do it; sure, she'd sign. She'd come this far, hadn't she? He felt his heart thudding against his ribs. He was so close, so damn close.

Representation, he thought—she had to go into Hurd's office with someone good, someone who knew the ins and outs. *He* knew them. Oh, yeah. And there was nothing that said that person had to be a member of the bar. Nothing stopping her from naming him as her representative. Nothing but her dislike for him, he thought, frowning suddenly, a little water thrown on his fire.

A larger bucket almost doused his flames when he sat at a stoplight on Speer Boulevard and remembered Heather.

The light was still red, and he had his right turn signal on, intending to drive out to the Carmichaels' and get Sarah's signature on the immunity document.

Damn it, Heather.

He switched off the turn signal, swore, and drove straight out Speer dreading the chore, but knowing he'd be very wrong not to let his sister know exactly what was going on.

He found her tending her spring garden, planting, digging, lovingly handling her prize roses. There were dirt smudges on her face and arms and perspiration stains on the collar of her workshirt. She looked young. He gave her a smile and hated himself.

"Oh, Jake," she said, looking up from where she was kneeling, "it's you. I knew the day was going too well."

He let that go. "I just thought I'd stop by and bring you up to date. You want to go inside? Get a drink or something?"

"Do I need a drink?"

"I meant iced tea."

"Mm. I think I'll stay right here on my knees and let you beat me down some more."

"Heather . . ."

"Just tell me. What is it?"

"I brought the witness back to Denver," he said. "She's scheduled to give a statement to the DA. Tomorrow."

Heather bit her lip. "So soon?" And then she laughed, a high, hysterical laugh. "My, but you are quick when you want something."

He met her stare, but it was difficult. "I should probably tell you that someone already made an attempt on her life."

Heather ducked her head for a moment and then looked up. "Well, Jake, I'm ahead of you on that. I already know about it. Someone shot her in Aspen."

"How . . . David? Did you talk to David or his wife?" Jake cocked his head, thinking. Why would David . . . ? It took him a couple of moments, then suddenly he knew. *Good God.* Heather was still seeing Disoto. That had to be it. *Disoto. Son of a bitch.*

Aloud, he said, "Barry Disoto?"

She shrugged. "Are you shocked?"

"No. God, no. I always liked the guy when you two, you know, went out in high school. I guess I heard something about it later. Did, ah, Scott . . . ?"

"No, he had no idea," she said. "He really couldn't be bothered."

"Huh," Jake said. "So you've had your, shall we say, knight in shining armor keeping you informed?"

She nodded again.

"And that must be how Disoto knew what David and I were up to. I wondered. So did David. *You* told him."

"Yes, I did. Did you expect me to sit on my hands while you went merrily on your way? It's *my* life, Jake, *my* reputation. Barry . . . cares."

He could see her bottom lip quivering, and the great effort she was making to keep her dignity intact.

She looked up. "I'll ask you one last time: Must this witness of yours make that statement?"

He sighed heavily.

"I see. So it doesn't matter who gets hurt along the way, just so long as you're vindicated?"

"You know this isn't about me."

"Oh? Don't tell me you aren't hoping to get your license back. Don't you dare tell me that."

"If I can prove I was set up, I will. But that's not the issue. Murder is the issue. I'm afraid the picture is larger than your reputation or my career. I can't change that."

"Of course not." She turned away from him and began

digging again. "I think you're done here now" was her last comment. And she stabbed the earth with her trowel.

He ran into rush-hour traffic on University Boulevard outside the country club grounds and his jaw locked. He couldn't be that wrong, damn it. Okay, so Heather's outrage was sincere. But, hell, she'd stayed with Scott all those years, stayed because she'd envisioned herself strolling around the Rose Garden at the White House.

He paused mentally. That wasn't entirely fair. His sister's life had a certain tragic slant to it. She'd always wanted children but wasn't able to have them. And Scott had refused to adopt. That had hardened her, made her bitter. He had often thought how ironical it was: Both he and his sister wanted children, but neither of their spouses had been interested. The Savelle Greek tragedy.

If Jake could protect his sister now he would. But the truth was, in this case, Heather's emotional state was secondary to the pursuit of justice.

Now he knew Disoto's role in this affair. Ever since Taylor had been murdered, the man had discreetly hindered both his and David's investigation. Protecting his lover. Protecting Heather.

Son of a bitch.

He himself had given up everything for this investigation, sacrificed it all to uphold the law. Hell, he had even sacrificed the best thing that had ever happened to him—Sarah.

The traffic crawled along University until he finally turned onto I-25 and made some headway.

Everyone thought he was wrong. He cut into the left lane, damn near causing an accident, then he forced himself to calm down. He might be the only man on the face of the earth who gave a damn about justice, but one was better than none. And screw the cost.

Roger had been trying to cut down on the booze—for years. Recently he'd had mild success, only allowing himself his first drink of the day at five P.M. He'd slipped a few times, he acknowledged, but he'd managed to enact his new personal rule most of the time.

Until Bill Lovitt's call.

Worse, he *still* hadn't told Elisabeth about Sarah. His wife was too emotionally fragile, crippled, actually, to deal with this news. And he still didn't know exactly what had happened despite a half dozen inquiries he'd made to well-connected friends in law enforcement. The only facts he possessed were that Sarah had disappeared immediately after the murder of the senator—hiding out at Lovitt's retreat—and now someone had shot her. He'd phoned the hospital last evening, but she'd already checked out. And Lovitt only knew she'd gone to Denver with that Savelle character and a friend of his, a Denver homicide detective, Carmichael something.

Only one thing made sense to Roger as he sat in the April evening by the swimming pool and sipped on his third double martini: Sarah, his surviving daughter, was mixed up in the Taylor murder. She had either heard something or seen something eighteen months ago. Now she'd been found out. No thanks to that Savelle.

His child was in trouble. But had she called him for help? *Hell no.*

What was he going to tell Elisabeth?

He watched two does grazing in the pasture below the house, barely visible in the waning light of day, and he tried to swallow his anger and frustration. The truth grated on him. If Sarah had not been screwing that senator none of this would have happened. As it stood, she was involved in the ugly affair and it could well become tomorrow's headlines. The press—especially the Philadelphia press—would gleefully crucify the prominent Jamisons.

The alcohol running hotly through his veins, Roger finally stood up and turned toward the house. He couldn't put off telling Elisabeth any longer. But, damn, he was dreading it.

He took a breath, strode across the flagstone patio, and then he heard his wife's cry, "Oh, my God, oh no!"

Roger rushed inside, banging the screen door behind him, sweat popping from every pore. He found her in the living room, sagging onto the couch, an arm flung across her eyes. And there, standing over her, was his son, Phillip.

"Elisabeth," Roger said, his gaze moving rapidly between his wife and son, "what the devil is going on here?"

"Sarah," she sobbed, "Phillip says Sarah was . . . shot. Oh, God, oh, Roger, I don't understand."

"Elisabeth," he tried, kneeling beside her, "there, there, Sarah is fine. She's not even in the hospital. It was an accident." But as he spoke, his eyes lifted to Phillip's. How did the boy know about Sarah? And what in hell was he doing here, anyway?

Roger patted Elisabeth's head and stood back up. He teetered a little. "All right, boy," he said, "I want to know exactly how *you* know about your sister. I want the truth, too."

Phillip met his glare and shrugged insolently. "I talked to Muriel Lovitt is how. And I can't believe you haven't told Mother. How was I supposed to know you hadn't?"

Phillip had spoken to Muriel? But . . . Roger searched his clouded mind. Then Phillip must have known where Sarah had been all along. He must have been in contact with his sister.

Phillip was grinning. He looked as though he'd been drinking, himself. That stupid sophomoric grin, the blood-shot eyes. "I know a lot more than you think," the boy said as if in answer to Roger's unspoken question. "A lot more."

"Go on." Tightly.

"I know she was with Taylor when he was killed, for one."

Roger grimaced as if he'd been struck.

"Oh, you're so pathetic," Phillip said. "You always thought she was sleeping with him. But you got it all wrong. Sarah was never *with* him. She went to Denver to work on his campaign. Period. And she was just in the wrong place at the wrong time."

Elisabeth said something unintelligible and sat up, wiping at her tears, looking from one to the other. "Roger? What is Phillip talking about? What have you been keeping from me? I want to know."

"He's not going to tell you," Phillip broke in. "But I will. You're damn right I will. Sarah went to Denver with the campaign to get the hell away from *him*." He glowered at Roger. "But Father here, who'd no more give someone the benefit of the doubt than fly to the moon, thought she was having an affair with the senator, so he made a bunch of calls to his good ol' boy politician friends and tried to put the pressure on Taylor to dump her."

"That's a goddamn lie," Roger hissed.

"Is it? Well, Sarah didn't think so. But that doesn't matter. Taylor was murdered and that was that. She never called you, but she called *me*. Did you know she witnessed the murder? Of course you didn't. But I did. She confided in *me*. I was the only one she trusted."

Roger kept staring at his son. And staring. And the pieces of the puzzle began to slip into place. Someone had put that Savelle on to his daughter, someone who knew she'd witnessed the murder and also knew where she'd been hiding ever since. It sure as hell hadn't been *him*, and it sure as hell hadn't been Elisabeth. That left Phillip. Who'd just stood right here and stupidly let the cat out of the bag.

"You," Roger said, facing his son across the coffee table, "*you* put that disbarred DA on the scent. Jesus H.

Christ, boy. Why? Why would you do such a disloyal thing?'' His hands formed fists at his sides. Phillip had gotten Sarah shot. Her own *brother*.

"Phillip?" Elisabeth said in a thin voice. "Did you do that?"

"I need a drink," Phillip spat.

"Oh, no, you don't," Roger said harshly, "not until I know why you did it."

"Worried your good name is going to be smeared all over the headlines?" Phillip shot back.

"Why?" Roger repeated.

Phillip grit his teeth. "Because, damn it all to hell, she's all I have."

"Phillip?" Elisabeth whispered.

"That's right, *Mother,* Sarah is the only real family I have. Sarah *loves* me. She cares, damn it. She's the only one who ever cared."

"And you thought . . ." Roger formed his words carefully through his rage, ". . . you thought that by exposing her she'd come back here?" He didn't wait for a reply. "You damn stupid fool. You're the reason someone tried to . . . to kill her. You did this."

"You did it. You did it with your drunken rages. You treated us all like crap."

"Phillip, no," Elisabeth cried. "Don't . . . darling, don't do this."

But Phillip was on a roll. *"His* parents"—he thrust a finger at Roger—"treated him like crap and he took it out on us. You know he did. And you're too weak to do a damn thing about it. Why do you think Constance—"

Roger lost it. He reached for Phillip and caught him by the front of his Ivy League sweater.

Phillip threw the first punch and struck Roger on the collarbone. Roger, who outweighed him by thirty pounds, shoved him, and he stumbled over a tilt-top table, and one of Elisabeth's priceless Chinese vases shattered on the stone hearth.

Phillip was blubbering by then, all control gone. He righted himself and lunged for his father, his mother's cries falling on deaf ears, and the two men were locked in a struggle that had begun three centuries earlier, when the first Jamison male had begun to resent his domineering father and had sworn that it would be different in his own family. But it hadn't been.

The fight ended when Elisabeth flung herself on top of the two of them, and an elbow struck her in the side of her head. Roger rolled away, while Phillip scrabbled to his feet, sobbing, mucus running from his nose, his face crimson.

"I hate you," the youngest Jamison male shouted. "I hate you."

"Go to hell," Roger panted, his head reeling, his wife, his fragile wife, weeping hysterically against his bruised ribs.

He and Phillip had fought once before, another drinking situation, when the police had brought the sixteen-year-old Phillip home on drunk driving charges. The fight had been physical, but not as bad as this. Elisabeth had sobbed then, too.

Tonight she was unable to stop the hysterical tears. They came in wave after wave, a torrent of emotions she usually kept well bottled up. Nothing either Roger or his son did seemed to be able to stem the flood.

She lay there on the floor, wailing, "Oh, Phillip, oh, please, oh, bring Sarah home. Oh, God, oh, Phillip, you can make her come home. I need her so much. I need my baby girl. Oh, please bring her home. I want my family, I want my family . . ."

They finally got her to her bedroom and forced a sleeping pill on her. It didn't do much good. "Oh, please, I want my family together. Oh, poor, poor Constance . . . I need Sarah . . ."

Roger was still mad with rage at Phillip, and worried sick that Elisabeth had truly lost it this time. He took his son into the hall outside the bedroom and issued an order. "You get in your car, get down to the airport, and get on a flight to Denver," he said.

"Me? Are you crazy?"

"Don't lip me, boy, not after what you've done to your mother. You heard her. She wants Sarah. You bragged about how much she loves you. Now get going or by God—"

"I . . . I don't even know where to find her. How . . . ?"

"How the hell should *I* know? Find that Savelle character of yours. Look in a phone book, for the love of God. I don't care how you do it, just find your sister and tell her she has to come home."

"But, what if she . . . ?"

"Hell, I don't know. Tell her I'll hire the best damn lawyer in the country to represent her. Tell her this Taylor case can wait. Tell her, Phillip, just tell her whatever you have to, but get her here. Elisabeth . . ." He stared toward the bedroom, the bedroom they'd hadn't shared since the night Constance had slit her wrists. "Tell her, tell Sarah her mother needs her."

Phillip looked at him for a long moment and then finally nodded. Then he went back into his mother's room, spoke to her for a minute and returned. Roger said nothing more to him. There was nothing to say. He stayed by Elisabeth's bedside, his head in his hands, and nothing made sense anymore. As if in a dream, or another lifetime, he had the vague memory of his own father's funeral, of standing over the man's coffin thirty-odd years ago and feeling nothing, perhaps a twinge of pain colored with dislike, but for the most part nothing. Elisabeth had suggested to him at the time that he was in denial, but he'd gruffly told her she was searching for something that wasn't there.

He had said, "I really never liked the old man, and he didn't much like me, either. What am I supposed to feel?"

Now, so many years later, he sat by his wife and wondered what Phillip was going to say over his casket. That they disliked each other? Hated each other? But he didn't hate his son. He wished Phillip were more of a man, but he didn't hate him. And Sarah. He really did love his little girl. He didn't understand her, but they had never fought. She kept things to herself, that was true. Once, a while back, he'd even thought she was the smart one to have escaped.

What if he'd done the same, Roger wondered, what if he had left Philadelphia forty years ago and never looked back? Would it have changed anything?

SIXTEEN

Barry Disoto saw Paula Granato sitting at a table in the far corner of the crowded LoDo sports bar, waiting for him. He made his way through the young, extremely noisy crowd, finding their juvenile cheering at the early-season Rockies game on the big screen TVs annoying.

But that was why he'd chosen this hangout: No one he knew would frequent the place, and no one would hear what he had to say to the *Denver Post* reporter.

When he reached Paula's table she stood up, gave him a bright smile, and held her hand out. "Good to see you, Captain Disoto. I appreciate you doing this, taking time to—"

"Sit down, Paula." He shook her hand briefly. "Let's make this quick, all right?"

"Of course." Her pen and pad materialized out of thin air.

"This is all off the record. If my name is mentioned, if the Denver Police Department is named, I'll deny it."

"Of course. That goes without saying. I know the drill."

A pretty waitress in a tight Rockies T-shirt approached. Impatient, Barry ordered a soda water; Paula already had a drink. When the girl was gone he leaned across the table; he had to speak louder than he liked because of the din.

"You remember the Scott Taylor murder?"

"How could anyone forget it?"

"Right, well, a witness has surfaced. A witness who was in his hotel room that night."

Paula stared at him. An attractive, gray-haired woman, a reporter who'd been around a long time, she knew the ropes, and she followed the rules. But right now she looked stunned. "My God," she said slowly, forgetting to jot anything down.

"The witness is a young woman named Sarah Jamison." Barry gestured at her pad, and Paula snapped to and began scribbling furiously. "That's J-A-M-I-S-O-N. She has an appointment to speak to the DA."

"What's she going to say? Do you know?"

"I can't disclose that."

"Christ, this is amazing."

"Yes, it is."

"This'll be the scoop of the millennium, hot damn. Where's she from, this woman?"

He paused. "Near Philadelphia, I believe."

"And you know she was there, actually saw the murder?"

"Yes."

"Okay, do I get first dibs at her statement?"

"We'll see. The fact that you're alerted should be enough."

"I'll need to confirm this. My editor will never let me go to press without confirmation." She frowned, and then she glanced at her watch. "God, not much time to make the morning edition. Any suggestions who I could call?''

"Hell, Paula, that's your problem.''

"The DA's office,'' she said, "they have to know what's going down.''

He arched a brow.

"Okay,'' she said, again glancing at her watch. "Can I assume the case will be reopened?''

"Probably.''

"Then there will be a grand jury convened, won't there? Will there be leaks? It might be hard . . .''

"You'll manage, I'm sure,'' Barry said drily.

"Anything else? Let's see. Why did she wait so long? It's been, hell, it's been a year and a half.''

Barry shrugged.

"Scared, didn't want to get involved. Was she a hooker?''

"I don't know.''

"Sarah Jamison. I'll try to find her on my computer, but I don't have much to go on.''

"She's in hiding right now, but you know it'll be out as soon as Tom Hurd reopens the case.''

"This is great stuff, captain.'' Paula paused a beat. "But I can't figure out why you'd let it out. Doesn't it compromise the safety of the witness? I mean, if the murderer's out there, and he knows there was a witness . . .''

"It's police business,'' Barry said in a taut voice.

Paula tapped her chin with her pen. "I get it. You're trying to flush someone. No, no, don't say a word. I understand why you can't.''

"I appreciate your discretion,'' he said stiffly.

"Hell, discretion's my middle name. You know that. Have I ever broken my word to you?''

"No, Paula, and that's why we're here tonight.''

"Is there anything else you can tell me? Like how you found her, who found her?''

Barry hesitated, thinking. "I can't tell you yet, but suffice it to say Denver Homicide was deeply involved.''

"Is this woman a willing witness?"

"I'll leave that to your judgment."

"I guess not. Hiding for all that time then dragged to the DA. Fun and games." Paula stuck her pen behind her ear. "Thanks, captain. This is a coup."

"Pulitzer Prize stuff, Paula."

She nearly ran out of the bar, and he watched her go, thinking, ruefully, that he'd still, no matter the risk to himself, go to any lengths for Heather. He owed her that much and more. He'd let her down at the most important time of her life, destroyed the girl he loved, deserted her when she needed him, and now he had to care for her and cherish her, try to make up for the pain he'd caused her so long ago, the pain she still suffered.

He sat there, his soda water untouched on the table, with baseball fans cheering around him, the huge TV screen flickering luridly on the faces of the spectators.

Tomorrow morning, or the next day if Paula could not get immediate confirmation, Sarah Jamison's name was going to be on every tongue in the nation. She'd run before, and he prayed she'd run again.

He sat there for a moment longer, took a roll of antacids out of his pocket, and put two in his mouth. The whooping and hollering mounted around him, and he shut his eyes. Was there any level he wouldn't stoop to where Heather was concerned?

Run, Sarah, run, he thought. And then he mused darkly that getting shot hadn't deterred her. Now it was becoming a high-stakes chess game. Barry had just moved a pawn. But Savelle . . . he had cleverly exposed his queen early on in the match. The question remained: Was he willing to sacrifice his queen to topple the king?

Jake's absence that day only succeeded in hammering the knowledge of him into Sarah. She knew he'd be arriving at the Carmichaels' soon, any minute, because Nina had told her so. He'd been at the district attorney's office, arranging for her to go in, to give herself up.

What had he said to the DA? How had he presented her? Would he be able to get her immunity?

She'd gone to her room and closed the door, with the excuse that she was still tired, but it was because she couldn't bear the pretense any longer. Fear lurked in the back of her mind, a cry that rang without end, and she couldn't keep up her act in front of Nina another minute. She had to save her store of strength to face Jake.

She heard, from downstairs, the boys come home from school. Their voices were loud then abruptly quiet, and she knew Nina must have warned them that she was trying to sleep. She regretted them having to do that in their own house, but she'd be gone soon, out of their lives.

David arrived home an hour after the boys, his car rumbling into the driveway, the garage door going up. She lay there, her heart beating, and waited for the time to pass. Fighting the urge to go to the window and scan the street, because she knew with a kind of fatalistic certainty that when they came for her she wouldn't recognize them anyway.

Her arm didn't hurt as much this afternoon, being an annoyance rather than a handicap, and her head was clear, clearer than it had been since she'd left the hospital. The absence of drug-induced cobwebs only served to bring home the gravity of her predicament. If only she could forget for a minute.

She heard Jake come into the house, recognized his voice, muted as it was. She could pick it out amidst the others with such ease she was ashamed of herself. She knew, then, that she'd been waiting all day for him to arrive. The way a convict must wait for his executioner. With a dreadful anticipation.

Rising, she brushed her hair. Her face in the mirror looked old, acid-etched by fear and fatigue. But she would do this thing that fate apparently required of her, and she'd get through it.

When she finally made her way downstairs, Jake was sitting at the kitchen table with David while Nina prepared dinner.

"Did you get some rest?" Nina asked her.

"Not really." Carefully, she avoided Jake's gaze.

Sean came in then and grabbed an apple from a bowl and disappeared again.

"You look better today," David offered.

"Thanks," she murmured.

Jake sat there silently, his eyes as intrusive on her as hands. She felt as though they'd been talking about her and had quickly changed the subject when she'd entered the room. Their unspoken words still hovered in the air. She gave Jake a surreptitious glance then and thought that he had no right to look so damn good sitting there, still the handsome dark-haired man she'd met in Aspen, who'd skied with her, who'd gone to that terrible Swedish film with her, who'd laughed so easily with her. God, it hurt. A lot more than she dared to acknowledge to herself. *Damn you, Jake, damn you.*

"I'm working on the safe house," David was telling her. "It'll take a couple of days."

She leaned against the wall and held her bad elbow. A defensive stance. "Will it be in Denver?"

"Not too far. I'm not sure yet."

She switched her attention to Jake. "Did you make the appointment with the DA?"

"Yeah, I did. Tomorrow morning, ten o'clock."

"Okay." Fear ran through her like an electrical current at the thought.

"Let's go into the living room and talk," he said.

She sat on the couch and he stood in front of her.

"I got a Writ of Immunity for you. Signed by the DA. You have to sign it, too."

"Thank you," she said stiffly. "Was it difficult to get?"

"Not once he heard that you witnessed the murder and

would give a statement to that effect, naming names."

She looked away, unable to bear his scrutiny.

"I want you to read the offer of immunity very carefully, Sarah. Before you sign it, you have to understand what you're doing. There's no backing out after that."

She cut her eyes to him, surprised. "You're warning me? Now? Isn't it a little too late?"

His brows drew together, and he considered his words before he spoke. "I may be disbarred, but I haven't forgotten the code of ethics, the responsibility a legal counselor has toward a client. If I were your attorney, I would advise you to read the writ carefully."

"You're not my attorney."

He rubbed his hand across his face. "Look, Sarah, you need legal representation when you go to the DA tomorrow."

"A lawyer? But I don't know any here."

"You know me."

"You're not a—"

"I can protect you as well . . . better than anyone else. I know how that place works. I practically ran that office. I know how they think. And there's no law that says I can't represent you." He paced back and forth in front of her. "You have the right to the representation of your choice. Bottom line."

She stared at him.

"I swear, if it looks like there are going to be any problems, I'll call in the best criminal guy I know. Pro bono. But this should be a simple interview. I can't foresee any complications."

She tried to sort out emotion from reason. She detested him for what he'd done to her, but she knew he was right. He could protect her—legally. He'd be the best person for the job.

God, how she hated the power he held over her.

"Let me see the offer of immunity," she said to stave off the need for an answer.

He handed it to her, a simple letter on the stationery of the Denver district attorney's office. Signed by Thomas Hurd in an illegible scrawl. This piece of paper was both her freedom and her prison. She read it, all the legal jargon: "Immunity from prosecution on the grounds of a full and clear statement . . ."

"Do you have a pen?" she asked without looking up.

"You understand what you're signing? This is a binding document."

"I understand that I don't have any choice."

"You always have a choice."

"You've seen to it that either I sign this and talk or I go to jail. What kind of an option is that, Jake?"

He said nothing.

"A pen?"

He reached into his breast pocket and handed her one. It was warm from his body. Quickly, she signed the letter before she lost her nerve.

"Okay," he said, as if he'd been holding his breath. "You're safe now."

Safe. "I'm not safe," she said. "I've probably just signed my death warrant."

"We'll protect you," he said fiercely.

"You'll try."

"No one knows you're here, no one that will hurt you."

"I'd like to believe that, but I don't. If they found me at the retreat they can find me here."

"We weren't alerted then. It's different now. You're under twenty-four-hour protection."

"Okay," she said wearily, suddenly sick to death of sparring with him. He'd never understand her fear; he only forged ahead come hell or high water. "Whatever you say."

"Sarah . . ."

"Yes?"

"Nothing. Uh . . . about me going to the DA with you tomorrow?"

"Sure," she said, and she hoped her tone was bored, "it doesn't matter, anyway."

Jake stayed for dinner, roast pork and potatoes and baby carrots. He seemed subdued to Sarah, quiet, even in the face of the boys' teasing. But the Carmichaels respected his reticence, as they respected hers, and the family chatter went on over the heads of the two guests.

"Dad, what's the Spanish word for church? It's in my homework."

"Look in your dictionary."

"Come on, Dad, it's easier to ask you."

"Iglesia," David said.

"Oh, yeah, I knew that."

"Can I have some of that crispy stuff, Mom? Please?"

"David, I got your navy blue suit back from the cleaners, and they couldn't fix that tear. It's ruined; honestly, a perfectly good suit."

"I'll wear it to work, babes. No one will ever notice."

"Is there ice cream for dessert?"

"Uncle Jake, which is your favorite, chocolate or vanilla?"

"I like that cookie crumb stuff," Jake said, "with the Oreos in it."

"And I bought chocolate chip because it was on sale," Nina said. "Oh dear, now no one will eat it."

"Yes, we will," the boys chorused.

The men went into the living room after the meal, and Sarah insisted on helping Nina with the dishes. She could at least carry things to the sink with one hand and put plates into the dishwasher. She'd have done anything to keep distance between Jake and herself.

But he was still there when she and Nina took their cups of decaf coffee out to the living room. Talking quietly and earnestly to David. The television set was on, a

Rockies baseball game flickering on the screen, but no one was watching.

"Go get yourselves coffee, guys," Nina said, setting herself on the sofa. "It's Colombian, your favorite, Jake."

David came back with his cup, sat down beside his wife, and laid a casual hand on her thigh, the kind of loving gesture that Sarah had never seen between men and women. Not in real life. She looked away, unaccountably embarrassed, but neither the Carmichaels nor Jake seemed to notice. Jake stood by the front window, holding his cup, staring pensively out. He looked, she thought, as if he were trying to read the future. Silence fell on the room, broken by an exclamation from David.

"Damn, three outs, the bases loaded. They've lost their last goddamn chance tonight."

Sarah pretended to watch the game, but her eyes kept straying to Jake. He was clean-shaven for a change, for his visit to the DA, she supposed. He wore jeans and a blue V-neck sweater; he must have changed his clothes before coming over here.

She hated him for what he'd done to her, but she hated him even more for letting her care about him. She understood now why he'd stopped her that night, stopped her from kissing him. Even Jake wasn't that much of a bastard. Grudgingly, she gave him his due for that.

And she had to acknowledge her own role in this ugly drama. She'd chosen to run from that hotel room, to hide, to try to forget it ever happened. She could have come forward at any time in the last year and a half, or she could have made an anonymous phone call to the police or sent an anonymous note.

She hadn't, though. She'd chosen to stick her head in the sand and pretend it hadn't happened, that Scott Taylor hadn't been shot in cold blood and left bleeding on the floor in the Brown Palace Hotel. She was a coward, a small, frightened thing.

She could hate Jake Savelle, but she couldn't blame him for her faults. And she didn't know whether or not to admire him for his unbending devotion to the truth.

She felt Nina's gaze on her; she let out a pent-up breath and tried to smile. Nina glanced from her to Jake and raised her eyebrows. Was the strain between them so obvious?

"I better go on home now," Jake finally said. "Thanks for the meal, Nina." He came over, bent down, and gave her a kiss on her upturned cheek. Then he turned to Sarah. "I'll be by to pick you up in the morning. Can you be ready to leave by nine-thirty?"

"Yes."

"Don't worry, Sarah. Just remember, you're doing the right thing."

"Uh-huh."

Then he was gone, and David got up to lock the door carefully behind him.

She sat there on the couch, her legs drawn up under her, aware of David and Nina talking softly to each other. But all she could think of was tomorrow, what she would say and how she would say it, what their reactions would be when they knew. What Jake's reaction would be. Then would he understand why she'd run? Or did his quest for justice render him blind to the weakness of ordinary people?

This was the most dangerous time for her—before she talked. Did *he* know she would tell her story tomorrow? Did his tentacles stretch as far as the Denver district attorney's office? Who was the other man who'd been there, the silent one, the man who'd shot Scott Taylor, the one with the thinning brown hair and tweed jacket? Was he waiting out there for her, lurking in the dark, waiting?

Over and over she repeated the words to herself: *I'm safe, I'm in a policeman's house, there's an armed patrolman out front, the doors are locked. I'm safe.*

Tomorrow she'd give her statement, and the world would sit up and take notice. Perhaps that would be enough. Once his name was known it would be too late to come after her. Wouldn't it be too late then?

"Come on, babes, let's go to bed," David said.

"Are you okay, Sarah?" Nina asked.

"I'm fine. I'll go to bed in a minute."

"I'll check the doors and windows," David said. "Don't you worry."

They left then, and Sarah sat watching the screen. She would get up in a minute and go upstairs to her bedroom. She'd try to sleep, to make the night pass. It was worse at night.

She heard the water running, a toilet flush, and then all was very silent. She finally rose and walked to the drapes and moved them aside an inch. Yes, there was the patrol car. Okay. Everything was okay. She dropped the drape back into place and then hugged herself, producing a dull pain in her arm. Okay? Was she crazy? Nothing was okay.

SEVENTEEN

Jake was panting, focused inward to the rhythm of his breathing, one foot in front of the other, one more block and then he'd walk the last two, a cool-down.

It was a cold morning, the sun perched to rise on the eastern horizon, the light still mother-of-pearl over Denver. Exhilarating.

He felt good. This was the best morning run he'd had in months. His brain was sharp, clear, and he knew in his gut that once Sarah gave her statement to Hurd today she'd feel immensely relieved. It had to have been a god-awful burden carrying around the knowledge all by herself. So alone. So afraid. But she'd realize today she wasn't alone; she'd have the backing and protection of every government official, every law enforcement officer in Denver. She'd have his backing, too. He hoped she believed that. He hoped she trusted him. She didn't have to like him to trust him. Right? *Right,* he thought, rounding the corner onto Lawrence.

Later, he'd try to regain the confidence he'd felt at that

moment, before it had all started to unravel. But at the time he was merely baffled when he saw a figure sitting on the front steps of his apartment building, a familiar figure.

Still cooling down, breathing hard, Jake walked up to the figure. When he realized who it was, when the knowledge hit his oxygen-starved brain, he felt as if someone had punched him in the gut.

"Phillip?" he stammered. "Phillip Jamison?"

The kid looked up sharply. "Oh, thank God, you're here. I rang and rang, but no one—"

"Phillip," Jake cut in, "how the hell did you get here?"

"I took a red-eye flight, got your address from the phone book—"

"I mean, *what* are you doing here?"

"I've got to find my sister." The college kid stood up then, hands in his jacket pockets, shoulders hunched in the cold morning air.

Jake glared at him. He did not like this at all. Not one goddamned bit. He mumbled something and then said, "Hell, you're freezing out here. Come on up, I guess, and you can tell me what's going on."

Jake made coffee. While the pot brewed, he turned to Phillip, leaned against the kitchen counter, and folded his arms across his chest. "I'm all ears," he said, an edge to his voice.

The boy was a wreck. His eyes were red-rimmed and tired looking, and his hands trembled. Cold? Jake wondered. Or was it something else?

"My mother," Phillip said, "she's very ill." He looked up from where he was seated on the couch. "She . . . she had a breakdown last night, and she needs Sarah."

Jake glowered at him.

"Do you know where she is?"

Grudgingly, Jake nodded.

"I have to talk to her."

Jake did not answer immediately. He could see the handwriting on the wall. Oh, yeah. And he didn't like what he was seeing.

"Your sister," he finally said, "is under police protection. She's got an appointment this morning with the Denver district attorney. A very important appointment. Her safety depends on this, Phillip."

"I have to see her, Mr. Savelle."

"It's Jake."

"Okay, Jake. I have to see Sarah."

"Did you listen to what I just said?" Jake ground out.

Phillip bowed his head. "Yes, yes I heard you. But my father, he doesn't want her to do anything without a top-notch attorney, and then there's our mother . . . she's very sick, and Sarah really needs to be there now."

Jake glared at him for a long moment and then said, "Shit," between clenched teeth.

He didn't give Phillip an answer, deciding through his frustration and anger to get in the shower, get dressed, and mull all this over. In the shower he figured, okay, he could hold this spoiled brat off for a few hours. Sure. But shaved, dressed, and fumbling with his tie, he thought: What if Elisabeth Jamison really was ill and something happened in those few hours?

Then Phillip was at his bedroom door, disheveled, his face haggard and his eyes frantic. "Can you at least give me a number where I can call her?"

"I'm thinking," Jake said.

"This is really important. My father—"

"Go on down and get into the BMW, the green one across the street." He tossed him the keys. "Go on, I'll be there in a minute."

"You'll take me to see Sarah?"

"What the hell do you think I'm doing? Now go on. I need a minute here."

Time, however, was not going to cure Jake's problem. He checked his watch—an hour and forty-five minutes till Sarah was due at the DA's—and his stomach sank to his feet. It didn't take a rocket scientist to figure what was going to happen. Sarah would hear about the offer of a top-gun attorney, a Johnnie Cochran type, and she'd grab the chance. It was suddenly as clear as the nose on his face. Sweet Sarah with her Mona Lisa smile hadn't been screwing some flunky state representative. She'd been screwing a United States senator, a top runner for the White House. She knew what her father's money could buy, and she knew how to read the cards. She'd leap at the chance to get out of this appointment. He could see a hot-shot criminal defense attorney tying the whole thing up in court for years. The lawyer would say she'd signed the Writ of Immunity under duress, and might even convince her to claim she'd never witnessed a damn thing.

He took the steps down to the street slowly, his mind working, circling. He tried to give her the benefit of the doubt, to tell himself that maybe her father's money didn't mean a thing to her; maybe she really had left all that behind. After all, she hadn't contacted her father for help after witnessing the murder.

Frustration gnawed at him, the need to know what she'd seen that night at the Brown Palace. *Who* she'd seen. So close. In a little over an hour she'd name the man. Jake couldn't believe it. Finally.

But his spirits spiraled earthward when he saw Phillip waiting in the car.

Hell. At best, even if she didn't take the offer of a big-shot attorney, she'd still be so worried about her sick mother—if Elisabeth was really sick—that she'd beg off the appointment, and then what could the DA do? Have her arrested? No way. Sarah was going to be the biggest material witness in his career and, knowing Tom Hurd, he'd already set his sights on a Supreme Court seat. Piss off Sarah Jamison?

He got into his car, jammed the key in the ignition, pulled away from the curb.

"Thank you," Phillip said.

"Do me a favor," Jake replied, "don't talk, okay? Don't say another damn word."

David Carmichael was pacing the living room carpet.

"Oh, sit down, honey," Nina said. She shrugged at Sarah. "Jake is only hung up in rush-hour traffic. He'll be here any minute. God, but you're nervous today."

David let out a breath. "Things go wrong," he said tightly.

"Oh, you're just being a cop, is all. Settle down."

Sarah said nothing. She was as anxious as David, more so. He was only worried about getting her to the DA safely, but she was the one with everything on the line here. Her life, for God's sake. And where was Jake, anyway?

As if to punctuate her thought, they heard him pull into the driveway, parking directly behind the awaiting patrol car that was to be their escort.

"Ah, here's the culprit now." Nina went to the door and pulled it open.

Sarah saw Jake first, looking like an elegant stranger in a dark suit, white shirt and— Her thoughts ground to a halt. Behind him—she blinked—behind him was Phillip. Phillip?

Jake strode in and only then did she recognize the scowl etched on his face.

Everyone seemed to speak at once then. "Jake?" Nina began.

"Who the hell?" David asked.

"Phillip?" Sarah whispered.

"Your brother's here to pay you a visit," Jake snapped.

Before she could begin to grasp the presence of Phillip—here, in Denver—he'd crossed the space between them and thrown his arms around her, causing her to wince from the pain in her arm.

"Sarah," he said, "thank God you're all right. I was out of my mind when I heard you'd been shot. It's my fault. I never should have made that phone call. Oh, God."

For a second Sarah didn't know what he was referring to, then she realized she'd forgotten all about his anonymous call to Jake. She couldn't even muster up anger. Her situation was far past that.

"Yes, yes, it's all right," she said automatically.

When she'd finally extricated herself from his arms, awkward introductions were made. Then she registered Jake's expression, and something about her brother's presence there made her feel as if a crevasse had suddenly opened beneath her feet, bottomless and dark, and she knew instinctively that if she faltered, if she took a wrong step, the abyss was going to swallow her.

She talked to Phillip in the kitchen, out of earshot of the others, but she was aware of the heavy silence that emanated from the living room.

"Listen, Sarah," Phillip said in a low voice, "it was real bad this time. The old man and I got into a little tussle, you know, and Mother went nuts, couldn't stop crying, screaming. And he was very upset. Very upset. He wants you home. He'll get you the best lawyer there is, the best in the country. You can't talk yet. You can't tell them what you saw."

"Phillip, look—"

"No, Sarah, listen, he's right. But it's not just that, it's Mother, too. I was really scared. I think we should call them right now. You don't have to make this appointment with some district attorney. Let the old man help."

Sarah began to shake her head. She put her hands over her ears. "No, no, no," she breathed. "I won't let them do this. They're trying to manipulate me. Don't you see that?" The black crevasse began to widen at her feet, and she rushed away from Phillip, into the living room, her heart racing. It was all a lie, a trick to get her to bend to her father's will.

She sat on the edge of the couch, dressed in her city slacks and blazer, her face in her hands, barely cognizant of the people in the room, who were silently staring at her.

Her mind raced, searching for a way out. Maybe Elisabeth wasn't sick at all. Her mother had had these breakdowns ever since Sarah could remember. And her father was using this, exactly as he used everything to his advantage. The offer of a good lawyer? Typical. Money could buy anything.

All a trick.

She looked up abruptly and met Jake's troubled eyes. Of course he was worried. And David. He appeared disgusted, getting his first taste of the Jamison sideshow—on the road. Nina looked . . . sympathetic. But no one could help Sarah combat the force of Phillip's plea. That was her battle alone.

David finally said something. "Sarah, listen, why not phone your folks and find out what's going on? What harm can it do?"

"*David,*" Jake warned.

"No, he's right," Nina said. "This is important. It's family. The DA will understand if Sarah has to postpone the interview."

"They're right," Phillip said. "There's no law that says you can't put this off. Sarah?"

And Jake. Jake scowled and swore.

Sarah moved her gaze from one to the other and experienced the flickering beginnings of a fight-or-flight panic—*cut and run,* screamed a voice from one corner of her mind. *Rotten coward,* came from another.

"I . . ." she began, the voices battling in her head. "I think I should . . . postpone the meeting." She locked gazes with Jake. "Just until I talk to my mother. Okay?"

Nina patted her on the shoulder.

"It's the only rational thing to do," David said.

"Where's the phone?" Phillip was asking.

Jake. He studied her face for an endless, horrible moment, and then he said, "Don't, Sarah, for God's sake, don't do this."

But it was too late.

Barry pulled into Heather's drive. On the seat next to him was the *Denver Post,* but the story had not broken yet. Obviously Paula Granato had not been able to get confirmation of Sarah Jamison's existence before the paper had gone to press last night. He had no doubt Paula would eventually get the story verified; there were more leaks in the DA's office than in a sieve.

Okay. So the story hadn't broken yet. But something even more fortuitous had just happened. Thirty minutes ago, Barry had been in his office when David had telephoned, giving him the news: Sarah Jamison's brother had arrived in Denver and she was postponing her interview. Barry had almost slipped and said aloud: *Thank God.* Instead, he'd done the requisite amount of cussing and told David to keep the guard on her until this was settled.

Heather, who was busy in the laundry room where Barry rapped on the back door, sagged against him when he gave her the good news.

"She's postponed her interview?" Heather breathed against his chest. "Does that mean she could still . . . ?"

"Shh," Barry whispered into her hair, "everything is going to work out. There *will* be a little flak, I'm afraid, plenty of media speculation about Scott's . . . death, but . . ."

Heather's head came up and her blue eyes met his in question.

He sighed. "The papers are going to get the story. I'm sorry. But it's going to be speculation unless the woman actually gives a statement. You can ride out a little gossip, darling; you've done it before."

"I'll hate it. You know how the media is, Barry, they'll make up whatever sells the most papers."

"They can only make up so much before they get into legal problems."

"But . . ."

"No, no, don't worry, this will blow over in a few days."

"She could *still* come forward."

"I don't think so. Once her name hits the news, she's in more peril than ever. If she's smart, if she's getting good legal advice, she'll shut up and let things drag out for years in the courts."

"Her name . . . Scott's name will still be dragged through the mud, you know it will."

"Gossip. Malicious gossip. That's all you have to tell people."

"I hate this."

"I know you do," he said soothingly, "but we'll ride it out together."

He kissed her forehead then. And she made a soft, purring noise, leaning into him. "That brother of mine," she whispered, "he's so crazy. I feel as if I've been on an emotional roller coaster for weeks."

"I know, I know." He kissed her cheek then and the tip of her nose. She laughed a little, complaining that it tickled. He knew he was due back at police headquarters in a half hour for a briefing with two of his detectives. There was no time for this. No time.

She turned her face up to his, her eyes so blue in the vivid light of morning, her lips parted slightly, an invitation.

"Can you stay for a few minutes?"

"I really can't."

"Please? Just a little while?"

He'd never been able to resist her, especially when she was like this, natural, no makeup or fancy hair that couldn't be mussed, her clothes casual—a white shirt open at the collar, slacks. Almost as if she were a high school kid again.

"Barry?" she breathed, and he bent his head and took her mouth with his in a hard, demanding kiss.

She sighed deeply and leaned back against the countertop, then she pulled away and looked at him for a moment. She smiled, carefree, young, as she'd been when they'd first met, before the abortion, before Scott, before everything. Heather had been his first, and she his, and sometimes they recalled that early love in tender words and shy smiles until she remembered her loss, their loss, and her childless years.

They came together in her bedroom, on the king-sized bed. It was odd, because they rarely made love during the day. Heather's urgency was odd, too. It was as if, Barry thought, she needed this to erase reality, to bolster herself against what was going to take place.

Lying there afterward, spent, he squeezed his eyes shut. But he knew what was going to happen. What always happened an instant after his passion ebbed. He'd see *her,* his wife, her face branded on the inside of his eyelids, the pain there, the accusation. *You bastard.* It was in her eyes.

He pulled away from Heather, fighting his guilt, trying to banish the image that tormented him. It never worked. It never would work, not as long as he was married. And he knew he'd never get a divorce. He didn't even want to. He loved Madeline. Somehow he loved his wife.

"Oh, Barry," Heather said as she gathered her clothes, "I love you so."

He said the right words as he, too, got dressed again. He always came up with the right things to say. Here. At home. Always. How could he love and cherish and protect two women at the same time? Year after year. He accepted that he could, though. He even accepted the lengths to which he would go to do just that.

EIGHTEEN

Jake sat brooding in his favorite chair. The bent and dusty blinds were drawn, and he hadn't turned the lights on. Only a diffused glow came from a streetlight outside, casting barred shadows on the wall.

Rage ate away at him like a hungry wolf. He couldn't quite put a finger on why he was so angry. It was partly due to the frustration of seeing all his plans collapse. Also because justice was once more being subverted, and he still didn't know the name of the murderer. The name he'd tasted on his tongue. He raged at the loss of Sarah— her trust, her need, the last fragile tie that had bound them together. He'd completely lost control of the situation, gone over the fine line of control he'd been so carefully walking. He'd stepped over into madness and self-doubt and defeat.

His stomach growled with hunger; he hadn't eaten all day. After he'd phoned Tom Hurd, he'd only tasted bile.

Nina had told him to come back for dinner and to talk to Sarah.

"What for?" he'd asked. "What the hell for?"

"Jake, she's upset. You don't realize how hard this whole thing is for her. Calm down and talk to her and Phillip. You'll be able to straighten things out."

"The hell I will," he'd said, and he'd stalked out of the Carmichaels' house, shaking with fury.

That goddamn sick family of hers, showing up like a bad penny at the last second in the guise of little brother. He should have tied Phillip up and shoved him into the trunk of his car until Sarah was safely in Hurd's office. Or strangled the son of a bitch.

He nodded to himself at the thought, and on the wall his wretched shadow, imprisoned by bars, nodded with him.

He'd been wrong again, blown his chance for redemption, for his life back, for the truth. He'd lost it, and this time he wasn't sure he'd get over it.

"We're going to have to postpone the meeting," he'd had to tell Hurd on the phone.

"Now, wait a damn minute," the DA had yelled back at him, and it had escalated from there. The same sick humiliation and despair, relived like a stale TV rerun.

He swore out loud, the words grinding out of his mouth as if he were chewing on stones.

And the goddamn doorbell rang.

"Jake," he heard, "Jake Savelle, are you there?"

Who in hell . . . ?

He pushed himself up out of the chair and padded over to the door, pulling it open. There stood Phillip Jamison.

"Hello, good evening," Phillip said, and Jake knew instantly that he was drunk. Contempt filled him.

"Go on, kid, get your ass out of here. I have nothing to say to you." He started to push the door shut.

"Wait," Phillip said, standing right in the doorway. "I know you're pissed. That's why I'm here. I wanna apologize." He wavered slightly and one eye wandered out.

"You little creep," Jake said. "You have the balls to come here stinking like booze?"

Phillip grinned stupidly and spread his hands, raised his shoulders.

"Go to your sister," Jake tried.

"Don't think I'm welcome there."

"Get a motel room then."

The kid just stared at him as if a Jamison had never heard of a motel.

"Shit." Jake stood there in old sweatpants and a T-shirt, no shoes, and looked at the scion of the blue blood family. Disgusting. "Come in."

"Thanks, Jake. I knew you'd let me stay. I could tell you're a really good guy. My sister said so."

"You're lying, you little shit."

"Yeah, I am. Boy, you're sharp." Phillip sprawled onto the couch, his well-worn leather jacket hanging open, his legs straight out in front of him. Two hectic spots of red stained his cheeks.

Jake turned his back and went into his tiny kitchen to brew a pot of strong coffee. No way did he want Prince Phillip here vomiting on his furniture.

"I wanna 'pologize," Phillip repeated. "I shouldn't have come here. Ol' man made me."

"Christ, you're a big boy. What did he do, handcuff you and put you on the plane?"

"Ha!" Phillip got out a scornful laugh, but his chin was sinking lower and lower onto his chest.

The coffee was brewing, and Jake came around and stood in front of the young man. "Okay, so tell me the truth, why did you call me that night?"

"Yup, I did that, all right."

"Why? Why me?"

"Oh, I figured you had the most to gain, being disbarred and all." The kid hiccoughed then. "See, I read the papers after Sarah told me about Taylor. She didn't, but I did. So I knew." He looked up at Jake, bleary-eyed.

"I almost called the district attorney's office, but I thought they might bury it. But I figured you wouldn't."

"Pretty clever, weren't you? But between you and me we almost got your sister killed."

"That's what my father said." Another hiccough.

"He was right."

Phillip shut one eye and peered at Jake. "He called you some choice names."

"Who, your father?"

"Yup, the Honorable Roger Jamison the Third, Esquire."

"I bet."

"We're all cowards, you know, all the Jamisons. Except Constance, because, you know, I often think what she did took more courage than hanging round."

Constance, the sister who committed suicide, Jake thought. He poured coffee into a cup, stirred in some sugar, and brought it to Phillip. "Here, drink this."

"Is it a latte?" Phillip asked drolly. "I don't drink anything but latte."

"Shut up and drink it."

Jake sank down into his chair across from Phillip, elbow on the arm, fist under his chin. "So, why'd you come, kid?"

"Told ya. The ol' man."

"Cut the crap."

Phillip sipped at the coffee, apparently found it too hot, and blew on it. "It's not sweet enough."

"And this ain't Starbucks. Why'd you come to Denver?"

Phillip closed his eyes. "I told you I'm a coward, didn't I? And I'm spoiled, too. And I'm afraid of Roger the Third, who is a sick, sick man. So, I came because I thought if I did this whole thing, and you found Sarah, I thought she'd come home. She's all I got."

"Jesus Christ."

"And my mother had a nervous breakdown, and it scared the hell out of me."

"Drink up."

He drank, his eyes still closed, and Jake saw that the color had drained out of his face.

"I think you misjudged your sister," Jake said. "I don't think she's going to go back to live near you no matter what."

"You know what, Jake? I think you're right."

"You can't hold on to people if they don't want to stay with you. Regardless of how much you love them," Jake said. "Believe me, I know."

"But, hey, it was a good idea, wasn't it? Theoretically." It came out *theretcally.*

"It was a lousy idea, kid. You nearly got her killed." Jake paused. "Did she ever tell you who she saw in that hotel room?"

Phillip opened his eyes, stared at Jake from under drawn brows, and wagged a finger at him. "Naughty, naughty. She won't tell you, so you try to get it from me."

"Well, do you know?"

"Nope."

"Don't lie to me, kid."

"I'm not lying. I have no idea who it was. Some scary dude, I guess."

Jake got him another cup of coffee.

"I'm going to need to pee pretty soon if you keep giving me this stuff."

"Shut up and drink it."

"You're pretty tough, man, not like my family. We're soft. Inbreeding. Shit, Jake, you know the truth? We're a dying breed, a smaller minority every year, us Mayflower folk."

"Yeah, yeah, I really feel bad for you sad sacks."

"I speak the truth." *Troof,* he'd said.

"You lied to me that day I came to Princeton."

"Uh-huh."

"Why? You could have helped me locate her sooner."

"I got scared she'd find out. And hate me."

"She'd have found out sooner or later."

"Later's better."

"You're a pain in the ass."

"I know. And I'm getting pretty sick of myself." Phillip pulled himself up laboriously, sloshing some coffee onto his sweater. "I've decided to . . . ha! turn over a new leaf. That's it. First thing I'm gonna do is tell Sarah to go give that statement. 'Bout time a Jamison took responsibility. Face fuckin' reality. Hell with the ol' man."

"You should have done that this morning, you moron."

"Had to get sloshed to think straight." He drank some more coffee. "Alcohol destroys my inhi . . . in-hi-bi-tions, so I . . . my head is clearer."

"Makes perfect sense."

Phillip stared at him with the glimmerings of sobriety in his expression. "Nothing makes any sense, Jake. Nothing."

Then he lay his head on the back of the couch and in a few minutes he had passed out.

Jake stared at Phillip, somewhere between resenting and admiring him. It took guts to show up at his door. It took guts to admit you're screwed up and you want to change. It took guts to tell the truth, and Jake judged Phillip's drunken ramblings to be the truth.

He got up and went into the bedroom where he found a blanket, which he put on the kid. He felt slightly paternal standing over him, looking down at his slack, open-mouthed, perspiring face. Then he was a little embarrassed at the notion. Phillip *had* a father. Maybe a flawed one, but better than a kick in the pants.

Of course, Jake's father had died when he was very young, but he didn't feel that it had done him irreparable harm. That was due to his mother, he knew; whereas Elisabeth Jamison was no help at all to her children.

Phillip moved and muttered in his sleep, and Jake lifted the young man's legs up onto the couch. He didn't wake up. Grudgingly, he had to give Phillip credit for facing the truth, for exorcising his demons.

He wandered around his apartment, putting the coffee away, getting ready for bed, and he realized that he wasn't so full of wrath anymore. Maybe Phillip's promise to advise Sarah to talk was the reason, but he didn't think so. What was it, then? Why would Phillip's drunken visitation bleed away his own anger?

Hell, he didn't know. Maybe it was as simple as being faced with problems worse than your own. Phillip had taken a step tonight, a step toward breaking out of old, ingrained destructive patterns. Jake had patterns like that; he had his own demons. His demons were twofold. He had an unbending drive to see justice meted out. And, he didn't kid himself one second, he wanted vindication.

He'd used people every step of the way. He'd used prosecutors and judges and the office of the district attorney to impose his own idea of justice on society at large. He'd used Shayne as a companion and to fulfill his need for children. He'd used Phillip and the Jamisons and Sarah's friends and Sarah herself. Wielding his Excaliber of justice no matter the consequences.

Well, he wasn't going to use her anymore. He was, as Phillip had said, going to turn over a new leaf.

He watched the kid sleep for a moment longer, then switched off the lights in the living room. Tomorrow morning Phillip was going to feel like something the cat dragged in. Jake shook his head then ambled back toward his bedroom.

This time, no matter what Phillip said to her, Sarah's decision had to come from her heart and her gut and her mind.

●　　●　　●

The media sharks smelled blood the moment the *Denver Post* hit the newsstands the next morning. The *Post* scooped the *Rocky Mountain News,* its archrival, with giant block headlines that read: *Eyewitness to Scott Taylor Murder Comes Forward.* With Paula Granato's byline.

It had taken Paula an extra day to get the confirmation demanded by her editor, but she'd gotten it, exactly as Barry Disoto had suggested, through a contact in the DA's office. A source that would go to the grave with her.

In the story, Paula named Sarah Jamison, thirty-three, of the Jamison banking clan of Philadelphia, Pennsylvania, as a witness to the murder of Senator Scott Taylor on that October night a year and a half ago in the Brown Palace Hotel.

She went on to say that Ms. Jamison's whereabouts were unknown at present, but it was known that District Attorney Thomas Hurd had had an appointment to take her statement, but that it had been postponed.

All proceedings were being carried out with the strictest security. Ms. Jamison would not be appearing in public, according to Paula, and informed sources felt that the Taylor murder case would undoubtedly be reopened.

Some of the early Denver TV newscasts picked up the story, but the national network morning shows, all broadcast from the East Coast, missed it.

When Paula Granato walked into the newsroom that morning to report to work, she got a standing ovation. Her colleagues who applauded the loudest hated her guts with the most fervor.

"My God," Nina said, holding the morning paper out, "look. I can't believe . . ."

David read the headlines and swore, got up from the breakfast table, and walked across the room to the phone.

"What?" Sarah asked. She was tired, wrung out by

worry over her mother, by lack of sleep, by the awful indecision tearing her apart.

Nina handed her the front section without a word.

Eyewitness to Scott Taylor Murder Comes Forward. The words sprang out at her, and it took a heartbeat before her brain registered their meaning. She drew in her breath and dropped the paper on the table. Who? How? Could Jake have . . . ?

David was talking on the phone, and she heard him telling someone about the headlines. "No, I haven't read the whole article, but she's named. Yes, named. Who the hell did this?"

Sarah closed her eyes, her body rigid with fear. Why? Who knew she was here?

Everyone knew now. Everyone. Nina was turning on the television to the local news, clicking channels until she stopped on one.

"Oh, my God, David," she said, "it's already on Channel Nine."

Sarah put her face in her hands and tried to think. What did this mean? Her name, plastered all over the news. And *he* was going to know it, know for sure she was in contact with the DA, not still hiding out in Aspen.

Desperately she tried to put herself in his position. What would *she* do if she were him? *Get rid of the witness.* He'd tried in Aspen. And missed. He might have believed he'd frightened her off. But now . . .

It struck her with the force of a blow. There was nowhere she could hide anymore. No corner of the earth he wouldn't find her. Until he was tried and convicted and behind bars, there was no way out.

"That was Jake on the phone," David said. "He's on his way. He wanted you to know this wasn't his doing."

She looked up. "It doesn't matter who did it. It's done."

"He's got Phillip with him, by the way. Somewhat the worse for wear."

"Phillip . . ." she murmured. Phillip and her father and mother, the whole ugly mess. She'd spoken to her mother yesterday, and Elisabeth was fine, the "breakdown" had passed. But that didn't matter anymore, because now she was trapped. The newspaper article had forced her hand.

Nina was staring at her, perhaps with the same thoughts, when the two boys came thumping down the staircase, ready for school. It was Nicky who saw the troubled looks on the three adults' faces.

He picked up his lunch bag and stopped short. "What's up, Mom? Are you okay?"

"I'm fine. Don't worry. It's not me." Nina tousled her son's hair.

"Okay." His eyes went from his mother to David to Sarah.

"Let's go," Sean said, "the school bus is going to come."

After the boys left, Nina looking at the paper, asked, "Who's Paula Granato?"

"I don't know," David replied.

"I thought maybe if she was on the police beat, you know, you might recognize her name."

"I have to go in," Sarah said abruptly. "Right away. Today. He knows now."

"Who . . . ?" Nina asked.

"The man who shot Scott. If he didn't know where I was since I left the retreat he knows now."

"Let's wait till Jake gets here," David suggested.

Suddenly she felt cold all over, and her hands shook. "I have to go in, David. You know that. Soon."

He looked at her and nodded slowly. "I guess you do."

Jake arrived twenty minutes later, disheveled, the skin of his face stretched tight across the bones, his mouth grim. Phillip followed and he looked hung over.

"Let me see it," Jake said harshly, reaching for the paper. He scanned the article quickly then threw it on the table and swore. "Who in hell did this? Who leaked it,

David? Who knew?'' David was about to say something but Jake cut him off. "You think Hurd did it? To force her to come in? If he did, I'll kill the bastard.''

"I don't see how he had time, but it's possible,'' David said.

"Who knew about her in Homicide?''

"Barry. And my partner. That's it.''

"No way would either of them do it,'' Jake stated.

Sarah sat there, her head bowed, as the anger, the questions, the force of Jake's outrage ricocheted around the room. Finally she spoke. "It doesn't matter who did it. I have to go in.''

Jake turned to her for the first time, as if she were the least important piece of this puzzle. "Yes,'' he said, inadvertently repeating David's words, "I guess you do.''

"Call the DA, Jake.''

For a long moment he held her gaze and then he looked up and nodded at David. "Check on the safe house okay? And more security. See how much manpower Disoto can spare.''

"Done,'' David said.

And then he turned to Nina and Phillip. "Can I have a minute with Sarah?'' he asked, and they silently disappeared while Jake sat down across from her at the cluttered kitchen table. He leaned back in the chair, his dark blue eyes pinioning her. The ticking of the clock patrolled the silence.

"How's the arm?'' he finally said.

"Better.''

"Good.''

She eyes him tiredly. "I hope you're satisfied.''

"I'm not satisfied, Sarah.'' He hesitated, his voice quiet. "No, satisfaction is the wrong word. Proud is more like it. You're very brave.''

She looked away, her stomach, her heart, her whole insides clenching, and a flush heated her skin. His words were like an intimate caress.

His gaze was still on her vigorously. "This has to be your decision now," he said. "I won't force you. I won't even tell you it won't be dangerous. It will be."

"I'm going in."

"You're positive? You've considered the ramifications?"

She nodded.

"We'll keep you safe. I swear to God, I won't let anything happen to you. Do you believe that?"

"I want to," she said, and she knew suddenly and irrevocably, that she still cared for him. Then, for a suspended moment there in Nina's kitchen, she was back at the Highlands Ski Area with Jake, on top of the world, and her whole body was alive with the thrill of what lay before her, and Jake was with her, laughing, admiring her, and the nightmare hadn't begun yet. Had that Jake ever existed?

"Are you going to make that call?" she asked.

"Yes, right now."

She watched as he got up, went to the phone, and dialed the number he obviously knew by heart. She heard him ask for Hurd's office, then he waited. She held her breath. There was no backing out this time, no putting it off.

"Tom?" he was saying. "It's me again. Yeah, I saw the papers. She's coming in. Today, right now, if you want her." He paused, listening. "I expect full security. The works. And no public statements. Okay, an hour. That's fine. She'll be there."

He hung up and pivoted to her. "An hour." He glanced at his watch. "Ten forty-five."

She rose from her chair shakily. "Okay," she said, "let me put some decent clothes on." She turned to leave.

His hand on her good arm stopped her. "Don't worry. I'll keep you safe, I swear it."

"Yes, I know, Jake, that's what you said before." Then she gently disengaged her arm and left him standing there.

NINETEEN

Sarah hardly remembered the drive into downtown Denver; it was all a blur. Nina was giving Phillip a ride to the airport. David was . . . yes, he was working on a safe house or something. But Sarah couldn't think about any of that. She sat next to Jake and stared out of the window, but registered nothing. The patrol car led the way. *As if one lonely policeman could protect her,* she thought.

She and Jake didn't talk; there was nothing left to say. He'd hear it all soon. Very soon.

A deputy DA, obviously known by Jake, met them in the lobby of the imposing building and whisked them upstairs.

"Is the place secure?" Jake asked.

"Jake, trust me, Hurd's done everything humanly possible," the young man said.

"I don't trust anybody."

Sarah tried to concentrate on breathing deeply, framing the words in her mind. Telling herself she was safe here. *Safe.*

Thomas Hurd was a handsome man, dark-complected, with black eyes and a neatly trimmed mustache and goatee.

"Miss Jamison," he said, rising from behind his desk, "or do you prefer Ms.?" He held his hand out.

"Either," she said, and she shook his hand. Firmly, she hoped.

"And your lawyer? Jake said you'd have representation . . ." He let the question hang in the air.

"I'm her representation," Jake said. Somewhat belligerently.

"You? But . . ."

"I know he's disbarred, Mr. Hurd," Sarah cut in. "I still want him to represent me."

"I advise you to reconsider, Miss Jamison. I think . . ."

"Let's get this over with," she said. "My mind's made up. Jake's my choice."

Hurd glared at Jake. "All right, but I want my protest noted."

"So noted, Tom," Jake said. Then, "Can we get going? I want Sarah out of here fast and set up in the safe house."

"Of course." Hurd shot Jake an angry look. "I want Miss Jamison to be comfortable. Let's not rush into anything."

"And *I* want all these people out of here," Jake said, an edge to his voice.

He was referring to Hurd's secretary, four assistant DAs, and the policeman who'd followed them.

"My staff should be here. They're the ones who'll be dealing with the case. You know that, Jake."

"Yeah, and I'd bet everything I own that one of them is responsible for the *Denver Post* headlines this morning."

"Like hell . . ." Hurd began.

But Jake held up a hand. "Let's not argue the point, okay?"

"No one's arguing. I just don't like the implications . . ."

Sarah felt impatience rise in her breast. Jake and the DA, bumping chests like two sumo wrestlers.

"They go or we do," Jake was saying.

"All right. Sharon stays"—he was referring to the court stenographer—"the rest of you leave the room. You can read the transcription later."

"Okay," Jake said when the room was cleared. "That's better."

"Christ, Jake, they're going to know what she says anyway," Hurd protested.

"Let's not make this a three-ring circus, Tom."

The DA sat on one side of a long, polished table, Sarah and Jake across from him and the stenographer with her machine at the end.

"Miss Jamison, Sarah, if I may, just tell your story as you remember it. Don't worry about details, we can go over those later. And I may ask some questions when you're done. All right?"

"Yes."

"You're aware of your rights in this matter?"

"She signed the offer of immunity," Jake said. "I have it here." He took it from his inside pocket and handed it to Hurd.

The DA glanced at it and said to the stenographer, "Please note that on this day at"—he checked his watch—"eleven-fourteen A.M. Sarah Jamison delivered a duly signed Writ of Immunity. And now, Sarah? Jake? We're ready to begin." He switched on a tape recorder that sat in the middle of the table. "Go ahead, anytime you wish, Sarah."

She drew in a deep, quavering breath. This was it, the time she'd imagined, dreamed of with sick sweat popping out on her skin, run from, denied ferociously. This was the time to tell the truth.

She swallowed convulsively, began to talk, then had to

clear her throat. She was aware of the stenographer's fingers poised over the keys of her machine, of the tape spinning in the recorder. Waiting.

"I first saw Scott Taylor at a rally in Philadelphia that fall, September, I think. I was very impressed with him, and I went to his campaign office and volunteered to work for his campaign. I met him in person there, and I told him how much I believed in his platform. I was at several other rallies and dinners, and I spoke to him, oh, a few more times. He was always so polite, as if he really appreciated the whole crew of volunteers." Sarah sat very still, her hands clasped tightly in her lap to quiet their trembling, her voice wavering a little as she told the story, how she'd gone to Denver to work on his campaign, how he'd remembered her name that fateful night, how thrilled she was when he'd wanted to talk to her about campaign strategy. Privately.

"I know you think I was dumb or naive, but I went. Scott gave people the feeling that they could help, they could *do* something, change things for the better.

"So I went to his room, we had drinks, and the phone rang. I remember he was annoyed."

"Would you like a glass of water?" Hurd asked.

"Yes, please." She took a sip when he handed it to her, then forced herself to go on. To the part that she'd relived over and over, every day since that night. And as she spoke the scene came alive in her mind. She saw it all again, every horrible detail.

"I went into the bedroom and stood behind the door. I heard a knock and two men came in. At first I couldn't hear them, but then they argued. About politics. Scott threatened the man."

She was aware Jake and Hurd were quivering like hounds on the scent. *Who?* they wanted to know. *Who?*

"Then Scott said something sarcastic and the man said something, I don't remember—angry—and . . ." She put a hand to her forehead. "I could only see through the

opening between the wall and the door, so all I saw were
snatches. The other man, I never saw his face, his back
was always to me, he was the one who shot Scott. I heard
two pops, not very loud, and I heard Scott's body fall.
Oh, God.'' She stopped for a moment, closing her eyes,
seeing the vertical strips slide before her eyes, smelling
the wine, feeling her purse strap dig into her hand, hearing
the drumbeats of her heart.

"Take it easy, Sarah." Jake's voice.

"I'm okay," she breathed. "Then the man, the shooter,
came into the bedroom. But he didn't look behind the
door. He didn't see me, then I heard them, messing up
the living room, I guess, because everything was thrown
around when I came out. I stayed there, behind the door,
for a long time. Hours. Then I got up, and I had to walk
by Scott's body on the floor. And I left the hotel. I just
left.''

They waited for her to continue, but she was finished
with her story. Except for one thing.

"I never saw the shooter's face," she said, looking
from Jake to Hurd. "I can only tell you he was tall and
thin and had brown hair, thinning brown hair, and he
wore a tweed sport coat.''

"And the other man?" Hurd pressed gently.

"I saw his face, and I wasn't sure who he was at first,
but then I remembered, I'd seen him on television. He
gave the order to kill Scott." She stopped and clung for
a beat to the safety of her secret, then she told them. "It
was Vaughn Ridley, the director of the CIA.''

There was stunned silence, then a shocked exclamation
from Thomas Hurd, a choked curse from Jake.

"Ridley?" Hurd whispered, disbelieving.

Sarah nodded, but no one in the room seemed to notice.
It was deadly quiet, everyone trying to fit his thoughts
around the enormity of her revelation. She felt, oddly, a
surge of satisfaction. Now they knew, she thought, now
they all knew why she'd fled that room.

She looked at Jake. What was he thinking? Her stomach clenched.

He finally blew out a breath. "Ridley. Jesus. Vaughn Ridley. No wonder . . ."

"You're certain of this, Miss Jamison?"

"Yes, I'm certain. I've seen him since, on television, his picture in newspapers and magazines. I'll never forget his face, not in my lifetime. It was him."

"Good God," Hurd said, then turned to Jake. "You told me I could prosecute him, you told me he wasn't protected. Jake, for chrissakes, the CIA director?" Then Hurd caught himself. "You didn't know either. You didn't know until this very moment, did you? She didn't tell you either?"

Sarah suddenly rose from her chair. "Excuse me," she said, "I don't feel very well. Could I . . . ? Is there a . . . ?"

"Sharon, show her the ladies' room," Hurd said quickly.

Sarah was aware of a cold sweat breaking out on her body, of her stomach rebelling, of a terrible weakness. Unsteadily she followed the stenographer, out of the room, down the hall, the policeman asking, "What's going on? Where . . . ?" Following her. The entire staff standing around, buzzing, murmuring, staring. But she didn't care, she only wanted to get to a private place.

Then they were in the ladies' room, and thank God no one else was there.

"Are you . . . ? Can I . . . ?" the stenographer stuttered.

"Please, leave me alone."

She vomited into a toilet, her insides heaving, relieving herself of the burden she'd carried for so long. She vomited from fear, too, then she flushed it away and rinsed her mouth at the sink and splashed cold water on her face.

In the mirror her reflection appeared cadaverous, greenish white, every imperfection in her skin standing out. She imagined, looking at herself, that her bones would actu-

ally appear beneath the ugly film that was her skin. And
she imagined, too, that the drops of water were tears. For
Scott Taylor? For herself?

Eventually she had to go back out and face the world.
She'd done it. It was over—for now. David would take
her to the safe house. Maybe she'd be able to sleep.

Jake was waiting outside the door for her. Pacing im-
patiently, that energy of his sparking from him.

"Are you okay?" he asked, worried. So very worried.

She smiled wanly. "I've been better."

He took her hand then, grasped it gently, and she could
feel the warmth of his fingers, the strength, the certainty.
He stroked the back of her hand, his head bowed. Then
he looked up, right at her, and he said, "I understand
now."

And, despite everything, his understanding mattered.

Vaughn Ridley was at a power lunch in downtown Washington when his pager went off, and he excused himself
graciously. "Sorry, I'm going to have to return this one.
No, no, finish your lunches, everyone. Put it on my account, will you? We'll complete this talk tomorrow, all
right, gentlemen?"

He went back to Langley to make the call on a secure
line; he'd recognized the number on his pager in a flash
of panic and knew he needed privacy.

Brushing past his secretary as he told her, "Hold my
calls, please, Linda. And put off my three o'clock for as
long as you can," he entered his inner sanctum, closing
the heavy door behind him.

Things were coming to a head out in Denver. And this
call in the middle of the day was not good, not good at
all. He sat down in his chair and wiped the beads of sweat
off his upper lip with the back of a finger, then picked
up the phone and punched in the number.

"She made her statement this morning," came the familiar voice. "I just left a meeting with Savelle, and she

named names, all right, yours, to be precise. Not mine. She didn't see my face.''

''Christ.''

''All hell's breaking loose. The DA is going to convene the grand jury, and the press will get your name. Any minute.''

Ridley collapsed back in his chair as if he'd been pole-axed. He could feel the blood drain from his face. His mind whirled feverishly, desperately.

''You there?''

''Yes, I'm here,'' he said hoarsely.

''Got any ideas?''

''Kill her. And don't miss this time. Kill her and get rid of the body. Everyone will think she ran again.''

''She'll be guarded like the crown jewels.''

''You can do it. You have to. If she isn't around to testify there's no case.''

''They'll still try to get at you.''

''Maybe not. Regardless, I can handle that. What I can't handle is a goddamn eyewitness. And don't think for a minute I'm going to take this fall alone, you understand?''

''You'd do that, wouldn't you?''

''You better believe it.''

''Jesus Christ. All right, I'll see what I can do.''

''I have confidence in you,'' Ridley said bitterly. ''You better come through this time. Or we're both dead men.''

''It may take me a while.''

''Not too long.''

''I'll do my best.''

''Of course you will.'' He hung up and drew in a deep breath and saw his life flash before his eyes. All the choices and decisions, all the maneuvering and prevaricating. To get here, in this chair, behind this desk. To wield unheard-of power.

And it was all dependent on one woman's testimony. She was, in a word, expendable.

• • •

"Honey, it's for you," Madeline Disoto said to her husband.

"Who is it?"

She shrugged. "Some woman."

Some woman. Barry got up from his comfortable armchair in front of the television set and took the cordless phone from her.

"Hello?"

"Barry, it's me. Barry, my God, I'm sorry to call you at home, but—"

"You know, I'm not at all sure I'm interested in your product at this time."

"Can you talk?" Heather's voice was panicky.

"Well, I may be in the future." Barry rolled his eyes at Madeline as if the call were from a pesky telemarketer and walked into his study, closing the door.

"Barry? Is she there, can you talk now?"

"Okay, Heather, calm down. I'm in the den." She'd never called him at home before. So she'd heard. Hell, the whole damn world knew.

"I can't stand it, Barry. They've been calling me all evening. CNN, ABC, CBS, *Dateline, 60 Minutes.* You can't believe it. It's a feeding frenzy." Her voice was shrill with hysteria.

"What did you tell them?"

"Nothing. No comment. I hung up on everyone."

"Don't answer the phone. Leave it on your machine."

"I will. I did. But it'll be in the papers tomorrow. My name, Scott's name, Sarah Jamison, Jake. The whole awful, sordid mess. Only worse this time. Barry, they *know* there was a woman with him."

"In her statement she said she only worked for his campaign."

"And you believe that? Knowing Scott? No one else will believe it either, and you know that. A pretty young woman alone in his hotel room? What should I do?"

"I told you this was going to come up, but it's just gossip and innuendo so far. The statement hasn't been made public. It's all leaks. There's nothing concrete."

"*Yet.*"

"Just hang in there. You'll weather it. Why don't you leave town for a while? Take a vacation."

"I will not leave my home because of a two-bit tart!"

"Now, Heather, it'd only be temporary. Look, there'll be a grand jury, but that's a secret proceeding. The trial, if there ever is a trial, will be months away. A lot can happen between now and then."

"What do you mean? What could happen?"

"How many times have I told you horror stories of witnesses, key witnesses, disappearing before the trial comes up?"

"What do you mean, Barry?"

"She might disappear again. She hid out for eighteen months, and it sure as hell wasn't her idea to come in. She could easily run. She isn't under arrest, so we can't hold her. And then everyone will figure she was just a slut out for some free publicity, a liar cashing in on Scott's notoriety. No one will believe her."

"I can't stand it. I . . ." Her voice broke in a sob.

"It'll be all right, believe me." His heart clenched at the thought of what she was going through. "Look, change your phone number. Call the phone company tomorrow. An unlisted number."

"Barry?"

"Yes. I'm here."

"You'll help me through this? You'll be there for me?"

"You know I will. It'll work out. Be strong. It'll pass, and everything will be back to normal."

"Promise?"

"I promise."

"I'll let you go. I know you have to go, Barry. She's

probably wondering . . .'' Heather never said Madeline's name.

"Yes, I have to go."

"I'm sorry I called. I couldn't help it."

"That's all right. Everything's going to be fine."

When he hung up he sat there for a minute, head bowed. His tactics hadn't worked. Sarah had talked and maybe now it was too late to remedy the situation.

Barry walked out of the den, phone in hand.

"Who was that, honey?" Madeline asked.

"Oh, one of those damn salespeople. You can't get rid of them."

"You're much too nice, dear."

"Yes, I suppose I am."

TWENTY

A safe house was only effective if its occupants could come and go inconspicuously.

A house situated in a suburb or a city neighborhood was a poor choice. One curious neighbor could blow the whole thing, endangering the person under police protection. Many police forces therefore used hotel rooms to house witnesses, where it was expected that the faces in the halls would change daily or weekly, and strangers were the norm. The city and county of Denver had elected a variant route. They leased, in conjunction with three other Front Range counties, a rental apartment in downtown Boulder, thirty miles north of Denver, where residents came and went frequently—students from the University of Colorado, visiting parents, visiting professors, businessmen in town for short periods of time, a barrage of new faces. A place where no one, not even the building manager, was particularly interested in either the business or the identity of the residents. As long as the rent was paid on time, as long as no one disturbed the others, everyone was left alone. Certainly no one took notice of occasional new faces in apartment 3E.

Sarah was still shaky when Jake and David, along with a friendly young patrolman named Gary Pacheco, walked across the downtown Boulder mall and entered the four-story, clapboard apartment building, carrying duffle bags.

"This is my first witness protection assignment," Gary Pacheco said as he held the door to the small lobby open for Sarah. "I want to get into security, you know? It's exciting work."

Behind them, David said, "Exciting? I'm afraid you're in for a surprise, patrolman. It's a lot of sitting around and eating junk food."

Pacheco smiled. "Hey, there have to be exciting moments once in a while."

"Let's hope not," Jake said under his breath.

David produced a key ring and shook it out, selected a particular key, and handed the whole ring to Pacheco. "Go on up to the third floor, very end of the hall, and open the door."

"I should secure it, right?" the patrolman asked.

David shot him a glance.

"Right," Pacheco said, "gotcha."

Sarah followed the young cop with her eyes as he disappeared up the stairs. She knew she should feel safe surrounded by armed policemen. But her palms were slippery on her purse strap, and her heart was beating a furious tattoo against her ribs, as if she'd just finished a workout instead of sitting in a car for the last forty-five minutes.

Pacheco appeared at the top of the first flight of stairs and nodded. She was aware of Jake behind her, his hand at the small of her back as they began the climb. Jake, her protector, her nemesis. She had no real sense of how she felt about him anymore. The constant close proximity unnerved her, yet she was glad he was there. He had a certain presence, a confidence to him that was contagious.

David led the way into 3E, switching on all the lights, doing his own security check while Jake showed her into the larger of two bedrooms, placing her bag on a bench at the foot of the queen-size bed.

"Let's see," he said while she stood in the doorway, "looks like you have a bathroom in here, big closet. Window. Not bad. But you have to keep these blinds closed."

She said nothing, only drew in a quavering breath and glanced around the room. Oak dresser, matching bedside tables, neutral carpeting, sea-green lamps, a green-and-brown print bedspread, blinds. Functional. She wondered idly how many other witnesses had occupied this space. Had they all been as frightened as she was, their breathing irregular, sweat beading their upper lip?

"How long?" she finally said.

Jake turned to her. "How long will you be here? I don't know. We'll see what the grand jury does. If there's an indictment, and I'm certain there will be, then our CIA man is as good as nailed."

"We both know that's not true. It'll be months, years." She looked around the room. "I can't stay here."

"We'll see to it you're placed somewhere, somewhere safe, with a false ID until the trial is over."

"I can't do that, Jake. That's like being dead. I have a life. I *had* a life. I don't want to give it up."

"We're only talking temporarily."

"Bull."

"No, I mean that."

"You aren't in charge. The DA, the police, they'll try to run my life. You know it. It's out of your hands."

"You might be surprised," he said. "I'm not that easy to walk over."

She regarded him for a moment. "No, maybe you aren't."

He left her to get settled then, quietly closing the bedroom door behind him. She washed her face as best she could with one hand, then slipped the sling off and lay down on top of the patterned spread, cradling her bad arm across her chest, willing her muscles to relax.

She could hear the men talking on the other side of the door. Someone was going to the Safeway to stock the refrigerator, someone else—must have been David— phoned in to police headquarters and said she was now settled at the apartment.

She was exhausted, but her mind was still spinning feverishly. Today had been an ordeal. Saying the words that had been bottled up inside her for so long. Reliving that night. And Jake, sitting so still, silent, listening, his eyes on her vigorously, his dark brows drawn.

What exactly had gone through his mind when she'd revealed the identity of Vaughn Ridley? He'd waited so long for that moment. And lost so much in the interim.

She lay there and tried to re-create the scene in her mind. He'd looked angry. Yes, angry. At her? At Ridley? And he'd said something: "No wonder."

No wonder what?

She must have dozed off then, because a tentative tap on her door startled her, and she sat up and oriented herself. The apartment. The safe house. Boulder, with all the students and tourists milling around the downtown mall. A typical college town, but cosmopolitan, charming, even chic. And she was stuck in here. Couldn't even go out for a coffee or to stroll the mall with its pretty trees and planters ready to burst to life in the April sun.

Another tap. "Sarah? Are you awake?" *His* voice.

"Yes." She cleared her throat. "Yes."

"We got some Chinese take-out. Would you like to join us?"

"Ah, sure, give me a minute."

She didn't feel any less shaky when she joined the three men around a table in the alcove next to the kitchen. Her appetite was gone. What she really craved was sleep. That, and a way out of this whole awful ordeal.

David was sitting on her right, Officer Pacheco next to

her, Jake across from her. There was nothing wrong with *their* appetites.

Mouth half full of kung pao chicken, David said, "I'll be leaving at eleven, Sarah, and Gary here goes off duty at midnight, but not until his replacement arrives and completes his own security check. Jake's going to sack out on the couch. You'll see several faces coming in and out on eight-hour shifts, but you're not to worry. These men are pros and you'll be very safe here. If you want any books or anything at all, you just let Jake or me know and we'll be happy to pick up whatever you need."

"Thank you," she said, and she pushed some fried rice around her plate, her mind only half there. She couldn't think about books. How could she concentrate on anything with Ridley still a free man? And the shooter—where was he? The resources at Ridley's fingertips frightened her more than anything. *Could* these three men really protect her from the reach of the director of the CIA?

She looked up and found Jake studying her, his expression questioning. Could he read her mind? Did he know how terrified she was?

The men watched the late news while she showered and got ready for bed. She told herself over and over that she was okay here. This was, after all, a safe house. But the fear lingered inside her. It persisted with a will of its own, wholly separate from hers.

She combed out her hair and put on pajamas. There was a television set in her room, but she wasn't able to concentrate on the news, especially when the report came on about her, how she'd gone into the DA's office to give a statement. Someone, obviously, had leaked an awful lot of information, and she quaked inside and pressed the button on the remote control until the weak battery finally worked, and the screen went blank.

David left at eleven, peeking in to say good night and to let her know he'd be back in the morning. Officer Pacheco waved reassuringly from across the living room as

David stood in her doorway. And Jake was there, too, sitting in a chair, knees splayed, his fingers steepled on his lap. He was engaged in his favorite pastime—watching her.

She said good night to David and asked him to thank Nina for her hospitality. And then she started to close the door but paused. "Jake?" she said. "Could I talk to you for a minute?"

He came into her room, and she sat on the bed against the pillows, legs crossed, supporting her left elbow.

"I've been thinking," she began.

He nodded.

"I'm worried. It's as if everyone is forgetting that other man is out there, the one who pulled the trigger."

"No one is forgetting."

"But how will you find him?"

Jake smiled, a confident, reassuring smile that made him seem young and cocky and sexy. "Once the grand jury hands down the indictment on Ridley, and he's charged and brought in, he'll try to deal. My gut feeling and my experience say he'll give up the triggerman to save his own neck. Oh, he'll get life, but he'll deal out of the death penalty. Then we'll have both men, and you'll be out of danger. Like I said before, this whole thing may never go to trial."

"These are all possibilities, though. You don't know for sure."

"I know how things work. I know the legal system."

"You're just trying to make me feel better."

He met her statement with directness. "Yes, I am. And I know you're frightened."

She tried to smile, but it was too hard, too false. What she wouldn't give for the kind of confidence he had, she was thinking, when he reached out and covered her hands with one of his.

"Sarah," he said in a quiet voice, "I keep a gun in the glove compartment of my car."

She looked startled.

"Hey, a couple years ago some very bad men I was prosecuting made some very bad threats, and I bought the gun. The point is, if you'd feel better, and this can be our secret, I could sneak it in to you. David would have fits, but if—"

"God, no," she cut in. "I couldn't."

"You're sure?"

"Absolutely."

"You're one brave lady," he said.

She heard his words, but she was held hostage by the sensation of his hand on hers. He'd kept it there too long, and if it went on much longer she wouldn't be able to tell herself it was only a friendly gesture. The tension was mounting like a bill that had to be paid. She drew her hands away very deliberately.

"I'm a complete coward," she said to cover the awkwardness.

"You know the old saying," he said, "the person who's most afraid but does his duty anyway shows real bravery."

"It's the things that could happen," she whispered. "The not knowing. Where he is, what he'll do. If he knows where I am."

"He doesn't. He can't."

She looked up and met the intensity of his gaze then quickly averted her gaze.

"Well," he said, "you probably want to get some rest."

"Sure, yes, I guess I need it."

"I'll be right outside the door."

"Okay. And . . . thanks, really, for being there today with me."

His lip twitched in a half smile. "Hey, just doing the job I've been trying to do for eighteen months."

She wondered about that. Was it merely the job? Or had it been more?

"Sleep tight," he said, and he left her there, alone with her thoughts and the steady beat of her heart.

Over the next few days, time passed bizarrely for Sarah. The minutes seemed to drag while hours flew by. The police guards, all handpicked by David or Barry Disoto, came and left on their eight-hour shifts, greeting her, doing their security checks, eating, watching TV, leafing through magazines. Everything was terribly routine at the small Boulder apartment. Yet to Sarah the world seemed askew, tipped off its axis by unseen forces. She wondered in a singular desperation why it was that no one but her seemed to notice.

David was in and out, often looking harried, his caseload and the administration of the safe house taking their toll on him.

Jake was around a lot, too, but never alone. One or two policemen were always present. They spoke of the mundane: It had snowed four feet in the foothills, and Loveland Ski Area was hoping to stay open till Memorial Day. Sports was a favorite topic among the men. Newspaper sport sections were scattered everywhere. She often tidied up; the cops seemed oblivious to the mess.

There was more in the news than sports. *She* was a favorite topic. At first she had shied away from the stories in the tabloids. After a time she almost got used to the publicity—almost—and once she even laughed at a front-page story in a well-known paper that portrayed her as a Joan of Arc, saving the world from the old-boy network in Washington. Mostly she was a mystery woman. She knew that eventually the press would do its research, and she'd be disemboweled on the front page of every paper in the country.

She braced herself for that day.

Jake was also a hot item with the press. He was hailed over and over as a turn-of-the-millennium hero, a tenacious modern-day crusader who had given up everything in search of the truth.

Young Officer Pacheco teased him mercilessly. "The hero has arrived. Hey, I hear that magazine, what's it called—*People*?—wants to do a cover story on you. Is that true?"

Jake only shrugged.

"And, man, someone down at headquarters said there was a bunch of girls waiting in front of your apartment wanting autographs. Did one of them really faint?"

That made Jake grimace, but he didn't deny it either, and Sarah gave him a surreptitious glance from the kitchen. Jake with his five o'clock shadow and the dark, waving hair that curled a little behind his ears. The good shoulders and the blue of his eyes. The shy but knowledgeable smile that lifted a corner of his mouth.

Oh, yes, the ladies must love their crusader.

Jake kept her up to date on the legal maneuvering. "The grand jury is being convened," he said one morning.

"When?"

"A few days. Next week, I think. Hurd's pushing for it, but the jurors have to be gathered, so it takes some time."

"But Ridley knows about my statement."

"Oh, yeah, he knows. And he's hiring lawyers and denying everything," Jake said, "but it won't do any good."

He was right. The turmoil had already begun, high-up government functionaries officially denying everything, unofficially turning tail and distancing themselves from the director, washing their hands of the whole sordid mess.

The media went wild, bandying about speculations on nightly talk shows featuring top-notch criminal defense lawyers versus ex–government prosecuting attorneys.

On the fourth day after she'd made her formal statement and moved to the safe house, the first story that really delved into her life broke in the *Philadelphia Inquirer*. By that evening all the papers and TV stations had it off the wire services, and the next morning she learned that her life was not her own anymore—they had it all. There were interviews with former teachers and professors and old school friends. Cameras hounded her family, shooting long-range videos of her father getting into his Mercedes in front of the family home. Even her mother was caught peeking out a window. Elisabeth's sculpture was featured on a midmorning Martha Stewart–type show and Phillip, who was back at Princeton, was followed everywhere, though, to his credit, he said nothing to any of the reporters and kept his cool. The next evening, footage of her father aired, a video of him entering his bank headquarters and shaking a fist at the cameraman.

Sarah watched, horrified, and put her face in her hands. "Oh, God," she said.

Gary Pacheco was on duty, and he rose from the couch and patted her on the back. "Hey, it's all right. Everyone knows the press can be a bunch of assholes."

"My poor mother," Sarah breathed. "My father and Phillip, they can take it, but my mother . . ."

Jake was there by seven that night. He had seen the report on her father, and he was mad.

They talked quietly in the kitchen, Jake leaning against a counter, arms folded, Sarah in the same stance across from him. "I'm worried about my mother," she admitted.

"The news coverage."

"Yes. She's awfully frail. I can't begin to imagine what this is doing to her. If I could talk to her . . ."

"You know you can't, Sarah. It's too dangerous."

"What about a pay phone? I could . . ."

"I don't want you out in public. No." He shook his head vehemently. "That's exactly how I tracked down Phillip. He used a pay phone. It's too risky. Someone may have a tap on your parents' phone. There are ways of checking, of course, but nothing is ever foolproof. Too dangerous.''

She shut her eyes for a moment then sighed. He was right.

"In a while,'' he said. "I'm sure we can arrange something in a little while. But—''

"How did I get here?'' she asked, cutting him off. *"I'm* in jail. It's like *I'm* the guilty one.''

He rubbed a hand over his face. "I know.''

"Is that all you can say?''

He pursed his lips and looked at her from under his brows. "Yes.''

She turned away from him, feeling the heat of anger rising to her face, but it was better than fear, so she nursed it, fed the flames.

"Maybe you should have kept running,'' he said to her back.

"Maybe I should have,'' she agreed.

The following morning he arrived before she was even out of bed. He knocked softly on her door and then opened it a crack.

"You decent?''

"Jake?'' she said, and she sat up, sleepy-eyed. "What time is it?''

"Little after seven.''

"Oh . . .''

"Look,'' he said, and he came in. "I had an idea last night when I finally got home.''

"I didn't know you'd left.''

"For a few hours. David was here. Anyway, I brought you something.'' He reached in his jacket pocket and pulled out a cell phone. "I want you to keep this. I registered it in my name, and I'm sure it'll be safe to use to phone your folks. Even if the call could be traced, it will lead to me.''

"You're sure? You don't need it back?''

He shook his head. "I splurged, it's a spare. I even put

my other cell phone number into your autodial, just in case. All you have to do is hit this button and you'll get right to me.''

"Well . . . thanks. I hope I don't have to use it, though.''

"Call your folks,'' he said, and he left.

She got her mother on the line and talked for an indecently long time, reassuring her that everything was fine.

"You're certain you're safe?'' her mother asked.

"Absolutely.''

"And all this will end soon?''

"Very soon.''

"Will you come home then, darling?''

"Let's see how long this takes, Mother,'' she said evasively.

Elisabeth put Roger on then. "Well, well,'' he blustered, "we're keeping our chins up here. But this is a devil of a mess, Sarah.''

"I know,'' she said.

"How is your arm?''

"Much better now.''

"Um, good, good. Phillip said you looked well, considering.''

"I'm okay, really.''

"And this grand jury business? When will that take place?''

"Very soon now.''

"Good, good. But I don't like the idea of you having to hide out this way. Are the people you're with competent?''

"Oh, yes.''

"Is that man, that Savelle, still around?''

"Yes.''

"Mm. He's too pushy and underhanded. Don't like him.''

"He's all right.''

"That's your opinion."

She said nothing.

"Do you need anything? I could—"

"I'm all set. Well, I better get going. Tell Mother I love her, and Phillip."

"Of course. And your mother sends her love."

"Well, 'bye for now."

"You'll stay in touch? We Jamisons stick together, you know."

"Sure," she said, but when she was off the phone, she realized that he had not sent *his* love. Why couldn't he at least say the words? *Why?* She knew the answer, though. Roger Jamison, of the we-stick-together-Jamisons, was incapable of acknowledging anything remotely resembling love. It struck her then that she'd sent her love to her mother and to Phillip but not to him. Had she been punishing him? And had he in turn punished her? Sick, sick.

Jake asked her over a sandwich at lunch how her call went.

"Oh, fine."

"Your folks are okay? With the media and all that?"

"They seem to be weathering it."

"Glad to hear it."

Then she asked the question that had always lain between them: "How is your sister doing?"

He hesitated for a moment, apparently caught off guard by her question, and she could see the thoughts flitting across his face. He was wondering why the homewrecker, the slut who'd slept with Scott, would care about the man's wife.

"Heather's not thrilled with the situation," he said carefully.

She wanted to tell him then. She wanted to throw it in his face—"I didn't sleep with Scott Taylor"—but he wouldn't believe her. Why should he?

It was Gary Pacheco who handed her the morning edition of the *Denver Post* the next day.

The headline shouted a question: *Savelle to Be Reinstated to Colorado Bar?*

She stood in the living room and scanned the article, her pulse quickening. The female juror who had claimed Jake had sex with her during a case had come forward yesterday, offering to make a deal with DA Thomas Hurd in exchange for immunity from prosecution for perjury.

"Another rat deserting a sinking ship," Gary said when she looked up.

"I don't understand."

"Way I see it," the young officer said, "this chick got paid to tell a lie, and she's afraid she's going to go down now that the sh—stuff is hitting the fan."

"Will Jake really get reinstated to the bar?" she asked.

"Hey, I don't know about that stuff, but the guys at headquarters are talking. They think so."

What if Jake were a lawyer again? She considered the ramifications. He'd be the man she'd thought he was when she first met him. He'd been good at his job. A great lawyer, Nina had told her. A fearless prosecutor. He'd lost so much, and she could restore it to him. She *had* restored it.

No, *he'd* forced her to do it.

She found herself anticipating his arrival. She wanted to see the new Jake Savelle, the successful young chief deputy DA of Denver. Would he be different? Would he care as much about her now that he was going to get his life back?

She waited and waited for him. But the hours ticked by and Jake did not appear.

At three, a key turned in the lock, and her heart gave an involuntary leap. It was David. She cleared the disappointment from her expression and greeted him warmly.

"Heard the news?" he asked.

"News?"

"About Jake. About that lying woman juror finally coming clean."

"Oh, that, yes," she said, shrugging.

At four Pacheco went off duty and another cop, a quiet, tense man who made Sarah even more nervous, took over.

At five Jake was still not there.

Had he abandoned her? Gotten his job back and no longer needed her?

She tried to read, she tried to watch television, she did the pile of dishes left by the men. Tomorrow she'd be driven on the Boulder Turnpike to a courtroom in Denver; she'd sit in a witness box in front of twelve men and women and tell her story. And Jake had abandoned her.

At six-thirty he finally arrived. He was not alone. On his heels, tongue lolling out, was a dog, a big golden retriever.

"Well," David said, "if it isn't Peaches and Jake. At last."

The dog greeted everyone, tail banging into legs, chairs, knocking over a foam coffee cup on an end table.

"Sorry," Jake said, tossing his jacket haphazardly on the back of a chair. "Shayne caught me and made me dog-sit this afternoon." He got a sponge from the kitchen and cleaned up the mess, Peaches still by his side.

"So," David said, "how's it feel to be the new hero of the day? Vindicated at last."

Sarah sat next to David on the couch and patted her leg. Peaches came over, lay down, and rolled over, ready for a nice tummy rub. But it was Jake who held Sarah's attention. She had expected something—some sort of jubilant response from him, but he frowned and seemed, if anything, angry.

"Ah, hell," he said, tossing the sponge into the sink, "they're a bunch of hypocrites."

David looked skeptical. "Come on," he said, "you've got to be feeling pretty damn good."

Jake dropped into the easy chair, his legs stuck out, knees parted, and he snorted in derision. "It wasn't bad enough that a gaggle of reporters hounded me all day, but even my ex had to stick her nose back into my business."

"What'd Shayne do now?"

"Are you kidding? She told me to march into the DA's office and demand my old job back. At twice the salary."

"So?"

"I don't want the goddamn job back."

"You're telling me," David said, "that if the Colorado Bar Association offers you your license back, you're going to tell them to stick it where the sun don't shine?"

Jake shook his head. "Hey, I'm not that stupid. I said I didn't want the DA's position. Of course I'll take my license back, but I won't be a bureaucrat again. No way."

Sarah finally spoke. "What will you do, then?"

Jake looked at her. "Maybe I'll teach. Get a job right here in Boulder at CU and teach law. Hell, I'm a celebrity," he said with scorn. "They'll be happy to hire me on as a full professor."

"Teach," David said.

"Sure. Why not? Turn out some lawyers with integrity for a change."

"Geez, Jake," David said, "I'd sure hate to ever piss you off."

Sarah idly rubbed the dog's stomach and listened quietly to the banter. A curious relief filled her. He was the same; he hadn't abandoned her. And, she supposed, he'd been the same before he was disbarred. Jake didn't change. He had a core of strength that didn't shift with the wind.

A teacher. Yes, Jake could be a teacher. With his intensity and his certainty, he'd be a popular professor.

She watched him and she realized the pain he must

have suffered, the dishonor of being disbarred. The doubt cast on him. It must have been lethal.

She found herself staring at his face, his mouth, and she recalled with shocking clarity the feel of his lips on hers, the soft warmth of his touch before he'd pulled away.

She looked down at Peaches, who was drifting off, and she wondered what Jake's ex-wife had thought when she'd heard the news today. Had Shayne been glad? Had she made up some excuse to drop the dog off with Jake, because she was suddenly having second thoughts about their divorce?

A tidal wave of images struck Sarah's mind. Shayne— whom she imagined to be a tall, beautiful woman—congratulating him. Perhaps they'd hugged. Kissed. Perhaps it had gone even further.

Sarah bit her lip and tried to put away the images. Unconsciously, she patted the dog, unable to stop thinking about Jake and his ex. She looked up and caught his gaze on her. There was something in his expression, *something,* and for a moment she thought it was regret. But regret for what? That his marriage had been ruined over his disbarment? Or did it have something to do with her?

The pathetic reality was that everything he did or said, every glance in her direction mattered. Too damn much.

TWENTY-ONE

Jake sat next to her in the backseat of the unmarked van sent to transport them to the grand jury hearing. The van had been provided by the Denver police department, the driver also, and so were the unmarked cars ahead and behind. The patrolman who drove the van had a sidearm and a shotgun that he propped carefully against the seat next to him. Tom Hurd was taking no chances.

That was good, Jake thought.

It was a blustery, cold morning, a Rocky Mountain spring storm tearing down out of the mountain passes. Snowing in Boulder, turning to slanting rain as they approached Denver.

"It shouldn't take more than one day," Jake said. "It's not as if there are multiple witnesses and a lot of complicated testimony."

"No," she said, glancing down at her hands clenched in her lap, "there's only me."

She looked lovely, her curls pulled back with a clip, her face carefully composed. She wore a conservative navy-blue suit, a white blouse, even pearls. And matching heels. A Main Line lady from an old, established family.

He knew she was nervous, but she concealed it well. He'd prepared her, hell, *tried* to prepare her in every way he could think of. The questions they'd ask. The prying, embarrassing, insinuating questions.

He'd tried to tread carefully in that area, not wanting to say bluntly, "Look, Sarah, they'll suspect you slept with Scott, and they're going to ask about that." But he knew that's what would happen. And there was always a nasty old biddy in the jury who wanted to know—demanded—every detail.

"You okay?" he asked again.

"I'll get through it."

"I know that. I'd just like you to be as comfortable as possible . . ."

"Comfortable?"

"I know, I know. Damn."

"You're more nervous than I am."

"Maybe."

"Why?"

"I don't know. Maybe because everything's coming to a head."

"You got what you wanted, Jake. You're even going to get reinstated to the bar. Why should you be nervous?"

He shook his head. But he knew. Her statement to the DA had been easy. This testimony would be brutal.

The van dropped them off behind the downtown building, and they were met by more armed policemen who surrounded Sarah, swallowed her, really, and swept her upstairs to the courtroom.

The jury was already seated, the twelve men and women who would be presented with the bill of indictment. In this case, the bill would state that Vaughn Ridley and an unidentified accomplice had murdered Scott Taylor on the October night in question, nineteen months ago, in his suite in the Brown Palace Hotel.

There was only one piece of evidence for them to consider—the eyewitness account of Sarah Jamison—and if the jury was satisfied that the evidence warranted a trial, that is, if they believed Sarah's testimony, they would find the bill to be a true bill of indictment, and the DA's office would begin preparing its case against Vaughn Ridley and his accomplice.

Tom Hurd was running the show; three of his deputy DAs and an assistant DA were there also, and the court stenographer. No judge, no bailiff, no defense team. The grand jury was an instrument wielded by the prosecution alone. There would be no sidebars, no objections in this courtroom. Jake could sit in on the proceedings, but he couldn't open his mouth.

Hurd greeted Sarah and gave her a rundown of the process, but she already knew all that.

"We'll make this as quick and painless as we can for everyone involved," he said.

"I'm ready." Sarah smiled politely.

Jake had to sit behind the bar. Before he left Sarah, he said quietly, "Hang in there," and he gave her hand a squeeze. But he wasn't sure she'd heard him; she'd gone someplace inside herself where he couldn't follow.

Hurd escorted her to the witness box, and she was sworn in by the foreman of the jury, a hard-faced middle-aged woman, who read the familiar words from a sheet of paper. No clerk of the court at this proceeding.

Tom Hurd stood then, buttoned his gray suit coat in an elaborately long procedure, cleared his throat, and smiled at Sarah.

"Miss Jamison, I'm going to cover some very basic items first, to acquaint the jury with you, all right?"

"Yes."

He asked her a lot of questions, name, age, birthplace, education. Jake knew Hurd was only warming up, and he'd warned Sarah not to be lulled by the rote queries.

She replied clearly, her face pale, her voice a little husky. A voice that promised so much.

"Now, Miss Jamison, tell us in your own words how you met Senator Scott Taylor."

Sarah repeated the story she'd given in her statement, that she'd met him at a rally in Philadelphia and volunteered to work for his campaign.

One of Hurd's deputies took over the questioning then. Jake knew the man well; Jake had been the man's boss, for God's sake. Daniel Worthingham.

"Now, Miss Jamison, I'd like to know exactly how many times you saw Senator Taylor in Philadelphia and what those occasions were."

Sarah hesitated. "I'm not sure I can remember all of them."

"Please try."

"Well, there was the first time at the Union League."

"The Union League?"

"Yes, sir. It's a very old, prestigious men's club on Broad Street."

"I see. Go on, please."

"Scott . . . The senator . . . was giving a speech about reforming campaign expenditures. I met him afterward, when I considered becoming a volunteer. He was there in the campaign office in his shirtsleeves, drinking coffee with the volunteers. Very friendly, not the least bit pretentious."

"Go on please."

"Well, let's see, I saw him at a dinner at the Wyndham Franklin Plaza Hotel, because I was helping to pass out platform papers. There was always a sort of get-together after those things, for all the volunteers, and he'd come by to thank everyone."

"You admired Senator Taylor?"

"Very much. He would have done so much for our country."

"And you saw him again?"

"I was at the rally in Harrisburg. I took down names for donations there. And in, let's see, Trenton, New Jersey."

"And in all these places you spoke to him."

"Only a few words, you know, like 'Nice day' or 'I liked your speech today.' "

"Did he know who you were?"

"Yes, he had an incredible memory for names and faces."

"So, he knew your name?"

"Yes, he did."

"Out of all the hundreds of volunteers in his organization, he knew your name?"

"Yes, I told you, he had an incredible memory."

"Do you feel that he singled you out for attention, Miss Jamison?"

"No, he was friendly to everyone."

Jake saw where Daniel was leading the jury. He would have done the same himself.

"And then you went all the way to Denver to work on his campaign?"

"Yes, I wanted to be part of it."

"Were you a *paid* volunteer, Miss Jamison?"

"No, only the full-time pros were paid."

"Yet you traveled all over and worked on the campaign. What did you live on?"

Jake saw Sarah flush a little. "I have a small trust fund from my grandfather."

"I see." Daniel Worthingham frowned. "You didn't have to work, then."

"It was a small trust fund, a very modest amount. I had also saved some money from a resort job in the Pocono Mountains."

"And you gave up everything, your life, your work, to chase after Senator Taylor."

This is when Jake would have shot to his feet yelling,

"Objection," but he couldn't do that here. He clamped his mouth shut.

"I did not chase after Senator Taylor," Sarah said calmly. "I volunteered to work for his campaign. I didn't see him very often, certainly no more than any other volunteer did."

Her reply was perfect, unassuming, unflustered, not the least bit belligerent. Jake was very satisfied with her performance. He could imagine how difficult this was for her, her life exposed to these people, scrutinized, analyzed, judged. And he knew the worst was yet to come.

Even though Sarah was Hurd's star witness, he had to press her on some of the difficult points, or the jurors would not believe her story.

It occurred to Jake that he wasn't looking forward to Sarah's testimony about what went on in that hotel room. He'd been trying to ignore the reality of it for weeks, but it would come out today. And Sarah would have to answer, because she couldn't plead the Fifth Amendment in front of a grand jury. She had to answer the questions, she had to tell them what she and Scott Taylor had been doing alone in that hotel room. His mind shied from the idea.

Tom Hurd took up the questioning again. "Now, Miss Jamison, let's go to Denver. How long were you here before Senator Taylor was murdered?"

"Let's see. A week, ten days, something like that. We all stayed in the downtown Oxford Hotel except for the senator. He went home sometimes, but he had the . . . the suite at the Brown Palace as well."

"And did you ever meet Mrs. Taylor, his wife?"

"No, I never did."

"Where was she when all this campaigning was going on?"

"She didn't make the trip back East. I believe she was sick."

"And she wasn't at the rally in Denver that night?"

"I never saw her. She might have been there and left early. I don't know."

"All right." Hurd paced, hands clasped behind his back, head down. "Now, Miss Jamison, let's get to the night in question. It was a dinner at the ChopHouse, in lower downtown. LoDo."

"Yes."

"What, exactly, was your job that night?"

"It was a fund-raiser. I sat at the door with another volunteer and took down names and addresses, and we collected checks from the people who gave donations."

"This was within the normal parameters of your duties?"

"Yes, I'd done it before."

"Senator Taylor gave a speech and then he had to work the crowd, shaking hands and so forth?"

"Yes."

"And then, when it was over . . . ? Please tell us what happened then, Miss Jamison."

Sarah shifted in her seat, and Jake knew what was coming.

"There was the usual gathering afterward, to talk over how the evening had gone, to sort of analyze things. It was late and we were all tired, but Scott—Senator Taylor—was still really pumped up from his reception. He was very pleased, more than pleased. He was there in his shirtsleeves by then, as usual, pouring champagne for all of us. He could be very . . . exciting. That night"—Sarah paused and looked down then raised her head—"that night, he was particularly happy. He was convinced he had Colorado tied up for the election."

"Go on."

"Well, he liked to ask each one of us who'd been in contact with the guests, he liked to get our reactions to them. How they'd responded to his speech, for instance. He was asking me about that, what I thought, and I was really flattered. I hadn't talked to him for weeks, since we'd left Philadelphia, but he remembered my name, he knew who I was."

"He singled you out, Miss Jamison."

Sarah hesitated. "Yes, perhaps he did that night. He was a very charming man, very charismatic. And I believed so strongly in him, in what he could do for America."

"From your words, I take it he had you snowed, Miss Jamison. Would you characterize your reaction that way?"

"Yes, I guess so."

Careful, Jake thought.

"Please continue."

"That's when he asked me to walk back to the Brown Palace Hotel with him." She paused. "He knew my father, my family, were staunch right-wing conservatives, and he wanted to get a handle on why I'd switched my allegiance. He was very curious."

"Curious," Hurd repeated.

"Yes, he thought it might help him get more conservatives to shift if he understood my reasons."

"So it was a purely practical thing, him asking you to go with him that night?"

"I thought so."

Hurd walked back to his table, studying a paper, or pretending to study it, Jake decided. Then he turned and Jake knew he had a difficult question ready for Sarah. *Don't take it personally,* he said to her silently. *I told you what he'd do.*

"Now, Miss Jamison, you must realize that it has occurred to us here in this room that you were somewhat naive in going to Senator Taylor's hotel room with him. Alone. Can you try to explain to us what your reasoning was?"

Here it comes.

Sarah seemed to gather herself; her face became even paler, her mouth, her beautiful, soft mouth, twisted a bit, and Jake wanted to stop the whole thing right there. To save her from shame. And for himself, because he didn't want to hear her damning words.

"You have to understand," Sarah said, "that we, Scott Taylor and I, were two adults working for a cause, a very important cause. It was a heady time. We thought Scott might actually win the election. All the polls looked that way. We were . . . high, I guess you'd say. People get very close when they work together like that." She paused. "I mean close in the sense of, say, men in a war who depend on one another for their lives. Well, it was kind of like that."

"A *war*, Miss Jamison?"

"Yes, a war. A political war, and Scott was fighting for his political life." She went on. "So when he asked me for my opinion, I was thrilled to be able to help. I may have been naive, and in hindsight I realized I was, but at the time I didn't even consider it. The man wanted my help and I offered it."

She sounded so sincere, Jake thought, so absolutely straightforward. He damn near bought it himself.

"All right, so, assuming all this to be true . . ." Hurd began.

"It *is* true," Sarah said.

"Yes, of course, Miss Jamison. Now, please tell us what happened when you got up to his suite."

Sarah drew in a deep breath. "He offered me a drink, white wine. He had something, scotch maybe. I sat on the couch, but he was restless. He paced. He started telling me about how sick he was of the endless functions he had to attend. He called them rubber-chicken dinners."

There was a faint murmur of laughter from the jury.

"Then he told me"—she glanced down again—"he told me that he was staying in the hotel instead of going home, because his wife, Heather, and he didn't really live together. They only stayed married out of convenience.

He said she wanted to be the First Lady. He called it their bargain.''

Jake could imagine the scene, and he could imagine Scott saying these things. Oh yes. To a beautiful young woman. Certainly.

Sarah, you damn fool, he thought. Or maybe she had been sexually attracted to Scott. The scene was burned into his brain. Sarah in a great dress—black, probably— her long legs, the white column of her neck arched as she sipped her wine. And Scott. The senator's eyes riveted on her.

Shit shit shit.

"I started catching on then," Sarah was saying. "I was getting a little uncomfortable, because I could see where this might be heading."

"Now, Miss Jamison, were you at all aware of Senator Taylor's reputation?''

"I, well, no, not really. I suppose I might have heard something, but the press is so awful, I didn't pay it much attention.''

"So you were an unsuspecting innocent in this?''

"Yes, I thought, I really thought he wanted my advice. I thought I could help him win.''

"Now, Miss Jamison, you must realize how naive this sounds.''

"But it's true," she breathed. "I swear to you"—she faced the jurors and gripped the rail in front of her—"I swear on my sister's grave it's true. I only went to that room to help the senator. I never once thought he'd try to seduce me and, and as it turned out, I didn't have to rebuff him. It never even got that far.''

She'd sworn on her sister's grave. . . . She was telling the truth. He knew that; it had been his job to sift truth from falsehood, and he'd failed. He'd thought the worst of her, suspicious bastard that he was. He'd thought the worst and, he realized with painful certainty, Sarah knew it. Jake writhed inside.

The candidate's mistress. All crap. He wanted to laugh at the vicious absurdity of his own prejudices.

"Go on, please. What happened next?"

"The phone rang. Scott answered it. He was annoyed. He said something like, 'It's too late, I'm tired, I was going to bed.' Then he told the person—or, as it turned out, the *persons*—to come upstairs and to make it quick.

"When he hung up I grabbed the opportunity to leave. I said I'd go back to my hotel because he had guests coming up. But he thought they might see me leaving and misconstrue what I was doing there. He told me to go in the bedroom and hide. It wouldn't take more than two minutes. Two minutes, he said."

"And did he tell you who was coming up or why they were coming?"

"No."

"You had no idea."

"I had no idea. He just said an important man."

"Continue, please."

"I went into the bedroom and hid behind the door. I took my coat and my purse and my wineglass, so there wasn't any trace of me in the living room. I felt so stupid, trapped there. It was a ridiculous situation. But there wasn't anything I could do by then. There was a knock on the door. Two men came in. I could only see through the crack in the door, so my vision was very limited."

She's prepared herself for this, Jake thought. Her voice had gone curiously flat.

"I saw one man's face, but the other man always had his back to me, so I don't know who he was." She told the story all over again, the argument, her distaste that turned quickly to fear, the two shots, Scott's body falling. The shooter coming into the bedroom, the two men messing up the living room to make it look like a burglary. She repeated it, not faltering, her expression unchanging.

There wasn't a sound in the courtroom. No one shifted

position or coughed or cleared a throat. Every single person listened to Sarah's story, spellbound with horror. They believed her, all right, every last one of them, Jake thought in triumph. They'd indict.

"I stayed there for a long time," Sarah was saying. "I was frozen. I really couldn't move. I was so terrified. And then, finally, I got up and I left. I ran back to my hotel and packed my things and took the first morning bus out to the airport. I called an old friend of my family's from there, and I flew to Aspen. And that's where I was when Jake Savelle found me."

"The question, of course, is why you didn't go to the police with this horrific tale, Miss Jamison," Hurd said.

"Because"—Sarah closed her eyes for a moment— "because I realized who the man was, the one I saw, the one who gave the order to shoot."

She paused, and her gaze went to the jury box as if to warn them that they would share the knowledge with her now, and they would also share the responsibility. Then Jake saw her straighten her shoulders infinitesimally— only he could see it—and she spoke the name. "It was Vaughn Ridley, the director of the CIA."

A gasp, a rustling in the jury box.

"You're sure of your identification, Miss Jamison?"

"I am."

"I repeat, why did you not report the crime?"

"Because I knew he could find me anywhere if he knew I existed, if he knew there was a witness who'd seen his face. He had all the power, all the resources. He could have me killed at the drop of a hat. I knew that."

"Are you aware that it's a felony to leave the scene of a capital crime, Miss Jamison?"

"Yes," she whispered.

"But you did it anyway?"

"I was afraid. And I was right to be afraid, because I was shot last week. Only wounded, but the bullet was meant to kill me. Because, you see, now Mr. Ridley knows I exist.''

"So, Miss Jamison, you're testifying here today that you witnessed the cold-blooded murder of Scott Taylor by Vaughn Ridley and his as-yet-unidentified accomplice?''

"I am.''

"Thank you, Miss Jamison, I'd like to call for a lunch break now, ladies and gentlemen. After lunch we'll discuss the unknown accomplice further and then, ladies and gentlemen of the jury, you will have a chance to ask your own questions of Miss Jamison. All right, everyone? One hour, please.''

Lunch was delivered to Sarah and Jake in a private conference room. He sat down on one of the uncomfortable metal chairs across from her, and they looked at each other without speaking for a moment.

"I did my best,'' she finally said in a voice drained of all animation. She looked exhausted, a far cry from the self-possessed woman on the witness stand. And she still had this afternoon ahead of her.

He'd done this to her, put her on the stand, the prosecutors picking her mind, the jury judging her. His stomach turned over, aching. "You were perfect. Wonderful.''

"I just told them what I saw.''

"They'll indict Ridley. I'm sure of it.''

"And the other man, the shooter?''

"They can indict him also, in absentia. And, believe me, once Ridley is arrested, he'll give him up. Don't worry, they'll get him.''

"If he doesn't get me first,'' she said without inflection.

"You're protected. Don't forget that. We're all here for you.''

She ate a little bit of the sandwich that had been delivered. Jake tried to eat his, too.

"I'm not very hungry,'' she said.

"Me neither." He leaned forward and covered her hand with his. "It'll be over today, this afternoon. You're almost home free."

"Until the trial."

"Don't worry about that. There might not even be a trial. Ridley would be smart to cop a plea. If I were his lawyer that's what I'd advise."

"Oh, God, Jake . . ."

"What? What is it, Sarah?"

"I can't dare let myself believe it could be over soon."

"It is. It will be." He stroked the back of her hand with his finger, his head bent, studying her wrist, the fine bones under the skin, the golden hairs, then he looked up and met her eyes. "Forgive me, Sarah," he said softly.

"Forgive you?"

"I thought . . . what everyone did."

"I know. I know what everyone thought." She shrugged. "There wasn't anything I could do about that."

"You told the truth, that's all you had to do."

And then Tom Hurd came in, and whatever more Jake might have said was curtailed, and Sarah was occupied listening to the DA tell her how marvelously it was going.

Another one of the deputy DAs questioned Sarah after lunch. A small boiled egg of a man named Clinton Weber. Jake knew him, too.

"We're going to go more deeply into a description of the accomplice," Weber said. "You've stated you never saw his face, is that correct?"

"Yes."

"Can you describe what you did see of him?"

"I saw his back. He had on a tweed sport coat. Wool. Black-and-brown tweed. He was pretty tall, taller than Scott."

"Scott Taylor was five feet, ten inches tall," Weber said, "for the record."

"He was thin. Well, his back was narrow. And he had brown hair, medium brown. Thinning. I don't know if he was balding because I only saw his back.''

"And you wouldn't recognize him?"

She shook her head. "No."

"What about his voice, Miss Jamison? Would you recognize that?"

"I don't think so. I only heard him say one thing, something like, 'Nobody's in here.' I was out of my mind with fear. I don't believe I'd recognize it."

"And you know he was the one who shot Scott Taylor, who actually pulled the trigger?"

"Yes."

"Did you see him pull the trigger?"

"No, his back was to me, but I saw Ridley move away and then the tweed coat covered the whole crack I could see through, and I heard the shots—"

"How many shots?"

"Two."

"Go on."

"I could see his back tense when he pulled the trigger. I saw it. I know he did it."

"For the benefit of the jury, I wish to state that the law holds an accomplice—that is, an accessory before or after the fact—as himself guilty of the crime, as guilty as the party who pulled the trigger. And you may, if you are satisfied as to Miss Jamison's testimony, find the indictment against one John Doe, an unnamed accomplice, as a true bill in absentia."

Weber sat down and Hurd replaced him. "And now, members of the jury, you may ask questions of Miss Jamison. Please indicate by raising your hand that you have a question."

The foreman, the hard-looking middle-aged woman, raised her hand. "Did you receive immunity for testifying, Miss Jamison?"

Sarah looked her straight in the eye. "Yes, I did."

"Shouldn't we consider that when we judge Miss Jamison's truthfulness, Mr. Hurd?" the woman asked.

"I cannot advise you on that. However, I can tell you that immunity is pretty standard in a case like this," Hurd said.

An older man in the back row: "Miss Jamison, why didn't you make an anonymous call or send a note or something, so this murderer was caught sooner?"

"I was afraid. I wanted it to go away. I have no other excuse."

A pregnant woman in the back corner: "Can you describe the murder scene, exactly what happened?"

"There were some angry words. At the time they made no sense, but once I recognized Ridley, they did. Scott was threatening to reduce the CIA's funding. Too many screwups, he said. Then the two men seemed to be leaving and Scott said something like, 'See you in Washington.' Very sarcastic. And Vaughn Ridley said, 'I don't think so,' or something close to that, then he stepped out of the way. I saw the movement in the crack, his gray suit slid away and the tweed coat was right in front of me. Then the two shots. Pops, really. Then I heard Scott fall." She paused and swallowed. "A very heavy object hitting the floor."

"Excuse me for a moment," Hurd said, "I'd like to interject here that there was a wad of steel wool found on the floor near Taylor's body. Steel wool can be used by those knowledgeable about guns as a silencer."

A young man in the first row raised his hand. "Why didn't the shooter see you?"

"He didn't look behind the door."

"Why not? I mean, if he thought there was somebody there."

"To tell the truth, I don't think either Ridley or his accomplice thought anyone was in the bedroom," Sarah said. "And it was dark in there. I was lucky. I was just lucky."

"I guess," the young man said feelingly.

A white-haired man in the back corner: "What did you see when you came out?"

"The room was a mess, cushions all over, lamps on the floor, drawers open. As if someone had been looking for something."

"Now, let me know if I'm wrong, but nothing was disturbed in the bedroom, was it?"

"No, it wasn't."

"So, why in blazes did the police think it was a burglary all this time? If someone was after the senator's valuables, they would have searched the bedroom. Or his body. Was anything missing from his pockets? His wallet or anything?"

Tom Hurd stood up. "That's a valid point, sir, but since nothing was missing from either the hotel room or the senator's person, and we now know why, at this point in time there's no reason to belabor the issue. Next question?"

Yeah, Jake thought, *that's what I wondered. That's what I kept saying. And not one goddamn soul believed me.*

The foreman again: "Do you think Vaughn Ridley did this by himself? Was this a conspiracy?"

Sarah took a deep breath. "I have no way of knowing. But I've had a long time to think about it, and I believe Ridley probably had the backing of others in power. They were afraid of Scott Taylor. Everyone in Washington was afraid of him. It was a political assassination."

"What about the shooter?"

"Oh, I think he was just the mechanic, you know, the hitman. He probably did it for the money. Someone Ridley hired. But this is all conjecture."

Hurd spoke. "If we find that this was a conspiracy, that would probably become a federal matter, but we won't concern ourselves with that right now. Our objective here, the people of Colorado's objective, is to indict and charge Vaughn Ridley with murder."

A heavyset man had a question. "I'd like to know more about you being shot, Miss Jamison. You appear to be all right."

"It happened while I was walking from my cabin to the main lodge of the Rocky Mountain Retreat, where I worked. It was around two weeks ago, at ten or ten-thirty at night. There was a full moon, so I guess he could see pretty well. I don't remember much, a hard blow to my arm, then the sound of a shot, and I woke up the next morning." She touched her left arm. "It hit me here. I was fortunate. He was aiming for my heart."

"He?"

"I can only assume it was somebody sent by Ridley, maybe even the same man who shot Scott. I didn't see anything, and the sheriff in Aspen didn't find anything. It snowed that night and covered everything up. The sheriff figured it was a poacher."

Hurd again, holding up a folder. "I will provide you with the sheriff's report on the shooting. But keep in mind that the sheriff had limited knowledge of the situation. We do not believe it was a poacher."

"Do you have proof that it was a deliberate attempt to kill Miss Jamison?" the heavyset juror persisted.

"No, no proof. But we'd hope to get it when we interrogate Vaughn Ridley." Hurd went on, "You will also be supplied with the medical report on Miss Jamison."

"Wait a minute," the white-haired juror said testily, "how did this supposed shooter find Miss Jamison? After all, he didn't know she existed."

Sarah smiled sadly, the Mona Lisa smile. "He probably found out because Mr. Savelle started looking for me."

Jake winced visibly.

"But how did Ridley make the connection?"

"I don't know for sure, but when Mr. Savelle began poking around and asking questions, somebody obviously informed Ridley."

"And who in blazes do you suppose that was?"

"I don't know. The Denver connection." She shrugged.

"Well, don't you think you better ferret out this guy and pretty darn quick?"

"Yes," Sarah breathed, "my God, I hope they do."

"We're trying," Hurd interjected. "We have the entire Denver police force working on it, believe me. But there isn't much to go on yet, which is why Ridley's apprehension and interrogation is so desperately important."

"This sounds like some crazy spy novel," grumbled the white-haired man.

Yes, Jake thought. *It sure as hell does.*

There was a pause then, while everyone digested the information. Some of the jury members wrote on notepads, some just stared at Sarah. The pregnant lady raised her hand then seemed to think better of it and subsided.

Tom Hurd stood, buttoning his jacket, looking down at his feet, apparently studying the floor. He raised his head and asked, "Any more questions?" He waited a beat then started on his closing speech. "Ladies and gentlemen of the jury, I—"

The foreman had a question.

"Yes, Madame Foreman?"

The hard-faced woman stood up and leaned forward, resting her hands on the jury box in front of her. "I have one last question, Mr. Hurd."

"Certainly, go ahead."

She fixed her eyes on Sarah, but she didn't say anything for a time, a time that stretched out into seconds that were like beads strung on an attenuated wire, then finally she spoke. "Miss Jamison, what I'd like to know is why we should believe what you've told us."

"Madame Foreman," Hurd began.

"Because," Sarah interrupted him, holding the woman's gaze unwaveringly, "I told you the truth."

And so the grand jury hearing concluded.

TWENTY-TWO

It was David's idea that Officer Gary Pacheco had to be taken off the security team at the safe house.

Sarah was in the shower when David pulled Jake aside and said, "I don't trust him."

"What?" Jake asked. Pacheco, of all the cops on assignment to Sarah, was one of her favorites. Not trust him? The young man was extremely diligent.

"The kid's too damn talkative. I heard him down at headquarters yesterday, and he was bragging about the duty he'd pulled."

"But isn't he one of Disoto's protégés?"

David shrugged. "He *was*. But Disoto was forced to agree with me. We're going to pull him off this case, replace him."

"Huh," Jake said, still surprised.

"I'm afraid we're also going to have to move Sarah to another location."

"You're kidding."

"Nope. No telling how many people Pacheco talked

to. It's not safe anymore, not after her testimony. You know that. She's in danger. The shooter is still on the loose, and God knows how close he is to us.''

Jake swore under his breath.

"Disoto's going to lease a small house right down the street from here.''

"A house?''

"It's just off the mall, and it rents out all the time. No one's going to notice a few new faces.''

"Mm,'' Jake said. He didn't like it. The apartment here, at the end of the hall and three flights up from the street, was easily secured. But a free-standing house? With multiple entrances?

As if reading his thought, David said, "I guess Disoto has used it before. He must feel it's safe.''

Jake sighed. "Well, okay. I better go tell Sarah to pack up. She's not going to like this, though. New faces, a new location. It will be hard on her.''

He could still hear the shower running. He fixed a cup of coffee and stood at the kitchen counter, contemplating the situation. David and his captain were the pros here, and if this move was better for Sarah that was that. He wondered how long she would have to stay in hiding. If indicted and arrested, *would* Ridley deal and give up the shooter? There were no guarantees in this ugly business, and that worried him, a lot more than he'd let on to Sarah.

She'd been a real champ yesterday. He recalled every word she had said, every last question put to her. It had been a grueling ordeal, especially the pointed questions concerning her relationship with Scott. He grimaced.

And then there had been the bright, shining moment when he'd learned that she had never been Scott's mistress. He still couldn't quite fathom the enormity of his relief. It shouldn't matter in the scheme of things. But, damn it, it did matter.

•   •   •

"Why?" Sarah breathed when Jake stood in her bedroom that morning and told her she had to move.

Jake shrugged. "Normal procedures. Disoto is covering all bases."

"You're lying. Something's happened."

"No, nothing has happened. Really. It's time for some new faces at a new location. Hey, you never know if one of the cops has talked out of turn. At home. Or maybe in a bar. This is routine procedure."

She stared at him. "And Gary? Will he still be assigned to me?"

"No. Like I said, new faces."

"Something *has* happened."

"No, honestly," he said, but she noticed that his eyes slid away from hers.

"I liked him," she muttered. "I felt safe when he was here."

"I'm sorry," Jake said.

She moved after lunch. Despite questioning Jake's explanation, despite wondering how many more times she would be uprooted, and despite the awful sense that someone might be watching them, following them from the moment they left the apartment building, she couldn't help turning her face toward the sun and breathing in the fresh spring air.

Her reprieve only lasted a few minutes. David insisted they drive the two blocks. And then a cop—one of the new faces Jake had mentioned—opened the door of the tiny brick house, and she was ushered inside.

They gave her one of the two bedrooms on the second floor, and she would share a bathroom. There was a window overlooking a small, tidy backyard and the alley beyond, and one that overlooked the street. The curtains were drawn tight, and she had to put on the lights to hang up her clothes. She felt as if she were suffocating. And that line Jake had given her about this being normal procedure—what a bunch of garbage. Something had happened, something that had put her security in question. Why wouldn't they tell her? My God, she quailed inwardly, it was *her* life.

The news that the grand jury had just handed down a decision came that afternoon. Jake took the call from Hurd. "They did. Great," he said into the receiver, and then he listened for a minute.

Sarah listened, too, on pins and needles. *Great,* Jake had said. But how long would it be before Ridley was behind bars?

"They indicted," Jake said when he was off the phone.

"What happens now?" Sarah asked.

"The DA and cops put together their case and an arrest warrant will be issued."

"How long?"

"When they feel the evidence is watertight."

"How *long?*"

"A little while. Hey, everything is going along right on schedule."

That night she dreamed about a man with thinning hair and a tweed sport coat. He was tall and reed-thin in her dream, and he had no face. He was everywhere she went in her sleep—a dark alley, a deserted street, a park lined with some sort of flowering trees, but it was a black night and she couldn't identify the buds on the trees. They seemed sinister, a thousand eyes following her. The man moved toward her along a path. Tall, thin, the sport coat. One hand moved to the inside of his coat. Then he was face- to- face with her but featureless, no eyes, nose, or mouth, just a pale blank oval in the night.

She never saw him take out the gun; she was only aware of a sound, a *pop, pop,* and then she awakened, thrashing in the sheets, sweat pooling between her breasts and her heart racing. She lay there in the blackness listening, terror knifing through her. Who was downstairs on duty? *Who?* She couldn't remember. Jake had been there when she had gone to bed. Was he still there? Had he slipped out as he sometimes did during the night? Why was it so silent in the house? Maybe . . . maybe they were all dead.

Jake. Oh, God. Not him, please.

She was going crazy, turning into a paranoid nutcase. And she was obsessing about everything, every sound, every movement, every expression on her guards' faces. She was also obsessing about Jake. The more time he spent with her, the more she began to count the hours till he left. Then, when he was gone, she thought about him constantly, counting the minutes, ticking off the seconds in her head till he returned.

On her third night in the new house she sat behind the closed drapes in the dining room and played cards with David and Jake. The cop who was supposed to have been on duty had called in sick, and now there were only two men to watch over her. Someone was due at eleven, but that was several hours away.

"Two cards," she said, idly looking at her poker hand, trying to concentrate.

"I'll just keep these." Jake put on a neutral expression.

"Right," David said, dealing Sarah her two cards and snorting. "You're bluffing," he said to Jake.

"It'll cost you to find out."

Sarah folded and studied the men. They were putting on an act, trying to behave as if this were a normal poker night among friends. And she was trying to do the same. Only it didn't work for her; she couldn't pretend as well as they could.

"Three queens," Jake was saying, and he spread out his cards on the table.

David swore. "You cheated."

Jake grinned.

How could he be so calm? she wondered. How could he play the role so well? There was death lurking outside of this house, men sent to watch the house, to find a way in, to erase her as they'd erased Scott Taylor. Or perhaps only one man waiting out there. The one she dreamed about.

"Your deal, Sarah." David handed her the deck.

"Let's say twos and sixes are wild," she said, and both men rolled their eyes. "Okay, no wild cards."

"It's your call," Jake said.

"Don't patronize the little lady," she snapped. "Nothing's wild."

"Whatever you say."

If Jake was calm on the surface it didn't mean he wasn't on his guard. She could tell he was alert to the night noises. He was also alert to her. She sensed his constant perusal, and her skin felt sensitive. It was the tension, she told herself.

Her gaze swung to David. There were heavy dark circles beneath his eyes, and he was wearing the same shirt he'd had on yesterday. Or had that been the previous day?

She switched her attention to Jake. His five o'clock shadow would be a full-blown beard in twenty-four hours, and his eyes seemed to glint each time the house came alive with mechanical noises: the furnace coming on, the refrigerator, ice dropping to the bin in the freezer. He practically thrummed aloud as the wind whistled in the chimney. There was a particular tilt to his head and a set of his shoulders and then his eyes would meet hers for a moment before shifting away. What was he thinking when he looked at her so keenly? Could he tell she was changing, that this awful ordeal was aging her, forcing her to face the unpleasant realities of life? Did he know that about her?

She knew, of course, how most men viewed her. Pretty Sarah, the nurturer, always upbeat, fun-loving, but often unapproachable when things got a little serious. But could Jake see past that, see into her soul? Did he know how hard it had been for her to come forward with the truth? How she'd always run from the tough side of life, from commitment? But he'd forced her to take a look at who and what she was and she'd discovered she was stronger than she had ever dreamed. He had done that.

They played poker till the night-duty cop arrived. David left for home then, and Jake said he'd catch some shut-eye on the couch.

"There's the bedroom upstairs," Sarah said.

"Couch is fine."

"You'll be here all night? You aren't leaving?"

"I'm here."

"Good," she said, not even caring that she was giving herself away. He'd think she was worried about security. And she was, of course.

She slept poorly. She wondered if she'd ever get a decent night's rest again, or if she were doomed to lie awake waiting for *him* to come, with his tweed jacket and his blank face and his gun.

He'd gotten into her head, invaded her subconscious. For a year and a half it had been Vaughn Ridley who'd struck fear in her. But now all she could think about was the other one, the tall man who'd pulled the trigger. She knew in her heart and her mind that Ridley would send that man to finish the job he'd botched in Aspen. With her dead, the indictment would be useless. She was the key, the eyewitness. They had to kill her. The tall man, the quiet one who'd so cold-bloodedly murdered Scott, he would be the one. She could feel his closeness, as if his breath were fanning the back of her neck.

She tossed in the bed and willed him to get out of her mind. But he was the stuff that nightmares were made of and there was no escape.

She must have slept because she was suddenly jerked awake by a noise in the backyard.

She sat up, unaware of the sweat that slicked her skin or the wild thumping of her heart. She strained to hear in the silence. What had the noise been? Or had she dreamed it?

Jake, she thought abruptly. Was he here? *Yes.* He'd

stayed. On the couch. *Okay, okay.* Maybe she should go down and tell him about the noise, have him send the cop outside to check.

Jake would hold her, hold her against his chest, his rough cheek pressed to her. All she had to do was go to him. She trusted him. If nothing else, he would never let anything happen to her.

Go down to him.

In the end she couldn't. She just sat there in the blackness, the blood surging hotly through her veins, alone, so terribly alone.

TWENTY-THREE

"The whole weekend?" Madeline Disoto asked at dinner on Wednesday.

"I'm afraid so," Barry replied. "Friday through Sunday. The seminar will be going on the whole time and you know my division is one of the hosts, so I can't get out of it. I'm sorry, honey."

"I wanted to try that new Thai restaurant, you know the one. And I already talked to Felice and Robby about it."

"Next weekend, dear. I promise."

"All right, but I'm holding you to it. You've been so tense lately. You really need some downtime." Madeline patted his arm and went back to eating her dinner.

She was so amenable, that was one of the problems with his wife. She always gave way, sometimes pouting a little but more often graciously. He wished she'd yell and curse, because that might assuage his guilt. A little bit.

"Where will you be?" she asked.

"Breckenridge. That new convention center. I'll leave you the number."

"Won't it be cold in the mountains this time of year?"

"Probably, but we'll never be outside, so it doesn't matter."

No, he wouldn't be outside, he thought. He'd be inside with Heather. A whole, entire three-day weekend to themselves. The phone number he'd leave Madeline would ring at the Breckenridge Convention Center, where he was registered. He just wasn't going to be there.

The weekend had been Barry's idea. Heather was so unhappy lately. Depressed, alternating between rage and crying jags. Newspapers and TV networks, talk shows, magazine editors were all harassing her, and she'd had to change her unlisted number again.

She desperately needed this break.

"I'll be home to get my bag right after work," he said. "I should get up there as soon as I can."

"Do you need me to take anything to the dry cleaners for you?"

Ordinary family talk. The details, the nitty-gritty of life. The stuff that made the world go round. Not at all akin to grand passion. But maybe grand passion could not survive the minutiae of everyday living. Maybe if he and Heather were married they'd grow bored with each other.

"No, dear, I think I have everything I need. My good suit, the gray one."

"Maybe Terry will take me to a matinee this weekend. If the weather's bad, I know he will."

Terry was their oldest son. He was going to study film, and he and Madeline went to independent films at the art houses whenever they could.

"That's a good idea. Isn't there something new playing at the Mayan?"

"Um, I think so.

Two more days. The timing was everything. He could leave work early, pick up his bag. Madeline would remember the time. She'd also ask him a million questions when he got back late Sunday. That meant he'd have to put in a few appearances at the convention, make sure his peers saw him there. Just in case. But for the most part he would be with Heather.

The trip worked for him—perfectly. And he couldn't forget how much Heather needed this break, too. She would be able to forget the torture the media was putting her through and, by Saturday morning, maybe he'd be able to forget—even for just a few minutes—the resurrected Taylor case and the single witness whose life was his responsibility, that goddamn woman who caused untold trouble for everyone with whom she came into contact.

Two days, and he'd be free of her, he thought as he shook a couple of antacid tablets out of a bottle and began to chew them.

Later, when it was all said and done, Jake would try to analyze how it had happened, but at the time it seemed as if the fates—if there were any such thing, he mused wryly—had conspired to bring it all about.

It began Wednesday night as he lay on the couch and tried to sleep. A single question kept him awake, though: Why the hell hadn't Ridley given up the triggerman yet? Jake mulled over a dozen reasons. Discarded eleven of them. The only scenario that made sense was that Ridley had set into motion a plan to take the eyewitness out of the picture.

At three A.M. he sat up angrily, the blanket dropping off his shoulders, and he ran a hand through his hair. He needed sleep, goddamn it, he needed sleep.

"Anything wrong?" came the duty cop's drowsy voice.

"No, nothing," Jake said, then, under his breath, "not much."

He never did sleep very well. By afternoon his nerves

felt like sandpaper under his skin, and his brain was sluggish. It was bad enough being stuck in this close proximity with Sarah. But at times, such as now, when she was in the kitchen doing dishes, humming, her slender back turned to him, her jeans tight across her buttocks, it was downright torture.

Then there was an infuriating lapse in the safe house schedule, and he lost it.

David was due, but apparently delayed, and the duty cop had to leave on some sort of a family emergency before his replacement arrived, and Jake was left alone with Sarah.

He called Disoto immediately to ask what in hell was going on, but he only got the desk sergeant, who was totally in the dark.

"David's probably on his way." Sarah came into the living room and sat. "He'll be here soon."

Jake paced back and forth across the carpet, glowering. Then he checked the lock on the door, the windows, the back door.

"Calm down," she said.

"I can't goddamn calm down. There's supposed to be a minimum of two men here at all times."

"Stop it, Jake." She was watching him, her face pale and drawn, circles under her eyes. She wasn't sleeping either, he supposed. "Pacing won't do any good. You're making me nervous."

"Sorry." He willed himself into stillness, sat down across from her in an armchair, and leaned his elbows on his knees. "This better?"

"Yes."

"I'm just . . . worried," he said. "About you."

"I know. But David will be here soon, you know he will."

He studied her from under drawn brows. "You look tired."

"So do you."

"This is tough on you."

"Yes." She smiled wanly. "On you too."

"I don't count for much in this situation."

"Please, false modesty doesn't become you."

"All right, I started it, but other people have taken over now."

"Mm, and you don't like that."

He shrugged.

"So, Jake, how do you feel about getting your license to practice back?"

"*Maybe* getting it back," he said darkly. Where the hell was David?

"I heard you say you wouldn't practice anymore. You'd teach."

"Yeah, I might. I'd like to make a difference, you know? I tried making a difference prosecuting criminals, but I think"—he hesitated—"I think I'm soured on that. To face those jerks who disbarred me day in and day out." He shook his head.

"Teaching is an honorable profession."

The wry, slanted smile. "I thought law was an honorable profession."

"It can be, I'm sure."

"Yeah, estates and taxes. Can you see me doing that?"

"No."

"And you, Sarah, what will you do when this is all over?"

"Oh, God, I can't think that far ahead."

"If you could do anything at all, what would it be? Come on."

She glanced up and closed her eyes, thinking. The curve of her neck made him switch his gaze away. "I think I'd like to be a backcountry guide in the winter. But maybe in the summer I'd teach. Riding, that is. You know, horses."

"I hear teaching is an honorable profession," he said drily.

"I think someone said that once."

Silence fell between them for a time, and Jake broke it with a question. "How are you holding up? Really?"

She looked away for a moment, considering. "I don't know. I don't think I'll know till it's all over."

He sprang out of the chair. "Where's David? Where's goddamn David?"

"Sit down, Jake."

"I can't. This is driving me nuts."

"Please."

He sat. Across from her again, so close that their knees were almost touching. He didn't know which was making him crazier—the screwup on the guard schedule or being alone with Sarah.

She glanced at him and then looked away.

"What?" he said.

"Nothing. Really."

"What?"

"I was just, well . . . Jake, are you really that worried about me?"

"Yes," he said.

"Why?"

How could he tell her that for the first time in his life he'd come to a realization? He knew now, when it was too late, that she possessed all the conflicting qualities he sought in a woman—vulnerability and strength, naïveté and intelligence, coolness and warmth.

"You haven't answered me," she said softly. "Why are you really worried about me? Is it because I'm the star witness?"

"Yes," he said too quickly. Then, "No."

"Why then?" She leaned closer, and their knees were touching. "I want the truth, Jake. You taught me that I was living a lie, and now I want the truth."

"What do you want me to say? That I care about you?"

She smiled a little at his curt reply.

"Sarah, God . . ."

"Would you rather pretend we don't mean anything to each other?"

"You're killing me," he whispered.

She reached out, gently laying the back of her hand on his rough cheek. Her touch scalded him, making his heart buck in his chest.

"I've had nothing but time—time to think about everything. This may end soon. We don't know. And we have unfinished business."

He muttered something, something unintelligible, because all he could focus on was her hand on his face and the way she turned it over so that her fingers trailed across his cheek, lightly, hesitantly.

Unfinished business. The words were like a stone tossed into a still pond, and their meaning seemed to ripple out, and out.

He closed his eyes and stopped thinking entirely, and somehow his hand came up and covered hers. He said nothing. But he leaned toward her, pulled by invisible chains. Their lips brushed, then met, both of them now staining toward each other.

She sighed. And he groaned.

His hands went to her hair, feeling its soft silkiness. At last. And he knew he'd been waiting his entire life to feel those strands. She murmured and sighed again, and her mouth was so familiar yet completely new.

They kissed slowly, and it was like the ripening of fruit, sweet and full of nectar, promising the most exquisite flavor. He felt his limbs turn to liquid, tingling and yearning.

He stood, pulling her with him, and she wrapped her arms around him and turned her head so that it rested on his chest.

"Sarah," he said, his throat tight.

"Don't say anything," she whispered. "Can't we forget for a little while?"

His answer was to turn her face up and kiss her again. *Why?* he thought. *How?* But it didn't matter; he had to take what she offered.

Her eyes closed, and he saw her face become soft. He brushed a strand of her hair from her cheek and bent his head to her, to drink the honeyed elixir of her again. Her skin was hot, as if she had a fever, and he could feel her bones beneath her flesh.

He pulled away. "Sarah, this is crazy," he got out.

"No," she said, "oh, no."

He held her by her arms and examined her face. She met his gaze with a kind of challenge, then drew his face down to hers.

They made love on her bed with the door closed. Quickly, urgently, not even thinking or asking about precautions. Clothes in sighing heaps on the floor, their bodies barred by sunlight filtering through the blinds. As if nothing mattered but their joining. Not the daylight, the imminent arrival of David, not the danger nor Scott's murderer nor the folly of what they were doing.

Jake would think later that these things made their lovemaking more poignant, more passionate. But at the time thought was banished, and he felt only wonder and a cresting inside himself as if an ocean tide were rising inside him, rising and rising and spilling over.

She was one of those women for whom making love was not an isolated act. She made love with her eyes and her voice and her body and her hands. And when he was spent she lay on her hip beside him, a hand resting in the center of his chest, studying his face.

"Why?" he asked.

She lowered her face to his chest and licked a drop of sweat from his skin. "I think it has something to do with caring," she said. Then she laid her head in the hollow of his shoulder and he could feel the beat of her heart against his ribs. "I tried to hate you."

"I thought you did." The scent of her hair was in his

nostrils, and his body felt slack and empty.

"Mm."

"Sarah . . ."

"Uh-huh?"

"David's coming any minute."

"I know." She sighed.

When David arrived they were both dressed, sitting demurely in front of the television watching the local news. They did not look at each other, nor did they touch.

"You're late," Jake said when David unlocked the door.

"There was some kind of screwup. Christ, I had a fit when I heard about it. Got here as fast as I could." David pulled his coat off. "But everything's okay?"

"Sure, it's fine," Jake replied.

Then David halted in the midst of hanging his coat on a hook, his body abruptly still, tense and still. He swiveled his head and looked at Jake as if he'd never seen him before. He looked at Sarah then back at Jake.

"Shit," he muttered.

TWENTY-FOUR

Barry Disoto popped his car trunk, put his bag in, and turned to his wife. "Sorry about the weekend."

"I know, honey." Madeline straightened the collar on the Polo shirt that he wore under his tweed sport coat. "These silly seminars come up. At least there aren't that many of them."

"Don't forget to set the security alarm at night."

"You've told me that six times," she said with a wry smile.

"I know, I know, I just worry."

"Always a cop at heart."

They kissed, and the guilt and anxiety settled behind his rib cage, an acid burn that caused sweat to form on his brow.

He drove only a few short blocks and then pulled into the lot of a minimart and parked. He took a roll of antacids out of his pocket, chewed three, then picked up the car phone and dialed Heather's house.

"It's me," he said, and he checked the time on his watch.

"Are you on your way? I'm all packed. God, am I looking forward to this weekend. You can't imagine."

"Sure," he said absently. "But I'm afraid I'm going to be a little late."

"Oh. How late?"

"An hour. Maybe two. It's something unavoidable."

"Darn."

"I know, I know."

"Police stuff?"

"Ah, yes, and I better get to it or I'll be even later. Sorry. See you as soon as I can. Okay?"

"I'm counting the minutes."

Barry switched the phone off, replaced it on its cradle, then let his head drop back against the seat for a long moment. He'd never wanted to face this chore. He still didn't. But it couldn't wait another day. He'd already let it go long enough.

He lifted his head, felt the heartburn ease only slightly, and he put the car into gear. "Holy Christ Almighty," he whispered and turned into the heavy late-day traffic, his palms slippery on the steering wheel.

Sarah sat on the edge of the bathtub, turned the faucet on, and tested the water. When the temperature was right, she dropped the plug in place and stood, catching a glimpse of her face in the mirror.

She stared at her reflection as if viewing a stranger. The woman who looked back at her had a softness to her expression and a confidence that she could not really recognize in herself. The fear still showed through; it lurked behind the green flecks in her eyes; but her face had thawed, the lines were less visible, the hint of a smile played at the corners of her mouth.

She didn't lie to herself. She knew exactly why she

looked so different—she'd had sex with Jake Savelle. No, God, no, it hadn't been sex. They had made love. A love that seemed crazily embryonic, raw in its newness and promise. Had she been the only one to realize that, or did Jake know it too?

The tub was filling and she shook herself mentally and stepped into the hall, fully dressed, on her way to her bedroom to get clean clothes. Inconvenient. But the men were just downstairs. Well, David was down there. Jake should be on his way from Denver and George, the young cop on duty, had gone out to get a pizza from a campus spot that didn't deliver.

Pizza. She was sick to death of this diet of junk food and sodas and more junk food.

She got her clothes and went to the head of the stairs, intending to let David know she was going to be in the bath.

She opened her mouth to call his name but then hesitated, hearing his voice—he was on the phone. She shrugged, turned, and that was when she caught a snatch from his end of the conversation.

"Yeah, well, Sarah's really nervous, sergeant. I know, but now she's backing off."

What? she thought, *David is saying that I'm backing off?* She stopped where she was and listened more closely.

"Look, she actually threatened to run away. Said she wouldn't testify at all."

What?

"You better let Disoto know. I realize . . . Yeah, well, it's getting pretty tense around here," he was saying, and Sarah clutched the bannister, unable to fit her mind around his words. All she could think of was confronting him and asking him *why. Why, David, why are you telling them those lies about me?*

It was some time before she finally moved and went down to the living room, leaving the water still running in the tub. David was just hanging up, his back to her.

"David," she said, a little breathless, "why did you say those things on the phone? Who were—?"

"I thought you were in the bath," he cut in, the color draining from his skin.

"I want to know what on earth you meant when you said those things."

He didn't answer. His face was cast in stone, a white marble mask.

"David? What was that all about?" But even as she asked, an alarm sounded in her head, and a cold shiver crawled up her spine. And then, as if in a dream, she saw David reach inside his jacket and take out his gun and point the barrel straight at her heart.

Realization did not come for a moment. She stared dumbly down the barrel of the gun, endeavoring to clear away the confusion that paralyzed her brain. David was pointing a gun at her?

The dawning of comprehension came slowly, in disassociated fragments. She lifted her gaze to his face, to the face she thought she'd known, but it no longer belonged to David Carmichael; it was the blank face of her nightmares.

The picture began to coalesce: A tall man, thinning brown hair. Something about the way he'd held his shoulders. Something about David's shoulders as he held the gun now. Could it have been . . . David? *Could it?*

He said something then, and she shook her head in denial.

He said it again. "Go on upstairs. Go on. Just do as I tell you. And hurry up."

She did as she was told, a mindless puppet, wooden, her brain churning, her body going through the motions as David Carmichael issued orders behind her.

"Turn off the bath and drain the tub."

She did. David? This was her nightmare all over again, and she'd wake any moment.

"Get your bag and throw the clothes in. Everything. Your shoes over there. Hurry it up, Sarah."

The gun. Aimed at her.

David. The shooter. He'd been so reluctant for her to come forward to make her statement. All those sharp words between him and Jake, all the times David had told Jake to drop it. *Of course.* And their friendship? Had David befriended Jake during the investigation only to mislead him?

"Get that hairbrush off the dresser. Goddamn it, hurry it up. And that book over there."

David had been monitoring everything, distracting everyone, carefully picking the cops who pulled guard duty.

Gary. The best of them all. David had made up stories about him, filled Disoto's head with lies so they could move her to this house, a house much harder to guard.

"Zip the bag up and get your purse over there. Move it."

She did as she was told, an automaton, fear stabbing her in the heart. Where was George? The pizza parlor. Right. David had sent him.

All planned. Everything neatly planned.

Jake. Oh, God. David had told him, "Sure, go on back to Denver and get caught up. I've got it covered here."

"Down the stairs, Sarah. Go on. *Go.*"

He had shot her in Aspen. It had been David. *My God,* Sarah realized, he'd driven to Aspen, shot her, rushed back to Denver in time to catch a flight the next day. The circles under his eyes when they'd first met in the hospital, his edginess—she'd thought it was because of the danger she was in. My God, how he must have been sweating it, wondering if she'd recognize him from the Brown Palace.

"Out the back door," David said, and this time he shoved the gun into her ribs. "Close it. Now around the side of the house. We're taking my car."

He was going to kill her. That phone call. He was setting it up perfectly, a play, act by act. Setting it up at police headquarters to appear as if she'd gotten cold feet and slipped out the back door, her bag, purse, everything cleared out. Covered all bases. And when no one found her—maybe for years—everyone would believe she'd done a better job of disappearing this time. He could say Jake had scared her off by coming on to her. And what could Jake reply?

"You're driving."

"Me?"

"Shut up and get in behind the wheel. Keys are in the ignition."

"You thought of everything," she stammered.

"Get in, Sarah, for chrissakes hurry it up."

No one would find her. Ever. He had planned this down to the last detail. When George got back with the pizza, he'd find the house empty, and David would say he had taken off to search for her. It made perfect sense.

She slid in behind the wheel as he threw her bag in the backseat. Her purse was next to her, between her and the door. Her wallet jabbed her hip, but she barely noticed as she started the engine, her hands shaking so badly it was difficult to turn the key.

"Put on the headlights."

"I . . . Where are they?"

"There." He pointed. "Hurry up."

Dusk fell over the city, and she followed his directions west toward the red, jagged mountains called the Flatirons. Every time she slowed or sped up he jabbed the gun at her and demanded she keep to the speed limit. Her right foot was quivering on the gas pedal, and her hands were shaking so badly it was a wonder she could keep the car on the road.

The highway began to snake as she drove through the Flatirons toward the mountain hamlet of Nederland.

"Where are you taking me?" she tried, her voice high, not her own.

"You'll know when we get there."

A stranger. He was someone she'd never met, not the caring father, the loving, concerned husband. Or even the cop. Certainly not Jake's *friend*.

They drove through Nederland in an eyeblink and the car's headlights picked up a sign that read ELDORADO CANYON 3 MILES.

"Why?" she got out, "Why are you—"

"Be quiet."

Of course he didn't want her to talk. She'd seen it in a thousand Hollywood movies—don't let the victim get close to you. Don't humanize the victim. She'd thought they were friends. This was insane, mad. It couldn't be happening.

"What about Nina?" she tried, and she licked cracked lips. "Think of your wife and children. If you're found out think about what this will do to them. David, please, before it's too late."

He laughed, a gruff, pained laugh. "It's already too late."

"You mean the Brown Palace, Scott—"

"Shut up and turn there." He pointed with the gun.

There was a sign: ELDORADO CANYON LODGE. She turned. Too sharply. And he was almost thrown up against her. He swore.

Past the lodge and a spa. Both ominously dark. It was April. Off-season. The road narrowed and rose dramatically. He was taking her into the high country, into the wilderness. *Oh God oh God.*

"Don't do this," she begged. "I won't tell a soul. Just let me out and I'll disappear forever. Please, please, David, you can trust me, you know you can."

He stared straight ahead and said nothing.

"Jake will figure it out. You know he will. He's smart. He'll put it together and this will all be useless."

"Jake? I don't think so. He's too goddamned infatuated to think straight. Hell, he was in love by the time he got back from Philadelphia."

His words touched her consciousness but wouldn't stick. She knew they meant something, something significant, but her terror banished them.

"At least tell me why you're doing this, why you murdered Scott. You owe me that much."

The road kept rising and curving, tall evergreens standing sentinel on both sides. Beautiful dark country. Ghastly and frightening now. It occurred to her she could open the door and leap into that blackness. But he'd kill her first. Or the fall would.

"It wasn't political," she tried.

"That's brilliant, Sarah."

"It was for money, then."

No answer.

"Nina's surgery. That's it. You owed money." Her brain was working now, sharpened by terror.

Still no answer.

"That's it, isn't it? You sold out, David. The CIA bought you."

"Watch that goddamn curve."

"How much did they pay you?"

"Shut up."

"Was it worth it? You'll have to kill me and then Jake—he'll find out, and you'll have to kill him, too."

"I said shut up."

"David, there were better ways. You could have—"

"So you figured it out. What good is it going to do you? Or any of us?"

Her heart thudded for a beat. She'd just heard regret, that pain. If she could play on it . . .

Think. How could she get to him? He was a toughened cop. Where were his soft spots? Jake. No matter what he'd said about Jake being twisted, they were still friends.

Underneath it all she knew that. And Nina and Sean and Nicky. Yes.

She wasn't dead yet. And she wasn't going to make this easy for him. *I don't want to die,* her mind cried. It seemed as if she'd just begun to live.

She glanced sideways at David, whose nervous sweat was beginning to fog the windows. Or was that hers? And she started in again, working on him, rambling, promising anything that flew into her head. To hell with pride.

Gloria Mindon was testy on the best of days, but on a Friday, having just put in two hours of overtime, she was downright nasty when Barry Disoto found her in the police lab.

"I knew I'd catch you in," he said, cringing inwardly when he saw her coat half on, her purse and car keys sitting on a stool.

The veteran lab technician shot him a scathing look. "I'm not in, Disoto. I'm at a movie with my guy."

"This will just take a minute," he said apologetically.

She stuck her other arm in her coat and picked up her things. "No fuckin' way. I'm history. Whatever it is can wait till Monday."

If nothing else, Barry thought, Gloria could swear with the best of them. "It can't wait. Sorry, but I'm pulling rank here. Now let's get this done so we both can get out of here."

She hesitated.

"It's a matter of life and death," he said, meeting the icy glare of the older woman. "Honestly."

She took her coat off, draped it on top of her purse on the stool, and dutifully, resentfully, switched on the bright lights in the lab.

She turned to Disoto. "A few minutes. In my book that's three. Now, what have you got?"

Barry took an envelope out of his coat pocket and dumped the contents next to a microscope. "I need a comparison," he said, hands on hips, staring at the contents scattered on the table.

She looked askance at him. "What I see here are some lab photos of a spent round and a single round—the genuine article. You want me to compare a photo with this slug?" She picked up the spent round and eyed it dubiously. "Don't know where you went to school, captain, but there's no way this will fly."

"I'm not looking for court material, Gloria, just your best guess. Could they match?"

"I don't make guesses and you damn well know it."

She wanted him to beg. Okay, hell, he would. "Please, Gloria, give it a shot. This is really very urgent." He reached into his pocket for the roll of antacids.

She shrugged, seemed satisfied, and dragged a lab stool over, plumping herself down, the fluorescent lights catching her white hair and turning it to silver.

Barry watched with his pulse hammering as she looked over the police lab photos, blowups that had been made nineteen months ago of a bullet, and then she scanned the report clipped to them. He saw her raise her brows when she read the name of the corpse from which the slug had been removed. Senator Scott Taylor. But Gloria was a pro, a thirty-year veteran, and she said nothing.

She put the photos down then picked up the spent slug, turning it in her capable fingers until she seemed satisfied, and then she placed it under the microscope, turned on the light, and adjusted the focus to her liking.

"When was this fired?" she asked, face to the eyepiece.

"Couple weeks ago."

"And what was it fired into? Human flesh? A wall?"

This was the part he hated to face. She'd know. She'd know instantly it had come from a cop's weapon. "A range target."

"Firing range."

"Yes."

"Mm. Nine-millimeter. And judging by the land-and-groove rifling, I'd say it probably came from a Glock."

"It did."

"And these twists in the grooves right here. Hm."

She looked up, rubbed her eyes, and studied the photo for a second; then she went back to the microscope and the spent round, occasionally turning it a fraction on the platform. Barry hated it, every stinking second of it. He'd hated it when he'd told all the homicide detectives to get down to the firing range and put their hours in. He'd hated dogging David Carmichael's footsteps. He'd hated having the range director dig the slug out of the target. He'd avoided the man's eyes when he'd done it. But there had been too many discrepancies in these last weeks, all involving Detective David Carmichael.

It had started with a review of his detectives' health insurance premiums. Boring paperwork. Nonetheless, he'd noted the huge unpaid claim from the bone marrow transplant Mrs. Carmichael had undergone right around the time of Taylor's murder. And then, by that summer, the bills had been paid up. At the time, Barry had concluded perhaps a parent of David or Nina had come to the rescue.

But then there were more oddities, and all of them circling the Scott Taylor case. There were, of course, the 9mm slugs taken from his head. Lots of the cops were switching to 9mm's, Glock being a current favorite as a service revolver.

And the steel wool that could have been used as a silencer. A cop would be savvy enough to use it. But not a burglar.

The clincher in Barry's mind, however, had been the night Sarah Jamison was shot in Aspen. David's partner had spent half that night looking for him. Barry never would have noticed, except that in the partner's report on a late-night homicide, he'd mentioned doing the prelims alone. And when Barry had asked him where David had been, his partner had shrugged.

The idea to have the men use the firing range had come to Barry after that. He'd been keeping the slug with him, hating to seek a comparison to the one taken out of Taylor's brain, hating it so damn much that he'd put it off and put it off. But now, after David's manipulation of the safe house cops, it was time for the truth.

"Huh," Gloria said, lifting her head, rubbing her eyes with her fists.

"What?"

She picked up the photo again and studied the markings on the slug.

"Well?" Barry pressed.

"None of this will hold water in court, you know."

"Gloria, goddamn it, could they be a match?"

"Maybe."

Shit. "On a scale of one to ten, ten being a match?"

"Oh, a nine and a half," she said, and before she could blink, Barry had snatched up a phone, pulled a slip of paper out of his pocket, and was dialing Savelle's cell phone number.

Goddamn, he thought, *goddamn it to hell.*

Jake was on the Boulder Turnpike when he took Disoto's call on his cell phone. He heard what the man was saying. He heard every word. But he couldn't believe it.

"Wait a minute," he said harshly, pulling around a stalled van in the heavy rush-hour traffic. "You're telling me that the ballistics from David's gun and the bullets that killed Scott match?"

"That's what I'm telling you, Savelle. David Carmichael is our man."

"But . . ." he began and nothing else came to him, not a goddamn thing.

"He's been manipulating us from the word go."

"There has to be a mistake." *Not David. Jesus.*

"There's no mistake," Disoto said in a hard voice.

Jake kept trying to think, to make his mind work, but his brain was stalled, a vehicle without a drop of fuel.

"I'm sending a squad up to the safe house. Where are you now?" Disoto asked.

"Ah, Boulder Turnpike."

"Okay. I'll be right behind the squad, but you've probably got thirty minutes on us. I don't want you to do anything, Jake, you hear me? You just wait till backup arrives."

"What the hell . . . ?"

"The man is dangerous. Let us handle him."

Not David, was still pounding in Jake's head.

"Have you got that, Savelle?"

"Ah, yeah. But, listen, it's got to be a mistake. Someone set him up. I don't know."

"There's no mistake," Disoto said, and he broke the connection.

It couldn't be, Jake kept thinking, his mind grasping onto the thought as if it were a life preserver. It just couldn't be. There was an explanation. David could explain it. He tried to reconcile the evidence Disoto had, the ballistics, against what he believed, what he *knew* about his friend, his best goddamn friend on earth. This was a mix-up, a typical cop screwup. And yet, certain incidents filtered into his head. He tried to fight them off, but they kept coming back, battering at his defenses.

The way David had befriended him, tried to curtail his investigation, tried to stop him from seeking Sarah—and where had David been the night she was shot? *Where?*

More recently: manipulating the guards, moving to another house. Why? Damn it, *why*?

Jake shook his mind free of the questions. *Not David.* And yet . . . What about the Denver connection? What about *that?* And what about Ridley—why hadn't he given the shooter up by now? Because he knew, he damn well *knew* the witness was about to be eliminated.

Wait, Disoto had said. Wait for backup. *Fuck that,* Jake thought, and he swerved onto the breakdown lane and stepped hard on the accelerator. All he could think was Disoto was an idiot, a moron—someone was setting David up.

But was he willing to stake Sarah's life on it?

TWENTY-FIVE

The headlights of the car swept across the black ranks of trees then stabbed the road ahead.

"Look," Sarah breathed, "there's no reason for this. I told you I'll disappear. You know I will. David, listen . . ."

She took another sharp curve and became cognizant of her purse grinding into her hip. She shifted unconsciously. "I disappeared before. I didn't tell anyone, I'll—"

"Shut up."

She was chattering, desperately trying to breach the wall he'd erected around himself, when it came to her with the suddenness of a lightning strike: *the cell phone.* Jake's spare cell phone was in her purse.

Her mind raced. Could she use it? How would she dial Jake's number? She didn't even *know* his number, for God's sake.

How how how . . . ?

Oh, my God, hadn't he said he'd put it on autodial? Could she—?

"Watch that deer!" David yelled, and she swerved sharply, almost hitting the doe that was standing mesmerized at the edge of the narrow road.

How how how? Feverishly she hit on possibilities, but she had to cast them aside—David was too close to her, he'd see her hand move, he'd hear the distinctive beeping as the phone powered up. And where was the autodial key? It wouldn't work. It would never work.

She found herself hyperventilating, sweat running down the back of her neck. There had to be a way. If she could turn it on, open the line, the receiver would pick up their voices. If she spoke loud enough, if there was even cell service in these mountains, if the battery was still charged, if . . .

"Stop the car up there," David ordered, and she spotted a metal Forest Service gate ahead, a chain and padlock hanging on it.

Oh, dear God, was this it? Was this where . . . ?

"If it's open we drive. If not," he said coldly, "we walk. Park right there." He pointed to where the pavement ended.

She did as she was told, her mind working, her fingers shaking on the gear shift lever. He reached over and switched the key off and pulled it out of the ignition.

"Stay here," he said, "and remember, I've got the gun on you, Sarah, so don't try anything funny."

He was true to his word. He got out, leaving his door open, the interior light on, and he walked the few feet to the gate, his eyes on her, and began to yank at the padlock.

She moved with catlike quickness, reaching into her purse, groping for the phone, frantically searching for the power button in the poor light, while keeping her head and shoulders as motionless as possible.

She pressed power, heard the mechanical beeps, saw only one battery icon light up—*just one*—then found autodial, hit it, and pressed send. She had no time to raise the antenna, no time to even see if a connection was made, before David was back.

"Damn gate's locked till summer. We'll walk. Get out of the car." He gestured with the gun barrel.

She did as she was told, dropping the phone into the pocket of her red fleece jacket. No time to zip it up. "Don't do this, David," she cried as loudly as she dared, and he came around to the driver's side and snatched her arm. "David, no! Why Eldorado Canyon?"

"Shut up and move," he said harshly, pulling her away from the car, her purse falling to the ground next to the driver's door, its contents scattering. Thank God the phone was in her pocket. *Oh, please Jake, be there, be listening . . .*

"But why Eldorado Canyon?" she cried, too loudly again, and David paused.

Her heart stopped. He knew. He knew, he knew. . . .

"You're making this harder than it has to be," he said, "now let's go."

"My . . . my bag. It's in the back of your car." Too loud, too loud.

"Leave it." He tugged on her free arm, and she knew—her purse, her bag, he didn't give a damn. When she was dead he'd get rid of them.

She talked incessantly, her voice high, shrill, as they inched around the side of the gate and he pulled her toward a footpath that led up and away from the rocky dirt road.

There was plenty of snow still on the path from the recent storm, but with the partial moonlight it was negotiable.

How far up the trail would he take her? How far till he felt it was safe to shoot her and cover her body? A terrible fear bludgeoned her—he wouldn't have to cover her at all. The wildlife would leave nothing to find. Coyotes, foxes, bears, ravens, magpies. She'd be scattered bones in a matter of days.

"Get moving, goddamn it," he snarled at her back.

The trail rose steeply for perhaps a hundred yards, snaking through a stand of spruce. It was very dark, hard to see even in the moonlight, the wind moaning in the treetops, her feet sinking in soft spring corn snow, a winter's worth of deadfall barring her way. In places the route was practically impassable, and she went as slowly as she dared, praying, hoping against all hope that Jake had gotten the call, kept the line open, heard her cries and was even now speeding through Nederland, only minutes behind. In her brain she knew the odds were against her, but her heart had to believe. She'd never wanted so badly to live.

Hurry, Jake, hurry.

Sarah's entire focal point became survival. She put one foot in front of the other and thought only of how to save her life. If it weren't for the gun trained on her, she had an edge. She knew the woods; in the last year and a half the wilderness had become her friend. She'd taken dozens of winter cross-country trips on moonlit nights, guided people safely, fearlessly. David knew nothing. He was a city boy, a cop. He knew the pavement. But here she was in her realm.

Except for the gun.

What if Jake didn't come? What if . . . ?

"Get going," David panted at her back, "through there."

Ahead they could see a meadow now, a high-country park. Moonlight lay in long swatches across the clearing, settling in silver ribbons over rocks and stumps. The trail became less distinct, and the snow was even deeper in the open space.

David was breathing hard now; she could hear him rasping. He wouldn't go much farther. He didn't have to.

Think, think, her mind screamed. The car was at the trailhead: Jake couldn't miss it. Nor could he miss their tracks. He'd be rushing, whereas they were going at a snail's pace. And he was a jogger—he'd handle it. Minutes. He'd be here in minutes. If he'd gotten the call, if he hadn't hung up, if he'd heard her voice. *If if if.*

It was up to her. *Think.*

She stepped over a fallen tree. Snagged her jeans. Let herself tumble awkwardly to the ground. Behind her David swore.

"Oh, God," she breathed, "my ankle, I think it's sprained. Oh, God."

He stooped, tugging at her arm. He didn't care about her ankle. He cared only about getting her into that next stand of trees. And there, he'd shoot her. They'd gone far enough.

She groped in the snow, her fingers burning at the icy cold, the coarseness, and she felt a branch. If she could twist it off . . . But it wouldn't budge.

And then her hand touched something. Hard. A rock. Could she . . . ?

"Get up, Sarah. Quit stalling." He pulled harder on her free arm.

"I'm trying, I'm trying, damn you," she wept, and the rock was in her hand.

Ordinarily it would have been too heavy for her to lift with one hand, but she barely noticed its weight. She let him drag her to her knees, moaning in pain, and then she swung the rock up with everything in her and slammed it into the side of his head.

David went down.

The wild thought flew through her mind that she could finish him right now, crash the rock down on his head again and again and again, but she knew she couldn't do it. For a beat she looked at him struggling to rise, then she ran, tripping and sinking and tripping to her knees and righting herself, toward the trees, toward the dark of the tall trees. Toward life.

•   •   •

Jake flew past Nederland doing close to sixty, his mind working like a machine despite the acid fear churning in his gut.

The canyon. Christ, how far, *how far?* He'd hiked it dozens of times as a young man, camped, climbed the peaks. How far—damn it, why couldn't he remember?

His headlights streaked across the sign to Eldorado Canyon just as the BMW's tires squealed around a sharp curve.

"Okay, okay," he whispered harshly, *"hold on, Sarah, hold on."*

Scenarios flew into his head despite his efforts to keep his mind in the moment. David finding the cell phone, the line open, shooting her. *Shooting Sarah.* Or he didn't find it, but he and Sarah were twenty minutes ahead of Jake, and David had reached the site he had in mind, and he was lifting his gun, pulling the trigger . . .

"Goddamn it, no," Jake ground out.

He tore past the darkened lodge and spa and flew up the curving road toward the Forest Service entrance to the canyon. Sick panic kept rising in his gorge, and he had to fight it down. She was smart, she was a survivor, she'd figure something out. David couldn't kill her. Jake couldn't lose her. Not now, God, not now.

Though it was only minutes, it seemed to take hours before his lights glinted off the bumper of a car. David's car. The gate, the barred metal gate. Jake slammed on his brakes and the car skewed violently sideways.

He flung himself out and looked around. Dark, the end of the plowed road, the gate. Open in the summer but locked now. And there by the driver's door was Sarah's purse, its contents spilled on the asphalt. He stopped for a second to make sure it was hers, then looked beyond the gate. The ground was covered with melting patches of snow from the storm.

He ran to the gate and tried to pull it open, but a chain held it firm. So David must have gone around it. With

Sarah. He was going to take her into the woods, far off the road, and shoot her and leave her body for the coyotes.

No.

He could make out footprints beyond the gate, two sets, leading up to the trail. His eyes were growing used to the darkness, and the moon had risen, glowing pale silver on the uneven terrain. He rushed back to his car, fumbled at the glove compartment, pulled his gun out. Bullets. With shaking hands he loaded it. Could he shoot it? Could he shoot *David*?

He edged around the gate and looked for the faint trail of footprints. They disappeared along the path, under trees, in shadows, on bare patches. He ran up the trail, lungs screaming in the cold, thin air, sweat freezing on his skin. Stopping, losing the trail, tripping over deadfall, sinking, righting himself. Up. Up. *Don't die, Sarah.*

There was light ahead now, brighter moonlight through the stand of trees lining the path. How far had they gone? How goddamn far before David . . .

Jake heard the echo of his voice before he actually saw him, and he froze at the edge of the trees.

Again. David's voice. More clearly now with a faint shift of the wind. "No point hiding, Sarah, I can follow your tracks . . ."

Relief flooded Jake, pure, molten joy. She was alive! She'd gotten away. Clever, clever, Sarah. And he ran on, slipping on the snow, legs churning, breath pluming.

He shot out into the clearing before he could stop himself. White, calm, bathed in moonlight, encircled by the black trees. There was a shadow on the far side of the clearing that was detaching itself from the blacker shadows. Moving stealthily, hands forward and together, and a moonbeam glittered on something metallic in his grasp. Jake moved toward him, across the snowfield, crouched, lungs burning. *Don't turn, David, don't . . .*

It was too late; Jake saw David whirl toward him, gun

rising, and Jake raised his own weapon in a primitive survival reflex. Then they both stood there in the moonlit clearing, guns pointed at each other in the panting silence.

"I should have known," came David's voice, and there was unutterable sorrow in it.

"Why?" tore from Jake's throat.

David laughed a bitter and humorless bark. "Money, pal. Isn't it always money?"

"My God," Jake got out, and his arms shook. How much longer could he hold the gun up?

"I only made one little mistake. I didn't check that goddamn hotel suite well enough. One little mistake and everything's gone to hell."

"Look, David, put the gun down, I'll do my best for you. I'll get you the best defense, I swear. This never happened, do you understand?"

"Cut the crap, Jake."

"No, I mean it. Just—"

"Jake?" came a voice. Sarah. From over there, behind David. He could barely see her; she blended into the trees.

"Sarah, get back."

But David was already twisting, aiming . . .

"No, David!" Jake's mind registered that there was no time even as his gun tracked David's movement and his finger tightened on the trigger, and the gun bucked in his hand.

The explosion was so loud, crashing in his ears, deafening him, and he thought for a second David had shot, too, he must have. But then he saw David fold and sink to the ground, a prolonged falling, an endless buckling of his body. A sob tore from Jake's throat, he threw his gun aside and ran to his friend.

Blood was already black on the snow. He rolled David over onto his back, adrenaline pumping, cursing, kneeling beside him.

"You got me," David said with faint surprise. "You fucking shot me."

"I'm sorry. Jesus. David, where . . . ? Is it bad?"

"Yeah, it's bad."

He was aware of Sarah kneeling beside him. "Call nine-one-one," he said to her. "You have the cell phone? Call them."

She pulled the phone from her pocket, punched in the numbers. He heard her with one part of his mind, and that small part realized she was crying, but his attention was focused on David.

"Where? Can I do something? David, talk to me, man. We've got help coming. Don't worry. You'll be okay." His words came out like vomit, rushed, tumbling over one another.

David shook his head slowly. "No," he whispered, "no good." He choked and coughed, and blood trickled from the side of his mouth. Jake wiped it away with his hand, thinking irrationally that if he kept the blood away, if he kept David free of it, he'd be all right. He had to be all right.

"Hang on. Come on, David, help's on the way. Sarah? Sarah?"

"Yes," she choked out, "I got through."

"Tell Nina . . ." David murmured.

"Yes, what, tell her what?"

"Loved her. And the boys."

"You tell them, David. You'll tell them yourself."

"No." His body convulsed under Jake's hands.

Sarah leaned forward beside him and put her folded-up jacket under David's head. She was crying, and Jake realized he was, too, his eyes leaking hot tears, his chest heaving.

"Oh, God," he said, "oh, God. I'm sorry, David. I'm sorry."

"Better this way," David said and his breath came unevenly, stopped, started, like an engine running roughly, out of fuel.

"No, no," Jake rasped.

"I loved them," David said strongly, then he coughed and a flood of black came from his mouth, wetting Jake, wetting his hands and his clothes, and then he was very still.

"David?" Jake shook him. "David? Hang on, they'll be here soon. David . . ."

He felt Sarah's hand on his arm through a haze of disbelief and horror. "No," he protested.

"He's gone, Jake."

"No, he can't be. He . . ."

"He's dead."

Jake looked at her, at her eyes shadowed in the moonlight, at the tears that glistened like pearls on her cheeks, at her bowed shoulders. He looked down at David's face, peaceful now, then back at Sarah.

"I killed my best friend."

"You saved my life."

"But I . . ."

She put her arms around him, kneeling in the snow, and they embraced, and he felt as if she were a lifeboat on a boundless sea. He held on with all his strength, crying out his anguish.

And then they sat there wordlessly on the cold snow watching over the lifeless body for a long time, a very long time, it seemed, until they heard the far-off warble of sirens.

Too late, too late.

TWENTY-SIX

It was nearly five A.M. by the time Barry Disoto drove Sarah away from the lights and noise in Eldorado Canyon.

She was still shaking, her senses acute despite the rescue operation taking most of the night. She kept pivoting in the passenger seat, checking to make sure Jake was directly behind them in his car. She'd argued that he shouldn't be driving, and especially alone, but he'd just muttered something, annoyed, and insisted he was fine.

He was not fine. None of them were.

"He blames himself," Sarah said, more to herself than Barry. "Once he gets hold of an idea he won't let go. I'm afraid . . ."

She glanced behind them again, expecting Jake's car to suddenly veer off the black road, something. But he was right there, his low beams right behind them.

"He's going to have to deal with it," Disoto said. "We all have ghosts in our closets."

"Yes," she said, thinking of her own ghost, now in

the full light of day. "But we don't all have to live with killing our best friend."

"Cops have to kill people," Disoto pointed out.

"Jake isn't a cop."

"You learn to live with it."

"I hope you're right."

"David brought it on himself. Jake was one of his victims."

"Yes," she said again, but when she thought of Jake's abysmal anguish she shuddered.

"Nina Carmichael doesn't deserve this," she said after a time.

"No, she doesn't."

A heavy silence pulsed in the car, and she put her face in her hands for a moment. All she could see was David lying in that snowfield, the moon glistening on the blood as it spread beneath him. His last words. Awful, awful. And who was going to tell Nina? Jake? After he'd pulled the trigger? It would kill him.

"We have to do something for Nina," she said. "We have to. No more innocent victims, please. I can't bear it."

Disoto was silent.

"What good will the truth do now?" she demanded.

Silence.

"No one knows what went on up there. Only the three of us. What if . . . ?"

"What if . . ." Barry repeated.

"It doesn't matter anymore what David did. He's dead. We could say . . . that he was trying to protect me. That he saved me. Something. There's got to be something you can do."

The quickness of his reply took her totally by surprise. "Yes," he said, "there is something. But it's up to you, Sarah, it's entirely up to you now."

• • •

It was barely dawn when Jake followed Barry Disoto down the walk in front of the Boulder safe house and got into Disoto's car. He glanced back at the house, the front window, and he saw Sarah standing there, holding the curtain aside, Gary Pacheco right behind her, no doubt telling her to stay away from the window. He saw only Sarah, though. With her elusive smile. He knew what it was now: an acceptance of the past and the will to go on.

Disoto pulled away from the curb and Jake turned to him. "What about my gun?" he asked. "What about the ballistics on my gun? The lab will match it to the bullet from David."

"What gun?" Disoto said mildly.

"My goddamn gun that you've got in that evidence bag in the trunk of the car."

"What evidence bag?"

Jake stared at him for a moment. "I see," he said. "It can't be this simple. Someone's going to figure it out."

"Who?"

"I don't know."

"Look, Jake," Disoto said as they drove toward Denver and the Carmichael house, "as David's captain, it's my duty to lead the investigation and conduct the search for David's killer and Sarah's abductor. We have two obstacles to pulling this off. One is the gun. And the gun can disappear. The second is Sarah's ability to identify the man who kidnapped her from the safe house. I think she's made it plain to us that the man wore a ski mask and she never got a look at his face."

"Okay, okay, but where was David when the kidnapping occurred?"

"Sarah said she was upstairs running a bath, and she thought she heard a heavy thud. As the lead investigator, I have to assume it was David's body hitting the floor when the kidnapper got him from behind."

Jake blew out a long breath. "And when I arrived at the safe house Sarah was already gone?"

"Yes, and both you and David went after her and her abductor."

"I don't like it."

"None of us *likes* it, Jake. But this isn't for us or for David's memory or even for the reputation of the police department. This is for Nina and her sons. Hell, we got the bad guy. *You* got him, Jake. It's over. And Sarah can still testify against Ridley."

"Jesus. *Ridley.* What if he talks now? What if he blows the whole thing?"

"Come on, Jake, who'd believe him? If Sarah sticks to her story, who the hell would believe him? He'll clam up tight now. He's got nothing left to deal with."

Disoto was right. Jake stared out the window as the light over the city quickened, and he knew in his gut that Disoto's plan—Sarah's plan—was workable. Amazing. The amazing Sarah Jamison. And he wondered why, exactly, she was doing this. Was it for Nina? Yes. Because David had paid the ultimate price for his crimes. But was she also doing it for *him,* for Jake, to help him shoulder the burden of killing his best friend?

Maybe. Maybe Sarah, the nurturer, was at work here. Or maybe, as she'd said, she shared in the blame for David's death. If she hadn't run in the first place, none of this would have happened.

Didn't they all share the guilt? Jake wondered. Or maybe they were merely human beings, caught in an untenable situation, and handling it the best way they knew how.

By the time Jake and Disoto got to the Carmichael house, just after seven A.M., Nina was composed. David's partner, who had arrived an hour earlier, opened the door and greeted them somberly.

"How is she?" Disoto asked.

"She's one great lady," David's partner said. "She's doing okay."

Lynn Erickson

She must have heard them arrive, because she came into the front hall then. Despite the early hour she was dressed, and Jake wouldn't have known how she felt except for her pallor and the expression in her eyes.

"Good morning, Mrs. Carmichael," Disoto said. "I wanted to stop by to give you my condolences and the condolences of the entire department. David was a fine officer, and he died bravely in the line of duty."

"Thank you, Captain Disoto," she said. Calm, gracious.

Jake started to say something, but his voice got choked up; Nina had to take his hand, and then all he could do was put his arms around her and hold her tightly and try so very hard not to blurt out the awful truth and his terrible, tearing guilt.

"It's okay, Jake," she whispered. "Every policeman's wife knows this could happen."

"Oh, God, Nina," he said.

She stepped back and gave him a weak smile. "We'll be all right, Jake."

"The boys?" he asked, suffering.

"They're in the living room. They'd love to see you."

How could she be so self-controlled? Her life had just been demolished; she was a widow, her sons fatherless.

The boys sat together on the couch, Nicky in tears, Sean looking angry.

"Uncle Jake," Sean said, "are they going to catch the guy who killed Dad?"

"I don't know," he said, his heart breaking, the truth rising in his gorge. "They're sure going to try."

"I want them to catch him," Sean said furiously. "I want that guy to die."

"Sean," Nina said, "that's enough. That kind of thinking isn't going to help matters."

Barry Disoto put his hand on Jake's arm as if to steady him, then introduced himself to David's sons. "Your father worked under me for over ten years. He was a good man and a fine officer. We were all proud to be associated with him. I want you boys to remember that all your lives.''

''Thank you,'' Nicky mumbled.

''Are they looking for the killer?'' Sean asked.

''Yes, the whole force is on it,'' Disoto assured him.

My God, Jake thought, he wasn't going to be able to bear it. The only thing keeping him sane, the thought he clutched to him like a talisman, was that the lie was better than the truth. A thousands times better.

Ironic that he believed this to be true, despite his life-long, headstrong, compulsive quest for the truth. Look where the truth had gotten him.

Barry Disoto kissed Nina's pale cheek. ''I'll wait outside in my car, because I know Jake has a few things to say to you,'' he told her. Then, to Jake, ''Take your time.''

David's partner also kissed Nina on the cheek and left with Disoto, and Jake had to face her alone.

''Nina,'' he began, ''there's nothing I can say. I'm sorry, very sorry.''

''Thanks for coming over so soon,'' she said. ''It means a lot to us.'' She hesitated. ''Come into the kitchen for some coffee, will you?'' And she nodded her head toward the boys.

He knew what she wanted.

''You were there,'' she said quietly. ''Is that true?''

''Yes.'' *Oh, God.*

''Was he . . . did he . . . ?'' She switched her eyes away, her voice catching.

''He wasn't in pain,'' Jake said, swallowing. ''His head was clear.''

''Oh.''

''He said . . . he said he loved you . . . and the boys.''

She cried then, silently, tears sliding down her cheeks, and Jake took her in his arms. ''I'll always be here for you," he said. "You can depend on me, Nina. You can call on me. Anytime. You know that."

"I know," she murmured.

"He was my friend."

"Yes, he was."

He patted her back, then held her arms and looked her straight in the face. "I'll be there for the boys, too. Anything. Like they were my own."

She wiped away her tears. "They'll need you." She tried to smile then. "Jake, you better get back to Sarah. She must be a mess. I've got a lot of calls to make." She closed her eyes and took a deep breath. "David's parents. My parents. And there will be a lot of people here soon."

How could she think about anyone else? Jake wondered. How could she?

"I'll stay if you want."

"No, really, there will be so many people here, and I'd like to make the calls now, while it's quiet."

"You're sure?"

"Yes."

"I'll leave you my cell phone number and the safe house number. In case you have to get hold of me."

"I'll be okay. As long as I have something to do, you know." She put her hand on his arm. "I'll talk to you later today."

"We all loved him, Nina," he choked out.

"I know. And that helps, it really does."

He left the house, walked out into the sunny spring morning. He was shaking when he opened the passenger door to Disoto's car.

"Rough, huh?" Disoto said.

"That was the hardest thing I've ever . . ." He hesitated, catching the distracted expression on Disoto's face. "What?" Jake asked. "What the hell now?"

"It's Ridley. I just got a call. It seems one of the news stations got wind of Sarah's abduction, and it came out . . . that David was killed, and, well"—Disoto turned and stared Jake directly in the eye—''an hour ago Vaughn Ridley was found in the basement of his house, dead from a self-inflicted gunshot wound.''

Sarah heard Jake open the front door of the safe house around ten o'clock in the morning. He was talking, his voice low, perhaps thinking she was still resting.

''I'm not sleeping,'' she called out from the kitchen, where she'd been pouring herself a cup of coffee.

He appeared in the doorway, and she recognized in his countenance the agony he'd just undergone. He was unshaven and his eyes were rimmed in red. ''How did it go?'' she asked quietly.

''About the way you'd expect.''

''What . . . what did you tell her?''

''That David wanted her to know he loved them, her and the boys.''

Sarah closed her eyes and took a breath. ''It's the truth.''

''There's something else, though,'' he went on, and the tone of his voice made her brace herself. ''Vaughn Ridley committed suicide this morning.''

''He's . . . he's dead?'' Her legs felt suddenly weak, and she slumped into a kitchen chair, trying to grasp the news. ''Oh, my God.''

''That about sums it up,'' Disoto said from the door.

''Then . . .'' She tried to be logical. ''That means . . . there's no trial? And I'm safe, I'm free to go?''

''Yes,'' Disoto said.

''Yes,'' Jake said.

''I'm safe, just like that? I can go and live my life?''

''It would seem so,'' Disoto replied.

''We don't want to . . . bulldoze you,'' Jake put in.

''No, no, you're not. I don't want David's family to suffer. He's dead. Ridley's dead. They've paid for their crimes. It's over.'' She felt tears well up in her eyes, and she put her face in her hands. ''It's over.''

"I've got to get back to headquarters," Disoto said, "and make my report. It's going to be wild there. And David's funeral. A lot of planning to be done. I'm sure the commissioner and mayor will call for a parade, the whole nine yards. A lot to do. No doubt there'll be national coverage."

Jake said nothing. He only winced and then walked into the living room and flung himself in a chair. Sarah followed and watched as he rubbed a hand across his face, as if to wipe away the torment.

"Well," Disoto said, "I've also got an overdue visit to make." He looked at his watch and then met Jake's eyes. "I think your sister will want to know that it's over now."

"Yes," Jake said distractedly, "I'm sure Heather will be relieved."

"This has been rough on her," Barry went on, and Sarah had the distinct feeling that there was a wealth of information passing between the two men, something to which she wasn't privy.

"Tell Heather," Jake was saying, "tell her I'll be by later. I want her to know it really is over for good now."

Barry nodded. "Yes, it is." Then he paused, as if lost in thought for a moment. "Yes, your sister can finally bury her past now. And find a little more happiness."

"I hope so," Jake said.

Barry smiled tiredly. "Well, I'll leave you two to sort things out. Sarah, you can stay here for as long as you like, until you figure out exactly what you're going to do."

She walked him to the door, where Pacheco awaited him. She thanked the young officer she'd gotten to know so well and then met Barry Disoto's eyes. "You're a good man," she said meaningfully.

"That's what my wife says," the captain replied, and then he shook her hand, gave her a faint smile, and left with Pacheco. For a long time she stood in the hall and hugged herself, her brain trying to assimilate all that had happened. *Insane. Unbelievable. Awful.* And yet she was safe. Free. For the first time in all these months she was free.

It occurred to her as she stood there that she needed to phone her parents. And Phillip. And the Lovitts, too. Everyone would of course know about Ridley's suicide— and probably her abduction, too. They'd be worried. Yes, she needed to make those calls.

And then there was Jake.

He was still sprawled in the easy chair when she went back into the living room, all the demons of hell rending him.

She sat quietly across from him, in the same chair, the same position, as she had that day they'd made love. It seemed an eternity ago.

"How are you?" she tried.

He focused on her. "Pretty bad."

"It was . . . ?"

"Horrible. Nina cried. She loved him so much. And the kids, ah, Christ, Sarah, it ripped my heart out."

"Don't blame yourself."

"Sure." Harshly.

"You had no way of knowing."

"I thought . . . I'm supposed to be a good judge of character," he said bitterly.

"David was a better judge. He knew no one would ever suspect him."

"I'll never get over it."

"No, you won't, but in time you'll understand it better. And maybe you'll forgive yourself."

He sat there motionless for a time, and she could see how exhausted he was. She felt, suddenly, protective of him.

"You should go home and get some sleep," she said.

"Sleep."

"You're going to need it."

But he brushed aside her concern. "What are you going to do, Sarah?"

"I'm not sure yet. I haven't had time to even think."

"Home to Bryn Mawr?"

"No." *Home, what a joke.*

"Back to the Lovitts'?"

"I don't know. I could, I suppose, but it's off-season now, and they don't need me. And after the way I left . . ."

"Stay here then. Disoto said you could. Think of all the money they're saving. David dead. Ridley dead. They won't have to pay for a trial. Nothing," he said darkly.

"Mm."

"Did you get any sleep?"

"A little."

"Did I tell you how goddamn smart you were to use that cell phone?"

"No."

"I'm telling you now, okay?"

"Okay."

Silence fell between them and with it a certain discomfort that held them hostage. She got up to refill her coffee cup. From the kitchen she had a clear view of him. "Do you want a cup? I made a pot in case—"

"Sarah," he interrupted.

"Yes?"

"Will you"—he paused as if to gather his thoughts—"will you go to David's funeral with me?"

She busied herself stirring sugar into her cup, fixing one for Jake, though he hadn't answered her. She rinsed the spoon and left it in the sink. Finally, she walked back into the living room and handed him the coffee cup. "Yes, of course I'll go with you."

"And will you consider . . . going home with me afterward?"

For a moment she wondered if she'd heard him correctly. "Go home with you . . . ? I'm not sure I . . ."

He gave a half laugh. "I'm too goddamn tired to beat around the bush, Sarah. I want you to move in with me. I want to explore that teaching position here in Boulder, and maybe you could check into the riding instructor thing right here. I don't know. My place is really a dump, but we could look around."

Sarah gave him a little smile, and she put her coffee down then sank onto the floor on her knees in front of him. "Are you sure you know what you're asking?"

"Yes, of course. I'm just afraid I'm such an obsessive idiot that I'll drive you crazy. Look at what I already did to you."

But she was shaking her head, smiling and shaking her head.

"What?" he said.

"Oh, Jake, you are an idiot. Don't you know that because of you, for the first time in my life, I know who I am and what I'm capable of? You gave me that. I owe you everything."

"Is that a yes?"

"That's a yes."

"In spite of everything?"

"No, *because* of everything."

And then he leaned forward, and she put her arms around him and held him. She heard him sigh, and she heard him whisper against her that he loved her, and they stayed that way for a very long time.

It's over, Jake thought. David's funeral was over, and he'd made it through the minister's words, Barry Disoto's eulogy, the mayor's tribute, the whole long, endlessly long litany of loss and grief, the human need to make sense of what was inherently incomprehensible.

Death.

He thought of the funeral as a dark tunnel full of fearsome dangers, a trial he had to undergo to prove himself worthy. Worthy of what?

Of Nina. Of Sean and Nicky. But mostly, he had to prove himself worthy of Sarah.

He'd held her hand throughout the ceremony, standing there with her at the graveside, and he'd squeezed her fingers so hard that her fingers had been white. But it was over, and he'd gotten through it.

He didn't think he could have done it without Sarah, though. He couldn't have spoken those calm, measured, loving words to the Carmichaels, he couldn't have borne the honor guard and the twenty-one–gun salute.

Disoto had carried it off without a hitch. No one in the department would ever question the death of a fellow cop, not when there was a family that needed the pension.

"You okay?" Sarah asked as they walked to his car.

"Yeah." He tried to smile at her, but his face felt stiff.

"You're not the least bit okay." Her voice was quiet. He opened the car door for her, but she didn't get in. She stood there, close to him, her eyes locked onto his, tendrils of her hair blowing in the mild spring breeze. Then she brought her hand up and laid it on his cheek "You will be, though."

"Promise?" he asked, trying like hell to lighten the situation.

But Sarah wouldn't play that game. "Yes, Jake, I promise." Dead serious.

She slid into the car, and he walked round to the driver's side. It was warm and sunny, a perfect spring day, a few white fluffy clouds over the mountains to the west of the city. He sat behind the wheel and stared blindly out through the windshield "Where to?" he finally asked.

"Home," Sarah said.

Home. His small, grubby apartment—*home.*

All Sarah had with her were the same bags he'd stowed in the trunk of his car when they'd left Aspen. It seemed so long ago, but it wasn't, only a few short weeks. A few weeks that had changed his life irrevocably.

When they got to his apartment, he put her bags down in the bedroom and turned to find her standing right behind him. "We'll look for a new place soon," he said. "I know this isn't much . . ."

"It's fine," she said.

"Hell, it's a mess, but I didn't care before."

She took his hand and led him to the bed, and they both sank down onto it. Her green eyes fixed on him for a moment, then she asked, "Are you regretting that I'm here, Jake?"

He leaned his forehead in his hand. "Good God, no. I couldn't have gotten through that without you. I've never been more sure of anything in my life. I want you with me, always." He raised his head, "But what about you? Are you sure, Sarah?"

"Jake, I will never leave you," she said emphatically.

He turned and they kissed, then he rubbed his cheek against hers, drawing in her scent. "We're starting over. Today. The two of us. A new life."

She laid her head on his shoulder. "A new life," she echoed.

They sat there, close together, looking out the dusty window at the wedge of splendor, the sun shining on the distant snow-capped peaks of the Rockies, and Jake knew peace.

His search had ended—he'd found Sarah Jamison.

Penguin Putnam Inc.
Online

Your Internet gateway to a virtual environment with
hundreds of entertaining and enlightening books from
Penguin Putnam Inc.

While you're there, get the latest buzz on
the best authors and books around—

Tom Clancy, Patricia Cornwell, W.E.B. Griffin,
Nora Roberts, William Gibson, Robin Cook,
Brian Jacques, Catherine Coulter, Stephen King,
Jacquelyn Mitchard, and many more!

Penguin Putnam Online is located at
http://www.penguinputnam.com

PENGUIN PUTNAM NEWS

Every month you'll get an inside look at our upcoming
books and new features on our site. This is an ongoing
effort to provide you with the most up-to-date
information about our books and authors.

Subscribe to Penguin Putnam News at
http://www.penguinputnam.com/ClubPPI